The
Barbarian
&
The Angel

Dr S. Fern

Acknowledgements

I would like to thank Roman Sznober for his editorial support and Rebecca Elise for the cover art. Thanks should also be given to Tom Flemming for giving his permission to use one of his pictures as my author photo.

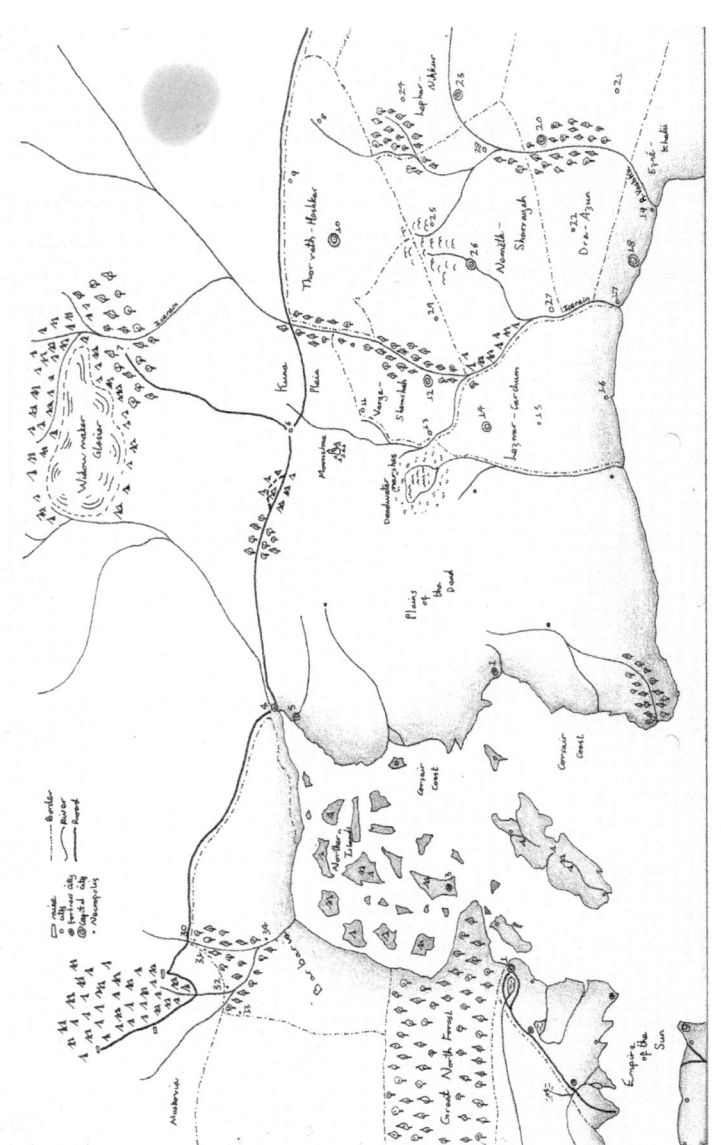

Settlements numbered on map

Chapter 1

It was mid-winter's eve and fierce winds had brought snow from the glacier they called the Widowmaker down onto the lands of the Northmen. It seemed as though the whole world had frozen. In Vorde, as in many other northern settlements, the thick carpet of snow was broken solely by the solitary form of the great hall; the heat of the large fire that blazed within, fierce enough to melt the snow settled on its roof. Smoke from the large blackened chimney was quickly carried away by the relentless wind. Fingers of light flickered from the vents below the eaves. In the occasional lulls between gusts the sound of raised voices and laughter could be heard coming from the hall, amid a commotion of metal on wood. Tonight the men of the north were celebrating mid-winter.

The hall was heaving; the entire tribe had gathered. Tables laden with various foods and casks lined the sides of the hall whilst a roaring fire blazed at its centre. It was around this fire that the tribe's menfolk were gathered; the women and children kept to themselves.

An icy blast cut through the festive warmth of Vorde's great timber hall as the heavy double doors were opened to admit a pair of men. The first to enter was a tall, well-built man with a shaggy tan beard. His companion was slightly shorter and leaner; he was clean-shaven and had a youthful aspect about him. Both were wrapped in heavy fur cloaks and covered in snow. A particularly powerful gust blew the long blonde hair of a brutish looking man into his drinking horn. He spat, cursing.

'Close those damned doors!'

'Stifle your whining, Olaf!' the larger of the two newcomers replied.

Olaf turned, 'Ragna, you're late! What delayed you?' he chided.

'The water troughs were all frozen over. We had to break the ice before we could leave.'

'Cold work.'

'Aye,' Ragna agreed before turning to his companion, 'Son, fetch two horns of mead, we've earned it this evening!'

As Ragna's son moved off through the crowds Olaf said, 'Surely you know the custom, Ragna? A boy is not allowed strong drink until he has come of age.'

'Olaf, is your memory failing you? My son begins his rites of passage tonight; he will pass into manhood next summer.'

'He is that old already?' Olaf asked, somewhat shocked.

Ragna smiled, 'Chronis waits on no man, my friend, and we'll all have to repay the Old Father of Time one day.'

'That we will.'

'But not today! Today all is well and there is mead a-plenty!' proclaimed Ragna as he accepted the horn the boy offered him when he returned. Turning to his son, he asked, 'Thurion. What is there to say regarding time?'

'We do not live in the past for that is where the dead live. Neither do we live in the future for our fates are not written. Rather we seek to live today, with honour,' Thurion recited with conviction. Ragna looked at Thurion, fatherly pride written on his face.

'Well said! You'll make a fine man,' Olaf bellowed, before draining his horn and making his way to the edge of the hall on unsteady legs in search of another drink.

'Come Thurion, let us eat and drink our fill and I will introduce you to Magnusson. This will be your first step towards manhood: standing before the chieftain without fear,' Ragna said as he led his son through the crowded hall.

Thurion had been to many a mid-winter feast but only as a boy, in the company of his mother. He had fought mock battles with other children with blunted wooden swords and had never really given any consideration to the significance of the festival. Those kinds of things were for adults; what he and the other children were interested in were playing games, eating and sleeping. Following this festival things were going to be different for him however. His father had taken him aside a few months earlier and explained the real significance of the feasting and the festivities.

'Thurion,' his father had begun, 'the mid-winter feast is a celebration of the potential that lies sleeping within every living thing. The plants and trees lie dormant, but within each one is the promise of new life. The earth is solid but locked within lies everything we need to grow our crops for another year. And within each of us, Thurion, lies dormant everything we might achieve in the coming year. With the passing of mid-winter we begin to see the slow waking of this potential as winter gives way to spring. All this you have heard before but do you understand it, do you believe it?'

Thurion thought for a moment before

answering. 'I had not really given it much thought in the past but I think I have come to understand more this last year. Yes father, I do understand and I do believe.'

'That is good, I think you are ready.'

'Ready for what, Father?' Thurion had asked, not realising what his father was hinting at.

'I've been talking with your mother and the family elders, and we are in agreement,' Ragna paused and a smile spread across his face. 'Son, you are ready to undertake the rites of passage, beginning with this year's mid-winter feast. You are ready to begin awakening the potential within you that will see you pass into manhood next summer,' he said with pride.

A smile now also spread across Thurion's face. 'Really, Father, you think I am ready to become a man?'

'Yes, Son, you are ready. Come, there is much you need to know.'

Ragna had walked Thurion around the perimeter of the corral in which the family's herd of oxen were kept, and explained what would be expected of the boy in the coming months. He explained that the rites of passage would begin at the mid-winter feast; symbolically representing Thurion's awakening to manhood. In the months that followed he would learn how to fight and how to hunt. He would learn of the gods and of the ancestors. All of this would be undertaken under the scrutiny of one or more of the tribal elders.

It begins tonight thought Thurion as he followed his father though the press of feasting men to where Chieftain Magnusson was standing. The chieftain was a huge man with long plaited hair and a full beard. A large scar ran from his left cheek down his face and ended halfway across his bare chest. He wore thick winter boots and heavy trousers that were held up by a leather belt clasped with a giant tooth. He was bare from the waist up but for a long wolf pelt cloak that hung from his shoulders. As Ragna and Thurion approached the chieftain they overheard the end of what looked to have been a heated debate.

'It's true enough! Have you received *any* news from Dramm or Holmsberg this last year? I tell you we'll see Muskovian banners before this next year is out,' Magnusson stated.

The man to whom he was talking responded, 'I fear you're right, we'll suffer at the hands of those cursed slavers before ere-long.'

'Suffer?! I said we'd see their banners, not that we'd be carried off into slavery! Look around you, Bramn!' the chieftain said in a loud voice, 'are these the faces of men who would be cowed by a rag-tag mob of thin-faced slavers?'

Magnusson's question was answered by a chorus of roars and spilled mead as the tribesmen within earshot assured their chieftain that they would not be cowed so easily.

'You see, Bramn, it will be bloody work but we'll not fall as others have – you can be sure of that!' The chieftain turned from his companion to regard Ragna and Thurion who had managed to approach him through the press.

'Hello, Ragna, you old goat! Glad to see you made it. Who's that hiding behind you?'

'Chieftain Magnusson,' Ragna began, 'I would like to present my son, Thurion. He is to undertake the rites of passage this coming year.'

The chieftain looked Thurion up and down

before he spoke.

'Do you fear me, boy?'

Thurion thought for a moment or two before answering, then in his bravest voice, he slowly replied, 'I respect you, sir, you are mighty and honourable. But I have done nothing to cause offence to either you or your family nor have I dishonoured our tribe. So, no, I don't fear you.'

'You answer wisely. You seem to know the difference between respect and fear. I will be watching you, Thurion, son of Ragna, and expect to see you attendant at mid-summer as a man of the tribe.' He nodded to Ragna before turning and heading into the crowd.

'You have done well, son, the chieftain approves. Now we celebrate, for tomorrow there is much to begin!'

And so Thurion celebrated his first mid-winter feast alongside the men of the tribe. This appeared to involve a lot of story-telling and yarn spinning about times gone by: hard winters, poor crops, battles fought, and lost friends. There were burnt fingers when men got careless and used their knives to roast strips of meat over the hot flames. There was a lot of banter aimed at the women who served the mead and vittles, most of which was ignored but some drew yelled retorts which Thurion did not understand. The feasting also seemed to involve the consumption of prodigious volumes of mead and ales; he joined in with this – but not for long.

The following morning the men of the tribe rose late, many waking to the pain of a throbbing head or a churning stomach. The great hall looked like the aftermath of a battle; detritus was strewn everywhere, men were passed out all over the floor, some were even asleep on the serving tables. Many of the casks had been broken open and a few of the mead benches had been wrecked. Dogs lay with bloated stomachs, surrounded by bones. It had been a good feast.

Ragna and Thurion had left the great hall just after first light and tramped through the soft snow to reach Ragna's vron, or homestead, in just over an hour, stopping briefly whilst Thurion threw up again. Ragna took pity on the boy when they arrived and helped him with his chores.

Once the morning's tasks had been completed, Ragna led Thurion into one of the barns and up into a loft. Thurion followed his father up an old wooden ladder to discover that, far from being another feed store, this was where his father stored his wargear. Broad round shields were hung from one wall, weapons of all types were mounted on racks on another whilst at the far end, on a stand, hung a fine suit of chain mail and an open-faced helmet. It was the first time Thurion had been allowed up into his father's armoury and he was in awe of what he saw.

'Am I to have my own sword, Father?' Thurion asked.

'In time. First you must learn how to use each and every weapon in this room. Have you heard it said that each man has his own preferred weapon?'

'Yes Father, I have heard that said,' Thurion paused before continuing, 'So once I have learned how to fight with each of these weapons, am I to choose one that I prefer?'

'No, Son, *you* do not choose your weapon. Your *weapon* chooses you.'

'I don't understand.'

'You will, trust me.'

Over the following dark weeks that led out of winter Ragna taught Thurion how to fight. Thurion learned the strengths and weaknesses of each of his father's weapons and how to use them effectively.

'Almost, you've almost got it, Son. Try again,' Ragna said as Thurion picked himself from the ground, and reclaimed his greatsword from where it had fallen from his grip.

'I'm just not feeling it, Father, it's...' Thurion trailed off, at a loss for words. 'It's not the weight or the length. I just don't feel comfortable.' A thought came to him as he swung the huge sword around in slow, precise arcs. 'I'll be back in a minute father, I've had an idea.'

Thurion jogged off to one of the outhouses and returned a minute later with a massive log splitting axe. 'Let me try again.' With a wry grin in the faces of both father and son the two began to circle each other. They sparred for a while before Ragna lowered his greatsword and raised his hand to his son.

'Enough, Thurion! Enough!'

'Father, I think...'

'The axe has chosen you.'

Ragna finished off his son's thought for him between heavy breaths. 'You've some of your grandfather's blood in your veins, that much is clear. Rannweig preferred a greataxe; you seem to be developing his taste for unsubtle weapons!'

Thurion grinned as he rested the axe head on the ground and leaned on the haft. 'You haven't told me much about my grandfather. Why not?'

'You may be undertaking your rites of passage, son, but you are not yet a man. Some tales are not for the ears of children. It is enough to say that he lived and died with honour. I promise you I will tell you everything once you have come of age.'

Thurion did not press the issue but chose to wait patiently until he came of age at the mid-summer festival.

Winter was drawing to a close when Thurion accompanied his father to Helme's forge. Helme was the tribal blacksmith and had agreed to help the boy forge his first set of wargear. It was gruelling work and Thurion came home from the forge each night covered in soot and smelling of smoke. By the time the first blossoms were appearing on the trees however, he had his own coat of mail and a helmet mounted in his father's armoury. Unlike his father, Thurion had chosen an all-enclosing spectacled helmet with a length of mail hung from the eye guards. As well as a two-handed battleaxe, Thurion had made for himself a single-handed axe and a small hatchet.

Some weeks later spring had arrived and the trees were covered in blossoms. There was still a chill in the air and the nights were still cold, but people began to move around more and the livestock was allowed to graze the new grass during the day. It was at this time that the men of Vorde began to venture out on hunting expeditions again after the austerity of winter. Thurion, like so many of the tribe's older boys, had accompanied his father on a number of last year's expeditions but had been little more than an observer. He had remained at the overnight camp and not ventured deep into the forest with the men. This year, however he was expected to take an active role in the hunt: another rite of passage into manhood.

The first expedition of the year gathered in the cold light of dawn one spring morning. The hunting party consisted of a dozen men, including Thurion and his father. Ragna had advised his son to bring with him only a bow and a couple of spears which he had gifted to him earlier, and his own single-handed axe. Thurion felt both excitement and trepidation as he was introduced to the rest of the expedition. These men included some of the tribe's most renowned hunters. Jhorm Henrickson was present, the only man known to have taken down one of the great wild hogs single-handedly and survived. He was a bear of a man, almost seven feet tall with a jagged scar running down the right-hand side of his face, closing his eye in a mangle of scar tissue. Kjeri Tojitson, known as 'the bowman', had also joined the hunt. He was not the size of Jhorm but the mighty seven-foot longbow slung over his shoulder made him look taller.

Their plan was fairly straightforward, they would head into the nearby forest and set up camp a day's walk from its edge. Early in the morning of the second day the party would split into smaller groups and make their way deeper into the forest. After a day's hunting they would return to Vorde, by dusk of the third day.

This was the first time Thurion had entered the forest proper. Until now he had only ventured into its outer reaches. Strangely he felt at home under the boughs of the forest's ancient trees. He found he had a natural talent at moving swiftly and quietly through the undergrowth, much to the annoyance of Jhorm, who tended to barrel through it like a troll or an ogre. As the sun set at the end of their first day's trek, the men of Vorde had set up camp in a small clearing near a forest pool and were settling down for the night.

Dawn was an hour away when Thurion rose

along with his father and shared a simple breakfast of cured meat and bread. By the time the rest of the hunters had formed themselves into small parties, Kjeri Tojitson had already left the camp. This, Thurion was told, was entirely expected; Kjeri, whilst being a sociable and well liked member of the tribe, always hunted alone. The remainder of the party split into three groups. Thurion found himself in a party with four others; Sigri, Alden, Brinwir and one of the tribal elders: Nunden Ackerstedt. The parties separated and made their own separate ways into the forest. After several hours Thurion's party came across a path through the undergrowth that looked to have been made by passing deer. Alden was elected to scout ahead of the rest of the group. A short while later he returned and announced that a group of around eight deer were grazing in a clearing, a little way along the track. Quietly the party stalked towards the clearing to find it just as Alden had said.

'Boy, make your way round to the other side and when I give the signal flush them towards the rest of us. We'll try to separate one of the adults and bring it down,' Nunden said to Thurion.

'Yes, Sir,' the boy replied before melting into the forest.

Silently he made his way through the forest, using the natural cover of the trees and the understorey. As he approached the edge of the clearing opposite where his companions were now lying in wait, he noticed that one of the ancient trees possessed a mighty branch that reached out a little way into the clearing. With a hunter's guile he climbed the tree and silently made his way along this branch until he was squatting at the branch's extremity, over the clearing. He settled down to wait.

After some time one of the deer wandered over and began to crop the grass under the tree in which Thurion was hiding. Suddenly, a white stone arced into the clearing from where the three hunters were concealed. The deer instantly stood erect, searching for the danger. Before it could make off, Thurion had reversed his grip on his spear and dropped from the branch onto its shoulders, spitting it. The beast cried in pain and surprise as Thurion landed on it. The others made to flee back into the safety of the forest, but before they had cleared the open expanse of grass Thurion's four companions burst from hiding and hurled their javelins at the closest animal. As the four men occupied themselves with their kill, Thurion finished off his deer with his axe.

The forest was soon quiet again. Thurion was cleaning the blood from his axe and spear when Nunden, the elder, walked up to him from across the clearing.

'When I said to flush the quarry towards us do you think I meant for you to make a kill yourself?' he asked, his voice stern.

'I saw an opportunity to achieve a kill whilst flushing the others towards you. If I have done wrong, I'm sorry,' Thurion replied.

The elder's face lightened and he smiled. 'Boy, you've not done wrong! You did flush the rest towards us as I asked; it's just that, er, I didn't expect you to do it in quite this fashion that's all. I can see you've some natural talent as a huntsman but it needs some polishing!' the elder jested, pushing the mangled form of the deer with his boot.

'I needed to finish it off,' Thurion said, trying to justify the large number of axe wounds along the deer's left flank.

'There are cleaner ways to finish off a kill, but you will learn them in time. For now, you can be proud of your first kill. Come, I'll show you how to prepare it so it can be carried back to camp.'

Taking out his hunting knife, Nunden pulled the deer over on its back, and holding its forelegs made a long cut down the belly. He opened the body cavity and allowed the guts to spill onto the grass, then, grasping the slimy innards he severed them from the diaphragm and all the way down to the vent. Using Thurion's axe, he severed the head at the nearest point to the shoulder.

'These,' he said, pointing at the guts, 'We don't eat. By the time we get this carcass back to Vorde their contents would have gone off and tainted the meat. And *that...*' indicating the doe's head, 'Would weigh us down on the walk back, so we leave both these parts for the scavengers, and as a token of our gratitude to the wild spirits for their bounty.'

They joined the others in searching for long branches on which to sling the deer. The journey back to the camp site was no swifter than their morning's journey out because, although stealth was no longer required, the weight of two full-grown deer carried between the five of them slowed progress considerably.

* * *

By dusk the hunting parties had started to return. Jhorm's party returned first carrying the huge carcass of a full-grown wild hog. The second arrived after them with a pair of smaller hogs.

'Couldn't you find anything smaller?' cried

Jhorm, the mock humour evident in his tone.

'Not all of us have the appetite of an ogre, Jhorm!' retorted one of the party, as he put down the hog he was carrying.

Ragna's party returned shortly afterwards empty handed. One of their number was being carried on a litter and looked badly wounded.

'What happened?' asked one of Jhorm's party as the litter was laid onto the ground.

'Troll,' Ragna announced. 'We were stalking a herd of deer as they drank from one of the rivers a little way north when they suddenly scattered. Arton couldn't get clear in time; his foot snagged on a root and he fell.'

'Bad luck,' said Jhorm as he leaned over the litter, 'Did you get the bastard, at least?' asked the hunter.

'Aye,' Arton said weakly. As Jhorm knelt beside the litter the wounded hunter drew a hand from under the cloak in which he had been wrapped and handed something to him.

'We got it to the ground but Arton finished the job; caved its head in with his axe,' explained another of Ragna's party.

'Arton – Troll Slayer!' Jhorm announced, as he unwrapped the package he had been handed to reveal a single huge yellowed tooth. The returned hunters cheered and banished the gloomy mood that was threatening to set in. They immediately set about collecting kindling and within a short time a camp fire was blazing. One of the smaller hogs had been skinned and butchered, and joints and pieces of meat were being positioned near the flames on makeshift skewers when Thurion and his party walked into view.

'It looks like you've killed enough for the both of us, son!' Ragna jested when he saw Thurion's party returning with their kills. As the two deer were laid out in the centre of the camp, alongside the other kills, Jhorm noticed the mangled left flank of Thurion's kill.

'Aye, you may have two – but look, it seems to have been mauled as badly as Arton here! Looks like a wolf or a mountain lion got to it first.' Jhorm observed.

'You'd do well to reserve judgement on the quality of the handiwork, Jhorm,' warned Nunden. 'That kill is all Thurion's work. He stalked it, he struck it and he finished it. Yes, it does look like it has been butchered by a blind man, but it is a novice's kill on his first hunt. Not many here can boast that. Can you, Jhorm?' The elder turned to Thurion's father, 'Ragna, your son has some skill as a hunter, you should be proud.'

Jhorm turned to regard Thurion.

'This is your first kill then? I take back what I said. Well done. I'm sure your father can show you how to finish the job a little more cleanly though!'

'Of course I can, Jhorm, all in good time.'

Kjeri returned last of all. He stalked into the camp almost unseen by the others for it was now quite dark. The elder was the first to spot him approach.

'At last, you grace us with your presence, Kjeri!' Nunden exclaimed, as the lone hunter almost staggered into the firelight.

'It's good to see you too, Nunden, help me with these would you?' he asked as he began to unbuckle two heavy leather belts that were strapped cross-wise across his chest. Nunden got up from beside the fire and helped him with his burdens.

'You've had a good day it seems,' said the elder. The two men each carried one of Kjeri's belts to where the party's kills were piled. From each one hung six good-sized geese.

With their evening meal finished the hunters set a watch and bedded down for the night. The journey back to Vorde was tough but spirits were high; Arton had not died in the night – which was seen as a good sign that he would recover from his injuries – their youngest member had made his first kill which had brought him another step closer to manhood, and they were coming back laden down with game. The expedition had been successful and none of them could have asked for more than that. Upon their return, the hunters were welcomed with cheers and horns of mead; as if they had been gone for three months instead of just three days. The villagers could not remember there being such a bevy of game from previous spring hunts. They took the success of this first hunt of the season as a good omen for the coming year.

Chapter 2

The sun was shining brightly in the sparsely clouded sky. A warm breeze gently rustled the leaves in the gardens of Sharrayah's citadel, causing the dappled shade to dance across the ground. At the centre of a small lawn surrounded by well-tended hedges grew a great old tree, its lowest boughs almost touching the ground. Under one of these heavy branches knelt a young angel clad in a moss-green dress. She held her snow-white wings around herself, concealing her head and hands.

The sound of hooves approaching at a brisk trot caused her to lower her wings slightly, and look up as a solitary horseman checked the pace of his grey horse and rode onto the lawn. He wore a white tunic under a deep blue robe. Sunlight glinted from the simple silver circlet that held back shoulder-length auburn hair.

Looking down at the kneeling angel he spoke in a clear, authoritative tone.

'Princess Celene, there you are. Your maids have been searching the citadel for you. Come, we may just make the opening ceremony yet.' He paused, asking as he dismounted, 'Have you been crying?'

The young princess rose to her feet, her long blonde hair catching in the breeze. As she did she stretched out her hands to the robed rider.

'Holy Sandar, I've done it, look.' She opened her hands to reveal a tiny baby bird. It was weak but it was alive. 'I found it at the foot of the tree; it had fallen from its nest and broken its wing.'

'You healed it without recourse to your focus stone?' Holy Sandar asked.

'Yes, Seneschal, I left it in my chambers after my last class,' she confirmed as she gently passed the bird to Sandar for inspection.

'It will live,' he concluded, 'Celene, you have never before managed to heal without channelling your will through your focus stone. What was different this time? How were you able to achieve this?' he asked, handing the bird back.

'I don't know, Seneschal. All I know is that it broke my heart to see it suffering, I had to do something, it was almost as if...' she trailed off, lost for words.

'As if Ios were calling you to act?' Sandar finished her thought for her.

'Yes, it felt like that. Was she, Seneschal?' the young princess asked.

'The Mother of all Life speaks to each of her children differently, Princess. Now return the youngster to its nest and hurry back with me to the citadel. We can discuss this on the way,' the seneschal said, impatiently.

'Are you not pleased for me? Is this not what all your lessons have been working towards?' she asked, a little put out by the seneschal's seeming dismissal of her achievement.

'Of course I am pleased for you, Celene! But if I don't get you back for the start of the opening ceremony, your father will have me confined to the citadel for the next year!'

The young princess's face brightened and she rose gently into the air on her great feathered wings. Gently she returned the bird back to its nest, and glided to where the seneschal was now riding off the lawn, easily keeping pace with his horse.

'Do you think the Holy Mother was really speaking to me, Seneschal?' she asked as they made their way back to the citadel.

'I do, Celene; as I said, she speaks to all of her children in different ways. All you have to do is recognise the way in which she speaks to you. Did it hurt?' he asked.

'Yes, it hurt a lot; the little thing was almost dead,' she admitted.

'Celene! What was the first thing I taught you?' Sandar asked, exasperated.

'Healing is a transference; whatever we heal we take on ourselves,' she replied, almost by rote.

'But we cannot bring anything back from death; that transference is forbidden,' Sandar said, finishing the sentence.

'Although the chick only needed to sustain slight injury to incapacitate it, the fact that it was almost dead made the transference extremely dangerous to one as inexperienced as yourself. Had it died as you were healing it then you too may have died. Please, do not try anything like that again. Your heart was in the right place, Celene, but you still have much to learn,' Sandar chided.

'I am sorry, Holy Sandar,' Celene apologised, using Sandar's official priestly title.

It did not take them long to reach the citadel. The fortress was more a collection of vast towers enclosed by a curtain wall than a single structure. Each sandstone tower reached many hundreds of feet into the sky, the tallest seeming to kiss the few clouds as they processed on their way across the bright morning sky.

The gardens immediately adjacent to the citadel's wall were the scene of frantic preparation as the seneschal and the young princess made their way through an ornate gateway. Pavilions were being erected, seating was being arranged, cold food was being set out whilst the rich smells emanating from the kitchens spoke of the many hot wonders being prepared there.

Inside the citadel of Sharrayah it was light and airy thanks to a clever arrangement of small defensible windows and carefully placed mirrors that reflected the light to maximum effect. Moving through the main atrium, Sandar led Celene up one of the two main stair cases, to the fifth floor where her chambers were located, and knocked on the rich red timber door. A middle aged woman wearing a simple light blue dress opened it.

'Seneschal Sandar, you have found our errant princess, I thank you!' she said, relieved.

'It was no problem, Lady Sara, she hadn't gone far; just down into the gardens.'

'You shouldn't go wandering off, Princess, not with the ceremony little more than an hour away!' she said, ushering the young angel into her chambers.

'Princess Celene, Lady Sara, I bid you good morning; I have preparations to oversee.' With a bow the seneschal excused himself.

'Holy Sandar is not just your mentor, Princess Celene, he is also the head of the Nemeth Order of Life *and* seneschal of this fortress, as you well know! He can't be expected to go running off after wandering princesses who have no sense of timekeeping!' Sara continued as she ushered Celene into her dressing room.

'Lady Sara, you have been my head maid for

many years; I trust you to have everything in order, so we have plenty of time!' Celene replied as she walked to the foot of her bed and regarded the myrtle-green dress that had been neatly laid out. 'Myrtle? You know I think there is too much blue in that colour for my taste, can I not wear... this one?' she asked, removing a forest green dress from one of her wardrobes.

'Princess, you know myrtle is your father's favourite colour. Today may be a celebration of your coming of age but he is still your father, and the High Prince of Nemeth-Sharrayah, or have you forgotten?' Sara asked.

'No, Lady Sara, I have not forgotten! I will wear the myrtle to please father, but he must wear forest green on my wedding day!' Celene replied as she changed into the pretty green dress that had been prepared.

'Wedding day? My Princess, you have barely come of age and already your thoughts are turning to weddings! Need I remind you that you are not to go around teasing all the young princes. You will tour the principalities to find a suitor in good time—'

'...as has been the custom for centuries!' Celene interrupted, doing her best impression of Sandar as she finished Sara's sentence with one of his often-used phrases.

'Celene! You should not mock the seneschal!' Sara chided.

In just over an hour the princess had prepared herself for the opening ceremony that would begin the day's festivities and the celebration of her coming of age. Dressed in a beautiful myrtle-green dress with a light-green shawl of gossamer silk around her shoulders, and a small tiara studded with sapphires and emeralds on her head, Princess Celene Nemeth descended the staircase from her chambers and crossed the atrium towards the garden where everyone had gathered. Her father met her at the door to the gardens. His wings were flecked with silver, as was his hair. He was dressed in fine myrtle-green robes, trimmed with gold.

'So you decided to attend today's celebrations after all!' her father jested as they embraced.

'I couldn't be late father, not with all these guests waiting!' Celene replied.

'That's just like my daughter, to take the light things in life seriously and the serious things lightly!' he reflected as they turned to enter the gardens.

Father and daughter stepped out into the bright sunlight of mid-morning as trumpets sounded their entrance.

'High Prince Raparké Nemeth, ruler of Nemeth-Sharrayah and Princess Celene Nemeth!' Seneschal Sandar announced as Raparké and his daughter made their way to the largest of the pavilions that had been erected in the citadel's gardens, the sound of cheers and applause filling the air.

The gardens were packed with foreign dignitaries, princes, members of the Nemeth Order of Life, and members of the High Order of Life. All of the principalities held the Mother of all Life, Ios, as their god. Whilst each principality had its own priesthood, the High Priesthood of Ios held supreme authority. Each principality was under the care of a single Elder of the High Order who had a number of high priests, priests and deacons under him (or her).

The priesthood comprised mostly of men and women who were gifted at birth with a deep sense of connection with Ios, and as a result had an innate ability to care for others. Helping others less fortunate than themselves was their principal aim. In reality, most of the priests and priestesses worked either in the royal palaces or the temples, leaving the daily social contact with ordinary folk to the many deacons they employed. Today, all the deacons and priests of the Nemeth Order of Life, as well as High Priest Paterios, the head of the High Order of Life himself, were present.

High Prince Raparké led his daughter to one of the three thrones that had been placed at the centre of the great pavilion. She took her seat next to her mother, High Princess Tamura, who was already seated. Unlike her husband, the High Princess was wearing a dress of light teal with a white silk scarf over her shoulders. She kept her wings folded behind her, sitting with great poise, waiting for the ceremony to start.

'How did you manage to convince father to let you wear *anything* other than myrtle-green?' Celene asked in a hushed tone.

Celene's mother turned her head a fraction and replied in a low voice, 'I *always* wear teal to occasions such as these, darling,' she said.

'And I *always* wear forest-green to official occasions …' Celene began.

'Celene, you are your father's daughter, *I* am your father's wife; there is a difference. Surely you have noticed this over the years?' her mother asked. Celene's only reply was to smile with just a hint of blush appearing in her cheeks.

Mother and daughter sat up straight and turned to Raparké as he began to address the gathered crowd.

'Your Royal Highnesses, High Priests and

Elders of our Orders, lords, ladies and gentlemen, I welcome you here to the gardens of Sharrayah to celebrate the coming-of-age of my daughter, Celene!' There was a loud applause which slowly petered out as the High Prince made to continue, 'My daughter has come of age and has passed from childhood into adulthood. She has cast off her childish ways and assumed the ways of a true Princess of the line of Nemeth!' Again there was an applause that slowly died away. 'I hereby invite each and every one of you to join myself and my wife, as we celebrate today with our daughter!' The applause was deafening as High Prince Raparké concluded his brief opening speech.

Raparké turned and gestured to his wife and daughter, who both rose and took his proffered hands. He led them out of the pavilion into the bright mid-morning sunlight where they were immediately approached by various guests. This was the first time Celene had been present at a royal function in an official capacity and so she said little, merely exchanging pleasantries with those guests who approached her to congratulate her. Many of these guests were young princes. Despite the fact that this was not an event where courting was accepted, it was clear that the young princes' approaches were designed to leave an impression on the young princess.

'Celene, you mustn't lead them on so!' her mother whispered as yet another young prince departed after introducing himself.

'I don't know *what* you mean,' Celene replied.

'You know *exactly* what I mean my dear; your smile says more than your lips – and you know it!'

'Oh Mother, I'm not saying anything

improper; whatever those fine young princes may assume is entirely up to them,' she replied in a playful tone.

'Just be careful, one day you may meet someone who is taken in by your forwardness... and then you'll both get hurt,' Tamura warned her daughter as yet another prince approached through the crowds.

'Mother, every prince from the angelic caste knows what to expect. They wouldn't be here otherwise!' she replied, dismissing her mother's warning as the young prince stopped a pace or two from her and bowed extravagantly.

'I am Prince Asmos of Dra-Azun,' he announced. Prince Asmos wore a vermilion tunic under a vest of finely woven silver mail. His hair was plaited and reached just below his shoulders. His wings, which were the same russet-brown as his hair, were flecked with black.

'Prince Asmos, you appear to have come dressed for battle!' Celene joked, gesturing to his mail and the rapier that hung from his belt.

'Not so, princess, I assure you! The princes of Dra-Azun are always armed. It is a -'

'Tradition?' Celene cut in, laughing.

'Why yes, Princess Celene, it *is* a tradition! You seem to have me at a disadvantage, you appear to know more about me than I about you. Would you tell me of some of your traditions?' the young prince asked eagerly.

'My dear Prince Asmos, a princess does not give up her secrets so easily, but perhaps we will chance to meet again at some point?' Celene replied.

'I would like that,' Prince Asmos replied. Blushing, he bowed politely saying 'Till then!' before turning away and heading back into the crowds.

'I like him Mother, he has a certain nobility about him,' Celene remarked as they strolled through the gardens towards one of the food pavilions.

'Celene, you appear to have liked every young prince who has introduced himself to you this morning, and all for completely different reasons,' she replied, somewhat off-handedly, 'Now, where is your father?'

'I saw him talking with Seneschal Sandar a few minutes ago.'

'Ah, he must be sorting out the blessings then,' her mother replied, as the two of them entered the shade of the pavilion and made for a table arrayed with bowls of prepared fruits.

Some little while later High Prince Raparké entered the pavilion, approached the pair and turned to his wife.

'Is it time for the blessings?' she asked him.

'We have a few minutes, there's no need to rush,' he replied. He then joined them and helped himself to some fruit.

A few minutes later the High Prince, along with his wife and daughter, walked back towards the main pavilion where he had previously opened the ceremony. This time Celene did not sit down with her parents but stood off to one side along with her two elder brothers, Erakos and Iraudis. Erakos was slightly taller than Celene, whilst Iraudis was taller still at just shy of six feet. Both young princes kept their hair cropped short, above their shoulders, giving them a somewhat militaristic look. Once Raparké and Tamura had taken their seats, Sandar entered the pavilion and addressed the gathering crowd.

'As is the custom on state occasions such as

today, it is the pleasure of High Prince Raparké and High Princess Tamura each to bestow a single blessing onto one of their subjects!'

A middle-aged man and a young woman were escorted into the pavilion by four soldiers wearing long coats of bright mail under snow white tabards. The scabbards that held long, straight swords clanked against their sides as they marched in step.

'Thank you,' Sandar said, dismissing the guards who then turned and took up positions a few yards away. He took the young woman by the hand and led her up to where Tamura was seated. As she approached the woman turned her eyes towards the ground before kneeling.

'How would you have the Mother of all Life bless you?' Tamura asked with stately grace.

'I… I am barren Your Highness,' the woman replied.

'Stand and receive the blessing of Ios,' Tamura commanded. The woman did as she was bade and stood facing the High Princess. Tamura rose to her feet and took the woman's left hand in her right.

'Holy Ios, Mother of all Life, hear thy child now,' the High Princess began as she placed her left hand over the woman's womb, 'remove this woman's barrenness and bless her with fertility,' she continued. A second or two later Tamura began to moan and, letting go of the woman's hand, doubled over. Immediately two priests in white robes rushed over to support her but she brushed them off. Slowly she regained her poise as a faint golden light began to emanate from her body. The glow only lasted for a moment or two before fading.

'I have taken your barrenness and our Holy Mother has taken it from me. Go, in the fullness of life,' she said to the woman who was now standing incredulous before the High Princess.

'Thank you, thank you,' she repeated as a priest led her out of the pavilion.

As the woman was led out of the pavilion to the waiting guards, Sandar led the man to Raparké's throne. Like the woman before him the man lowered his eyes to the ground before kneeling in front of the High Prince.

'How would you have the Mother of all Life bless you?' he asked. The man pulled the sleeve of his tunic back to reveal his arm. It ended at the wrist in a mangled lump of scar tissue where his hand should have been.

'I was a miller, Your Highness; I caught my hand in the millstones some years ago and haven't been able to work since,' he said.

'Give me your arm,' Raparké commanded. 'Holy Ios, Mother of all Life, hear thy child now. Restore this man's hand so he may work again, I beseech thee.'

The miller's arm was immediately surrounded by a faint golden light and the hand slowly began to regenerate. The miller looked on in a mix of wonder and horror as his missing hand was restored, and as the High Prince's hand began to wither and die. A look of pain crossed Raparké's face as he held his now-withered hand to his chest. Slowly, the golden light that had surrounded the miller's hand transferred itself to his. Those who could see looked on in wonder as the High Prince's hand was restored to its original form.

High Prince Raparké turned to the man, 'You have received the blessing of Holy Ios, go now, miller, and take up your profession again.' The miller was speechless as he was led out of the pavilion, gazing in wonder at his restored hand. As the soldiers escorted the two civilians out of the royal gardens the crowds slowly began to disperse, since the blessings of Ios marked the end of the official celebrations.

Tomorrow would see Celene attend her first royal council. She went to bed with mixed emotions; excitement because of the new freedoms that coming-of-age permitted but also apprehension because of the responsibilities that she had now inherited.

Chapter 3

With the heavy curtains drawn, the richly furnished bedchamber was in almost complete darkness. She had been ill for some time. The sickness had slowly incapacitated her until she was bed-ridden. Her husband, High Prince Seratos Leznar, had been by her bedside for months now, neglecting all of his responsibilities. At first he had prayed daily to Holy Ios for aid but his prayers became less frequent as the Holy Mother remained silent. In truth he had never really expected an answer. She had never heard him before, so why would she listen now?

Although he had ruled Leznar-Carchum for some years now, since the death of his mother, all thoughts of his responsibilities faded as his beloved Saruké grew weaker and weaker. The more withdrawn he became, the more concerned his seneschal became. Eventually he became so concerned that he felt compelled to act in his prince's stead, though he could not make any decisions regarding matters of state on his behalf. He was forced to turn messengers and emissaries from neighbouring provinces away after his prince refused to grant any of them an audience. Over the course of a few months High Prince Seratos had managed to isolate the principality of Leznar-Carchum from its neighbours, thanks both to his refusal to see anyone other than his priests, and his insistence that all of his principality's available resources be turned to searching for a cure for his beloved wife.

High Prince Seratos knelt by her bedside, his ebony hair falling across his face concealing the tears that ran down his cheeks. He clasped her cold hand gently in both of his own. She was now only breathing weakly. A stray lock of her long, blonde hair fell across her beautiful face as she turned to face him. Gently he brushed it back behind her ear.

'Saruké, my beloved,' he said, feeling her move for the first time in several hours.

'Are you still here?' she asked, 'I would have thought you had better things to do...' She was exhausted and could not finish her sentence.

'My love, I have barely left your side for weeks. I have the whole principality searching for a cure; no one will rest until you are well.'

'We all die, my love.'

'Surely the Holy Mother will hear the cries of her priests? Surely she will intervene?' he asked himself as much as his wife.

'Everything that lives must eventually die; it is the way of things,' she whispered before lying back, exhausted.

Seratos continued to kneel by her side and wept bitterly.

Where are my priests? Where is Tiran?

At that moment High Prince Seratos had never felt more alone. His god had abandoned him, remaining oblivious to all of his prayers and petitions. His wife was barely conscious and now his seneschal was late.

* * *

Some time later a knock sounded at the bedchamber door.

31

'Come,' Seratos said quietly.

The door opened silently and Tiran, seneschal of Carchum and Head of the Leznar Order of Life entered the room. He was a middle-aged man, clean-shaven with short-cropped hair. He wore the white robes of the priesthood girded about the waist by a belt of black leather inlaid with silver roses, which signified his dual rank of seneschal.

'Your Highness, I have done as you requested.'

'You have found a cure?' There was hope in the High Prince's voice as he gently placed Saruké's hand back on the bed and rose to face Tiran.

'I have ordered every member of the priesthood to help maintain a day and night prayer vigil in the temple,' he replied.

'That is not a cure, Seneschal,' Seratos replied slowly.

'Your Highness, only the Holy Mother can save the High Princess now; everything else has failed.'

'We have not tried *everything*.'

'*That* will not work, Your Highness. Surely you must see that? Attempting to heal her in such a way would certainly kill any of us who tried. It is highly doubtful that it would work.'

'High Priest Tiran, The Holy Mother does not hear me. She has not answered your priests though they pray day and night. There is no other option. Summon your best healers.'

There was an ominous note of finality in the High Prince's voice. Tiran left the bedchamber with a deep sense of foreboding. *This will not end well. The angelic caste, the children of the Holy Mother, are so very different from us mortals that we cannot hope to heal the High Princess. Has his grief blinded him so much that he would condemn innocent men to death?*

Being duty-bound to obey his High Prince, Tiran did as he was ordered and summoned the ten most powerful healers in the principality's Order of Life. Early one morning, several days later, they were all gathered around Saruké's bed in a semi-circle, holding hands.

'Think about what you are asking, Your Highness,' Tiran begged his lord in hushed tones, 'what you are asking has never been attempted before.' *She is* so *close to death.*

Seratos ignored the pleas of his High Priest and turned to the healers.

'Begin.'

The ten priests around the princess's bed began to pray quietly. After a few minutes a faint golden light began to emanate from the High Princess. This light grew in intensity before gently suffusing into the room and settling around the gathered priests. A pained entered the voices of the ten men. One by one they began to visibly wither and grow old. Eventually, they all collapsed and lay still. The golden light settled back onto the High Princess.

'What happened?' Seratos whispered.

'They failed, as I warned you they might, Your Highness.'

Tiran tried to keep his voice even but could not hide an edge of bitterness.

'You think I was wrong to sacrifice these men? I had to try EVERYTHING!'

'Your Highness I was only—'

'Get out. You have failed me, Tiran.'

High Prince Seratos turned from his seneschal as he dismissed him, stepped over the bodies of the dead healers and returned to his wife's bedside. *The Holy Mother has failed me.*

Tiran returned to the temple to pray and so did not hear the cry of anguish three hours later when High Princess Saruké died. He did not hear his High Prince tearing the bedchamber to pieces in a grief-stricken rage. Neither did he hear the sounds of breaking glass that would have told him of Seratos leaping from the chamber window to fly off, weeping all the while.

Seratos flew aimlessly for hours until he found himself crossing the Plains of the Dead. Eventually he landed on a little dirt lane and began to walk, too immersed in his own grief to care exactly where he was going. His eyes were glazed, not focused on anything. His feet traipsed over the path.

'Hail, he who weeps!'

Seratos looked up, blinking. He had been so engrossed in his grief that he had not noticed the old crone walking towards him. She was haggard and leaned heavily on an old gnarled, twisted staff. The filthy rags she wore hung loosely from her skeletally thin body and she spoke with a dry rasping voice.

'What did you say?'

'Hail, he who weeps!' the old woman repeated.

'What do you know?'

'I know many things. I know that you are bereaved. I know that your god has forsaken you, that those around you have failed you, and that you find yourself wandering alone seeking answers to questions that you don't yet know how to ask,' she replied.

Seratos was silent for some time. He was about to ask how she knew so much about him, but before he could she turned and carried on down the road.

'Keep walking, High Prince. Let your grief guide you,' she rasped.

Turning from the old crone, Seratos continued to walk down the dusty lane that led out into the plains. His grief was so great it caused him actual pain deep inside; it felt like his guts were knotted up. He could not reconcile his loss with what he had always been taught about the loving benevolence of The Holy Mother. She had let Saruké die. She had ignored his pleas and his prayers. Why would she abandon her children?

He was so lost in his own thoughts that he only realised that he had approached the great Necropolis when its cold shadow blotted out the pale afternoon sun.

The city was a ruin of crumbling stonework, decaying timbers and rusting iron. To say that it was entirely abandoned was not entirely accurate. Seratos noticed gaunt, mangy hounds slinking in and out of shadows and the occasional raven perched high up on the remaining columns. He was also sure he heard the tell-tale skittering of rats.

He laughed bitterly. His armies had joined forces with those of High Prince Raparké many times in the past to drive the denizens of these plains back into the graves from which they had risen. Now he found himself wandering the streets of a Necropolis bereft of that which, if he was honest, was his sole reason for living. He paid no heed to the hounds that trailed him or to the ravens that circled overhead as he wandered deeper and deeper into the city, losing himself as much in his own thoughts as in its narrow, twisting, rubble-strewn streets.

High Prince Seratos eventually found himself standing in front of what once had been a great palace. Now, however, it was nothing more than a crumbled ruin. Its great gates had rusted off their hinges centuries ago and nothing but the ironwork now lay on the sand, barely visible under a covering of the sickly-looking ivy that eked out a meagre existence in this accursed place. The palace, at one point, had undoubtedly had many floors. These had collapsed over time and now nothing remained but a rutted ground floor almost completely hidden by fallen masonry. There also had been towers that probably reached towards the clouds, but these now lay as a mix of stones and broken tiles on the landscape. Across the outer courtyard could be seen the outline of what once had been a grand entrance-way, but was now little more than a pair of columns forming a perilous gap amongst the fallen stonework.

As Seratos stood regarding the ruined palace, his mind reconstructing an image of the how the palace might have looked in its former glory, something made him start. There was a man standing in what remained of the palace entrance-way. The High Prince was sure he had not been there a second ago. He appeared to be wearing long dark robes although from this distance it was hard to tell. The figure gestured for Seratos to approach. Slowly the prince passed through the gateway, stepping around the rusted gates and made his way across the courtyard towards the palace and its mysterious occupant.

Chapter 4

The evening meal had been eaten around the fire in their large, single-storey roundhouse. Thurion's mother and younger brother had gone to bed and the fire was beginning to die as Ragna sat down beside it and motioned for Thurion to join him. Offering a cup of wine to his son, Ragna asked, 'What do you know of the ancestors, Son?'

'Only that they judge us when we die.'

'Then it is time that you learned about them more fully,' said Ragna. 'Our ancestors reside in the underworld, in a great hall. Each family has their own ancestors, residing in their own hall. All however hold Naeror, the god of the dead as their patron. Upon death we are brought before our ancestors for judgement. If they deem that we have lived an honourable, noble life we are welcomed into our ancestral hall as one of them, to feast. If, however, our ancestors find us wanting in these virtues we are banished into the cold wastes beyond the borders of Naeror's domain.'

Thurion thought for a few minutes before asking, 'So we become immortal after death, like the gods?'

'No son, nothing is immortal. Death is merely a transition, from one life to another. It is true to say that our spirit is not subject to the natural laws of age and decay but it can still be killed,' Ragna explained. Thurion was taken aback by this revelation. 'Do not fear, son, so long as you live your life with honour, so long as you respect your ancestors and your patron god, then your future lies in Naeror's domain. Nothing has ever truly threatened Naeror, for he is mighty.'

Thurion was visibly relieved and ventured a further question. 'Who is my patron god?'

'That is a decision you must make once you reach manhood. Every man gives this deep consideration for there are many gods, all of whom are to be revered as we revere our ancestors, but a man can only take a single god as his patron. Do not worry about this now; now is not the time. It is late,' Ragna observed, before rising and making for his bed.

As the weeks went by and mid-summer drew closer, Thurion was called to train with a number of the tribe's mightiest warriors and to hunt with the likes of Jhorm and other huntsmen. As soon as he was away from the settlement Thurion felt somewhat more relaxed, somewhat freer. He would often join hunting expeditions only to go off on his own, much as Kjeri was known to. Members of the hunting expeditions would see him melting into the forest just before dawn as they rose and broke their night's fast. Before long Thurion took to going off hunting alone, often being away for a few days at a time.

He took his weapons training seriously, steadily becoming more and more proficient in the use of the axe until he was called to spar with Ovlur, one of the tribe's elders. Ovlur was a broad-shouldered man who kept his head shaved bare which accentuated his long plaited beard and deep-set eyes. Ragna accompanied his son to the great hall where Ovlur was waiting outside. Chieftain Magnusson was there, as well as a small crowd who had turned up to witness this next stage in the boy's rites of passage.

Thurion sized up Ovlur. The elder stood at a little over six feet tall and his broad shoulders made him look huge in comparison to himself. He was bare-headed and wore a thick leather sleeveless tunic with a V-shaped neck. The tunic was fastened tightly around his waist which showed the beginnings of a paunch taking shape. Thurion noted this with interest: clearly the elder liked his ale and had not bothered to exercise much over the winter months. Ovlur carried a shield and a mace, which had been wrapped in a padded sheath of cloth and leather. Whilst it was understood that injuries could very well be sustained in these mock duels, inflicting crippling injuries was not the objective.

Ovlur was to push Thurion to his limit, to see just how much he had learned. The elder also wore a sheathed seax on his belt. Every tribal warrior – including some of the women – wore one of these knives in a long sheath slung from a waist belt. Most seax were a palm's length and one width long – about eleven inches for a man and seven inches for a woman, and had a handle made of either wood or bone, usually with elaborate carving on.

The seax was a versatile tool that could be used for slicing vegetables, skinning game or gutting an adversary. Thurion carried one when he was out hunting, but his was only a short-bladed version that boys of his age were allowed to have. He craved for the day when he was granted the right to wear a warrior's seax, and he knew this was only a short time away, for he had excelled in the hunting skills test. The handle of Ovlur's seax was clearly visible; it was made from deer horn decorated with fine inlays of silver and copper and carved to depict a hunting scene. His lack of armour demonstrated confidence in his own ability: he had no intention of getting hurt today.

For his part, Ovlur ignored the lad and was engrossed in binding his hand with a thin strip of rawhide – presumably to improve his grip on the mace.

Slowly, the crowd encircled the pair and they turned to face each other, standing at ten paces distance. Magnusson stepped into the forming arena and, in a loud voice, addressed Thurion.

'You have been training with some of our tribe's mightiest warriors. It is time to see what you have learned. Are you ready?'

'Yes, Sir, I am ready,' Thurion replied, trying to hide the apprehension he felt at the thought of facing Ovlur in single combat.

'Ovlur ?'

'Aye, Chief. I'm ready to give him a *proper* workout!'

'Then begin,' commanded the chieftain.

'Come on, boy, let's see if you are as good as they say you are with that log-splitter of yours.'
Thurion was not drawn in by the elder's taunt, and instead of rushing foolishly at his opponent he held his ground. The two combatants began to circle cautiously and exchanged a number of blows, getting the measure of each other. Like Ovlur's mace, Thurion's axe blade had been sheathed in leather for this mock duel.

Steadily each warrior's attacks became more deliberate and aggressive. Ovlur swung his mace in easy circles around his wrist, holding his broad shield out in front of him, rim towards the younger warrior. Thurion took a step towards Ovlur and began to swing his axe in a great figure-of-eight pattern in front of him. All of a sudden he lunged in towards Ovlur and swung at the warrior's unprotected right side. The elder stepped backwards out Thurion's reach.

'You'll have to do better than that if you're going to bring *me* down, boy!'

This time Thurion did respond. He swung his weapon straight at the shield arm of his opponent aiming to splinter his shield. Ovlur however, being a seasoned veteran, was prepared for this and angled his shield to deflect the axe up and away, over his head. This was the opening he needed. He rushed Thurion, mace swinging low. Thurion saw Ovlur's attack and released his grip on the axe haft, letting the weapon swing wide. Stepping into the elder's attack, Thurion grabbed hold of Ovlur's mace-wielding right hand and struck out with his knee into the other man's chest.

Axe and mace went flying into the gathered crowd and the two men fell, grappling to the floor. Ovlur let go of his shield and attempted to recover from his opponent's unorthodox counter attack. Thrusting his great shoulders upwards he heaved Thurion off backwards. Thurion broke his fall and using his body's momentum, rolled over and quickly regained his feet. Ovlur was slower to recover and had barely got up, still down on one knee, when Thurion seized his chance and in two quick paces skirted the struggling warrior and mounted his shoulders. With a feral snarl he drew his opponent's seax and raised it above his head, ready to strike, when a shout came from the crowd.

'ENOUGH!'

Chieftain Magnusson strode up to the combatants closely followed by Ragna. Magnusson grabbed Ovlur's wrists whilst Ragna took hold of his son's raised arm.

'Enough, Son! It's over. Enough. You've gone too far!'

Thurion turned to his father with a wild look in his eyes. Ragna tightened his grip on Thurion's arm and spoke softly to him, 'Easy, Son, easy. Catch your breath, take control; there's no need for this.' As he looked at his father his heart rate dropped and he visibly calmed. The chieftain, meanwhile, helped Ovlur to his feet.

'You're getting slow, Ovlur. You let a boy half your size take advantage of you!'

''E got lucky, that's all. If my knee hadn't locked when it did I would have thrashed him,' responded the bewildered elder.

'But you have to admit the boy has the spirit for combat – he didn't back down once – all he lacks is self-discipline. He'll make a good warrior, don't you think?'

Ovlur wasn't happy at being defeated in front of his peers – especially by one of the novices. Not only was he defeated but also disarmed and nearly wounded by his own weapon. The second rite was a bout between an experienced warrior and a novice, staged to demonstrate both how well the novices used the techniques taught them during their training, and how much mettle the young men showed when faced with an opponent of greater skill. Usually, the experienced warrior would lead the novice on and allow himself to be struck once or twice to give his opponent some confidence, then he would probe their moves, searching for weaknesses. This usually resulted in the novice suffering cuts and bruises, sometimes broken bones, but never any serious injury. If the novice acquitted himself to the satisfaction of the warrior and two adjudicators, he would pass to the next stage of the passage. Ovlur had just experienced his first humiliation in years and he wasn't feeling generous.

'You've a fierce spirit within you boy, that's clear to see,' he growled.

'Aye, a fierce spirit indeed!' said the chieftain to Thurion. 'You fought well, Thurion, son of Ragna. The bout goes to you. You have passed your second rite. Now, return Ovlur's seax to him.'

Ragna let go of his son's arm and Thurion looked down at the dagger still in his grip. He flipped it quickly, caught it by the blade and tossed it back to Ovlur.

After recovering his weapons, Thurion walked back with Ragna in silence until they were nearly back at the vron. Once they were back home Ragna asked the question that had been burning in his mind as they walked.

'What happened, Son? You appeared to lose control when Ovlar deflected your blow.'

'I don't know, Father, it didn't feel like losing control, more like something within me awakened, something basic, deep within me, something that guided me and showed me where his defence was weak and where I could strike. I feel something like it when I hunt,' he said.

His father listened to his son's explanation but, ever thoughtful, said nothing.

As the weather warmed up Ragna and Thurion would go out hunting together, enjoying the sights, sounds and smells of the grasslands and shrubland that fell away from the forests.

Preparations were being made for the mid-summer feast. One evening, about a month before the feast was due to take place, Elder Ovlur came to visit Ragna as the family sat eating their evening meal around the fireplace.

He rapped on the door frame. 'Evening! Something smells good! May I come in?'

Ragna looked up. 'Ovlur? Of course, come in and welcome. Will you eat with us?' he asked as the elder entered the roundhouse.

'Thank you, but no, I have a number of other families to visit tonight,'

'Oh? What news?'

'It's regarding your son,' Ovlur replied ominously, casting a quick glance to where Thurion sat with his plate.

'My son? What could you possibly want with Thurion? Surely you must have gotten over that incident during the bout? I have spoken with him about that many times and he meant you no harm; he felt he had to show that he was ready. He reckons he dented your pride more than anything else!'

'No, it's not about that, I got over that fairly quickly. By Krorsch, I've had more than my pride dented in lesser squabbles over a skin of ale. No, I have just come from a meeting of the tribal elders. It has been decided that Thurion has successfully completed the rites of passage. He will enter into manhood at the coming festival,' Ovlur announced, evidently enjoying the tension he had just created. Thurion could not suppress a wide grin.

'Thank you, Ovlur, thank you,' Ragna said, overjoyed.

'Good evening,' Ovlur replied and left.

'I knew you were ready, Son. Ermill, open the wine we've been saving!' Ragna said to his wife.

As Ermill went to fetch the wine, Ragna got up and retrieved a small cloth-wrapped package from a wooden chest at the foot of his bed. He returned to the fire and presented the package to Thurion who carefully unwrapped it. Inside the package Thurion found a gold ring. The ring itself was plain but the relief that adorned it was exquisitely made. Fashioned from gold, it took the form a Norshorn; a great rhino with a single large horn and long shaggy fur. As Thurion examined the ring, Ragna detected a frown on his forehead.

'Son, the ancient Norshorn is the symbol of your paternal line. You have earned the right to bear its likeness,' Ragna explained as a warm smile spread across his face. That night the family celebrated.

The mid-summer feast was a grand occasion. Held outside it was a much larger affair than the mid-winter feast had been. A large trench was dug outside the settlement and in it was set a fire. Over this fire was cooked all the food that had been prepared in the preceding days. This feast was traditionally, not only where boys that had successfully undertaken the rites of passage entered into manhood, but where couples betrothed to each other in the previous year would be married. As such the mid-summer feast was the highlight of the year for the Men of the North.

As the feast was reaching its zenith Chieftain Magnusson made his way up to where Ragna and his family were standing. Together with Thurion he was drinking mead and picking the meat off a roasted hog leg.

'Thurion, I officially pronounce you a man of the tribe. Congratulations.' The chieftain pulled from his belt a small pouch and handed it to Thurion. The pouch contained a flint and steel. 'You are now to light your own fires, in your own home, Thurion. I hereby give you the right to pick a plot of land as your own and on it to raise up your own house,' the chieftain explained with a smile.

'Thank you, Chieftain,' answered Thurion, the implications of his symbolic gift sinking in.

'Remember your training and never let up. Keep honing your skills; always strive to better yourself. Live with honour. Now, I have something your father asked me to keep safe and bring with me today.'

With that, Magnusson produced from his tunic a long, flat object wrapped in cloth; obviously heavy. He handed the packet to Ragna who took it from him and thrust it at Thurion.

'What's this?' he asked. He was already aware that the ceremonial pouch he had received symbolised his independence and his coming-of-age, but was not prepared for another surprise.

'Go on, open it, Son,' encouraged Ragna.

Thurion passed him his drink to hold whilst he used his other hand to unwrap the cloth. As the last fold fell away, the gleam of metal filled his hand. The tip of the seax poked through the end of the sheath and the leather was freshly oiled. The handle was made from deer horn and was slightly curved. He pulled it out and admired the long blade and turned it to appreciate the sharp edge that had been honed to perfection. His eyes lit up when he saw the Norshorn carved into the horn and marvelled at the detail of the trees and plants that stood out around it.

'It seems our new man is lost for words, Ragna. I'll leave you to it – see you later.' With that Chieftain Magnusson merged back into the crowd, looking for the next young warrior he was to inaugurate into manhood.

Thurion stood speechless for a long time. He cradled the seax as if it were made of eggshell. It all came together there and then for him. The Norshorn ring, the flint and steel, and now the seax. He felt complete. All the effort he had put into the previous months had been worth it. The result of which was encapsulated in four objects he now held. *Manhood, the acceptance into the full social life of my tribe and equal standing with other warriors – no more a boy.* Tears welled in his eyes as he looked up at his parents but he stifled them quickly. 'Thank you,' he managed to croak as he tried to hug them both.

Thurion took leave of his parents and proceeded to work his way through the lively crowd in search of the rest of his peers who had undertaken the rights. Those who had successfully passed into manhood, he found in twos and threes, all as jubilant as he. Together they celebrated, eating and drinking into the night.

Once the feast had drawn to a close life returned to normality in Vorde. Thurion took some time to choose the location for his house but eventually settled on a site at the edge of the forest. To begin with, he constructed a small shelter and moved his few possessions into it. As the summer drew on he spent more and more time away from the settlement, initially joining hunting expeditions but later simply leaving Vorde for a week or two at a time. His home began to resemble little more than an extension of the forest under whose shadows he had built it. As summer drew into autumn his excursions did not abate with the worsening of the weather. He simply wore a heavy fur cloak over his mail shirt and wandered regardless. As winter approached Ragna and Ermill became concerned for their son. They had seen him rise to manhood but then grow ever more distant.

When asked about his wanderings Thurion would respond by asking if the whole of life were not simply a journey. He did not understand his parents' concerns. He was well, fit and healthy. Moreover, he assured them, he was content when he was wandering; more content than he had ever been.

Whilst Ragna respected his son's decision he could not shed the feeling of growing concern for him. It was reaching the time when a young man was expected to select a patron god for himself. It was not his son's wandering alone for weeks on end that concerned Ragna, but more the fact that he was alone without a god to watch over him. At the mid-winter feast Ragna spoke to Borii, the tribal sage.

'I understand your concern, Ragna,' Borii said, 'It is not something I think you need to concern yourself about over-much, however. You are right when you say that by now a young man should have chosen for himself a patron from amongst our pantheon of gods. In Thurion's case I think he has chosen another path. I believe something has awoken in your son, Ragna; the wilding. Some call it the wanderlust. In truth it is the accepting by someone, like your son, of the spirits of the wild. Ragna, it is my belief that your son has accepted those feral, primal spirits of the wilderness as his patrons. There is nothing to fear, but much to discuss. If this is the case, we need to bless him and send him out into the wilderness. Only there will his true potential be realised.'

Ragna thought on this for some time before finally talking to Ermill about it. Together they explained the situation to the family elders. After some discussion it was agreed that Ragna would talk to Thurion when he next returned to Vorde. They were to wait a full month before Thurion reappeared. It was a cold morning in early spring when Ragna walked to the edge of the settlement, as he did every morning, in search of his son. As he approached Thurion's shelter, he noticed his son's belongings were outside but there was no sign of his son. He made to return home when a call from the forest checked him.

'Father! It is good to see you!' Thurion came striding out of the forest with a small hog slung over one shoulder. 'Will you breakfast with me? There's plenty!' he asked, gesturing to the carcass.

'Thank you, Son, I would like that,' Ragna replied as a smile crossed his face that spoke of a father's love for his son. Soon there was a fire burning and sticks of hog meat around it. In the entrance to Thurion's shelter father and son enjoyed a breakfast of roast wild pig.

'Son, I have been talking to Borii. I was concerned for you,'

'It's alright. Borii has spoken to me too. I met him a way north a few days ago, and he explained about the wilding, as he put it. Everything makes sense now.'

'That is good, Son, that is good. So you will agree to accept the tribe's blessing?' Ragna replied, evidently relieved.

'Agree? I would be honoured, Father,' replied Thurion, smiling. The two men continued their meal in silence for a minute or two before Thurion spoke again.

'Father, you promised to tell me of my

grandfather, Rannweig, once I had passed into manhood. Will you tell me of him now?'

'Aye son, I'll tell you of Rannweig's Rage,' Ragna said, putting down his skewer of meat. 'Some years ago, when I was barely older than you are now, life was not as peaceful as it is today. Vorde would come under frequent attack by Nightmares, those dark daemons of the Shadow World. They would come out of the west, singly or in packs to ravage our farmsteads and possess or kill our families. Over the years the attacks became more and more frequent until we found ourselves in a state of perpetual war. We were forced to set up a watchtower at the westernmost point of the settlement and man it day and night. In this way we would have warning of an impending attack and have time enough to gather our warriors and secure our families in the great hall. As I have said, I was a young man then but my brother, Esgar, was a few years older than me.'

Ragna looked pained as he recalled the memory of his brother.

'It was a little after dawn one autumn morning when the watchtower bell began to sound. My father, your grandfather, roused us all and saw my mother and sisters safely into the great hall. The three of us, my brother, your grandfather and myself donned our wargear quickly and ran to the watchtower where the rest of the tribe's warriors were gathering. Through the mists our foes came at us, braying and howling. There were many of them, several hundred at least, though some swear there were many more. Battle was joined and the fighting was fierce. I fought shoulder to shoulder with my brother and father, their greataxes rising and falling in great bloody arcs. My own spear had been lost early on in the battle, embedded in the chest of something that resembled a bear – it was odd; a great beak crowned with long tentacles took the place of its head.

That nightmare would have claimed my life that day were it not for my brother. My mace was heavy in my hand and my strength was beginning to wane. Esgar stepped in front of me as I was forced onto my knees, the beast's tentacles threatening to rip my shield from my arm. He swung his axe in a great arc, and buried the blade deep in the bear-thing's face. It fell with a choked cry and did not rise. We fought like this all morning, the three of us shoulder to shoulder until *it* came. A troll it may have been once, but now it was possessed of a spirit not its own. With black eyes from which heavy black fumes billowed, it came at us…'

Ragna stopped, tears forming in the corners of his eyes.

'Father?'

'Esgar stood against it but he fell. Rannweig saw him fall and his heart must have broken, for he let out such a cry of pain as I had never heard before and pray never to hear again. He flew into a berserk rage, cutting the monstrosity to pieces in his fury and grief. Then he fell to his knees and wept for his fallen son. It was all I could do to fend off further attack as he wept in the blood and mud of the battlefield. Eventually Rannweig rose from the ground and, taking Esgar's greataxe in one hand and his own in the other he vent his rage. He became an avatar of death; grief fuelled him to feats of endurance none could ever hope to match. Where he stood nightmares were banished by cold steel, their thick black blood flowing freely, staining the ground. None could stand against him and so they fled, back away west. We could not stop him. He pursued them into the west and we never saw him again,' Ragna concluded, his voice thick with emotion. 'That said, we were never attacked again, not from the west.'

Thurion looked down at his ring thoughtfully.

'Don't fear, son, he rests with our ancestors. I am sure of that. He may have been driven mad by grief but he fought with honour and I am sure he died well.'

After their meal Ragna left to find Borii whilst Thurion began the process of drying and smoking the remains of the hog. That evening the whole family met in Ragna's house and Borii explained what would be involved in Thurion's blessing. The hour was late when the sage finished but the relief amongst Thurion's family was evident. Thurion's path was not one of dishonour, he was not rejecting his ancestral gods; he was merely walking a different path. Thurion agreed to return to Vorde in time for the next mid-summer feast at which he would be formally blessed by the tribe and sent off into the wilderness.

Winter passed and true to his word Thurion returned to Vorde in time for mid-summer. Towards the end of the feast Borii found Thurion and informed him that the time for his blessing had come. Once he had gathered his few belongings he accompanied the old sage to a valley several miles outside of Vorde. One side of the valley was heavily wooded whilst the other was not. Chieftain Magnusson as well as many other members of the tribe had gathered to witness the blessing for this was a rare occasion.

Borii led Thurion a little way along the valley before setting a number of leather straps of varying lengths down by his side, blindfolding him and taking several paces back.

'Thurion, it is clear for all to see that the wilding has come upon you. Do you hereby embrace the spirits of the wild?' the sage asked in a loud voice.

'I do,' Thurion answered with confidence. The gentle breeze that had been rustling the taller grasses began to grow in strength.

'Will you answer them when they call?'

'I will.'

The wind grew stronger.

'Will you accept their blessing now?' Borii shouted, struggling to be heard over the howling gale that had suddenly risen up.

'I will!' cried Thurion.

Then there was silence. The wind died down. Borii was silent and Thurion could hear little more than hushed mutterings from the gathered crowd behind him. Slowly he took off his blindfold and saw, standing before him a colossal norshorn with long shaggy fur and a single large horn situated on the end of its nose. Thurion turned to Borii in surprise, who took a few steps back.

'Truly you have been blessed, Thurion. No one has seen such a beast for many years. They were all thought to have died out long ago.'

Thurion stepped up to the beast and placed his right hand on the side of its head and stroked it. The great beast responded and nuzzled him gently.

Chieftain Magnusson stepped out from the crowd and approached Borii. Turning to Thurion he pronounced in a loud voice, 'Thurion, you have been blessed by the wild spirits. Accept now the blessing of your people as we send you out into the wilderness to follow your calling and commune with your gods!'

Thurion bowed low to the chieftain before picking up the longest of the leather straps that Borii had lain down next to him. Calmly he slung them over the norshorn's back and secured them in place under its chest. Once he had lashed his few belongings to these straps he reached up and rested a hand on the shoulder of the great shaggy-haired beast. In response it lowered itself onto its knees to allow Thurion to climb onto its back.

Raising his spear into the air he saluted his tribe and called out, 'May all the gods bless you!'

He turned and rode away down the valley and into the wilderness. Loud cheers rang in the valley, as the tribe sent out one of their own into the wild. As he rode off the sun caught Thurion's golden ring and a tear of pride came to Ragna's eye as he saw his son riding away, embracing his calling.

Chapter 5

The council chamber was a vast room dominated by a huge circular table of dark wood. It was mid-morning and High Prince Raparké was dressed in a simple pale green robe but was still every part a High Prince. When Celene entered, her father was talking to one of the dozen councillors that had already gathered. The main doors to the chamber were closed silently by a pair of soldiers who left after admitting Celene.

Raparké ended his conversation when he noticed his daughter approaching the great round table and turned to address the gathered councillors,

'Gentlemen, welcome. Allow me to officially present my daughter, Princess Celene, at her first Royal Council meeting.'

'Welcome, Princess,' the dozen councillors said, almost in unison.

'Celene, have you seen your brothers? They should be here,' her father asked.

'I saw them at breakfast but I have not seen them since, father.'

'I'm sure they'll be here soon. In the meantime however, let me introduce you to my council.'

Placing one hand lightly on her shoulder the High Prince led his daughter around the room and began introducing her to his councillors.

'This is Councillor Hashen.'

'Welcome, Princess,' the councillor said. Celene smiled and bowed her head slightly before her father led her on.

'Councillor Mahrad, Princess Celene,' Raparké introduced his daughter.

'Princess, it is an honour to welcome you to the council for the first time,' the old man said.

'Ah! This is Lord Commander Rhodos; commander of the army.'

'Lord Commander,' Celene said, a little apprehensive. The Lord Commander was a large man, easily over six feet tall with broad shoulders.

'Princess Celene, welcome. Don't be nervous; my bark is worse than my bite, I assure you!' the lord commander said, trying to put the young princess at ease.

'It's true, we haven't had a war in Nemeth-Sharrayah for centuries! My Lord Commander is usually employed keeping the dead out of Leznar-Carchum. There is little to do in this principality other than keeping the peace!' the High Prince joked. Nodding to his lord commander he turned to Sandar.

'You know Seneschal Sandar well, I believe?' Raparké asked as they approached the seneschal.

'Holy Sandar, we know each other well,' Celene affirmed.

'This morning, My Princess, I am acting in the role of the Seneschal of Sharrayah and not as the head of the Order of Nemeth. That aside, yes – we know each other well.'

Raparké was about to introduce Celene to another of his council when the chamber doors opened and Celene's two brothers entered.

'Erakos, Iraudis, you are late,' their father said as the doors were closed behind them.

'We are sorry, Father, we have no excuse,' Erakos apologised on behalf of his brother as they approached the table.

'The council has a lot to get through and cannot be kept waiting by young fly-aways such as yourselves. Now, apologise to the members of council before you sit down,' Raparké said.

'We are sorry, gentlemen,' the young princes said.

'Don't be late again,' Raparké reproached before turning to address the council. 'Gentlemen and Celene, shall we begin?' he said.

They all took their seats at the table and waited for the High Prince to begin.

'Fortunately, the agenda is fairly short this morning,' Raparké began, 'Counciollor Hashun, is High Prince Asaros still looking to divert the River Vashaka at Himo to better irrigate his land?'

'So far as I know, Your Highness, the last I heard he had dispatched an envoy to High Prince Damakos of Dra-Azun with a view to bringing the High Prince around to his idea,' Councillor Hashun reported.

'Councillor, you must organise a deputation and head to Azun immediately. You must convince High Prince Damakos that he would be ill advised to allow the River Vashaka to be diverted. That river provides fresh water and a livelihood for countless settlements downstream both here in Nemeth-Sharrayah, in Dra-Azun, and Enzé-Khalii. It is a major source of food during the upstream migration of the species that ascend it, especially the Vaska salmon. Its diversion would be a catastrophe. I want you to counter any ideas of digging wells in the affected settlements as an alternative source of fresh water. That is an unacceptable compromise. Impress upon him there *must* be another way. All the principalities must work together to conserve the river,' Raparké replied.

'It will be as you wish, High Prince; I will lead the deputation personally. We will leave at first light tomorrow morning,' Councillor Hashun promised.

'Thank you, Hashun. Lord Commander Rhodos, is there any news from Leznar-Carchum or is everything still quiet on the border?' Raparké enquired.

'All is quiet, Your Highness, quieter than it has been in a long time in fact. It may sound counter-intuitive but that unsettles me.'

Raparké thought in silence for a minute or so as he took in this news. 'It is not counter-intuitive, Lord Commander. For a reason I cannot quite place your news unsettles me as well. Perhaps Councillor Mahrad can shed a little light on this situation?'

The High Prince turned to another of his councillors.

'Councillor, it has been your responsibility to organise Princess Celene's tour of the principalities. We will welcome your report in a few minutes. First, I would know what reply you have had from Leznar-Carchum. You must have received responses to the invitations you sent out last month?' Raparké asked.

'Your Highness, as you are aware I sent messengers out to all of the surrounding principalities inviting them to entertain the Princess as she tours in the next few months. I have received positive responses from all of the surrounding principalities except Leznar-Carchum. I have heard nothing from that principality. My messenger was not permitted an audience; he returned without a response, which is most unusual and somewhat concerning.'

'You are right to be concerned, Councillor,'

Seneschal Sandar interrupted, 'Your Highness, I know I am here as your seneschal but I feel I must speak now as the head of the Nemeth Order of Life, with your permission.'

'Speak, Holy Sandar, what have you to say?' the High Prince asked.

'Many of my priests have had troubled dreams of late. They have woken in the small hours, images of an angel in mourning clear in their minds,' the high priest reported.

'Holy Sandar, the angelic caste are Children of Ios and as such we are intimately connected with her. It is not unheard of for the Holy Mother to communicate the passing of one of her children, in dreams, to the priests of her order. I am sure you are aware of this. What is really troubling you? You may speak openly here.'

'I know of what you speak, Your Highness, I have experienced what you have described before. This was not like that. This was grief the likes I have not encountered before. It is almost as if...' the high priest trailed off.

'As if?' Raparké prompted.

'As if the Holy Mother herself is in pain,' Sandar concluded.

'That is concerning. Keep me informed of any further developments. Celene will pass through Leznar-Carchum on her tour in a few months' time. Hopefully this will be resolved by then,' Raparké said before turning to Councillor Mahrad again.

'Now, on to happier things! Councillor Mahrad, we would have your report on the preparations for Princess Celene's tour of the principalities,' the High Prince announced with a smile on his face.

'Your Highness, barring Leznar-Carchum, I am happy to report that all is in order.' The councillor turned to Celene, 'Princess, as you are no doubt aware, it is tradition that you tour the principalities once you have come of age. The purpose of this tour has many objectives. For example, the tour will provide you with an excellent opportunity to get to know the geography you learned in school, to meet with subjects in other principalities, and to get to know the ruling families of the surrounding principalities. It will also provide you with an opportunity to get better acquainted with the princes that were in attendance yesterday,' he explained, a wry look creeping across his face.

'As I have already said, all the preparations for your tour are now in place. I have arranged for you to leave in two days' time. Your route will initially take you east into Lephar-Nihkur, then south into Dra-Azun, then further south along the Vashaka into Ezné Khalii, west into Leznar-Carchum, north into Varga-Shemshah and finally north-east into Thorvath-Heshkar before returning home before autumn gives way to winter.'

'It does indeed look like you have everything in hand, Councillor,' Raparké complimented with a satisfied look. 'I suggest we conclude here, gentlemen. Celene, I would ask you to go with Councillor Mahrad; he will explain to you the particulars of your tour.' The look of pride on Raparké's face was evident for all to see.

Chapter 6

High Prince Seratos Leznar followed the figure into the crumbling palace. It reeked like a mausoleum inside; the air was dry and many surfaces were heavily cobwebbed. The furniture and disintegrating wall-hangings had an ancient look about them; nothing about this palace appeared to have changed in many centuries. He was led from the palace's antechamber into what appeared to be a small hall of some kind. The roof was still intact. Huge bookcases lined the walls, reaching up to the ceiling. A number of heavy wooden tables stood in the centre of the room. Cushioned chairs were arranged around each of these tables whilst two, more ornate, chairs stood to each side of the hall's grand fireplace. A number of candles mounted at intervals along the walls gave out barely enough light to see by. Although most of the palace was ruined and abandoned, Seratos observed signs that the ground floor was – or had been – in recent use. Routes through the dusty, grit-strewn floor were visible like deer paths through a forest. A number of the chairs showed signs of recent use as did one of the heavy round tables. The fire place however had obviously not been lit in a long time.

Seratos' mysterious host turned to him as he entered the hall, removing his deep hood to reveal a completely hairless head.

'I am afraid my lord is away at present, though I expect him to return before nightfall,' he announced, his parchment-dry skin threatening to crack as he spoke. 'May I get you some refreshments while you wait…uhh?' The thin voice trailed off.

'High Prince Seratos Leznar' Seratos replied, in answer to the implied question.

'Vorn, Steward to Lord Vilhern Dach. I will return momentarily,' the old man said before turning and leaving the hall.

Once Vorn had left Seratos began to inspect his surroundings more closely. Without exception, everything in the hall was several hundred years old, including the books which were all bound in an archaic manner. As he was perusing a shelf of what appeared to be philosophical texts, Vorn returned carrying a notched silver tray. Walking over to one of the more recently used tables he set down a tarnished silver goblet, a chipped glass decanter and a plate of what looked to be cured meats. Vorn poured a glass of thick, dark coloured liquid and turned to Seratos.

'If it is not too impertinent a question, Your Highness, may I ask what brings you to My Lord's palace? It has been, until now, unheard of for a child of Ios to enter this city voluntarily.'

Seratos was silent for a minute before he replied. 'I have been guided by grief,' he said finally, recalling the words of the old crone.

'I see you are bereaved,' Vorn replied. 'Your grief hangs over you like a cloud. I believe my lord will be able to help you. Please, take a seat.' He handed Seratos the goblet and gestured with a skeletally-thin hand to one of the chairs by the fireside.

Mutely, Seratos took the proffered drink and sat down by the ash-choked fireplace. Sipping at his bitter drink he stared into the middle-distance and sank into a deep melancholy. Silently, Vorn left the hall. Quite some time passed before the old steward returned.

'My Prince, please permit me to escort you to the main audience chamber; Lord Dach has returned.'

Seratos rose form his chair in silence, still lost in melancholy. He allowed Vorn to lead him through a number of apparently disused halls and corridors. The steward seemed entirely un-phased by the almost complete lack of light in the disused areas of the palace. Eventually Seratos was escorted into the relatively well-lit main audience chamber.

The audience chamber was a long, relatively narrow hall with a number of curtained recesses set into its walls. A few candles burned in sconces set in the walls but they did nothing to banish the funereal atmosphere of the place. On an old stone throne at the end of the hall sat Lord Vilhern Dach. Seratos turned his gaze to him slowly, almost mechanically, but as soon as his eyes met those of the desiccated figure sitting on the throne, he started. Recognising the wolf rampant embossed on the figure's aged crown, surprise tore him from his melancholy.

'YOU!' Seratos cried.

'Yes, High Prince Seratos, it is I,' Lord Dach replied, his face permanently fixed in a rictus grin, 'I must say, I am almost as surprised to see you, as you are to see me.'

Seratos was shocked to recognise Lord Dach, although he shouldn't have been; the two had met on the battlefield a number of times. He, alongside High Prince Raparké, had repelled many raids launched either directly or indirectly by this macabre lord over the course of his time as High Prince. That he – a child of Ios, the God of Life – should be standing before Lord Vilhern Dach, a disciple of Nhurkhu,

God of the Dead, in such civil circumstances was unimaginable.

'May I ask what brings you here, Child of Ios?' The dead lord asked, his verdigris-covered armour creaking as he moved.

Child of Ios? How hollow that title sounds. I have never felt further from my spiritual mother as I do now. 'I... I don't know,' Seratos admitted. Though his host was the antithesis of everything he had been raised to believe and despite the fact that he had fought him on the battlefield many times, Seratos realised that he did not hate him. Rather he felt a disquieting ambivalence towards him.

'I sense that death has been your companion of late, Prince Seratos; can it be that the Holy Mother has failed to take care of one of her own?' Dach asked, the slightest hint of malice in his voice.

'She abandoned me and left one of her daughters, my wife, to die of a fever,' he admitted, tears welling up in his eyes as the memory of Saruké's last few hours came to him again.

'Life is so fleeting, so brief. Surely you did not expect her to live forever?'

'Forever? No, but I did not expect to lose her so soon. Why?' he asked himself as much as Lord Dach.

'Because Ios is the god of the brief, the fleeting, and the ephemeral. She is a weak god, far inferior to Nhurkhu,' Vilhern answered with conviction.

'How can death be more powerful than life?'

'Life is finite, Prince Seratos, as you have painfully witnessed so recently. Death, whilst inevitable, is eternal. This palace is more than eight hundred years old, its foundations are older still. I myself was born nearly four hundred years ago. I sit before you as a testament to the power of Nhurkhu.'

Seratos took in what Vilhern had said and considered it for a few moments. Slowly, as if scales were falling from his eyes and he was seeing clearly for the first time, he began to understand. *I must have known this all my life but never admitted it; surely that is why Ios ignored my prayers and petitions? She feared the truth. For so long I have been enslaved to a transient god, one that will one day fail all those who place their faith in her. I will no longer be a slave...*

'You are right, My Lord, I have believed in a lie and fought against the truth for so many years.' Seratos fell silent as a thought occurred to him, 'Nhurkhu is far more powerful than Ios, you say?'

'He is,' Lord Dach confirmed, allowing the grief-stricken prince to continue.

'Could he return my wife to me, from the dead?' he asked, a note of desperate hope in his voice.

'Her body but not her soul. She was a follower of Ios and so her soul returned to Ios when she died. No one, mortal or god, can claim a soul that has been pledged to another. It is a law that is inviolate.' *His grief has blinded him to that fundamental truth; life cannot exist without death and death cannot exist without life... The death of his wife has started him on a path that can only lead in one direction...* 'Nhurkhu cannot return the soul of your wife but he can vouchsafe your own and in so doing bless you with great power; power you can barely comprehend...' The Lord of the Dead left the last enticing thought hanging in the air.

There was a heavy silence for some minutes.

'Show me,' Seratos said.

'Follow me,' Lord Dach replied, rising from his throne.

Chapter 7

Thurion travelled the wilds for many weeks with his appointed mount. Sometimes he would ride his great shaggy-haired norshorn and sometimes he would walk alongside it. He did not feel any pangs of loneliness as his family feared he might, having left his tribe behind him seemingly for good. *Truly life was a journey* he mused, one warm afternoon in late summer, *a journey with seasons.* Just as spring gives way to summer or autumn to winter so he had embraced his nomadic existence and accepted that all things change. For now, life was good.

As autumn gave way to winter Thurion's bond with his mount grew stronger. He came to call it Rimehorn, because of the layer of frost that would form on its horn in particularly cold weather.

Occasionally Thurion would come across small settlements where he would be greeted with the offer of hospitality: a drink, a meal, and a place to sleep. Although he was treated with kindness, as any wilder was, he always sensed a feeling of suspicion behind the front of cordiality. Perhaps it was the sight of the great axe that he carried slung over his shoulder, or was it Rimehorn? The sight of the enormous norshorn was enough to send the faint-hearted running for cover.

He had been welcomed into one such settlement, Salmo, far to the north of Vorde and it was here that he celebrated the mid-winter feast. It was a small village of no more than a couple of dozen small vrons and about a hundred and twenty inhabitants. The feast was held in the largest roundhouse and Thurion contributed to the occasion by hunting a large hog for the roasting spit. The autumn had been mild so the winter winds were late and the snow was thin on the ground. During the feast he spent a lot of time talking to the elders about his life at Vorde, and giving some good advice to the youths who were about to undergo their rites of passage into manhood.

The night following the feast, just before dawn, he woke to the sound of thunder. The ground shook underneath his bed roll and terrified screaming and shouting could be made out coming from the nearest roundhouse. Rising, he quickly wrapped his sleeping cloth round his waist, fastened it over his shoulder, picked up his great axe and ran out into the night.

Outside there was utter chaos, with fire and smoke everywhere; men and women carrying children were running in all directions into the night. Hawk-faced men on swift horses were riding around the buildings hurling flaming brands onto the thatched roofs, their slanted eyes glinting in the firelight. Thurion ran over to where a man he had spoken to during the feast lay crumpled against the side of a burning house. He was wounded, clutching his belly, his guts spilling out between his fingers.

'What's happening?' demanded Thurion of the wounded man.

'Muskovians,' the wounded man gasped. Thurion gave him a blank look. 'Slavers,' he spluttered, spitting blood before going limp in Thurion's arms.

Soon enough he saw the truth for himself. As

families fled their burning houses mounted raiders would ride them down, haul them over their saddles and ride off into the night. Seeing one such moustachioed raider haul a young girl off the ground by her hair, Thurion reacted. Almost instinctively he reached down, pulled a rock from the mud and hurled it at the fleeing raider. The stone hit him in the side of the head, knocking him from his saddle. The slaver was getting to his feet as Thurion charged out of the night towards him. The man managed no more than a surprised cry before Thurion cut him in two from neck to waist. Turning to the girl who had slipped from the saddle of the rider-less horse, he shouted 'Go! Run and hide!'

He ran towards a group of villagers being circled by two of the raiders. Raising his axe high he caught the nearest Muskovian as he wheeled his horse in a tight curve, taking the man's right arm off at the shoulder. The raider fell and his horse galloped off into the darkness. The other Muskovian saw what had happened and charged Thurion from around the group, but the barbarian was already swinging his weapon as the man came at him. The slaver was following his partner in a left-hand circle and raised his hand high to strike Thurion a blow with a wooden baton. Thurion's axe continued in its arc and the blade caught the Muskovian's arm as it swept down, severing it at the elbow. The rider screamed but kept his seat and managed to ride off. Thurion strode over to the first slaver who was writhing around in a futile attempt to stem the flow of blood from his shoulder, and with a short swing of his mighty axe he severed his head, curtailing the man's suffering. Blood spurted over the slushy ground and the children screamed.

And then it was over. Thurion watched the

slavers ride out into the night and vowed to give chase and avenge the villagers who had fallen during the raid. It did not take him long to pack his belongings and strap his bags on Rimehorn. The ground shook as Thurion galloped north in pursuit of the fleeing slavers; the first cold rays of dawn just lighting the horizon.

There was never really any chance that he would catch the Muskovians on their swift steeds; Rimehorn could travel for many hours without tiring but he was not a fast beast. However, the slavers were easy to track in the thin snow and it did not take long for Thurion to discover their camp. He was following the tracks made by their horses through a lightly wooded forest when the trees came to an abrupt end. He pulled Rimehorn up in the light shade of the trees at the edge of the wood and surveyed the country before him.

The land dropped away onto a vast grassy plain, now lightly dusted with fine snow. The slavers' camp was clearly visible at the foot of the slope. At the far edge of the camp he could make out a makeshift pen; it was full of men, women, and children, corralled like cattle. In the distance beyond the camp Thurion thought he could see a wide river that wound through the plain from east to west, but it was white and the other rivers he had come across were still flowing. So it had to be something else; he guessed that it was a broad, well-made road. Evidently it was for this road that the slavers were heading. Drawing his great-axe he urged Rimehorn into a gallop. There was no cover between the edge of the forest and the Muskovian camp but now was not the time for guile or cunning.

The ground shook as Rimehorn pounded down

the slope. A horn sounded from the camp and then another. Some of the slavers ran for their horses, some didn't, preferring instead to string their curved bows and try to shoot the barbarian before he reached them. Many shafts flew at Thurion and Rimehorn as they thundered down the slope towards the slaver's camp. A number whistled past his head and a few hit Rimehorn. The great beast appeared not to notice, his thick shaggy coat gave him effective protection from such darts. Those slavers that had remained on foot made to flee when they realised that nothing they possessed could halt this thunderous threat, but it was too late. Rimehorn slammed into their camp, splintering carts and ripping up tents. Thurion laid about the Muskovians amidst their confusion, his heavy axe taking a deadly toll.

Once all the slavers had either been slain or driven off, Thurion brought his great mount to a halt and looked around at the devastation he had wrought. A shocking sight greeted him as he approached the corral where the captives were held; they were tied together like cattle. Never having witnessed the enslavement or brutal captivity of people – especially women and children – he felt suddenly sick. He knew about incarceration from what his father had taught him, but had never seen it practised. He knew about justice – he had seen it dispensed by Magnusson. Ears and fingers had been hacked off perpetrators after they had been caught committing crimes in Vorde, but these events had been rare in his childhood.

What he saw not only made him sick but also made him mad. He freed the captives and then proceeded to destroy the camp. As he was torching the last of the tents Thurion noticed a man crawling away, making for the cover of a nearby ditch. He quickly caught up with the bleeding man, turned him on his back and pinned him to the ground with a heavy, booted foot.

'Where were you taking these people?' asked Thurion.

The man gave a pained grunt.

'WHERE?' demanded Thurion once again.

'To the road,' said the man, pointing in the direction of the road he had seen from his vantage point on the hill. 'There's a slave train passing by in a week's time.'

'A slave train?' Thurion asked, 'what's a slave train?'

The Muskovian's face contorted in disbelief, but he made no answer.

'Answer me!'

'It's how we move the slaves. We chain the men together in lines and walk them to where we are going. The women and children we put in carts to keep them fresh, they fetch more that way.'

'Where were you taking them?'

Another silence.

Thurion pressed down on the man's chest. The slaver gasped for breath and muttered Muskovian curses, then, 'Will you get off me if I tell you?

'Only if you tell me,'

'Alright, I'll tell you – now get off.' The boot slid off the man's chest and Thurion took a step backwards.

'The mines, up to the mines, over to the north-west, at the foot of the mountains,' explained the man, half sitting up. 'What's it to you anyway? They're ours, or are you planning to take them for yourself? There are plenty to go round and the demand is always high; they don't last long in the mines. Some of the women last a long time though – if they co-operate!'

Thurion's mind tried to picture what the slaver was saying. The thought sickened him. The Men of the North respected courage and honour, some of the women carried weapons, usually seaxes, and none would stoop to harming children. There was a strong work ethic and a man earned the respect of his peers by his deeds and through his skills. Not by exploiting the weak.

The Muskovian read the look on Thurion's face as he tried to stem the bleeding from his leg. 'It's not worth it, boy, when the train arrives Eukmen Artumn will have your head on a spear and that beast of yours on a spit. He's none too forgiving.'

'Who is he, this Heyukman?' Thurion struggled with the Muskovian pronunciation.

'He's trouble, as far as you're concerned. He's only the biggest slave trader in Muskovia, and he doesn't like anyone interfering with his business. You'd better run now while you still have the chance. After I tell him what happened here he'll come after you, he won't stop until he has your head. They're not worth it, they're only slaves.'

Thurion roared as he pulled his single-handed axe from his belt and split the man's head in two. *I said I would get off you but I didn't say I would spare you*. A dangerous look settled upon Thurion as he stalked back to the burning camp. Some of the people he had just freed came to meet him.

'Thank you, we thought ourselves lost. How can we repay you?' asked an older man with a deep gash across his crown.

'You can return home and summon all of your fighting men. Send them here as soon as you can.

There is a slave train passing this way a week from now. It must not reach the mines,' Thurion said.

'Now just a minute, we're grateful for all that you've done, that's true enough. But why should we march out to fight someone else's battles?' asked a young man.

'There's no reason you should. But you have the freedom to choose. I will destroy that slave train with or without your help... but without will be harder. A week from now,' he said as he turned and walked to where Rimehorn has grazing a little way from the wrecked camp.

'You're just leaving us here?' another voice complained.

'Your homes are three days that way, you'll not starve,' Thurion said, pointing up the hill towards the forest. 'Take what food and water you can find from the slavers' supplies, they must have ample, how else would they have survived without hunting for the coming week?'

The small group began to search through the wreckage of the tents and recover what was edible, and decanted water into small portable containers. Thurion helped them sort through the debris. After they had gathered all that they could find they began to walk up the hill, some grumbling that they had very little whilst others chided them for their lack of gratitude.

For the next week Thurion camped at the edge of the forest at the top of the hill overlooking the main east-west route. By day he left Rimehorn to graze on the grasses he uncovered with his hooves, while he scouted along the route looking for suitable places to set an ambush, being careful not to tread on the road where his footprints could be seen. Few travellers used the road now as the snow was falling thicker and the winds were gathering pace.

His progress was impeded by the drifting snow although the fall was light for the time of year. In the evenings he cooked dried meat and vegetables from the Muskovian camp. As the days passed and the coming of the slave train drew closer, there was still no sign of the help he had asked for. Indeed, he began to doubt that he would have any help at all in the coming attack.

Just before dusk on the seventh day a party of around two dozen armed men reached the edge of the forest overlooking the plain.

'So where do you suppose he is, Bjorn?' asked a tall, heavily-bearded man as he peered out across the plain.

'I have no idea, Bergil, he was supposed to be here. I can't imagine we've missed him, not if his beast is as massive as we've been told,' replied a heavy-set man whose bald head and chin reflected the moonlight.

'Can't you?' A voice asked from the darkness. Thurion stepped out of the gloom of the forest behind them.

'How did you? I thought…' began Bjorn.

'You passed me about twenty yards back.'

'We were looking for the great beast that the others told us about.'

'Ah yes, Rimehorn. He's grazing some way off, over there,' Thurion said, gesturing away to the east.

The bearded man stepped forward and introduced himself.

'I am Bergil Hjammerson of the village of Kornum, we are neighbours of Salmo, and these are my men,' he said with a sweep of his hand. 'I'm sorry we're late, but we were out on a hunting trip when word reached us of what happened at Salmo. We came as quickly as we could. There are others but they're further away and wouldn't have been able to get here in time. The boy who brought us the message told us that all of their able-bodied men were either killed or wounded defending their families.'

'Thank you for coming – all of you. I am Thurion, son of Ragna, son of Rannweig of Vorde. I am a wilder, my journey led me to Salmo; I was there during the raid.'

'What can you tell us of this slave train?' asked Bergil.

'It is vast and well-guarded but the slavers are arrogant and keep a poor watch. I have ventured far, let me show you what I have found.'

Thurion led the score of warriors down the slope eastwards where the ground began to break up and thick shrubs stood like white statues. They came to a stretch of road that was flanked on both sides by deep drainage ditches. Much of ditches along this stretch of the road had become overgrown and were covered in snow. A man could still conceal himself well with a little thought however.

'The train is less than a day away and travels slowly. It should pass here by noon tomorrow. Do you think you can lay an ambush from these ditches?' asked Thurion.

'I would think so,' replied Bjorn. 'Where will you be?'

'Behind that hill,' replied Thurion, pointing to a small, fairly steep hill that rose close to the road a few hundred yards from where they were now gathered. 'Wait for my signal before attacking.'

'I expect we'll recognise your signal?' asked one of the Northmen, a note of humour in his voice.

'I would hope so!' replied Thurion as he turned and led the way back to where he was camped. The men of Kornum slept around Thurion's camp fire, whilst Thurion went to find Rimehorn and slept under a large bush on the hill in preparation for tomorrow's ambush.

The slave train was comprised of around ten ox-drawn carts, on each of which was mounted a sturdy timber cage. The Muskovians had managed to squeeze around two dozen captives into each cage, with men and women in separate carts. The captives were dishevelled and dispirited, their clothing torn and stained; sanitation for the prisoners was not high on the list of Muskovian priorities. It was true to say that the train was well-guarded. A vanguard of cavalry led by the imposing figure of Eukmen Artumn, the self-styled Slave Baron of Muskovia rode at the train's head. The vanguard wore boiled leather armour and carried stout spears with bows strapped to their saddles. Around two-score men escorted the slave carts on foot as they trundled along the road. These guards wore lighter armour but still carried the same stout spears and bows that the vanguard did. The train had been travelling west for a number of weeks and was close to the end of its journey.

Eukmen's journey had been a long but profitable one. Soon he would be home and relaxing in comfort. Having entered Muskovian lands he allowed himself the luxury of taking things a little easier. This was the part of his journey he enjoyed: the final leg home, in the security of his own lands with all his carts fully laden.

'My Lord! Who is that?'

Eukmen was jolted out of his reverie by one of his captains.

'Where?' he asked.

'That figure there on the hill top, to the right.'

'I don't know,' replied the slave lord with concern as he gazed at the figure of Thurion astride the massive, solid form of Rimehorn. 'But whoever he is, and whatever that *thing* is, I don't like it. Send a party of men to see what he wants!'

At that moment Thurion lifted his spear into the air and roared as Rimehorn reared, pawing the air. The ground shook as the great beast landed on its forelegs and began thundering downhill towards the train's vanguard. The Northmen, hidden in the ditches, hearing Thurion's roar and feeling the vibrations made by Rimehorn, took this as his sign. Shouting fearsome battle cries they rose up from where they had lain concealed and charged the lightly armoured foot guards.

Artumn's vanguard swung in the direction of the hill and cantered towards Thurion. The ground shook more and more as Rimehorn thundered closer. The cavalry's charge swiftly faltered as their mounts refused to face the primal fury of the oncoming norshorn. Thurion and Rimehorn hit them with the force of an avalanche. Men and horses alike were knocked to the ground. With his spear buried in the face of the vanguard's captain, Thurion drew his great-axe and laid about the nearest cavalrymen with brutal effect. Those who didn't taste his axe were crushed beneath Rimehorn's hooves.

Although the ambushing Northmen found themselves out numbered about two-to-one, their fury and heavier armour more than made up for their lack of numbers. Artumn's guards were fit, well-trained, and recovered well from the ambush, but the onslaught they faced was fierce and many succumbed to the the Northmen's onslaught. When the fighting was over, most of the Muskovians lay dead with the Northmen standing over them. A few were wounded and lay groaning in the snow. Although they had suffered wounds during the fighting, none of the Northmen were killed.

Artumn was gone. He had rapidly left the scene on horseback after seeing his men cut down. Thurion was disappointed that he could not reach the slave baron before he fled. *Still,* he thought, *it is good to leave someone alive to tell the tale of how a small band of Northmen defeated a large number of Muskovians,* as he split the skull of the last of the cavalrymen.

As the captives were being freed Bjorn strode up to Thurion, who was washing Muskovian blood from his mount's deadly horn with some snow. The ground where he stood was a brown and red slush. All around him lay the mangled bodies of men and horses. Severed limbs and fleshy parts stuck out from the snow – some of the hands still clutched swords.

'Our debt to you is paid, Thurion, son of Ragna,' he announced.

'There never was a debt. You have simply acted with honour and did what needed to be done,' Thurion replied. 'You have avenged the dead of Salmo and freed others from the clutches of slavers, whereas they would have suffered and died without hope, thinking their gods had abandoned them. Today you have helped me keep my promise to the villagers of Salmo, so if anyone is in debt it is I – to you, and the men of Kornum.'

'It was the least we could do and we could not have done it without you. What are you going to do now, Thurion?'

'The Slave Baron, Artumn, is still at large and whilst he lives no one is safe. I intend to find him and do what is necessary.' As he mounted Rimehorn Thurion turned to Bjorn again,

'For a season I will be the slaver's bane; no man should live in servitude to another. But winter is upon us and the slavers will not return until spring, so you are all safe till then. I have to do something else before then, something that calls me.'

With this pronouncement he turned Rimehorn from the road and rode north into the cold expanses of the northern wilds towards the glacier they called The Widowmaker.

Chapter 8

Councillor Mahrad explained to Celene the details of her coming tour of the principalities in minute detail. Her itinerary was to include six royal banquets held in her honour, three royal tournaments and three holiday fayres which were being held during her visit. There would be no language barrier although she might find the Thorvath dialect a little difficult at first. She was to be accompanied by a chaperone appointed by her father at all times.

Two days later the princess found herself in the main courtyard of Sharrayah with Seneschal Sandar, waiting for her carriages to arrive.

'Is all this really necessary, Seneschal?' she asked as half-a-dozen large carriages and as many wagons were driven into the courtyard from the stables.

'Of course, you are a royal princess: your tour is a state occasion,' Sandar replied.

'But six carriages and...' she paused as a troop of soldiers marched into view, 'two dozen of the Royal Guard?' she asked.

'The standard accompaniment for a royal dignitary such as yourself,' the seneschal replied as the troop came to a halt a few paces away.

The Royal Guard were clad in bright mail under white tabards. They wore silver-winged steel helmets and long straight swords hung from their belts. In response to a single order from their commanding officer, the guard brought their heavy spears round to stand smartly behind their black tower shields. The guards' shields were emblazoned with the emblem of the house of Nemeth; a silver rose twined around a silver feathered wing.

'Good! It would appear that everything is now in order,' the seneschal commented as he passed his gaze over the now-crowded courtyard, 'Princess Celene, allow me to introduce you to the commander of your guard, Captain Gadas.'

Sandar motioned to the guard commander who was a tall man of middle years with a well-trimmed moustache and short-cropped beard.

'Princess,' Captain Gadas said, bowing low.

'Captain, pleased to meet you,' Celene replied.

The seneschal turned from the commander to the gathered carriages which were surrounded by many maids and servants. He motioned for one of the maids to approach. As the woman approached, Sandar turned to Celene.

'May I introduce Arité, your Principal Maid-in-Waiting for the journey? Barring the Royal Guard, everyone in the caravan is answerable to her,' Sandar explained.

'But, Sandar, why isn't my Lady-in-Waiting, Sara, coming with me?'

'Because Arité is a more senior member of the priesthood than Sara is. She is also very organised and knowledgeable in all manner of things. Besides, it is your father's wish that she accompanies you.'

'Oh, very well. Arité, pleased to meet you,' the princess said.

'Princess,' Arité said curtsying. 'I understand your reticence, but please be assured that I have your best interests at heart. I am familiar with some of the customs of other principalities you will visit, and have travelled abroad many times. I have spoken with Lady Sara who has acquainted me with your preferences, and she has packed the garments that you will need on the tour, so please do not worry.'

'Thank you, Arité. I look forward to getting to know you.'

'It will be a pleasure to serve you, Your Highness. I shall be waiting by your carriage.' With that, she curtsied again before walking up the line of carriages.

As Arité left High Prince Raparké and his wife entered the courtyard, making straight for their daughter.

'Mother! Father!' Celene cried before rushing over and embracing them both.

'Do you think we would let you leave without saying good-bye?' her father asked as the three embraced.

'Of course we wouldn't, Darling,' Tamura replied, in answer to her husband's rhetorical question.

'Oh, this is so exciting, but also quite scary, I've never been away on my own before,' Celene admitted.

'You won't be on your own, Arité is very capable; she will ensure that everything is taken care of,' Tamura said.

'And Captain Gadas is a very dependable commander, you can rely on him to keep you safe,' her father added.

'Oh, Raparké, you do fret so, these are the principalities, Holy Ios is sovereign here; our daughter is in no danger!' Tamura reproved her husband. 'Your father worries over-much, Celene, but *you* needn't, everything will be fine. Now get going and remember: this is your tour, enjoy yourself!'

'Thank you, mother. Thank you for your concern, father; I will be fine, don't worry!' Celene said, her tone light.

Suddenly there was a commotion in the sky above Sharrayah. Celene looked up.

'Erakos! Iraudis!' she cried, rising up into the air on her snow-white wings. The two brothers swooped down, out of the sun towards their younger sister. 'Brothers! I'm so glad you're here to see me off!'

'We wouldn't miss this; our little sister off in search of a fine young prince!' laughed Erakos.

'I'm not going in search of a prince, Brother! This tour is... tradition!' Celene protested, blushing as she did.

'Yes, the traditional way for a young princess to find herself a husband!' Iraudis said, joining his brother in teasing their sister.

'You two are impossible!'

'Yes we are, aren't we?' Erakos replied with mock indignation.

'We are that, if nothing else!' Iraudis agreed as the three angels glided slowly towards the courtyard. 'Seriously, though,' he continued, 'we wanted to be here to wish you luck on your tour.'

'Yes, enjoy yourself; you only come of age once!' Erakos added.

'Well, thank you, Brothers, that is very thoughtful,' Celene replied, 'you can both be very sweet when you put your minds to it!'

'Enough, Celene! Now it's Erakos who's blushing!' Iraudis said, teasing his brother. The three siblings landed in the middle of the courtyard laughing.

'Late again, boys?' Raparké asked.

'Not late, father, just in time!' Iraudis answered for the two of them.

'Yes...' Raparké said as he and his wife walked up to their three children. 'It is time,' Raparké said to Celene.

'Yes, father,' she replied, then hugged each of her brothers and her parents in turn. Seneschal Sandar approached and gently took Celene's hand.

'Your father is right, Princess, it is time,' Sandar said before looking to Raparké. The High Prince gave a slight nod of his head as his seneschal led his daughter to the waiting carriages. He led her to the head carriage where Arité was waiting. After placing Celene's hand in that of Arité he turned to the Principal Maid.

'I hereby entrust Princess Celene into your care,' he said.

'I accept this duty and swear that I shall do all that is necessary to protect and cherish her, putting her well-being above all else, Seneschal Sandar,' she replied just as solemnly. 'Shall we, Princess?' she asked Celene as she led the young princess into the lead carriage.

High Prince Raparké, his wife, and sons looked on as the carriages and wagons of Princess Celene's caravan left Sharrayah's courtyard, flanked by Captain Gadas' Royal Guard.

Chapter 9

Lord Vilhern Dach led Seratos from the audience chamber, through the dimly-lit palace. His baroque bronze armour clanked and creaked as he strode purposefully through dark corridors and poorly-lit halls. They stopped and entered a chamber that turned out to be a small armoury.

'I notice you are unarmed, Prince Leznar. It is not wise to travel the streets of my city unarmed at any time of the day or night, especially a *Prince of Life*, such as yourself,' he advised. The emphasis on his official title amongst the priesthood of Ios was not lost on Seratos.

'I thank you for your advice, Lord Dach, but would caution you against using *that* title again; Ios abandoned me when she allowed Saruké to die.' A pang of grief came over Seratos when he spoke her name. Tears immediately welled in his eyes and he fought back the desire to weep. Gritting his teeth he fixed Vilhern with a steely glance, 'Ios is dead to me now.'

'We are about to venture out into the city; you are welcome to any weapon in my collection.' Lord Dach gestured to the weapons and other accoutrements of war mounted on the walls of the chamber. He had heard Seratos' renunciation of his god but said nothing. *He is walking a narrow path. I must see that he does not lose his way...*

Seratos walked slowly around the cold room examining the weapons that were mounted on the stone walls. He found his current situation perplexing. Ordinarily he should detest even being in the same room as this dead lord, and holding a civil conversation with him should be unthinkable. Try as he might however, he could not bring himself to feel anything remotely negative towards his current host: it was as if years of enmity and hatred had been suddenly erased. His renunciation of Ios had been an unconsidered act of passion. He considered the implications of the words he had spoken so fervently just moments before as he studied Lord Dach's armoury. Did he feel any remorse or regret for so ardently forsaking his god? As he turned a long, intricately worked pole arm over in his hands he realised something. He felt no regret, and no remorse whatsoever. In fact he felt a bizarre sense of liberation, as if he had finally found the strength to cast off a burden he had unnecessarily carried for many years. Smiling for the first time in months he brushed the dust and cobwebs from the shaft of the pole arm and turned to Lord Dach,

'This is a fine weapon, My Lord. With your permission?'

Dach recognised immediately the change that had come over his guest but still did not broach the subject. 'Take it, as a gift from one lord to another.' Vilhern smiled then, his already rictus grin twisting abhorrently as he did so. Turning to leave, he took down from the wall a matched pair of axes with curved handles and a worn leather belt to which was attached a pair of axe-loops. He buckled on the belt and slipped an axe into each of the loops as he led the way out of the armoury and towards the palace's antechamber.

As they entered the decrepit room they found

Vorn waiting for them.

'We are going out into the city, Vorn; we shall be some time,' Dach announced to his steward as he crossed the room.

'Of course, My Lord.'

Together they left the partially ruined palace and made their way out into the dead city.

'Where are we going?' Seratos asked, after they had walked for about half a mile down numerous twisting, turning streets.

'You asked me to show you the power available to one such as myself, who reveres Nhurkhu. We are going into the city so that I may do as you have asked.'

The moon was full as they walked along a deserted street and then into a large courtyard. Seratos breathed sharply and brought his pole arm up into guard when he noticed the large pack of hounds lounging in the courtyard. The pack immediately rose to their feet and started eyeing up the two figures that had just entered their territory.

'Fear not, Prince, through Nhurkhu we may have dominion over such beasts.' Stretching out his hand he muttered something under his breath. As if in response to his barely audible words, the great hounds turned and loped away down a side street leaving the two companions alone.

'Remarkable.'

'Not really; I haven't shown you anything yet,' Vilhern boasted as he led Seratos through the now empty courtyard.

'Can you control any creature in the way you did those hounds?'

'Only certain creatures: dogs, bats, crows, that kind of thing. But not ravens. I believe they have some connection or other with one or more of the barbaric northern gods.'

Eventually Lord Dach led Seratos up to the gates of the city's main cemetery.

'Now, Prince Leznar, allow me to illustrate the true nature of the power available from the God of the Dead,' he announced, as he opened the cemetery's ornate wrought iron gates. Leading the way through the maze of mausoleums and small self-contained graveyards he began to explain the nature of the power he possessed. 'I have already said that not even gods can claim a soul that has pledged itself to another. There are, however, weak, faithless souls who wander the vast expanses of the underworld alone. Those souls can be summoned, bound and controlled... then there are wraiths: souls that have been rejected by their gods; murderers, rapists, traitors. They can also be bound... *if* you are strong enough.'

'Are you, My Lord? I have faced your spirit hosts a number of times in battle but I do not recall facing wraiths. What are they?'

Vilhern's countenance turned even more grim than usual, if that were possible, as he listened to Seratos' question.

'I have summoned wraiths and bound them to my will before. They make excellent assassins. They are not easy to control for they are strong-willed. I am strong of will and can call upon a great power but even I will not summon a wraith lightly.' The dead lord paused for a moment to consider a thought that had just occurred to him, 'you, however, Prince Seratos, may discover that you surpass even one such as myself. You see, I was once a man, as mortal as any other. But you, Prince, you are something else entirely...' He left the thought unfinished, hanging in the air between the two of them.

Seratos' countenance took on a dark look, and his eyes spoke volumes, 'Yes, I am, aren't I?'

Lord Dach returned his look with one equally as dark and foreboding before continuing. 'You know of my ability to raise the dead; you have faced my troops in battle. What you may not be aware of is that the more directly the dead are enslaved to your will, the more independent they become. In this way it is possible to raise up commanders to take the weight off yourself and your necromancers.'

'Necromancers?'

'They perform a similar role to your priesthood. You will not have met any of mine for I do not tend to bring them to the battlefield; I find them just a little fragile.'

Seratos remained silent as Vilhern led him further into the graveyard. As he followed he listened as his host expounded the nature of death and its grim god. 'There is much to learn it would seem,' he stated finally.

So his decision has been made, Vilhern reflected, *it is time then.*

'Though you have yet to actually *show* me anything,' Seratos objected.

'Why would I choose to show you the *effect* of power, when I can show you the *source* of that power?' Lord Dach gestured towards a huge ornate mausoleum that stood at the very centre of the cemetery. To Seratos it resembled a temple more than a burial chamber.

'But the source of your power is...'

'Nhurkhu *himself,*' Vilhern emphasised the last syllable as if this information was common knowledge to everyone except Seratos. He began to mount the steps that led up to the doors of the great mausoleum.

Chapter 10

The air inside of the mausoleum reeked of mildew and old death. Seratos could see nothing until the tell-tale sound of flint against steel gave way to a shower of bright sparks and the *woomp* of a torch catching fire.

'I can see as well in the darkness as in the light, but you may need this.' Vilhern passed Seratos the torch he had just lit before turning and walking into the darkness. Seratos took the torch and held it out in front of himself. The light from the flickering flames illuminated the antechamber in which he now stood. It was a sizeable room, some ten yards across and about as many deep. There were a number of unlit torches identical to the one he now held, mounted in sconces on the walls. Other than that and the dozen soldiers that stood guard over a door in the far wall, the room appeared empty.

Seratos crossed over to the far wall. The door was open and Vilhern had passed through into the next room. As he passed the door guards he noticed that under their heavy, scaled armour they were little more than skeletons. Each held a stout spear in one hand and rested a tall oval shield against the stone floor with the other. Scrutinising their weapons, his eyes were drawn to the faded emblems painted on their shields. Though the ravages of time had worn the designs away in places and the paint had flaked off, he immediately recognised the shape of a black wolf rampant on a field of crimson. 'My Lord, is this—' he began.

'My tomb? Yes, Prince Leznar, it is. I was interred here more than three hundred years ago; however, thanks to the power of Nhurkhu my life did not end with the death of my body.' Vilhern answered Seratos' question in a matter-of-fact manner, his voice echoing from the next room.

These guards should have been little more than piles of rust and bones by now. They should not still be standing... Seratos thought, as he passed by them and followed Vilhern into the next room.

Seratos entered a large chamber, much larger than the one he had just left; easily three times the size. Once again unlit torches were mounted along the walls and the signs of age were present wherever he looked. In each corner of the chamber lay the mummified remains of large dogs, preserved to look as though packs of hounds were sleeping. Seratos did not consciously notice any of these details however, because his attention was drawn to the vast stone pedestal in the middle of the room. Atop this chipped construction rested a large marble sarcophagus.

'And this is my coffin, Prince Leznar.' Vilhern motioned almost casually to the ornate, finely carved coffin as he continued towards the back of the room.

Seratos pulled his gaze from the sarcophagus as he followed Vilhern to the far side of the burial chamber. They stopped, and in the flickering light of the torch Seratos saw they were standing next to a vast, bronze iris door mounted in the back wall. To its right, a heavy chain ran from an opening in the ceiling into a similar opening in the floor. Vilhern looked at Seratos and grasped the chain in his right hand.

'Will you follow me freely and of your own volition, Prince Leznar?'

'I will; Ios is dead to me,' the prince replied.

Vilhern turned from the prince and began to pull on the chain. Slowly the iris door began to open. As he peered through the aperture Seratos caught his breath, the cavern that opened up on the other side of the door was colossal; far too large to exist within the confines of the mausoleum.

'Welcome to the Underworld, Prince Leznar,' Vilhern said as Seratos stepped through the round doorway. His voice echoed in the vast cavern.

The atmosphere in the cavern was not over-bearing or oppressive but it was gloomy. The only light came from a few fire pits that had been cut into the rock floor. Seratos could not see across to the other side of the cavern, but he could see that there were a large number of other iris doors set into the cavern's wall, from where he stood he could count fifty at least. Vilhern began to walk around the edge of the cavern. As he did so he gestured to the doors that they passed.

'This is the Hall of the Gates. All these gates that you see belong to different lords; lords like myself. Upon swearing fealty to Nhurkhu, should you be of sufficient rank, you are permitted to build your own gateway, your own portal, if you will, into the Underworld. The gateways allow the Lords of the Underworld to travel effortlessly between the world of the living and that of the dead. Of course there are natural portals, but the location of these is somewhat random, both in this world and in the one above.'

Seratos listened as Vilhern explained. He looked at the gates he passed as he followed Vilhern around the cavern. Each was the same as the one he had just come through with the exception of the name engraved on the small plaque above it. These plaques declared who each gate belonged to. Above Vilhern's it had read Lord Vilhern Dach. From the names he read there appeared to be gates all over the known world. One that caught his eye read Lord Yusef Al-Ambar. Evidently the legends about 'Yusef the Mad' going in search of the Underworld were not just tall tales after all...

After about half an hour they reached their destination. Before them rose an enormous iron portcullis with a large number of narrow windows cut into the stone of the cavern wall to either side of it. Seratos got the unnerving sense of being watched, indeed if he strained his eyes he could just about make out the tell-tale shape of a cross bow in the gloom of one of the lower windows.

'Who approaches Deshra-Kardak, Fortress of Nhurkhu, God of the Dead and Lord of the Underworld?' a grating, foreboding voice challenged from the darkness beyond the gate. Undaunted, Vilhern took a couple of steps forward.

'I am Vilhern Dach, Lord of the Dead and ruler of the necropolis Emphar-Nek. I am accompanied by High Prince Seratos Leznar of Leznar-Carchum. We come seeking an audience with Nhurkhu himself.'

After a moment of silence the huge portcullis began to rise slowly on clanking chains.

'Enter,' the voice commanded. They did as they were told and entered the forbidding darkness of Deshra-Kardak's gatehouse.

Chapter 11

A cold, mournful wind greeted Prince Seratos as he stepped out of the gatehouse of Deshra-Kardak. Built into a cliff-face, the gatehouse exited onto a vast curtain wall that ran along the cliff before curving out to enclose a vast fortress-city. The wall, on which Prince Seratos and Lord Dach now stood, rose some hundred feet from the desolate, boulder-strewn plain below. Many of the stone buildings that comprised Deshra-Kardak were almost as tall as the curtain wall itself whilst a number of the larger buildings rose higher still. The tallest towers had their summits some hundred feet or so higher still and appeared to reach up into the grey, leaden sky.

'Follow me,' Vilhern said, as he made his way towards a set of steps built into the side of the wall. Seratos followed as his guide descended the slippery steps that descended the inner face of the curtain wall. Without a guard rail the descent was perilous and had to be undertaken with care.

With the stone walled buildings rising above him, Seratos followed Vilhern as he led him through the city. The atmosphere was damp and spoke of mildew and decay. The few people they passed shuffled rather than walked and were careful to hide their faces under deep hoods as the two nobles passed. As careful as they were to cover their faces their hands were plainly visible. They had a dry, almost cured, look to them that unsettled Seratos slightly.

After about an hour or so, Seratos and Vilhern stepped out into an open plaza that was surrounded on three sides by the tall, imposing buildings of the city and on the other by the vastness that was the main palace. Vilhern confidently led Seratos across the plaza and up the steps to the huge gates that led into the palace. Although the rotten-looking heavy gates were open, their path was blocked by a line of guards armed with halberds, standing at ease. Covered from neck to foot in scale armour their skeletal faces were just visible underneath the ornate helmets they wore.

As Vilhern and Seratos approached the guards barred their way with their halberds.

'Who seeks to enter the palace of the Lord of the Underworld?' one of the guards challenged.

'I am Lord Vilhern Dach and this is High Prince Seratos Leznar. We seek an audience with Nhurkhu,' Vilhern replied, his tone authoritative.

'Wait here.' With that simple order given the guard turned and entered the darkness of the palace's entranceway. A couple of minutes later he emerged, accompanied by an ancient looking man in ornate, moth-eaten robes.

'Ah, Lord Dach, welcome. It has been some time since we had the pleasure of your company here at the palace,' the old man said, the familiarity clear in his voice.

'Malitaa, it has been too long,' Vilhern replied, 'Malitaa, may I introduce High Prince Seratos Leznar, ruler of Leznar-Carchum.' Malitaa bowed politely but could not suppress a look of consternation. 'Seratos, may I introduce Malitaa, arch necromancer to Nhurkhu.' Seratos bowed formally.

'My Lord, please forgive my impertinence, but I must ask why you have brought a child of Ios to our lord's capital city?'

Seratos shot the arch necromancer a dangerous look when he mentioned his forsaken title.

'Malitaa, please,' Vilhern began, noting Seratos' countenance, 'Prince Seratos is currently undergoing a… crisis of faith. I believe that our lord may be able to provide some guidance,' Vilhern explained.

A look of understanding passed across Malitaa's face and his tone became more cordial, 'I am sure I can arrange an audience with our lord before the end of the day. Please follow me.' The old necromancer led them through the mouldering palace gates and into a large hall where they waited for their audience.

Malitaa was as good as his word. Seratos had been waiting for a couple of hours when a figure entered the hall. It was wrapped in bandages that covered every inch of it. Over these bandages it wore a gold trimmed purple robe with a deep hood. The nauseating stink of embalming oils caught in Seratos' throat as it approached.

'Lord Nhurkhu will see you now,' it announced in a dry, gritty voice. Silently Vilhern and Seratos rose and followed the figure as it turned and led them out of the hall. As he followed, Seratos tried not to breathe too deeply of the pungent fumes their host left in its wake.

They were led across the hall to a large set of doors that appeared to be slightly less rotten than the ones at the entrance to the palace. The embalmed figure opened one door, stood to the side and announced them:

'Lord Vilhern Dach of Emphar-Nek and High Prince Seratos Leznar of Leznar-Carchum.'

Once they had been announced Vilhern led the way into the almost pitch black audience chamber. Although the path leading through the chamber was lined with bowls of burning oil mounted atop stone pedestals, Seratos could neither see how wide nor how long the hall was. For some reason the light from the burning bowls did not illuminate as far as it should have done.

Under the constant feeling of being watched, Seratos followed Vilhern as he walked through the hall towards the far side. At the end of the hall, barely visible in the gloom, was a large stone throne inlaid with bone. Large braziers burned to either side of it illuminating its occupant in a flickering light. Vilhern dropped to one knee reverentially once he reached the throne. Seratos, after a pause, also bowed as Vilhern had done.

'Rise,' commanded the deep, resonant voice from the throne.

Both obeyed and for the first time High Prince Seratos Leznar beheld Nhurkhu, God of the Dead and antithesis to his spiritual mother, Ios. Nhurkhu was barely visible underneath the heavy black aura surrounding him, an aura that seemed to drip from him and seep across the floor. All that was visible in the darkness was a pair of burning red eyes. At first Seratos thought the great folded wings he could see belonged to the god of the dead. He discovered he was mistaken, however, when from out of the blackness surrounding the Lord of the Underworld, a sinuous head and neck appeared. Almost reptilian in nature, the beast that clung to the back of the throne stretched its scaly, membranous wings and let forth a soul-rending screech.

'Why have you brought a child of Ios into my

realm, Lord Dach?' Nhurkhu asked.

'My Lord, Prince Seratos is not now a child of Ios, but an orphan,' Vilhern answered quickly, a note of panic in his voice.

'Orphan? Explain your presence here, Prince,' the dark god demanded.

'Ios has abandoned me, Lord. She could not save someone I loved dearly, someone who had served her faithfully her whole life. I did everything I could to save her, but in the end the Mother of Life was deaf to me, she paid no heed to my cries and let my beloved die. My grief led me to Emphar-Nek and Lord Dach. He has helped me to see clearly for the first time...' Seratos trailed off as the memory of Saruké surfaced again.

'That everything that lives eventually dies,' Nhurkhu stated, completing Seratos' unfinished sentence. 'You have come to realise that Ios is god of the temporary and the transient. I can see that this has been a painful lesson to learn, but take heart, Prince Leznar, it is a lesson that you have learnt nonetheless; many do not. What is your desire?'

'When I followed Ios I could not channel her power as others could, even the priesthood seemed closer to her than I. Now I am a Prince without a god, without a purpose...' Seratos let the implications of what he was asking speak for him as he found himself momentarily at a loss for words in the presence of this awful deity.

'You would swear yourself to me, taking me as your lord and master?'

'Just as my peers have sworn themselves to Ios.'

'You would accept me as your father?'

Seratos almost choked on his next words.

'You would take me as your son?'

'I will. Simply swear yourself to me, commit your soul into my care. You will never be lost as your wife is now lost. You will finally taste the power that has been withheld from you for so long.' Nhurkhu confirmed, his doom-laden tone laced with promise.

Seratos considered the implications of his next words for a second or two before casting aside all doubt and clearly declaring, 'I hereby swear myself to you, Nhurkhu, God of the Dead and Lord of the Underworld. I commit my soul into your care that I should never be lost but taste of the ultimate power that claims all who live, eventually!'

'Do you renounce Ios as your spiritual mother?'

'I renounced her before and I renounce her again, now!'

The fires that had until now been flickering sedately in the bowls and braziers suddenly burned hot and bright. The winged reptilian creature that had been curled around the throne cried out terribly and took to the air, revealing for the first time its lack of forearms or legs. Nhurkhu's eyes glowed more intensely and the aura that had been dripping from him and seeping slowly across the ground now poured from him to flood the floor of the entire hall.

Seratos screamed as harrowing emptiness slowly manifested deep inside him. For a couple of tormented minutes he realised that he had just sacrificed his very being, his soul, that which raised him above the beasts of the earth and the birds of the air, to the God of the Dead... for eternity. His torment was however, temporary, like life itself. Once he had given up his soul he found he had nothing else to lose, but everything to gain. His pained cries turned to exultant laughter as Nhurkhu infused him with a power he had never felt before. All thoughts of what he had just sacrificed dissolved in his mind as the darkness took hold of him. Turning back to the throne, Seratos Leznar, High Prince of the Dead, bowed to his new lord and master.

Chapter 12

Although mid-winter had past, the weather became colder and more bitter as Thurion rode higher into the mountains, towards the glacier. The vast grassy plains had long given way to broken, rocky tundra. Many were the days he rode atop Rimehorn, snow settling on man and beast alike. There were few noises to be heard in that bleak land barring the whistling of icy wind that gave Rimehorn his namesake. Thurion found himself, oddly, at peace in those cold days of late winter despite the harsh conditions.

They rode together as high as Rimehorn could manage, until the deep snow in the valleys and the incline of the mountainsides made further progress impossible. It was with a little regret that he turned back towards the south not having reached the glacier; the reason for its name still remaining a mystery to the Northman. On the downhill journey winter gave way to spring and a slow melting of the snow on the trees and rocks could be made out. Steadily the ground thawed as spring took its hold and Thurion found he needed his heavy cloak less and less. As the weather improved, so game became more and more abundant and hunting was less arduous.

Mid-spring found Thurion riding through a hilly country strewn here and there with great rocks. Passage south was slow for picking a route through the broken, rocky ground proved difficult. Thurion was in no hurry though and so enjoyed the slow progress of those fresh mid-spring days.

The sky was a mixture of blazing reds and oranges with dusk no more than an hour away as Thurion left the plain he had been crossing all day and entered a rocky terrain. Great piles of rocks and boulders rose up on all sides, obscuring the sinking sun. Suddenly Rimehorn stopped, sniffing the air.

'What is it?' Thurion asked, as much to himself as to Rimehorn. Sniffing the air he too detected a faint odour on the breeze. It smelled like stale sweat and was coming from the direction where the trail narrowed and the rocky walls closed in. He casually reined Rimehorn back, making him reverse slowly until they were obscured from sight from ahead.

Donning his spectacled helm, Thruion dismounted and allowed Rimehorn to back away from the rocks to more open country. He made his way carefully into the shadows of the rocks. He sniffed the air again. Yes, he could definitely detect it, the odour of an unwashed body – and it was getting stronger. Holding his axe in an easy two-handed grip he stalked further and further into the shadowy gloom, following the stale stench.

A sudden roar and it was on him; leaping out from the shadows, a troll of gigantic proportions swinging what appeared to be a huge thigh bone at the lone barbarian. Thurion ducked, deflecting the heavy, but poorly aimed, blow over his head with the haft of his axe. Taking a few steps away he drew the troll out of the shadows into the evening twilight.

Again the beast swung its crude weapon at Thurion and again the barbarian avoided the blow with reflexes more befitting a panther than a man. Seeing the beast swing wide, Thurion seized his opportunity and struck with a serpent's speed, sinking his axe deep into his adversary's chest. Howling in pain the beast staggered back. The troll's pained howls echoed around the ravine, the rocks amplifying the awful sound many times over. Knowing a little of troll physiology Thurion did not expect his first blow to be fatal and prepared to attack again. Once again the troll swung its club in a wide arc. Seeing another opening, Thurion stepped into his opponent's attack, deflecting the troll's swinging arm, he struck savagely at the beast's face. The axe's steel bit deep, cutting into the troll's jaw.

Dark blood flowed freely as he darted back, avoiding the troll's swinging left arm. The beast stood for a moment, holding his injured jaw before spitting a single bloody fang onto the ground. Thurion watched as the wound he had just inflicted closed up leaving little more than a small scar. With an ear-splitting roar the troll came on; hurling a flurry of blows at Thurion. Such was the fury of the troll's assault all he could do was defend himself. Then a particularly powerful blow struck him, hurling him ten feet through the air to slam into a large outcropping of rock.

Spitting a mouthful of blood through the mail hanging from his helm's eye guard, he got to his feet and picked up his greataxe from where it had fallen. Again the troll came at him but this time he was ready, dodging the bone club with a panther's grace he counter-attacked savagely. Time and again Thurion attacked, landing an unrelenting rain of blows on his titanic adversary. Thick dark blood ran from wounds which did not heal immediately and slowly the troll's attacks weakened until, with a moan, it collapsed to the ground. Thurion seized the opportunity and taking a wide swing with his axe, he decapitated the exhausted beast.

'Try healing that you stinking bastard!' Thurion cried, his words echoed down the small valley of boulders. Breathing heavily, Thurion stepped away from his fallen adversary and leaned on a nearby rock to calm himself down and allow the adrenalin to dissipate. Using some lichen from under the snow he cleaned the blood from his axe. He strode out of the shadows and onto the starlit plain in search of his companion.

Finding Rimehorn not far from where he had left him, he mounted and despite the darkness rode until midnight, giving the rocky ravine a wide berth. For where there was one troll, there may be others.

The further south Thurion rode the more open the land became until he was once again traversing open country. Summer was approaching and the tall grasses of the plains waved in the warm breeze. Herds of mountain deer came down to graze on the luscious greenery and to avoid the biting midges higher up in the forests. Here and there a solitary tree provided shade for birds and beasts alike. It was not long before he encountered the slaver's road again as it wound its way eastwards from the Muskovian mines of the northwest. He followed it until he came to a line of hills that ran parallel to the road for many miles. He nudged Rimehorn to ascend this ridge and as they rode, looked for signs of the approaching slave train. Whilst riding eastwards he realised that he had probably missed it as it made its way east, empty. He was not sure when it would be coming back west but when it did, he would be waiting.

The road wound south, away from the hills towards the city of the Merchants' Guild. It was along this gentle bend that he spotted the train, already embattled; a large band of men in lightweight lacquered armour were assaulting the slave cages. They were heavily outnumbered and were being pushed further and further from the wagons.

Urging Rimehorn into a gallop Thurion charged down the hill towards the embattled train. The leader of the train saw him coming and called out to his guards to warn them of the impending attack. The fighting was so fierce however that they did not hear his cries. Rimehorn crashed into the slaver's rear ranks. Those he didn't send flying through the air like rag dolls, he crushed under his enormous bulk. Thurion laid into them as well, his great-axe rising and falling in deadly arcs. The swarthy faced attackers initially fell back when they saw him, overawed by the display of primal savagery. It was only when they saw him slaying the Muskovians that they realised he and Rimehorn were not their enemy, and they once again took the fight back to the slavers.

As the last of the guards lay bleeding by the roadside Thurion rode up and down the train splintering the wooden cages. With the cheers of free men and women ringing in his ears, he rode up to the head of the train to find its commander lying on the ground, dismembered. He was disappointed that it was not Eukmen Artumn, the Slave Lord. A tall man in dark blue lacquered armour approached Thurion and removed his helmet to reveal sea-green, slanted eyes. He slid his gently curved sword into its scabbard before bringing his right hand to rest casually on its pommel.

'I thank you for your aid, friend, I am Xinsauh He, of the Su-tep island province.'

'I am Thurion, of the wilds. These are your people?' he asked, gesturing to the men and women that were being helped from the broken cages.

'Yes, the slavers attacked several coastal villages a little over a week ago, we have been following them ever since we received word of the raid. It is unlikely that we would have prevailed had you not intervened. What drew you here?' asked Xinsauh.

'I am the Slaver's Bane until such time as my life takes a different course.'

Xinsauh, somewhat confused by Thurion's answer, changed the topic, asking, 'Will you stay with us tonight? At least let our gratitude be reflected in our hospitality.' It had been a long time since he had shared the company of others, and not wishing to appear churlish Thurion gladly accepted the invitation.

After putting Rimehorn out to pasture, Thurion joined the islanders in their camp. Whilst they were very hospitable he found some of their customs strange. Their commander, Xinsauh, was always served first, followed by his lieutenants and finally the other men. The women would eat separately. With the exception of Xinsauh, none would look him in the eye when he addressed them, and when they did speak they addressed him as 'Mounsah' – something which he found quite disconcerting. Indeed everyone he dined with that night seemed to have a title as well as a personal name, though it was only by their titles that they were addressed. In truth Thurion found the whole evening far too formal and was relieved when those he was with began to retire for the night. The following morning he awoke with a new state of mind and a new direction. As he was breaking camp Xinsauh approached him.

'Thurion of the wilds, I bid you good morning. I am leading my people home. We will travel south, following the road for a few days before making for the coast. Will you join us?' he asked.

'Thank you, but no. I will continue to head east.'

'But there is nothing to the east except wilderness.'

Thurion simply smiled at the islander as he packed the last of his possessions and donned his helmet. He looked up before whistling long and piercingly into the warm morning sky. Rimehorn came trotting towards Thurion from out of a small copse. The ground shook as the mighty beast came to a halt mere inches from him. 'Good-bye, Xinsauh He, of Su-tep province,' Thurion said as he mounted the huge beast and rode away into the east.

As he left the islanders' camp and the Slaver's road behind him, Thurion realised that he was also leaving this latest season of his life behind too. By leaving the Slaver's road behind he would also leave behind his opportunity to liberate more poor souls captured by the Muskovians. He could have turned back though he chose not to. He decided, instead, to focus on this transition and look to what lay ahead of him, not behind. *As the world changes with the coming and going of nature's seasons, so a man changes with the coming and going of life's seasons.* Truly he had lived with honour, valour and pride this last year but he knew the season was passing. With a cheerful countenance and an open mind he struck out north east, the summer breeze fresh in his face.

Chapter 13

Celene sat in silence in the lead carriage as her caravan pulled slowly out of the gates of the citadel. She was apprehensive at the thought of going on such a long journey; she had rarely been out of Sharrayah before and had certainly never before travelled beyond the borders of the principality. However, apprehension was not the only emotion that she was feeling: excitement, expectation and elation were all bubbling up inside the young princess.

As the caravan made its way into the city surrounding the citadel, she realised that she had all the maids, and even Captain Gadas' Royal Guard at her beck and call. This new-found freedom and authority was almost intoxicating. She looked out of one of the carriage's windows and watched as the city's people went about their daily lives in the bright summer sun. The light sandstone of the shops and houses reflected the bright colours of the awnings, which had been erected over the stalls to keep the sun's heat off the stacked produce. Looking up into the clear summer sky she smiled and, rising to her feet, made for the door at the back of her carriage.

As soon as she opened the door she was hit by the sounds and smells of the city. She had seldom been into the city proper; a principality's ruling angelic family rarely interacted directly with its populace. The priesthood tended to act as intermediaries between the angels and the people. What she saw and felt excited her, she wanted to be close to it and decided to break with royal protocol. Stepping down from the rear of the carriage she walked up to the front of caravan and began to bask in the city's atmosphere.

'Is there something wrong with your carriage, Your Highness?' A voice asked from behind her. She looked over her shoulder to see a concerned Captain Gadas hurrying to her side.

Sensing his disapproval she replied, laughing, 'No, Captain, thank you; everything is fine. I didn't fancy staying cooped up in my carriage on such a lovely day, I thought I might walk a while.'

The captain was plainly not pleased but he could not admonish the young princess, 'Very well, Your Highness, I will arrange an escort immediately.'

'That won't be necessary captain, thank you. After all, we are still in Nemeth-Sharrayah are we not?' Celene asked in her best rhetorical tone.

'We are, Your Highness. Please forgive my over-caution; I gave my word to the High Prince that I would keep you safe during your tour.'

'Captain, I am sure you will keep me perfectly safe. Your concern for my well-being does you credit.'

'Thank you, Your Highness. You are correct of course, an escort is unnecessary here in your own city. However, I would ask that you consider one once we leave Nemeth-Sharrayah, and I will *insist* on you having one when we enter Leznar-Carchum.'

'So, Lord Commander Rhodos' fears are known to his captains then?' *It is probably not my place to enquire into the Lord Commander's concerns, I'm sure that father would be displeased... but he is not here, and I am,* she thought to herself as Captain Gadas considered his reply.

'Lord Commander Rhodos has made his concerns regarding the silence of Leznar-Carchum known to all his captains,' Gadas replied.

'Have you ever been to Leznar-Carchum, Captain?' Celene asked, as the caravan passed through a bustling market, smiling at everybody.

'Yes, Your Highness, I have. I was present when we repulsed the last invasion from the Plains.' Gadas could not stop his mind bringing back the bloodshed and the horror, and wondered where the princess was heading with the conversation.

'Do *you* think I will have anything to fear when we cross the border?'

The captain was silent for a moment before answering. 'Look at your guard, Your Highness,' he began, gesturing to the soldiers that were marching alongside the caravan. 'These are the finest soldiers in the whole of this principality. I have fought alongside them many times; I have complete confidence in them. They are brave and they are loyal.' He hesitated for a few moments before lowering his voice, 'May I be frank, Your Highness?'

'Please do, Captain.'

'I do not know what we shall find when we enter Leznar-Carchum, but I do know that if the worst were to happen, these soldiers would die to a man, protecting you. I honestly do not think you have anything to fear,' he concluded.

'Thank you, Captain, your confidence is comforting.'

She smiled and waved at the people who stopped what they were doing to wave back, there were many calls of 'Good luck, Your Highness' as the citizenry noticed who it was that was passing by. Men respectfully bowed and doffed their hats whilst women bobbed on their knees in quick curtsies. Children ran alongside the flanks of the Royal Guard to get a better look at the princess. Many young girls waved and threw lily petals in the path of the royal caravan. Word of her tour had clearly spread throughout the city; Councillor Mahrad had done his job well.

She wanted to stop and talk with the crowds of well-wishers but knew her captain would never allow it, and so had to content herself with shouting 'Thank you!'. The pretty petals of the Nemeth lily were symbols of good fortune and were usually showered over young women on their engagement, today they were wishes for success. She continued walking at the head of her caravan as it snaked its way through the city and out into the surrounding countryside.

Once the caravan had left the city it turned east towards the border with Lephar-Nihkur. It was almost dusk as they approached the village of Harashur. The caravan was crossing a small stone bridge over a river on the outskirts of the village when a cry went up from a little way up-stream.

'Sarushii!'

A splash was heard followed by a young voice screaming, 'Help! Help! Help me, PLEASE!'

Celene ran to the side of the bridge and looked up-stream for the source of the commotion. In the gloom she could make out a small shape being swept downstream towards the bridge and another shape waving its arms and screaming on the river bank further upstream. Without thinking, Celene spread her wings and jumped from the parapet. She swooped low over the water and plucked the struggling figure from the current. Climbing swiftly, she flared her wings briefly before landing a few yards from the hysterical figure that she had seen on the bank.

Looking down, Celene saw for the first time that the figure she had pulled from the water was a young boy, no more than five years old. The second figure came running up and swept the boy up in his arms.

'Oh, Sarushii, I told you to be careful by the river!' The young man then looked up to regard Celene for the first time. 'Holy Child of Ios, thank you, a thousand times – thank you,' he said, almost whispering, his head bowed. Celene lowered herself onto one knee and gently raised the man's head with her hand. She looked into his eyes and he began to cry.

'You are the boy's father?' she asked.

'Yes. Forgive me, I should… I should have…' he said between sobs.

'What happened?' she asked the soaked little boy, in a gentle tone. But the boy started coughing and shaking as he clung to his father who stroked his son's wet hair.

'I said he could play by the river bank before he had to come in, I saw him lean over the edge and then he slipped. I couldn't help him; I can't swim.' He was shaking.

She looked again at the boy's father. 'It was an accident, there is nothing to forgive.' She smiled and gently helped father and son to their feet.

'Thank you, again,' the boy's father continued, 'if there is *anything* I can do…'

'It is clear that you love your son very much. Continue to love your son. Go in peace,' Celene answered. Still uttering his thanks, the man led his son home just as Captain Gadas and six of his Royal Guard came clanking breathlessly up the river bank.

'Princess, are you alright?' the captain asked.

'Everything is fine, thank you, Captain,' she said. She was not ashamed by her rash actions, far from it. She tried to play them down because she did not like to acknowledge every kind gesture and act of charity she performed.

'I do wish you would give me some warning the next time you are considering throwing yourself off a bridge!' Gadas replied, somewhat irritated but evidently relieved.

Slightly amused, Celene looked at him and asked, 'My dear Captain Gadas, there really wasn't time. I couldn't ask one of your men to jump in and save the boy, could I? With all that metal on, they would sink like stones!'

'You are quite correct, Your Highness.' The captain paused and took a deep breath before he continued, 'Come now, it is getting dark; we should make camp. I think we all could do with a good meal and some sleep.'

Together Princess Celene, Captain Gadas and his attendant guards made their way back down the river bank to where the caravan was waiting for them. They made camp in a meadow a few hundred yards downstream from the bridge.

'I hear you have had an adventurous first day, Your Highness, if it's not too forward of me to say?' Arité asked Celene as she prepared the princess' bed that evening.

'It was rather adventurous, yes – and exhilarating!' Celene replied, 'And it was not too forward of you to say, Arité, you are my maid, not my servant!'

'Thank you, Your Highness. Will there be anything else?' Arité asked as she turned to leave

Celene's carriage.

'No. Thank you, Arité. That will be all, goodnight.'

'Very well, Your Highness. Should you need anything in the night, just come and wake me, I sleep in the second carriage, goodnight.'

The next morning the caravan made its way to the village only to find the way blocked by a crowd of people. Seemingly, the whole population had gathered to see the princess who had saved a little boy from the river; men, women and children thronged the single road that cut through the cluster of dwellings. All were cheering when the princess' caravan passed by. Looking out from her carriage Celene caught sight of Sarushii. He was with his mother and father, sitting aloft on his father's shoulders, waving excitedly. She smiled to herself, embarrassed by the warmth of the reception.

The caravan left the village behind and entered open country making its way east along the main road towards Nihkur. The countryside was, for the most part, rolling grassy lowlands stippled in places with areas of shrub and the odd small copse. Again, like yesterday, Celene had decided to walk rather than ride in her carriage. The bright sun seemed to accentuate her beauty, imparting an iridescent glow to her long blonde hair.

'Do you plan to walk for the whole of your tour, Your Highness?' Captain Gadas asked.

'At least while the sun is shining, Captain. It is such a beautiful day, is it not?'

'It is a fine day, Your Highness, long may it continue!'

'How far is it to the border?'

'From here, it's about one hundred and fort-five miles – about a week's travel. From the border, Nihkur is a further ten days journey. We should reach the bridge over the River Vashaka in about four days.'

For the next week the caravan made quiet, steady progress through Nemeth-Sharrayah, heading slowly for the principality of Lephar-Nihkur.

Chapter 14

Seratos Leznar, High Prince of the Dead took leave of his god and withdrew, accompanied by Lord Dach and Sisus, a necromancer from Deshra-Kardak. The bald and clean-shaven man, who appeared to be no more than forty or fifty years old, walked a couple of paces behind the two lords as they returned to the world of the living. Stepping out from Vilhern's tomb the small party was assailed by sheets of rain driven by a cold wind. Little had been said on their journey back to Emphar-Nek, indeed it was only when they reached Vilhern's ruined palace that anyone spoke.

'Can I persuade you to stay a while? There is much I may now show you,' Lord Dach offered, turning to Seratos.

'Thank you, Lord Dach, but no. As much as I would like to stay a while there is much that needs to be done in Leznar-Carchum.' His countenance darkened as he mentioned his home principality. 'And much to learn,' he added, turning to look at Sisus, who returned the look with a slight smile before bowing deferentially to his new master.

'In that case I will bid you farewell, and ask you to remember me if ever you need advice or aid of any kind; we are now no longer enemies, Prince Leznar.' Vilhern replied before turning and striding towards his palace where Vorn was waiting to welcome him back.

In silence Seratos and Sisus turned from Lord Dach's palace and made their way east, out of

Emphar-Nek. As he made his way through the necropolis he noticed that the hounds that had dogged his every step before, now kept a respectful distance from him, eyeing him from the shadows. Even the circling crows were silent as he passed through the dead city.

Eventually they found themselves on the road that led to the border of Leznar-Carchum. The surroundings becoming less and less desolate the further east they travelled.

Seratos broke the silence. 'I understand that you have been appointed as my... steward?... teacher?'

'Correct. I understand that you and your family are served by a priesthood,' Sisus began.

'*Were* served. That will change as soon as I return,' Seratos stated.

'My apologies, High Prince. I understand that you *were* served by a priesthood until recently?'

'Correct, what of it?'

'Think of me as the head of your *new* priesthood, so to speak,' Sisus explained, the wind whipping at the folds of his beige robes as he spoke.

'My high priest is also my seneschal. So you have thoughts on becoming my new seneschal?'

Sisus thought for a moment. 'Yes, precisely. I will help you to not only master the dark arts and raise your own cadre of necromancers but will see to the day-to-day running of your estate.'

'I see... Tiran served me well,' Seratos began, a slight note of regret in his voice, 'But he is deceived, just as the rest of the priesthood are. They must all be... replaced,' he said, his tone grim and soulless.

'What of your family, prince? If you will

permit me to ask,' Sisus did not in fact ask anything explicit, but rather let the implication of his words ask the question for him.

'I will tell them all that has been revealed to me and then allow them to choose.'

'Choose, My Prince?'

'Between life and death. They can choose to embrace my new faith and I will embrace them as a father does a returned prodigal son, or they can reject my faith in which case I will reject them.'

Sisus said nothing but the dark, scheming look on his face as he allowed Seratos to edge slightly ahead of him spoke volumes.

Carchum was not far from the border and so Seratos and his newly-appointed seneschal reached its gates in reasonable time. As soon as he approached, Seratos was recognised by the guards on duty who immediately opened the gates and sounded a fanfare as he passed through. Tiran was waiting in the courtyard by the time Seratos and Sisus had crossed the city and reached the palace.

'Oh, My Prince, we were so worried for you! The palace has been in turmoil ever since...' the seneschal trailed off, his gaze lowering as he recalled the dreadful day that Saruké died, the day when Seratos had fled in grief-stricken anguish. 'We are so relieved to have you safely returned. There were those who swore that they had seen you flying west, but they must have been mistaken.'

'They were not mistaken, Tiran. You will summon the priesthood to the audience chamber. Have them assemble at dusk,' Seratos ordered before walking straight past his seneschal and, followed by Sisus, climbing the steps that led into the palace.

Word of Seratos' return spread like wildfire

and no sooner had he and Sisus entered his private chambers than there was a knock at the door.

'Leave us,' Seratos dismissed the few priests that were silently waiting on him. The three men exchanged confused glances.

'Get out! If I need you I will call for you!' he snapped. The three priests quickly left the chambers by a side door. Seratos took a deep breath and calmed himself.

'Take a seat, Sisus, I expect I will have a great many people asking a great many questions before I can make my pronouncement this evening. If anyone asks, you are simply someone I met in my absence who helped me to accept the truth of what had happened, and accompanied me back to the palace.'

'As you wish, my Prince,' Sisus replied, withdrawing to a comfortable chair set unobtrusively in one corner of the luxuriously-furnished apartment.

Seratos crossed the room and opened the chamber doors.

'Brother!' The beautiful young angel flung herself at him, wrapping her arms tightly round him and held him close.

'Aldene,' Seratos replied with little emotion, as his young sister embraced him.

'We were all so worried about you. Father will be so relieved, he has hardly left the temple since...' her voice trailed off, 'well, you know, that afternoon,' she finished evasively. Breaking her embrace she kissed him lightly on the cheek and entered his chambers.

'Tiran has sent word to father, he will be up soon.' She paused and regarded her brother. 'What's happened, Seratos? There's something different about you.'

'I have been enlightened, so to speak. I have come to understand things that before, I had never even questioned. I have summoned the entire priesthood, at least all those who are currently in Carchum. I will reveal everything this evening, once everyone is present.'

'Oh, I am so pleased, Seratos, come, let's go to the temple and offer a prayer of gratitude. We will probably meet father on the way,' the young angel suggested, the smile on her pretty face a reflection of the relief in her heart.

'No, Aldene, I—' a knock at the door interrupted Seratos mid-sentence. Not bothering to finish what he had been about to say, he crossed the room and opened the door. Before it was fully open Seratos was embraced by an elderly angel with silver hair and wings.

'Father.'

'Son, I feared we had lost you. Ios be praised!' Seratos backed away at the name of his former god.

'Son?' his father asked, concerned.

'Father, there is something that you should know. I was just about to tell Aldene before you arrived. I have had an epiphany. I understand so many things now, things that I had not considered or really contemplated before. I was hoping to wait until this evening before announcing my new-found faith to the gathered priesthood, and our family. I should probably tell you both now though; it wouldn't be fair to keep you in suspense.' The briefest of grave looks crossed Seratos' face.

'Oh do tell us! To keep us in suspense would indeed be a mean thing to do, Brother!'

'Very well. I have come to see your Holy Mother for who she really is.'

'*Our* Holy Mother? What are you implying, son?'

'Father, please. I have been helped to see that Ios is a weak god with only temporary influence over those who show her deference.'

Aldene and Seratos' father caught their breath in their mouths – words failed them.

'She never spoke to me in all my years spent paying obeisance to her, and she either could not – or would not – intervene to save Saruké. No, father, your Holy Mother is not all she has led you to believe; life is temporary, fleeting, and doomed inevitably to come to an end. Death on the other hand, death is eternal.'

Seratos' pronouncement shocked the two angels standing before him so profoundly that neither spoke for some minutes.

'You... you can't possibly believe what you have just said. Please, Brother, tell me this is just some kind of sick joke.'

'It is no joke, Aldene. I never once saw Ios revealed to me but I have stood in the very presence of Nhurkhu, I have witnessed his power first-hand.'

'So... your pronouncement this evening,' his father began.

'This evening I will dissolve the Leznar Order of Life. From now on this principality will pay homage to Nhurkhu, God of the Dead and Lord of the Underworld,' Seratos declared.

'What is this madness that has overcome you, son?' Tears filled Seratos' father's eyes as he spoke.

'You dare to call me mad, old man? You, who have served a weak and frail god all of your life? A god that cannot save you from death's embrace, dare to call me mad? No, father, it is you who is mad, you have been deceived from the day you were born!'

Seratos roared.

His father began to weep, 'Please, son, repent, there is still time! She will still take you back! Ios will not forsake you!' the old man pleaded.

'She forsook Saruké and she has never shown the slightest care for my well-being! Get away from me you old fool!' In a bout of unfettered rage Seratos struck his father, hurling the venerable angel across the chamber and slamming him into the far wall with a crunch that spoke of frail bones and wings breaking. Throughout the exchange Sisus had remained in his chair quietly watching as the events unfolded. He smiled inwardly as Seratos took another step along that long, dark road that he himself had begun walking so many years before.

Seratos looked across the room at the broken body of his father and found that he felt no remorse or regret for what he had just done. The old angel had chosen to remain steadfastly loyal to Ios and had paid the price. He turned to Aldene who was frozen in shock.

'Wh- wh- what? Why?' She could barely vocalise her thoughts. Seratos walked over to his youngest sister and placed his right hand on her shoulder. She shivered at his touch.

'Aldene, in the end Ios betrays us all. Witness that betrayal.' He said, gesturing to the broken body of their father, 'would you also be so betrayed?'

'I, I don't understand.'

'Your father had a choice, he chose poorly. Now you too have a choice.' Seratos' tone became grim as his grip on his sister's shoulder tightened.

'You're asking me to forsake the Holy Mother? I... I can't, Seratos, I just can't.' Tears ran down her cheeks as she looked into her brother's cold, lifeless eyes.

'Then I am sorry, dear sister. I had hoped you would not have to suffer as our father did.' Seratos loosened his grip on Aldene's shoulder and gently moved his hand up to lightly stroke her neck.

'Seratos, please...' she sobbed as her brother tightened his grip. Her eyes took on a terrified look and she tried to pry his hand open. She failed, and slowly suffocated as her brother committed sororicide.

Without a single pang of grief Seratos opened his hand and let the limp body of his sister fall to the floor. In that act, a cold emptiness came over the High Prince of Leznar-Carchum that would never leave him.

Chapter 15

True to his word Captain Gadas halted the caravan at the border of Lephar-Nihkur three days after it has crossed the river Vashaka. The border was not fortified, as in the principalities there was little need for fenced and gated borders; peace prevailed in these lands where Holy Ios was revered above all other gods. There was a small gatehouse next to the road which was flanked by two large gate posts. The only sign that it was a border crossing was a small pennant fluttering on a short mast on one of the posts. Gadas approached the small gatehouse.

A border official came out of the house to greet the approaching caravan. The official wore a loose white shirt that was not laced all the way up at the front, and loose fitting beige trousers. A red cummerbund was wrapped around his waist.

'I lead the caravan of Princess Celene of Nemeth-Sharrayah to Nihkur.' Captain Gadas informed him.

'I hereby welcome you, on behalf of High Prince Taran Lephar to Lephar-Nihkur. We have been expecting you,' the border official replied, bowing low, trying to hide his dishevelled appearance with some semblance of dignity as Celene passed by just ahead of her carriage. A little way down the narrow road, in front a cluster of small, circular canvas tents stood a small guard of honour stood to attention, their armour gleaming in the sun.

The lands beyond the border were much the

same as in Nemeth-Sharrayah; rolling grassy lowlands interspersed with small areas of woodland. The people were the same as well; a ruling angelic caste, a priesthood and the rest of the citizenry. They differed in one respect: they expressed their devotion to Ios more outwardly than the Sharrayahan people. This was noticeable in the greater number of small shrines that the caravan passed as it wound its way to Nihkur. The journey from the border to the capital passed without incident. Captain Gadas did find the local populace more openly hospitable than the people of Nemeth-Sharrayah, which made his job of ensuring Celene's security a little more tricky because he did not want to appear ungrateful for the hospitality that these people were showing. In the end though, his worrying proved unnecessary and they arrived safely at Nihkur.

The two palaces were different. Where Sharrayah was a city surrounding a collection of vast towers girded by a curtain wall, Nihkur was a sprawling metropolis with the vast royal palace at its centre. There were no towers here, nor was the palace itself fortified as such. As the city came into sight late one afternoon, the caravan was met by a troop of cavalry. Clad in bright mail and holding tall lances, the escorting knights were an impressive sight. The emblem of the house of Lephar; a stylised angel holding a spear aloft on a field of jasmine-yellow was displayed proudly on the knights' tabards as well as on the long pennants fluttering from their lances.

'I am Lord Commander Asalion and I formally welcome you to Nihkur, Your Highness,' a knight in particularly ornate armour announced, before bowing to Celene as she stepped towards him.

'It is a pleasure to visit this fine principality,

Lord Commander, we have found its people to be most hospitable,' Celene replied with stately grace.

'I am please that you have found us so, Your Highness, we pride ourselves on our hospitality. May I escort you to the palace?'

'Certainly, Lord Commander, it would be a pleasure.'

As in Sharrayah, the streets of Nihkur were thronged with people all cheering as the young princess was escorted to the royal palace. In this foreign city though, with so much attention directed at her, Celene decided to remain within her carriage. She might have been enjoying all the boons that came with coming of age, but she found herself just a little shy in this foreign land.

At length the caravan was escorted into the main court yard of the royal palace. Lord Commander Asalion dismounted and waited to escort Celene to where High Prince Taran awaited her in the audience chamber. Celene got out of her carriage and stood, unsure of what to do. She looked to Captain Gadas for guidance. The captain walked over to her.

'Your maids will be accommodated with the palace servants, though Arité will likely be put up in a room adjoining your own. Myself and my men will be accommodated in the barracks,' he explained in a low voice.

'Am I to enter the palace on my own then?'

'Yes, but don't worry; just mind your manners and you'll be fine. Arité will be on hand if you need anything. Enjoy yourself, princess, this is *your* grand tour; you are High Prince Taran's guest and he will look after you,' Gadas reassured her.

'Thank you, Captain,' Celene said, squeezing her captain's hand before allowing herself to be led inside by Lord Commander Asalion.

Inside, the royal palace was bright and spacious, in a manner similar to Sharrayah. Where it differed, however, was in the prevalence of large embroidered wall-hangings that adorned almost every wall.

'They tell the history of the house of Lephar,' Lord Commander Asalion explained when he noticed Celene gazing at the vast hangings as she passed deeper into the palace.

'They're wonderful.'

'Some of them are many centuries old,' the lord commander replied, 'Seneschal Karsesh will be able to talk you through them better than I can; I will introduce you to him later should you desire it.'

'Thank you.'

Finally, Celene was escorted into the audience chamber where she was met by High Prince Taran and his son, Prince Rass. Taran was tall with shoulder length jet-black hair. Prince Rass was almost as tall as his father and sported the same black hair, though he kept it cropped short. Both angels were wearing formal attire. On Arité's suggestion Celene had changed earlier out of the forest green riding skirt and boots she wore on the journey, and was now wearing a long-sleeved formal court dress with high bodice, all in myrtle green. A small diamond tiara, trailing a short veil, sparkled amongst her golden hair.

'Princess Celene Nemeth of Nemeth-Sharrayah!' Lord Commander Asalion announced as Celene made her way into the vast audience chamber.

'Princess Celene, it an honour and a blessing to meet you,' High Prince Taran said as Celene approached the throne on which the High Prince was seated. Prince Rass was standing a pace or two behind and to the side of his father's throne.

'It is a pleasure to visit your principality, High Prince; your subjects do you honour; they are some of the most hospitable people I have had the pleasure of meeting,' Celene replied.

'It warms my heart to hear you say so, Your Highness; we in Lephar-Nihkur pride ourselves on our hospitality,' he explained, 'please allow me to introduce my son, Prince Rass Lephar.' The young prince stepped forward and bowed low, spreading his black-feathered wings wide as he did so.

Celene had to fight hard to stifle a laugh that threatened to break out at Prince Rass' show. *He is obviously trying to impress me... bless!* she thought to herself also bowing, as etiquette required.

'May I be permitted to take you on a tour of the palace, Your Highness? The banquet is not due to begin for another couple of hours,' Prince Rass asked, proffering his hand. Celene paused for the briefest of moments, just enough to notice Prince Rass's outstretched hand quiver nervously,

'Certainly,' she replied sweetly, taking his hand, 'It would be my pleasure to tour your fine palace.'

'But first, some refreshment,' the prince said, leading her towards a table set off to one side of the chamber, 'we have a choice of wines made from grapes grown in our vineyards and fruits picked in our gardens. There is mead made from honey produced in our apiary. Or perhaps you may prefer some fruit juice? Maybe you would like to try some spring water – it comes from forest springs that are fed by underground meltwater directly off the glacier far to the north.'

Celene was too tired to cope with the torrent

of information from the nervous prince, but she kept her composure and pretended to be perusing the labels before finally settling for a goblet of spring water – *directly off the glacier far to the north,* she mused to herself.

The prince led her from the audience chamber through one of the archways situated in the wall behind the throne. The chamber they found themselves in was smaller than the main audience chamber but no less impressive. The walls were covered with ornate embroidered tapestries whilst large mirrors reflected the evening light that came shining in from windows set high in the arched roof overhead. A number of servants could be seen lighting the large candelabras that would illuminate this hall as the early evening gave way to nightfall.

'This is the Hall of Greeting,' Prince Rass explained as he escorted Celene through. 'It is in this hall that we entertain visiting dignitaries and the like before they are granted an audience with my father.'

'You entertain your guests before they are granted an audience as well as afterwards?' Celene asked.

'Of course, it would not do to keep our guests waiting in a cold antechamber, Your Highness! Concerning your own arrival, we were aware of your approach to the city long before you got here so we were able to escort you straight into my father's chamber.'

'I see,' Celene said, trying to take in what appeared to be merely the surface of a very complicated etiquette.

Prince Rass escorted Celene through the royal palace, showing her the finest of his family's embroidered hangings, explaining the story each told as he did so. Finally he led her onto a high balcony that girded the entire palace. A gentle breeze brought the sweet scents of the palace's gardens up to the couple on the balcony.

'The view is magnificent; you can see the entire city from here,' Celene exclaimed.

'Isn't it, but I have yet to show you the most wonderful sight of all; come, follow me,' the young prince said enthusiastically. Celene was led along the balcony until she was standing above the main doors that led from the ground floor ballroom out into the magnificent gardens. The sun was just setting as the prince stepped behind Celene and, placing one hand at her waist he leaned in and pointed towards a large lake at the far end of the garden.

'See how the lake reflects the sun's last rays,' he said in a hushed tone.

It was a beautiful sight, there was no denying it, but his motives in bringing the young princess here were obvious. Celene gently removed the prince's hand from her waist and stepped away slightly.

'It really is beautiful—' she began.

'It is, isn't it?' Prince Rass interrupted.

'It is also getting late, Prince Rass, aren't we going to be late for your father's banquet?' she asked.

The prince's shoulders drooped slightly. 'We still have a little time, however, I will show you to your chambers – if you wish.'

'Thank you, Prince Rass, that is very courteous,' she replied. *I must not appear discourteous but I really don't want to be the subject of any more of this young prince's advances!* she thought to herself as Prince Rass escorted her down from the balcony and to her chambers.

'Did you enjoy the tour, Your Highness?'

Arité asked with a knowing look in her eyes.

'The palace is very impressive, Arité; it takes a long time to see it all, especially when the tour is so very *thorough*!' Celene replied in a conspiratorial whisper.

'What's Prince Rass like? – if you don't mind me asking, Your Highness; we maids were shown straight to our quarters, you see,' she said, making a poor attempt at mild curiosity.

'Prince Rass is… very polite and well mannered,' Celene replied obliquely.

Arité looked at the young princess, her eyes asking the obvious question that she thought she ought not to ask directly.

'He's *nice*,' Celene insisted. Her head maid simply smiled and passed her a long forest-green dress.

'Arité! Not like that!' Celene said, blushing.

'I'm not prying, Your Highness, just trying to make sure that you're well cared for on your tour.'

'Arité, you should feel free to ask questions! I've said before; it's perfectly alright. I'm not as stuck up as, say, Iraudis!'

'Princess, now that is no way to talk about your brother!' Arité chided.

A few minutes later a knock came from the door. Arité left Celene putting the final elements of her make-up on and went to see who it was. She opened the door and was met by one of the royal stewards. He was a member of the Lephar Order of Life; the priesthood that existed to serve the house of Lephar in the same way that the Order of Nemeth existed to serve the house of Nemeth.

'High Prince Taran sends his compliments and kindly requests that Princess Celene join him and his son in the banquet hall in fifteen minutes.'

'Thank you, please tell the High Prince that Her Royal Highness will be delighted to join him there shortly,' Arité replied.

The banqueting hall was vast and lit from end to end by huge chandeliers each holding a score or more tall candles. The hall was dominated by an enormous table, easily able to seat a hundred people on each side. As Celene was escorted into the hall a round of applause erupted which was begun by High Prince Taran who rose from his seat as she entered. Celene almost stopped in her tracks as the wall of applause hit her. To his credit the steward that was escorting her did not break pace but gently guided the young princess to her seat between High Prince Taran and his son.

The royal family and their guest took their seats at the head of the great table, the other guests sitting down after them. The banqueting hall was filled to capacity and the many guests strained their heads to get a look at the visiting princess. The atmosphere was electric as Celene found herself the centre of attention. Lines of liveried stewards carried in platters of cooked meats and vegetables, and placed them on tables arranged around the periphery of the hall, whilst others carved the great joints and serving staff placed the platters of sliced meats and steaming vegetables in the middle of the dining table. Celene found herself spoilt for choice as she perused the many platters that filled the huge table.

'I do hope the spread is to your liking, Your Highness,' High Prince Taran asked.

'It is wonderful, Your Highness. I have never seen such a spread before, in fact, I have never experienced *anything* quite so grand before.'

The fact that, barring her coming of age celebration, this was the first royal engagement that she had attended as an adult was politely overlooked by both Celene and Taran.

'I am pleased you approve,' he replied before gesturing to his son who was seated to Celene's right, 'Prince Rass, Princess Celene's glass is not quite full.'

'At once, High Prince,' Rass replied formally, gesturing to a waiting servant who hurried over and re-filled Celene's glass.

'Thank you, Prince Rass.' *Honestly, all this formality; 'High Prince' this and 'prince' that. This is a banquet not a court session!*

Although the House of Nemeth observed the strict etiquette of the principalities it did not follow them quite as strictly as the House of Lephar seemed to. It was all a little too much in Celene's opinion. That said, High Prince Taran definitely knew how to entertain! Seeing as she was only going to be in Lephar-Nihkur for a couple of days, Celene resolved to enjoy herself as much as possible.

The banquet lasted for some time. This proved to be an excellent opportunity for Celene to learn a little bit more about Prince Rass. Swallowing a mouthful of cured duck she put down her knife and turned to the young Prince,

'Tell me, Prince Rass, how do you spend your spare time?' she asked.

'I have many pursuits, Your Highness. I pursue the sporting disciplines of archery and the javelin. I enjoy whiling away the evenings at the artist's easel,' he boasted.

'So you are an artist as well as an athlete?' Celene said, baiting him a little.

'I am, Your Highness, in fact a number of my grander pieces are displayed around the palace; I would be delighted to show you them later on,' he replied.

'Possibly tomorrow, Your Highness, I feel this banquet will last long into the night,' she said, trying to deflect Rass's proposition.

'The night will still be young, much like ourselves,' he countered with a grin.

'Young we are, Your Highness, but I have had a long day and I have a feeling that tomorrow will be no shorter!' she replied. *If he doesn't get the message I may have to be more direct!* Thankfully Prince Rass got the message – just.

'Forgive me, you *have* had a long day, perhaps tomorrow?'

'Perhaps,' Celene replied with a smile.

Celene was not wrong; the banquet did last long into the night. If the House of Lephar had a flaw it was that they often got so swept up in their entertaining and hospitality that they would often lose complete track of time. Eventually however the long candles burning in the chandeliers began to gutter and go out.

'Princes, princesses, lords and ladies! The night is drawing to a close!' High Prince Taran announced in a loud, clear voice as he rose, slightly unsteadily, from his chair, 'lament not my dear friends, for tomorrow we will meet again at the Grand Fête!' A great cheer went up across the hall as glasses and goblets were raised in salute to the High Prince.

Celene was greatly relieved when she was able to leave the banqueting hall. Escorted by a royal steward to her chambers, she thanked him, went inside and closed the door behind her.

'You look like you have had a good evening, my lady!' commented Arité as she came out of one of the chamber's side rooms.

'I have had a good evening, thank you Arité – but I feel like I could sleep for a week!'

'It *is* late, I don't think I recall a Nemeth banquet going on for *quite* so long. Your bed is made and I can have hot water brought up if you wish to bathe.'

'Thank you, Arité, you are very thoughtful. I probably should bathe but it is so late that all I want to do is to collapse into bed, especially if tomorrow is to be as long as today has been!' Celene replied, yawning. With that she ambled into the bed chamber, sat on the bed, took off her shoes but before she had begun to undress her eyes closed and she gently slid back onto the bed.

Arité chuckled to herself, tucked the tired princess in and put out the candles before she too retired for the night.

Celene slept deeply and peacefully until something bright and blinding stabbed her eyes.

'Good morning, Your Highness, rise and shine!'

It was Arité. And it was daylight.

'Time to wake up, Princess. I have let you sleep as long as I dare!' chirped Arité, as Celene slowly came to.

'What time is it?' Celene asked, her voice groggy and her eyes half-closed.

'Four hours after sunrise. Come now, you'll feel much better after you bathe; I have prepared your bath, now come on whilst the water's still hot! Breakfast is in an hour.'

Last night was a long *night!* Celene recalled as

she shuffled into the bathroom.

Almost an hour later Celene had just put on a simple pale green dress and was brushing her hair when a knock came at the door.

'Coming, Arité,' Celene said, putting her hairbrush down, 'I'm ready.' But instead of her Principal Maid a royal steward greeted her as she opened the door to her chambers.

'Good morning, Your Highness, High Prince Taran and Prince Rass request the pleasure of your company at breakfast,' the steward announced.

'Of course, thank you,' Celene replied, somewhat surprised as she stepped out in to the corridor. 'Are we going to the banqueting hall again?' she asked the steward.

'No, Your Highness, breakfast will be served on the main lawn.'

Celene was led through the palace and out into the gardens at it's rear. Two large ornate doors led out onto a well-tended lawn. In its centre a fine selection of cold meats, breads, cheeses and fruit had been set out on a large cloth-covered table. High Prince Taran and his son were already seated, along with his wife, High Princess Ariyenne. Although she had been present last night Celene had not had an opportunity to really meet her.

'Good morning, Princess Celene,' Taran said as Celene was escorted over to the breakfast table.

'Good morning, High Prince,' she replied, recalling the formalities of the night before, 'High Princess Ariyenne, Prince Rass,' she greeted the others before taking her seat.

'Good morning, Princess,' Ariyenne replied.

'Good morning, Princess, you are well rested I trust?' Prince Rass asked as he offered Celene a plate of cured meats.

'Thank you, Prince Rass, I am well rested,' she replied, taking a few slices of ham out of politeness. Rich meat was a little too much for her this early in the day, but she did enjoy the collection of soft fruits on offer, and partook of the spring water she had enjoyed yesterday.

Exchanging polite small-talk, the four angels enjoyed a pleasant breakfast in the warm morning sun. Then as the servants cleared the breakfast table High Prince Taran turned to Celene.

'We would be honoured if you would join us for the Grand Fête later this morning.'

'I would be delighted to join you, High Prince. When does it start?'

'The Fête itself started yesterday, down in the city. We will visit in an official capacity later on; I will send a steward for you in about an hour's time.'

'I look forward to it, Your Highness.'

'Wonderful!' Prince Rass exclaimed. 'There is just enough time for that tour of my paintings I promised you last night.'

Celene's heart sank but she kept her composure, and managed to summon a smile. *Damn, I thought he might have forgotten about that!*

'That would be lovely,' she replied.

She took his offered arm and allowed him to lead her back into the palace.

The prince's paintings were rather good if the truth were told, although he did spend rather too much time talking about them, she thought. For the most part they were landscapes. *How much can you really say about a landscape?* Evidently, if you are the artist, you can find an almost endless number of things to talk about that end up leading back to how excellent your piece is…

It was with relief when, about an hour later, Celene espied a royal steward approaching them from other side of the hall that they were standing in.

'Princess Celene, Prince Rass. The carriages are ready, would you please follow me? High Prince Taran is ready to depart for the Grand Fête,' he announced.

'With pleasure!' Celene replied with barely concealed relief.

'What a shame, I haven't shown you my studio and some of my pieces that have yet to find their way onto the palace walls,' Prince Rass said as they made their way through the palace.

Thank Ios for that!

'Are you not looking forward to the Grand Fête, Prince Rass?' she asked, noticing a change in his countenance as they made their way through the palace.

'Not really. The city smells rather and its occupants are somewhat uncouth.'

'But, Prince Rass, your subjects are wonderfully hospitable people! I had the pleasure of meeting some of them on my journey across Lephar-Nihkur to the city.'

'They are as hospitable as they can be, I suppose,' he replied.

Well, that is a side of you that I haven't seen before, Prince Rass. She kept that thought to herself as the steward led them out of the palace towards the waiting carriages. Celene found Captain Gadas and a number of his soldiers waiting for her alongside her carriage.

'Princess Celene, good morning. I am to escort you into the city this morning.'

'Good morning, Captain. I would be delighted to have *you* escort me into the city.' She smiled as she entered her carriage. Captain Gadas was a shrewd man and read enough into what Celene had not said to know that saying nothing further was his wisest course of action. Arité was already waiting inside for her.

Escorted by the Lephar Palace Guard, High Prince Tamar's carriage led the procession of eight carriages into the city. As well as Tamar and Ariyenne in the first carriage and Rass in the next, several other members of the royal family were in attendance. As Celene's carriage followed the other seven out of the courtyard Captain Gadas and his men fell in step alongside.

'What a tiresome young man!' Celene said, as much to herself as to Arité.

'Prince Rass? Tiresome?' Arité asked.

'Yes, but don't get me wrong, he's a fine young prince but he is rather self-absorbed – for one thing.'

'Oh?' Arité said, allowing Celene to continue her diatribe.

'Whilst I cannot fault him as an artist, he does go on so! Honestly, Arité, don't ever make the mistake of accepting an offer of a personal tour of his work! And as for his, frankly offensive, views regarding his human subjects – what a pig!'

'Your Highness! You can't say things like that!'

'Arité, I know that my family and I are royalty as well as Children of Ios, but that is no excuse for treating our subjects poorly or speaking badly of them,' the young princess stated with firm conviction.

'Your Highness, may I be frank?'

'Of course you may.'

'You are a singular young woman; you have a grace and love for your subjects that I have never before seen in one of royal blood. Prince Rass is not the only angel to hold such views: these are commonly held by most of the royal angelic families. We as subjects have either simply accepted the fact that the angelic caste hold those views and live with it, or devoutly believe in your divinity, charity and infallibility,' Arité explained.

'Really? I thought that my brothers were just a little haughty. I never thought that they regarded the people as inferior. What do you think of me, Arité? You may speak freely.'

'Your Highness, I would not be here if I thought for a moment that you were as disingenuous as some of the other royals. I live to serve you. I honestly believe that you, and your family, are the Children of Ios, the Mother of Life. As such you are as divine as the Holy Mother herself. It is an honour to serve you,' she replied, a tear forming in her eye.

'Oh Arité, you have such a good heart! In you I see all that is right and noble in humanity. I am so glad I have you with me on this tour.'

'Your Highness, you are too kind—' Arité was cut off mid-sentence when a knock came from the front of the carriage. Arité wiped the tear from her eye and opened the carriage's front door. One of the Royal Guard was standing on the carriage's running board and leaned in as Arité opened the door.

'We are approaching the central plaza, ma'am.'

'Thank you,' Arité replied before turning back to the princess, 'we are approaching the central plaza, Your Highness. You may need this,' passing Celene a light silk shawl.

'Thank you,' Celene replied, taking the shawl and wrapping it loosely over her shoulders. 'Say nothing to anyone else. This is between ourselves. We can talk some more later.'

The carriage came to a halt. Tall white stone buildings surrounded the huge public square which was thronged with people, held back by a line of soldiers in bright armour. A large covered dais had been erected along one side of the square. The carriage train had stopped next to it. A roar of cheers and shouts erupted from the crowd as High Prince Tamar and his wife emerged from the first carriage and made their way up onto the dais to take their seats. The cheering continued as Prince Rass emerged from his carriage followed by the other members of the Lephar royal family.

Celene stepped out of her carriage amidst more cheers. The cheering crowds rather intimidated the young princess, and so she looked to Captain Gadas for guidance as she descended the steps of the carriage. Gadas gestured to three of his men who quickly fell in step behind him. Celene walked up to her captain, 'You will escort me to my seat,' she ordered.

'Of course,' he replied, understanding immediately. The captain took up position to Celene's left whilst the other three soldiers took up positions to her right, in front, and behind her.

'Thank you,' she whispered as they made their way towards the platform. Once Celene had taken her seat between High Prince Tamar and Prince Rass, Captain Gadas and his men stepped back to take up positions at the rear of the dais.

A dozen royal trumpeters sounded a fanfare

that announced the second and final day of the Grand Fête. A moment or two later a military band came marching into the square along one of the two roads that was still open. As the band entered the square playing a loud, brash military tune, Celene made herself comfortable in anticipation of what she expected to be the start of a long day.

Prince Rass, keeping his eyes on the marching band, said quite loudly in her direction, 'If you required an escort from your carriage, you should just have asked, Your Highness; I would have been happy to escort you.'

'I thank you for your offer, Prince Rass, but I have my Royal Escort for such duties and they are entirely adequate,' she said somewhat abruptly, well aware that she had probably just insulted her host, implying that she preferred to be escorted by humans over being escorted by him. Not that she cared any more at this point. To be honest, he was becoming more than a little tiresome.

The band finished and marched out of the square playing yet another rousing military number. It was followed by the rest of the day's entertainment which comprised of dancing troupes, circus performers, magicians, acrobats, a children's choir and a procession of floats from most of Lephar-Nihkur's administrative districts – a thinly-veiled exposition of regional agriculture and forestry which included a lot of livestock. Thankfully for Celene, Prince Rass didn't speak much to her after his offer of an escort was unceremoniously rebuffed.

Once the last float, followed by a splendid variety of cattle, had exited the square, another fanfare from the royal trumpeters signalled the end of the official events of the day. The Grand Fête would carry on until well after nightfall but this was the end of the royal involvement in it. A great cheer erupted as High Prince Taran and his wife rose from their seats and waved at the crowds. Their last official duty completed, they turned from the crowds and began to mingle with the rest of their family that was present on the dais.

Taran came over to Celene, 'I do hope you enjoyed the fête, Princess. Will you be joining us for dinner? I'm sure Prince Rass would enjoy your company.'

Celene smiled politely. 'I would be delighted to come, High Prince, but first let me confer with my captain about my schedule.' She turned to where Captain Gadas was standing at the back of the dais and motioned for him to join her.

'Captain,' she began as Gadas approached, 'I have been invited by the High Prince to stay for dinner. We are due in Dra-Azun in... a little over a week if I am not mistaken, are we not? When must we depart if we are to make good time, please?' She raised an eyebrow slightly. Gadas understood immediately and feigned deep thought for a few seconds.

'I am afraid that if we are to reach Azun on time, Your Highness, we must depart by mid-afternoon at the latest. I *am* sorry, but we cannot afford to lose a half day's travel,' he replied in the most apologetic tone he could find. Celene turned back to Taran.

'I am so sorry, High Prince, but it seems that we really *must* leave soon. It was a pleasure to visit Lephar-Nihkur; your hospitality does you credit.'

The High Prince's shoulders dropped slightly. 'It is a shame, Your Highness, but I know you have a schedule to keep. Prince Rass!' Taran said, motioning for his son to join him, 'Prince Rass, it appears that Princess Celene must depart for Dra-Azun this afternoon.'

'What? So soon? What a pity. I was hoping that we could spend more time together – there are so many things that I didn't get to show you. Nevertheless, it was a great pleasure to meet you, Your Highness. I do hope that you return to Lephar-Nihkur soon,' he replied, taking her right hand in his and kissing it. Celene managed to conceal a grimace as she took her hand back, just slowly enough to remain polite.

'I thank you for your hospitality, Prince Rass. If I have cause to return, you may be certain I will let your father know.' She turned to the High Prince, 'High Prince Taran, I thank you again for your hospitality. Please pass on my blessings to High Princess Ariyanne and the rest of your family.' Celene bowed and turned to leave the dais.

Captain Gadas and his men escorted Celene back to her carriage and they returned to the palace, whereupon he immediately gave orders that the caravan was to be prepared to depart as soon as possible. Celene apprised Arité of what had happened once they had finished packing, and the caravan was making its way through the city.

Arité was shocked, 'You said what?'

'I merely said that I would let his father know if I were in his principality again. Did I say anything wrong?' she asked, her countenance the picture of innocence.

'You intimated that you would prefer the company of the prince's father to his own!'

'Did I really?' Celene tried to sound coy.

'Princess Celene, I believe that you know *exactly* what you said!' Arité said, laughing as she cut up some fruit for her princess. Outside, the late afternoon light was starting to fade.

The caravan made good time, reaching the border of Dra-Azun in six days. It was the middle of a dry afternoon on the sixth day when Princess Celene's caravan halted in front of a gate that barred their way. Two guards dressed in infantry uniforms and holding ornate halberds stood to attention, one on either side of the road. Neither made any attempt to open the gate. Captain Gadas, having removed his tabard earlier in the day because of the heat, marched up to the gate in his dusty armour.

A young man in light mail and a peaked parade helmet exited a stone gatehouse and marched up to Captain Gadas who was waiting on the other side of the gate. He eyed Gadas up and down, noted the gold fringes of the captain's insignia on the tunic shoulder, the ornate presentation sword hanging at his side but he failed to see the crest on his breastplate.

Evidently some sort of unscheduled visit, he thought. *A trade mission perhaps?* He came smartly to attention and drew a deep breath.

'I would know your name, that of your highest ranking official and your proposed business in Dra-Azun,' he said with an air of assumed authority, trying his best to sound superior.

Gadas quickly sized up what he saw standing in front of him. A newly-appointed ensign, clean uniform, shiny boots, practically fresh out of a military academy, not top of his class but somewhere near the bottom; probably not deemed competent enough to be assigned to a prestigious unit such as the cavalry or a royal detail, but with enough common sense to run a border post. They had probably told him that border duty was vital to the security of the principality. So here he was; a reluctant border official, maybe a frustrated warrior on the inside, with a little piece of empire and the arrogance of youth. Gadas had seen subalterns like him before – lots of them. He and his sergeants had knocked many into shape on the parade ground and in the field. Most couldn't stand the pace, bought themselves out and either went into the civil service or the diplomatic corps. This one wouldn't have much of a career in the diplomatic corps. Gadas decided to take him down a peg.

'I am Captain Theos Gadas of the Royal Guard of the Royal Principality of Nemeth-Sharrayah. I am escort to Her Royal Highness Princess Celene Nemeth, daughter of High Prince Raparké Nemeth, ruler of Nemeth-Sharrayah. We are on our way to Azun as guests of High Prince Damakos as part of her royal tour. We are expected. When you address me, you will address me as "sir".'

The young officer visibly straightened and saluted sharply.

'YES SIR!'

Gadas returned the salute and said, 'Better, Ensign. Now, will you open the gate?'

'YES SIR!' The ensign repeated. Taking two ceremonial steps backwards, he executed a smart right turn and took two paces forward, halted, executed an about-turn and came to attention on the side of the road. He ordered the two guards to open the gate.

Captain Gadas marched forward ahead of the caravan, stopped in front of the ensign and addressed him. 'Where is the guard, Ensign?'

'In the barrack room, Sir.'

'Why aren't they out here?'

'Sir?' The ensign looked puzzled.

'It is customary that when visiting foreign dignitaries, such as royal princesses, arrive at the border on their way to an official engagement at the royal palace, they are met by an honour guard. This visit was planned months ago. So where is the guard, Ensign?'

The trembling ensign didn't answer but turned to one of the other guards and issued an order. 'Corporal! Turn out the guard – at the double!'

The corporal ran off into a long white building set back from the road and returned some minutes later followed by four soldiers carrying the same type of halberds as the others. They lined up beside the two duty guards and came to attention. Gadas looked at them then turned back to the ensign.

'Six men. Is that all you have?'

The young subaltern stared fixedly ahead and recited, 'A border contingent consists of seven able-bodied men; five halberdiers, one lance-corporal and one commanding officer. There are two guards on duty at all times. The contingent is a self-contained unit. The men take turns doing the cooking, the cleaning and the washing. Sir!'

Gadas had clearly rattled the ensign; but this was not what he meant. 'Ensign, just how long have you been stationed here?'

'Three months, Sir.'

'Three months. Surely you must have been informed at some time in the last six weeks that a royal tour would be crossing into Dra-Azun at this point, and that should have been long enough for you to have organised an official honour guard?

'Yes, Sir.'

'Aaannnddd...' Gadas was enjoying himself.

'Yes, Sir. I received dispatches seven days ago to that effect – but I was advised to expect you any time following the day after tomorrow. A colour guard was to have been dispatched some days ago and is expected to arrive some time tomorrow, in the afternoon, Sir. It appears that my orders were inaccurate, Sir.'

'No, Ensign. Not entirely. We left the palace of Nihkur earlier than anticipated and the caravan has made good time on the road, so we are a little ahead of the projected schedule. However, be that as it may, during your training you should have been taught to always prepare in advance, never leave anything to the last minute and always have a contingency plan. You would be well advised to remember these basic tenets.'

The ensign relaxed fractionally. Being unprepared was better than causing insult to visiting dignitaries; moments before, he had felt certain that a dishonourable discharge was looming his way, but now he only feared a reprimand. He was kicking himself for being so stupid: he should have recognised the crest of the House of Nemeth-Sharrayah immediately and not been so arrogant.

'Yes, sir,' he replied. 'I will in future. Thank you, sir. Please accept my apologies for my behaviour and please pass on my most humble apology to the princess for delaying her journey unnecessarily.' *Grovel you idiot, grovel.*

Gadas was impassive. 'Your apology is noted. I will pass it on. What's your name, Ensign?'

The ensign swallowed. 'Schenke, J. Ensign second class, B Company, North-east Border Patrol.

Would you like me to give you the name of my commanding officer, Sir?'

'Why would I want that, Ensign?'

'So you know who to report me to when the caravan reaches Azun, Sir.'

'That is a matter for the princess. It is her decision. As I have said, your remarks have been noted and will be passed on. Now, I must be getting along. Carry on, Ensign Schenke.'

The young ensign pushed his chest out, whipped up his hand and saluted crisply.

'Yes, Sir. Thank you, sir. Welcome to Dra-Azun. I am sure you will find our hospitality second to none. Blessings be upon the princess.'

Gadas returned his salute but did not reply. Looking to his right he signalled the caravan to move off, then turned and marched ahead, leaving the young officer to wallow in uncertainty.

As the caravan approached, Schenke issued commands to his men.

'Company! Order arms. Royal Salute!'

In crisp, neat moves the impromptu honour guard pushed their halberds out at an angle, pulled them back into their sides and drew their left arms across at a right angle and touched the shafts. He drew his sword and swung the blade high and straight, brought the hilt down to his chin, blade upright, and stood to attention as Celene's carriage rolled over the borderline. As it passed his position he rapidly rotated the blade downward bringing the point to rest near his right boot and bowed his head in salute. In doing so, he did not see Celene smiling out of her carriage window at him. He watched as the rest of the caravan rolled through his post, past the barrack room and the flagpole onwards into Dra-

Azun.

Dra-Azun was a lot more militaristic than Lephar-Nihkur. Every village had a garrison posted in it, who seemed to spend more time cleaning their kit than drilling and training, or so Gadas thought after speaking to some infantry officers when they stopped to rest.

'So, are you going to report that young officer when we get to Azun, Captain?' Celene asked, after they had camped for the evening.

'No, Your Highness, I won't,' Gadas replied. 'It's not worth it. I gave him what young subs like him need — a kick up the rear. Metaphorically speaking, of course.'

'Of course,' joked Celene.

With that, he bowed slightly, turned and marched off in the direction of the camp fire. Celene went back to her carriage, pleased with the fact that the young man was not going to get into trouble because of her change of schedule.

They met the ceremonial colour guard on the road the next day. The commander was a little perplexed to learn that his troop was too late to perform their task, but Captain Gadas apprised him of the situation and suggested that they ride back to Azun, and inform High Prince Damakos that Celene's arrival would be a day earlier than planned. They would get a second chance to form the guard of honour when the caravan entered the capital.

That will give you more time to polish your brasses thought Gadas as they rode away.

Chapter 16

'Where do we go from here, Necromancer?' Seratos asked as he turned from where his sister's body lay and strode towards his bedchamber.

Sisus followed his master. 'You must prepare for your meeting with the priesthood, it is no more than a few hours away,' he replied.

'Prepare? Why can I not merely slay them if they refuse to forsake their weak god?' he asked as he began to strip off the clothes he had been wearing since he had fled this room some days previously.

'You could, My Prince, of course, but in so doing you would miss an opportunity to illustrate the power of Nhurkhu over Ios. The choice is yours, however,' Sisus replied, turning his back to his master as he changed into a clean set of robes.

'And how exactly would you suggest I illustrate the power of Nhurkhu to the misguided sycophants that are already beginning to gather in my hall?' the prince spat, belting a long curved sword around his waist.

Sisus thought for a moment or two before a thin smile crept across his face. 'I believe there is just enough time for you to take your first lesson in the dark arts.' Sisus stalked out of the bedchamber and made his way over to where the two angelic corpses lay broken on the floor. 'Watch what I do, listen to what I say and then repeat *exactly*,' he commanded before standing over the body of Seratos' father.

From a pouch hanging from his belt, Sisus

removed a handful of what appeared to be dirt and lightly sprinkled it over the body of Seratos' father. With this preparatory act completed he opened another pouch and took a pinch of green powder between his thumb and forefinger. He began to speak in a harsh, guttural language that Seratos could not understand but to which he listened intently. As he spoke, the necromancer drew a complex circular pattern above the angel's corpse with the fingers he had dipped into the green powder. The green dust fell from his fingers to hang suspended in the air leaving the pattern clear to see. Throughout the ritual Seratos concentrated hard, committing all he saw and heard to memory. Although he was blessed with an almost eidetic memory, he found it exceedingly difficult to remember every detail.

Once the green ritual circle hung completed in the air, Seratos noticed the corpse begin to move, very slowly at first but as the seconds passed the movement became stronger and more obvious: as if it were awaking from a long sleep. Sisus stopped chanting as the old corpse rose to its feet to stand unsteadily, the spine clearly broken.

Seratos was incredulous. 'How is he standing? I broke him myself!'

'*It*, not he, Master. It stands infused with the power of the underworld. It is this power that animates it, that gives it the illusion of life. It stands now enslaved to my will.'

'It will do whatever you command?'

'That is possible. The ritual I have just performed is a relatively simple one and so the results are somewhat basic. In time I will teach you more complex rituals that will give you more flexibility. For now, simply repeat what you have just seen.'

With a look of intense concentration Seratos stood over the body of his sister, and taking a hand full of the graveyard dirt from Sisus, he began imitating the ritual he had just witnessed. It took every ounce of his concentration but he succeeded. He stood perspiring with the effort it had taken to enact the ritual, and stared at his sister who was now standing before him with dead eyes in a head that sat at an unnatural angle on a crushed neck.

'How do you feel?' Sisus asked his pupil.

'The power...' was all Seratos could manage. He turned from his tutor and, beckoning his sister to follow him, made for the door that led out of his private chambers, 'I have learned your first lesson, Necromancer, and I believe I know what you intend my second one to be,' he said as he entered the corridor and made his way towards the main audience chamber.

'I see you have an aptitude, My Prince,' Sisus replied, following his master through the palace. *An aptitude and great potential.*

By the time Seratos and Sisus arrived in the main audience chamber, Tiran had managed to assemble every single priest that was currently residing in Carchum. With a gesture and a thought Seratos commanded his corpse-sister to remain in a small atrium that led into the audience chamber, along with Sisus. This was something that he had to do himself.

An expectant silence fell over the audience chamber as Seratos entered and made his way to his throne. There were over three hundred of the priesthood present, including Tiran. As they gathered in front of the throne Seratos motioned for one of the guards that were in attendance to approach the throne.

A whispered order sent the man around the chamber locking all of the doors. With this done, Seratos addressed his assembled priesthood.

'I have lost much in the last few days but now I have returned, having gained so much more,' he began. Several of the gathered priests, offered up impromptu prayers of thanks at this news. 'I have learnt a great truth and my faith has been strengthened as a result.'

More prayers of thanks were offered up.

'I have gathered you all here to share this truth with you and to offer all of you here a choice.' Silence fell across the hall.

'Ios is a weak and frail god, unable to save even her most devoted from death's embrace. I was betrayed by her, my own beloved wife was betrayed by her. The truth I have come to learn is that whilst life is temporary and fleeting, death is eternal and everlasting.'

Shock and horror were written across the face of everyone present. Some of the women fainted at their prince's blasphemy whilst others began to weep.

'I am hereby disbanding the Leznar Order of Life and outlawing the worship of Ios across the whole of Leznar-Carchum,' he announced. Then he reassured them, 'However, I do not hold your past against you. I am now giving each of you the opportunity to renounce your faith in Ios and instead to embrace the eternal power that is Nhurkhu, God of the Dead, Lord of the Underworld!'

Tiran was the first to regain his senses. 'How can you say such a thing, my prince? Surely you have not come to believe that death is preferable to life? I... I do not understand. We were all deeply saddened by Saruké's passing but—'

'But *nothing*, Tiran! Watch and listen, perhaps you will come to see the truth as I have.' Seratos motioned for a priestess to approach the throne. She was approaching old age, her silvery hair almost blending in to her white robes. She climbed the steps to Seratos' throne and stood, obediently, awaiting instruction.

'Witness the frailty of life, Tiran.' In one fluid motion Seratos rose from his throne, unsheathed his sword and ran it up to the hilt into the chest of the priestess standing before him. Tiran looked on in horror as his prince slew the peaceful woman without a hint of remorse. With a strangled cry she fell to the floor and bled out, her heart spitted. Shrieks and cries filled the room.

'And now witness the power of death, Tiran.' Sheathing his sword Seratos took a handful of graveyard dirt from a pouch on his belt, passed to him by Sisus before he had entered the hall, and prepared to raise the priestess's body. The ritual was somewhat easier for the prince to perform this time, having performed it once before. The gathered priests looked on horror-stricken as Seratos raised the old corpse from death to undeath.

'Sorcery! This is sorcery!' one of the gathered priests yelled, 'we will have no part in this!'

'You all now have a choice,' Seratos declared, ignoring the outcry and unsheathing his sword meaningfully at the same time. 'Renounce Ios, abandon the path of weakness and frailty and stand with me, or remain enslaved to your feeble god and stand against me.' He looked every one of the gathered men and women in the eye as he made his pronouncement. Then, turning to Tiran, he addressed the man that had once been his closest counsellor.

'Tiran, will you stand with me?' A troubled look settled on the seneschal of Carchum and he remained silent for some moments.

'I'm sorry, Your Highness, I cannot renounce the Holy Mother. I just can't.' A tear rolled down the man's cheek as he looked into his prince's dead eyes.

'Such a shame,' Seratos declared coldly, before decapitating the man who had once been so close to him. Turning to the gathered priests, he cast his eyes slowly over them. 'Are you all as blind as Tiran was, or are there some among you that are able to see the truth?'

No one dared to speak for some minutes. Eventually, a young priestess stepped out from the crowd.

'Your Highness, if I may ask, Princess Aldene?' the young woman asked fearfully. Seratos recognised her as his late sister's head maid and motioned for one of the guards to unlock the door to the antechamber where Sisus and Aldene still waited. He paused for a moment and willed his corpse-sister into the audience chamber. Unsteadily, the un-dead angel shuffled into the hall.

'No!' the young priestess cried before burying her head in her hands and weeping uncontrollably.

'She was as blind as Tiran... as was my father,' Seratos announced.

Several of the gathered priests placed their hands on the young priestess's shoulders as she wept, trying to console her as best they could. At length she managed to control her emotions enough to turn to Seratos and look her prince in the eyes.

'I have been Princess Aldene's maid since before she came of age,' the young woman paused and took a deep breath, 'I will choose as she did;

praise be to the Holy Mother!' she declared defiantly.

'Praise be!' a voice called out from the crowd.

'Yes, praise be to the Mother of Life!' another voice called out. Seconds later the entire gathering was declaring their loyalty to Ios.

'You'll have to kill us all, My Prince, we will never submit to Nhurkhu or any of his macabre disciples!' someone cried out from the crowd.

'So be it,' Seratos whispered as he descended from the dais.

The slaughter was horrific. Seratos moved through the audience chamber like the hand of death itself.

Stabbing. Scything. Cutting.

Priests and priestesses fell screaming, clutching mortal wounds. Arms and hands were severed as they tried to put up a feeble defence, blood spurt from arteries and spattered in all directions. The few guards on duty in the chamber tried to intervene but were likewise cut down without a second thought by the rampaging prince.

Seratos lost all track of time as he slew. Eventually he stopped and, breathing heavily, looked around him. There was not a single square foot of the audience chamber that was not blood stained. Around him lay the hewn bodies of more than three hundred men and women of the Leznar Order of Life, nearly half of the entire order.

Sisus entered the room and breathed in sharply as he beheld his lord and master. 'Truly you have become an Angel of Death, My Lord,' he declared.

Seratos turned to regard his tutor and then turned his gaze upon himself, noticing for the first time that he was covered, head to foot, in the blood of the priesthood. Raising his sword to regard the blood-stained blade he began to laugh.

He laughed deep and well. 'Praise be to Ios indeed!' Seratos mocked before turning to Sisus. '*Angel of Death*. I like that, Sisus. From now on I will no longer be known as High Prince Seratos Leznar. I am now Lord Seratos Leznar, Angel of Death.'

'And so your conversion is complete, My Lord; your training in the dark arts can begin in earnest,' Sisus declared, his gaze passing over the bodies that covered the floor.

Chapter 17

'Show me more, Necromancer,' Seratos demanded, wiping the blood from his sword.

Sisus smiled before replying, 'In time, My Lord, first there is a task that needs completing.'

Seratos remained silent but motioned for the necromancer to continue.

'How many other members of your family are currently in Carchum, My Lord?'

'Only my two brothers, Goson and Phadinus, they govern Sursh and Laho respectively. I also have an older sister but she is married to High Prince Nabas Thorvath of Thorvath-Heshkar and lives there for most of the year. Besides a few cousins scattered in a few other principalities, that is all. Why do you ask?' he replied, returning his sword to its scabbard.

'You have begun a great undertaking; overthrowing your principality's patron god. There are however those who would resist the rule of Nhurkhu, should they get a chance. They must not be given that chance, My Lord.'

The implication in Sisus' voice was clear. Seratos unconsciously tightened the grip on the pommel of his sword. 'I must confront them, as I did my father and sister, they will not be easy to persuade...' his voice trailed off, deep in thought.

'There is another way, My Lord, a way to tip the odds in your favour,' Sisus almost whispered.

'Speak your mind,' prompted the angel.

'You could summon aid, aid that could be

employed to retrieve your brothers from their palaces, bring them here and ensure their, er, how shall I put it, submission?'

'Speak plainly, Necromancer, I am in no mood for guessing games,'

'I can show you how to summon and maintain dominion over the creatures of the night, My Lord. Would you be willing to give the upper floors of your higher towers over as roosts?'

'I would.'

'Then, My Lord, I believe that a flock or two of harpies may help solve your fraternal problems. Show me your towers.'

Seratos simply nodded and turned, indicating for Sisus to follow him as he picked his way carefully across the corpse-strewn audience chamber towards one of the still-locked doors. Unlocking the door, Seratos led the necromancer up many flights of winding stairs as he showed him the highest towers in the palace.

'The three highest should suffice,' Sisus said, heavily out of breath, upon returning to the High Prince's chambers.

Seratos stripped off his blood-stained clothing and bathed before changing. Once he had sent a servant off to the kitchens for food and another to ensure that no one went into the audience chamber, he sat down in a luxurious chair and motioned for Sisus to recline in another.

'As soon as we have eaten and refreshed ourselves we will summon my brothers.'

They will be as faithful to the Holy Mother as Aldene and Father were... I will probably have to break them in a similar way...

Looking Sisus directly in the eye he asked,

'What next? Surely, in order to maintain my hold over this principality I will need to eradicate every trace of Ios' taint? I will require loyal followers, men and women who will swear themselves to the new faith. That will not be easy.'

Sisus held his lord's gaze as he responded. 'The promise of power, My Lord, has bought the souls of even the most pious of men before now. The captains of your army – I suspect – are not as devoted to their god as your priesthood were. Show them something of your new-found power and promise a taste of it for themselves and I guarantee that most, if not all, will remain loyal to you. With that done, it will be a simple matter of sending them out across the length and breadth of the land to raze every shrine and temple they can find. Regarding the remainder of the priesthood, I have something else in mind which I think you will appreciate, but one thing at a time My Lord – I am famished!'

Seratos was too lost in thought to hear the knock at the chamber door, or notice the servants bringing in the platters of food. Eventually, the smell of cooked food pulled him away from his thoughts, and he joined Sisus at the table to enjoy his first well-cooked meal in some days.

Once he had eaten his fill, and received word that guards had been posted at every door leading into the audience chamber, despite the fact that it was still early morning, he allowed himself and Sisus to retire. Since neither of them had gotten any proper rest in the last few days, they slept quite soundly.

They rose a little after sunset and ate what would have passed for breakfast at a more civilised hour. Seratos insisted that they immediately begin gathering the colonies of harpies that would make the high towers of Carchum their permanent roosts. Sisus undertook the tutelage of his new master with great zeal. He summoned six servants with torches who accompanied the angel and himself to the top of the highest tower in the palace. On reaching the mezzanine chamber, instead of beginning to explain how he was to summon the flocks, Sisus insisted that Seratos record everything that he had learnt to date. He waited patiently while Seratos wrote on parchments brought up by the servants.

'From the very first, everything I learnt I committed to parchment, and had it bound. I therefore have my own manual, my own personal "Book of the Dead" – if you will forgive my use of such a clichéd term,' explained Sisus as Seratos carefully – but energetically – recorded everything he could recall. 'In time, you will not need to refer to your notes, but it is vital that you keep them and update them as you learn and understand more. My "Book" now stretches into many volumes as, doubtless, yours will too, in time.'

Some while later, as the moon reached its zenith, Seratos laid aside his quill and looked up from where he had been working.

'You have recorded everything that has been done?' Sisus asked.

'I have, everything up until this point is contained within these sheets. *Everything.*' Seratos declared.

'Excellent, then I suggest you have them sent to your chambers and we will begin.'

Seratos bound the pages he had just penned with a length of cord and had them sent down to his chambers. Having dispatched the servant, Seratos helped Sisus bind the wrists of the five remaining servants before gagging and stripping them. Finally, they tied long lengths of rope to the ankles of each victim. Sisus had already opened the shutters of the two large windows in the room allowing in the cool night air. Sisus issued more instructions. With two mighty flaps of his wings Seratos leapt up into the air, perched on the room's high rafters and began hauling the servants up by their their feet. Tying the ropes off, he leapt down and looked coldly at the suspended bodies of the three men and two women, writhing desperately, uncertain of their impending fate.

'What now?' he enquired.

'Now we wait. The smell of fear emanating from our bait should attract the nearest flock like flies to a corpse.' Sisus turned to regard the bound servants with a clinical look, 'the flock leader will enter first and try to claim what she wants before allowing the rest to fight over what remains.'

'Try to claim?'

'Yes, My Lord, she will *try* to claim what she wants but you must not let her.'

'Why, Necromancer? Explain everything to me; don't make any assumptions in your teachings.' Seratos was getting impatient.

'Of course, My Lord, I apologise. You must not let her take her choice of victim – at least not at first. You must first over-power her and thus depose her as pack leader. After you prove yourself as the pack alpha, then she, and the rest of the pack, will submit to you,' Sisus clarified.

Seratos was puzzled, unable to follow his tutor's logic. 'But why? When a predator finds its prey to be stronger than it initially thought or better prepared than it anticipated, surely it will back off, not wanting to risk undue injury. Why would a harpy act any different?'

'Because they are all female, My Lord.'

Sisus' reply elicited another blank look from Seratos. He went on to explain further.

'Whilst harpies will eat pretty much anything they can track down and kill, they have a preference for human flesh. A female victim will usually be torn apart and consumed as soon as she is caught, but the men...' Sisus trailed off, his gaze settling on the three men hanging from the rafters. For a second, a look approaching sympathy passed across his face. 'The male victims are raped before they are eaten, My Lord. Harpies have little choice; every male offspring that results from a union with a harpy is still-born.'

The necromancer looked ill as the images his words conjured up revolted him. The details of Sisus' explanation had no effect on Seratos however, who took in the information with a cold detachedness.

Sisus retreated from the top of the tower as soon as the cool night breeze brought the first harsh cries into the tower. Seratos prepared himself mentally for what was about to happen. A few minutes after Sisus had left, Seratos began to make out winged shapes hovering in the air a few feet from the open windows. It took a further few minutes before a shape swooped from the hovering mass and flew towards the tower's window. Landing on dirty taloned feet the flock leader was hideous to behold. Clad in scratched and heavily repaired leather armour the she-beast stalked into the room, her leathery, bat-like wings folding behind her. When she noticed Seratos in the gloom she rose up to her full height and let out a harsh, grating cry that sent shivers down his spine. She resented the angel being there, at her feeding ground; whilst angels and harpies did not compete for food she took his presence as a challenge to be dealt with. She unfolded her wings slightly, bared her teeth and moved towards him with her clawed arms outstretched.

Seratos responded to this challenge by spreading his wings wide and roaring at the top of his voice. She lunged at him suddenly, seemingly intent on ripping out his throat. As she closed, Seratos brought his wings together with a thunderous *CLAP!* The resultant shock wave knocked the harpy off her feet and sent her sprawling across the floor. Without waiting he leapt onto her prone form. The two combatants wrestled for a few minutes before Seratos' skill overcame the harpy's brute strength and ferocity. He finally managed to pin her to the floor, his hand to her throat, and stared into her eyes, daring her to do anything other than capitulate. She held his gaze for a few seconds before turning away and letting her tensed body go limp. Slowly, cautiously, Seratos rose to his feet and backed away from his opponent indicating for her to do the same.

'Mar-r-r-ster,' the harpy rasped in submission as she got to her feet. Her voice was dry and sounded like gravel.

'Yes, I am,' Seratos stated. 'You and your flock now answer to me, do you understand?'

The she-beast, not able to meet Seratos' piercing gaze, instead looked upwards at the five terror-stricken servants.

'DO YOU UNDERSTAND?'

'I understand, Master,' the harpy replied, still not daring to look at the angel.

'This is your new roost, harpy,' Seratos continued, 'from now on, you and your flock will live here and answer to me.' He then added in a dangerous tone, 'Should you disobey me, then by all the power of Nhurkhu I shall destroy you!'

The she-beast nodded. 'We will not fail you, master.'

'You already see that I have provided you with a meal,' Seratos indicated to the rafters. 'You may eat, but afterwards I have a task for you and your flock.'

'What would you have us do, once we have fed?' she asked having regained some of her composure.

'I have two brothers, one is the Prince Governor of Sursh and the other is the Prince Governor of Laho. You will bring them to me... unspoiled.'

There was a slight pause before the she-beast replied. 'As you wish, Master.'

Seratos gestured towards the servants who were now writhing even more in terror and invited the harpies into his tower. He turned and left the tower. As he descended the staircase he made out the sound of flapping wings inside the room, followed by terrified screams. By morning his brothers would be brought before him and he would settle the last of the familial obstacles to his new order. He met Sisus as he made his way back to his chambers.

'I have sent for my brothers.'

'Excellent, however, there is one more thing that needs to be done before they arrive, My Lord.'

'Yes?'

'The small issue of the current state of your audience chamber.'

'Ah yes, I must *re-make* my priests into something more useful.'

'Indeed, My Lord. I think this would be a

perfect opportunity for your next lesson – once we have eaten?'

'Certainly. But – my next lesson? Have you not already shown me how to re-animate the dead?'

'I have, My Lord. Currently, however, you have merely re-animated their bodies, they will respond only to simple commands directed at them. In order to make them useful you need to enslave them to your will; to make them, effectively, an extension of your own mind. However, the more bodies you have enslaved to your will, the less attention you can give to each. I will show you how to enslave the newly-raised dead to the will of another. For example, were you to raise some of your priesthood and enslave them to your sister then you would only have to command your sister; she would command those under her. You will come to understand the importance of hierarchy as your *following* increases,' Sisus explained as they entered Seratos' chambers. They sat down to eat what would have been a mid-day meal were it not taking place in the early hours of the morning.

Once they had eaten their fill Seratos rose, a dark light shining behind his eyes, and said, 'Teach me my next lesson, Necromancer.'

Chapter 18

For the next two years Thurion travelled the little-known lands south of Widowmaker glacier. Occasionally he came across signs of people; disused winter huts, shelters woven around tree trunks, broken pottery. He kept off any tracks he found. He lived off the land as if he had been born to it, content with only Rimehorn for company. Eventually he found himself travelling south once more, unconsciously following natural trails unknown to civilised men.

The climate became more temperate as he left the tundra behind. Late one afternoon he and Rimehorn were just skirting two small wooded hills, following a small brook that ran off their gentle slopes and enjoying the peace of early summer when Thurion spotted something strange on the horizon. At first it looked as if a rainbow was sprouting from the ground, but as he drew closer he could make out regular shapes and wisps of smoke rising from many camp fires. The camp was comprised of a myriad of tents in many colours; no two were alike. He was curious to see who these people were, but after such a long period of solitude he was reluctant to approach a large party. He remained a little way off, setting up camp under the boughs of a large solitary tree, before picking up his bow to go hunting.

Later that evening, with Rimehorn grazing a few yards away, Thurion sat roasting a small deer over a fire. The night was still, the sky clear.

Rimehorn's ears twitched and he looked up just as Thurion discerned the sounds of someone approaching the camp.

'Come closer to the fire, don't hide in the darkness; I'll not harm you,' Thurion called into the darkness. A lone man came out of the night to stand in the light of the camp fire. He was dressed in long flowing robes and had a loose scarf wrapped round his head.

'Forgive my intrusion but we saw you make camp a little while ago,' the stranger said.

'You are from that large camp?' Thurion asked, gesturing in the direction of the encampment he had seen earlier.

'Yes, we are a merchant caravan travelling east towards Hayesh Et-kun. You are welcome to join us; no one should travel these parts alone.'

'I thank you for your concern, but we are more than capable of looking after ourselves,' Thurion replied cordially.

'We?' asked the stranger. In response Thurion whistled into the night. A moment or two later Rimehorn approached the fire.

'*We*,' explained Thurion. The stranger took several paces back from the massive form of Rimehorn.

'I... I see,' he replied.

'Don't worry about Rimehorn; he's harmless – most of the time. I thank you for your offer, Friend. Perhaps I will come over tomorrow. Whom shall I ask for?'

'You may enquire for Elaim El-Shadur, although I would advise you to seek Magrivald the Magnificent.'

Thurion was puzzled. 'Who is Magrivald the

Magnificent and why should I seek him if I am looking for you?'

'He is the merchant prince to whom this caravan belongs. Anyone joining or leaving it must first obtain permission from him,' explained Elaim before bidding him 'good night' and returning to the encampment. Thurion mulled over the merchant's invitation, it had been a long time since he had been in the company of so many people. He felt a growing sense of unease at the prospect.

The dawn found Thurion eyeing the merchant camp with suspicion. He watched as men in opulent robes looked on whilst others took down the tents and prepared the caravan for travel. As the tents came down Thurion saw at the centre of the encampment, a vast array of wagons that had, until now, remained concealed from view. Like the tents that had surrounded them, the wagons were painted in every colour of the rainbow. Some were open topped, stacked with crates whilst others bore fabric-covered frames. As the caravan formed up in preparation for its departure, Thurion watched as the men that had taken down the tents armed themselves, ready to escort it on its way east.

Thurion mounted Rimehorn and slowly approached the caravan. He studied the men who now formed its guard. They were smartly attired wearing deep green tabards over white shirts and black breeches with black Capitano hats completing their uniform. Each man carried either a tall pike or a long musket. As he approached, several mounted men in the deep green uniform of the caravan guard rode up to him. Some of the horses were unhappy about Rimehorn and stopped short of the pair, rearing and snorting.

'Hold, stranger! We would know your identity, your reason for approaching Prince Magrivald's caravan, and the nature of the beast you're riding,' challenged one of the guards.

Ignoring the questions Thurion said, 'I am looking for Elaim El-Shadur, he came to my camp last night and invited me to seek him out today.'

'You will come with us,' another of the guards ordered.

'Where do you intend to take me?'

'You will be taken before Prince Magrivald. None may join his caravan without his permission,' explained the first guard. 'Give me your name.'

'Is that so?' Thurion said, the slightest hint of threat in his tone. 'I think I will meet this Prince Magrivald. Take me to him,' Thurion demanded, ignoring the guard's order.

Evidently put out by his refusal to be intimidated, the guards escorted Thurion towards the caravan where they were met by a score of guards in red tabards. As they approached, one of them, a man with a red silk sash worn across his chest, stepped towards the party and, ignoring Thurion, addressed those men escorting him.

'Who is this? Why have you brought him here?'

'We saw him approaching the caravan, captain. He wishes an audience with the prince.'

The guard with the red sash looked at Rimehorn with suspicion before turning to Thurion.

'Who are you and where are you from?'

'I am Thurion, son of Ragna, son of Rannweig. Formerly of Vorde, I am now of the wilds,' Thurion replied.

'Vorde. I've never heard of it. Where is it?

'It's a village away west, just south of the Muskovian mountains.'

'A barbarian, eh? We've heard of them. Godless savages, they say. What business do you have here?'

'I am here at the invitation of Elaim El-Shadur.' Thurion was getting rather tired of being questioned. 'Who're you?'

The man looked at him arrogantly, before responding. 'My name is Captain Phillipe Guntono, commander of Prince Magrivald's bodyguard. You are to dismount and follow me; I will escort you to the prince's carriage.'

'Very well,' said Thruion as he climbed down from Rimehorn.

'What about your beast? You can't just leave him here.'

'Why not? *You* brought me here, besides, he is not *my* beast; I do not own him. We travel together. He will be fine; he is more than capable of taking care of himself!' Thurion laughed as he ruffled the fur that hung down from Rimehorn's heavy eyebrow ridges. 'Just leave him be, don't aggravate him whatever you do, he will not approve,' he warned as he turned to follow Captain Guntono into the array of wagons.

After several minutes spent passing through the mustered wagons of numerous merchants, Thurion found himself standing before an ornately carved carriage of fine red wood. Two bodyguards stood guarding the door at the carriage's rear. Captain Guntono stopped before entering the prince's carriage and turned to Thurion, gesturing to the axes on his belt and the one strapped across his back, 'I cannot allow you to enter this carriage armed.'

'I am always armed, but you need not fear me,

captain. I am not here to kill your prince.'

'It is the law,' Captain Guntono said flatly.

'It may be *your* law, captain, but it's not mine.'

The guard to Thurion's right drew his sword and held the point to the barbarian's chest. 'Your weapons, savage,' he demanded.

'That was not wise,' Thurion growled. In one fluid motion he drew his single-handled axe and struck the man's hand, knocking his sword away. He stood glaring at the startled guard, his axe inches from his face. 'I could have killed you,' Thurion said, drawing his hatchet. 'But I did not.' He turned and addressed Captain Guntono, 'You may trust me, Captain.'

Guntono looked long and hard at Thurion. *He could have, that much is true but what am I to do? Do I allow him to enter, armed? What choice do I have?* After a pause, he said, 'I believe I can, Thurion of the wilds. Follow me.'

He turned and entered the carriage. Thurion replaced his axes, glared at the guards that followed him and turned to follow the captain into the prince's carriage.

The interior of the prince's carriage was as opulently adorned as the exterior. The carriage was furnished with finely carved furniture made from the same warm red wood as the coachwork. There were floral patterns made with intricate inlays of silver and ivory. All the furniture was varnished and well polished, reflecting the light from the small windows like a mirror. An overpowering floral scent hung in the air. Prince Magrivald sat at the end of the carriage on a luxurious settee upholstered in fine purple velvet trimmed with gold piping. He was dressed in a voluminous crimson silk robe made woven with gold thread, and wore a matching plumed turban adorned with fine gold chains. An elaborate livery collar made from gold and pearls hung around his neck; his fingers were covered with rings of solid gold, some encrusted with fine gemstones. He was certainly rich and had no qualms about showing it.

Thurion, however, noticed none of this initially. His eyes were fixed upon the prince's face. The prince had lightly tanned skin and wore a small pencil moustache across his upper lip. His left eye was deep brown in colour; his right, however, was made of solid gold.

As the captain and Thurion entered the carriage, closely followed by the two guards, the prince set down a goblet of wine.

Captain Guntono came smartly to attention and bowed. 'Magnificence, may I present Thurion of the wilds, formerly of Barbaria. He approached your caravan this morning so I had him brought to you.'

The prince was agitated. 'What is the meaning of this? This man is armed, Captain! You have brought an armed man into my carriage!'

Guntono bowed even lower. 'A thousand apologies, Magnificence, however, he has demonstrated that he means you no harm; see – his weapons are slung. I can vouch for him, Magnificence.' Guntono tried to sound confident. The two guards behind Thurion shuffled uneasily.

'I hope you can, captain, I certainly hope you can.' The fuming prince turned to face Thurion, eyeing his axes and his wild appearance. 'Thurion. That is your name you say?'

Thurion just nodded.

'What brings you to my caravan?'

'I was travelling east and came upon your encampment last night. One of your merchants, Elaim El-Shadur, approached me. He said I would be welcome. Seeing as we both appear to be travelling in the same direction, for now at least, I thought I would accept his invitation.'

'I alone have the authority to invite people into this caravan, barbarian; no one else.' The prince's tone was arrogant. He was obviously not used to others disobeying him. 'I will have to speak to Elaim El-Shadur. So, tell me, how far east are you travelling?'

'I cannot say how far, all I know is that I will travel east until my journey takes me elsewhere. I am a nomad, Prince Magrivald, I do not walk a set path and my destination is not fixed.'

The prince thought for a minute before responding to Thurion's somewhat cryptic answer.

'Ahh. You are a mystic – I have heard of such people although I have to say that I have not met one, though you do not strike me as one who sees into the future. How are you travelling? Are you on foot or do you have a mount? I presume you are travelling alone?'

'I am not a mystic. I am not sure of what you mean, Prince. There was a woman in my village to whom the gods would speak; we called her a soothsayer. I never spoke to her though. I am just a man; a warrior and a hunter. I ride my mount Rimehorn; we have been together now for over two years since my passage into manhood. I carry nothing other than the things I need to hunt and defend myself with; I ask for nothing except to travel with the caravan until our paths diverge. It has been nearly two years since I have spoken to another person, and I am intrigued by the variety of people travelling with you.'

As Thurion spoke the prince's demeanour lightened somewhat, and he listened with interest before replying.

'You say you have not spoken with another person for the past two years? Where have you been travelling all this time not to have seen another soul?'

'I crossed the upper reaches of the great river that flows down to the Merchants' City, heading for The Widowmaker after helping to destroy a couple of slave trains on their way to Muskovia. I didn't reach it, though.'

'Why, in the name of all that's holy would you want to?'

'I wanted to know why it's called The Widowmaker. But I wasn't able to find out; winter is grim that far north, and the trolls are troublesome!'

The prince was incredulous. 'You were attacked by a troll – how in the name of Bis'anturr did you survive?'

'We fought long and hard before I cut its head off,' Thurion replied simply, as if killing trolls was nothing to him.

Prince Magrivald wrinkled his brow. 'Seriously?'

'Yes, seriously,' Thurion nodded, 'I never reached the glacier, as I said, because of the deep snow and the lack of forage for Rimehorn, so I turned back and was drawn south, in this direction.'

'If that is so, then you are a very interesting character, Thurion of the wilds. You may join my caravan though I cannot spare you any provisions.'

'Thank you, Prince. I will not need your provisions; I carry all I need with me.'

'Good. I'm glad we understand each other.' The prince turned his gaze to Captain Guntono, indicating the interview was over.

'Captain, fetch Elaim El-Shadur to me at once.'

'Yes, Magnificence,' the captain responded, snapping to attention. He saluted smartly before motioning to his guards to escort Thurion from the prince's presence. Before he reached the door the prince called after him.

'Oh, and, Captain,' the Prince lowered his voice, 'If you ever allow anyone to enter my carriage armed again I will have you flogged. Do I make myself clear?'

'Yes, Magnificence,' the captain replied swiftly before turning and leaving the prince's carriage as quickly as he could.

As the men left the carriage a loud disturbance erupted somewhere towards the edge of the caravan. They heard shouts of anger and cries of pain mixed with the sound of timbers breaking. Amidst the noise of the shouting and destruction Thurion immediately recognised the snorts and bellows of anger that could only be his friend.

'RIMEHORN!'

He sprinted as quickly as he could towards the chaotic sounds, weaving his way through the crowded camp site. Heavily-robed merchants, trying to run from the disturbance, got in his way. When he reached the source of the commotion a scene of devastation and carnage greeted him. He saw Rimehorn surrounded by pike-armed guards who were desperately trying to drive him from the caravan. Injured men lay amongst smashed wagons. Rimehorn was snorting and thrusting his horned snout at the nearest guards.

Thurion shouldered two of the guards aside. 'What have you done?' he demanded.

'He just went mad!' someone replied.

'Nonsense! I told you to leave him be!' Thurion shouted back. He approached the enraged beast and patted his flank. He noticed ripped lengths of leather resembling a bridle hanging from his head. 'What is this? Why have you done this? Who ordered it?' Thurion yelled at the crowd.

A small, timid man stepped forward into the ring of soldiers.

'The animal started to wander amongst the wagons. We were afraid he would break the traces and the other harness, so we tried to tether him – but he just went berserk!'

'I told you to leave him alone. He is capable of taking care of himself. This is *your* fault – he was just trying to protect himself!'

Suddenly, a voice shouted, coming from behind and to the right of Rimehorn.

'Form two ranks!'

Immediately the ring of pikemen split, revealing two ordered ranks of musketeers.

'No!' Thurion bellowed as he ran towards the man commanding the musketeers, drawing his hatchet as he did.

'Stay back and you won't get hurt. That beast is dangerous!' shouted the commander.

Thurion stopped. He faced the commander, a captain, so that he was between him and Rimehorn. There were twenty paces separating them.

'Stop!'

The captain ignored him. 'Weapons ready!' He raised his arm in signal. The musketeers brought their pieces up to their shoulders.

'What are you doing? He means no harm. Put your weapons down,' Thurion pleaded. Behind him, although Rimehorn had calmed down somewhat since his appearance, Thurion sensed the beast lowering his head, preparing to charge.

The captain glared at him. 'That animal has killed people – if you don't step aside I will have my men shoot you along with it.'

Thurion felt more anger welling up inside. The captain was not willing to stand down, this was clearly an opportunity for him to prove himself in front of his men. Thurion tried to reason with him again.

'If these people had left my mount alone, as I told them to, this would not have happened. I cannot let you kill him. If you give the order to fire I will have no choice but to kill you and your men.'

The musket captain was somewhat taken aback at Thurion's bold threat but he was not about to be intimidated by a lone barbarian with no more than a hatchet. He now reckoned he had good reason to order his men to shoot both the wild beast and its barbaric rider, after all, he had just been threatened with death whilst in pursuit of his duty.

'How dare you threaten me, barbarian? I am a captain of the Prince's Guard. If you live after this, I will have you chained and flogged. Now stand aside or be shot.'

He had lowered his arm a little whilst he spoke, and the musketeers allowed their weapons to waver downwards. This was not lost on Thurion and, not knowing what else to do, he hurled the small axe straight at the captain. It hit him square in the chest and he fell to the ground. At the same time Thurion drew his seax, and ran towards the fallen officer. It only took him a few seconds to reach the captain, who was lying there with the hatchet sticking out of his cuirass.

Thurion quickly straddled him and pulled the hatchet out of the breast plate. He had deliberately thrown the small axe with force enough to knock him down and wind him but not kill him. With a few quick slashes he cut the straps that held the captain's ornate helmet on and stuck the blade under the stunned man's throat. Some of the musketeers had managed to follow the action and now pointed their pieces at Thurion.

'Tell them to lower their firesticks or I'll put out your eyes.'

'You wouldn't dare. My men will shoot you,' came the throttled reply.

Thurion was in no mood to be dared. He grabbed hold of the man's long hair, pulled his head back and stuck the tip of the blade under the captain's left eye. The man shrieked.

'Stop! Stop! Stop! I'll do it!'

'Tell them to lower their weapons and walk away – or do you want to find out how much use Prince Magrivald has for a blind guard?'

The captain finally capitulated to Thurion's demand and ordered his men to stand down. Behind them, Rimehorn rose up on his hind legs, pawed the air for a few moments then crashed back down again. The ground beneath his hooves cracked. Many of the caravan guards fell as the ground shook beneath them. Those that did not fall retreated from the enraged norshorn. Freed at last, the great beast ran from the caravan out onto the safety of the plains.

Thurion kept his grip on the captain. 'I am

here at the invitation of Prince Magrivald and as such I have a right to be treated as part of this caravan. From what I have seen, the prince does not tolerate failure or insubordination, so if you want to keep your position you will leave me and my friend alone. Understand?'

The captain went to nod his head but a sharp pain in his eye prevented him. 'Yes, I understand. You will he left alone. This-this w-w-was all a t-terrible mis-mis-stake,' he stuttered.

Thurion removed the seax's tip from the captain's eye and sheathed the weapon. As he stood up to sling his hatchet on his belt he was nearly overcome by a horrible stench. The captain had soiled himself. Cracking a wry smile, he simply walked off in search of his beloved companion. The remaining guards and onlookers were too shocked to say anything and parted before him, allowing him to leave the wrecked scene.

Thurion found Rimehorn at the site of the previous night's camp. He had collapsed the tree that Thurion had slept under whilst rubbing his head against it in an attempt to remove the pieces of bridle, now caught up in his long forelock. Blood flowed from the sides of his face, evidence of his exertions. Slowly Thurion approached him, speaking calmly, soothing his mood. The great beast calmed down and stood to allow Thurion to remove the remains of the bridle.

'I warned them to leave you be, but they didn't listen. You've done nothing wrong, my friend, nothing at all,' Thurion said as he gently cleaned the blood from the fur on Rimehorn's face. Placing one hand under his chin, Thurion led Rimehorn back to the caravan.

As they approached the merchant caravan a guard officer in green livery marched up to him. He looked about to speak, his look thunderous, but Thurion cut him off before he could say a word.

'I warned you to leave him alone. I assured you that he could take care of himself. He has never harmed anyone without a cause. You brought this on yourself. You're lucky he didn't kill you all.'

Without waiting for a reply Thurion walked off, leaving the officer speechless as he led Rimehorn to where the caravan was beginning to move off.

Out at the front of the convoy of wagons the air was clearer and Thurion rode alone, Rimehorn's presence unnerving the horses that pulled some of the wagons, although the oxen that pulled others seemed unaffected by his presence. He contemplated the morning's events. He decided that he did not like Prince Magrivald's contemptuous attitude towards others, or the attitude of some of the other merchants he had seen, for that matter. They seemed to him, possessed of an air of superiority that they had not earned. The way they lorded over the men under their command did not sit easily with him. *Why don't I simply ride off and leave them?* He didn't know. And so with no good reason to leave, he stayed, and travelled with the merchant's caravan as it snaked its way eastwards.

A little after noon Thurion slackened Rimehorn's pace and allowed one of the wagons to pull alongside. The wagon was open-topped and painted a deep shade of orange. A number of large wooden boxes were stacked in it, covered with a tightly secured canvas sheet. The driver and another man were sat at the front of the wagon under an awning. Both were dressed in long robes and had silk scarves wrapped around their heads; the passenger wore a richly embroidered tunic over his robe whilst the driver's clothes were plain and worn. Thurion turned to the man sitting next to him.

'Excuse me, I'm looking for Elaim El-Shadur. Do you know where I might find him?'

Not bothering to look at Thurion, the man gestured and replied, 'He's a cloth trader, you'll find him further back.'

The man's rudeness and dismissive attitude made Thurion instantly angry, but he controlled himself – just. After giving the merchant a withering glare he turned and rode back down the length of the caravan. As he passed by he noticed that, almost without exception, the merchants of the convoy sat as far apart from their drivers as they could. It seemed to Thurion that they saw themselves as somehow better than those that served them. This he did not understand. He slowed and turned Rimehorn towards the passing wagons until he was riding alongside a high-sided wagon with a canvas-covered iron frame. This time Thurion addressed the driver and ignored the merchant sitting beside him.

'Excuse me, driver, I am looking for Elaim El-Shadur. Do you know where I can find him?' he asked.

'Afternoon, sir. Elaim? Yes, I think you'll find him a little way back. He rides a red wagon bearing the initials 'E.S.'.'

'Thank you,' Thurion replied as he slackened Rimehorn's pace, allowing the wagons to slowly trundle past. A few minutes later a brightly painted red wagon bearing the golden initials 'E.S.' drew alongside.

'Ah! My lonely friend from the other night?'

exclaimed the merchant.

'Aye, I am he.'

'I did not catch your name last night.'

'I did not give it. Thurion's my name, Thurion, son of Ragna, son of Rannweig of Vorde and this is Rimehorn,' he replied, ruffling the neck fur of the giant norshorn.

'It is an honour to meet you, truly,' replied the merchant.

'Explain something,' Thurion said, 'seemingly with the exception of yourself, the merchants of this caravan – including your prince – appear arrogant, and show no respect for those who serve them. Why is this?'

'Ah yes. The merchants are a breed apart, friend Thurion. This you have already discovered it would seem. The wealthiest merchants of the guild are all barons or princes and so are above the likes of you or I,' explained Elaim.

'And you, you are not a baron or a prince?'

'No, my friend, I am not. I am just a man like yourself.'

'Like all of us. We are *all* just men, Elaim El-Shadur. I was born into a tribe with a chieftain and a council of elders. Those men earned their positions and were well respected within the tribe. These barons and princes, how did they earn their positions?' asked Thurion.

'Earn? They were born to their positions,' explained Elaim.

Thurion laughed long and hard. 'You joke, surely?! Men are not born to positions of power! Chieftain Magnusson, the leader of my old tribe, gained his position through ritual combat. His son will have to earn the title just as his father did if he wishes to lead the tribe.'

Elaim sat quietly for a minute or two before speaking again. 'I have heard some of the members of the guild refer to you as a savage, no more than an uncultured barbarian. I see now that this is not the case. It would seem, Friend, that there is much you could teach us.'

'Elaim, I *am* a savage! I would have it no other way!' Thurion laughed again.

'Say what you will. Call yourself a savage if you like; I see a principled man riding next to me who seems to understand respect.'

'I doubt your *well born* fellow merchants would agree with you. If they expect to see a savage I will show them one. However, there is one thing you have not explained yet. You are not like the others, why is that?'

'I am not a lord, a prince, or a baron. I was born as common as Jagada here,' gesturing to his driver who turned and nodded to Thurion. 'I began trading as a young man, travelling the perilous route between Hayesh Et-kun and the Fur Traders' camp at the foot of The Widowmaker. The camp has no permanent inhabitants, just those trappers who have returned from the wilderness with pelts to trade and the few merchants willing to make the journey up there. I used to buy dried vegetables, grain, and cheap toiletries and haul them to the camp where the trappers would exchange their pelts for them. I would sell the pelts on when I returned home. There was a fortune to be gained there, though I almost lost my life many times. The tundra plain up there is a cold and forbidding place, no place for a man on his own. I used to travel with a group of other merchants and together we fought off bears, bandits and wolves.

Now I travel the caravan road in relative safety.'

Again Thurion laughed.

'Why do you laugh?'

'I have travelled the tundra to the north for years. Cold? Aye. Forbidding? No! It is a peaceful place where the complexities of men do not reach. Granted there is always the risk that you'll be mauled by a sabre-tooth bear or fall foul of a wandering troll but it is no more forbidding than travelling along with all your barons and princes!'

Elaim looked at Thurion in surprise. 'You have travelled the tundra? On your own? It is said no one can survive there. How the trappers survive at the glacier's foot is remarkable. That you travelled for years, alone, is astonishing,' he said, a note of respect in his voice.

'The fur traders survive by being as hardy as a tundra pine and as tough as the glacier itself. I tell you the truth, I travelled the tundra for two years but I was not alone. I had Rimehorn for company,' Thurion said as he stroked Rimehorn's thick neck. 'He is all the company a man could ever need.'

The merchant looked wistful. 'I do not think I could survive for too long outside of the company of others, it would be a lonely existence,' he said, as much to himself as to Thurion.

'Well, I find the company of others just as taxing. Too many people make me nervous. But—'

'Then why are you here, in the midst of this caravan?' the merchant interrupted.

'It is where I find myself at the moment; where my path joins that of others,' Thurion replied before asking, 'this caravan is bound for Hayesh Et-kun you said?'

'Yes, where else?' replied the merchant.

'I have not been that far east yet. I think I will travel with you at least as far as the city – I might even venture in! Where will you go once you reach Hayesh Et-kun?'

'I think I will spend the winter there before travelling back to the city of the Merchants' Guild.'

'Do you ever travel up to the Fur Traders' Camp any more?' asked Thruion.

'I haven't for some years now, and I expect I never will again. As I said, I was a young man then, full of stamina and willing to take on anything the tundra threw at me because the rewards were big. In the end it all got to me, the bandits, the wild animals, the weather, and the monotonous landscape. I lost a lot of supplies, pelts… and friends up there. I came to accept that it would only be a matter of time before the tundra claimed me too, so I decided to try my hand at something else and went into the cloth trade. Now I travel as part of a caravan – I pay for the privilege but at least its safe and the route is less perilous.'

Thurion was incredulous. 'You *pay* to travel, Elaim?'

The merchant looked at him and smiled, 'You are naïve to the ways of the world, aren't you, Thurion? Yes, we all have to pay Prince Magrivald to join his caravan, and in return he provides the guard detail. To you it may sound strange, but to me it makes sense. I'm getting old and I want to live to enjoy some of the money I've made. I would rather pay someone else to take the risks so I don't have to. It's as simple as that.'

'Ah! I understand what you mean, I can see that it makes sense for you. I can also understand why you gave up fur trading: it must have been hard for you, losing your friends.'

'Yes, it was,' the old man replied before he sank into thought. Memories of rough tracks that passed for roads, lined with trees and rocks, came back to him. The safe camp sites, and the unsafe ones. Memories of still, crisp mornings on the tundra that later turned into driving blizzards. Memories of fighting off thieves and sabre-tooths, and leaving the bodies of his friends in the snow when the ground was frozen. The wagon suddenly shuddered as a wheel went over a stone, bringing Elaim back to the present.

'I see some of myself in you, Thurion, when I was your age; full of confidence, ready to take on the world – but you are more the warrior than I ever was. You are also comfortable being on your own with just your beast for company. I never saw myself being more than what I am now: a trader in goods that other people want to buy. But you are different, you do not see in me what you might become, do you?'

'No. I cannot see myself settling down and growing old. I cannot see much beyond today. I go where the wild spirits lead me.'

'Can you see your spirits? Do you hear them and commune with them?'

'No, I cannot. They are just feelings; feelings that are almost imperceptible, I can be by myself, but I am never alone. It's difficult to describe.'

'Well, whatever they are, they are doing a fine job looking after you,' concluded the merchant.

'Aye, that they are,' Thurion said before slipping into a reverie recalling his time wandering the tundra with Rimehorn.

Chapter 19

Azun was far more obviously a fortified city than either Sharrayah or Nihkur were. The city's eastern gate, which Celene's caravan was now approaching, was a fully fortified gatehouse flanked by tall towers. The lower windows were barred and the towers were crenelated. Arrow slits were visible all the way up to the ramparts. The city gates were already open and from the gatehouse, a chariot appeared, heading towards them on the road. It was being driven by a man in what appeared to be royal colours. Riding behind him in the chariot was a young looking angel with russet-brown wings and a vermilion tunic worn over a mail shirt. Captain Gadas halted the caravan as the chariot's driver slowed his vehicle and the young angel stepped off. The guard detail came to attention.

'I am Prince Asmos of Dra-Azun,' he announced.

Gadas nodded in the exaggerated manner that senior soldiers do when addressing junior royalty.

'Your Highness, I am Captain Gadas of the Royal Guard of the Principality of Nemeth-Sharrayah. I am escorting the Princess Celene Nemeth on her tour of the principalities. I am given to believe that your father is expecting us.'

'Yes indeed, Captain, we have been expecting you!' Prince Asmos replied, a broad smile on his face, 'Please, allow me to escort you to the palace.' With that, he smartly stepped back onto the chariot. The driver slapped the reins, brought the chariot about and began to return to the gatehouse at a slow walk. Gadas signalled his men and the drivers to move off, the caravan following the prince's chariot.

As the caravan emerged from the gatehouse into the city it was met by a mounted honour guard of knights resplendent in shining armour and carrying tall lances. Plumes adorned their helmets and pennants bearing the royal coat-of-arms fluttered from their lances. Even the horses looked resplendent in their plumed headstalls and lavishly embroidered saddle cloths.

Celene was looking out from one of her carriage's windows, her eyes wide with wonder at the spectacle. 'Arité! Come and look.'

Arité stood open-mouthed when she beheld the honour guard that had been laid on for her princess. As the caravan passed, the knights fell in behind the last wagon and formed a rear escort. They recognised some of the knights from the meeting on the road some eight days previously. The caravan – looking and sounding more like a military parade – with Prince Asmos at its head, wound through the city to rapturous cheering from the crowds. Celene enthusiastically waved back at them.

The royal palace was as fortified as the city itself, and Celene's caravan passed through yet another fortified gatehouse before coming to a halt in the palace courtyard. Celene stepped down from her carriage into the warm light of mid-morning. The young prince had dismounted and run back to where Celene was exiting her carriage.

He bowed slightly and greeted her. 'Welcome to Azun, Princess Celene Nemeth, I am Prince Asmos Dra. I believe we have met before.'

'Prince Asmos, thank you. Yes, you are

correct, we have met before, earlier in the year.'

'Yes, at your coming of age. How was your journey to the capital?

'It was marvellous, the people have been so friendly and welcoming and the guard of honour, well, that was truly magnificent.'

'Thank you,' he said, as if it was all his doing. 'May I escort you into the audience chamber? My father is expecting you.' He offered his arm which she gracefully accepted.

The inside of the palace was as militaristic as the outside. Ornate shields bearing the royal coat-of-arms hung everywhere with clusters of weapons arranged beneath them. Portraits of monarchs in expensive armour hung between the windows. Guards manned every door and lined all of the major corridors. They all came smartly to attention when the prince and Celene approached.

'Her Royal Highness, the Princess Celene Nemeth of Nemeth-Sharrayah!' a steward announced, as Prince Asmos escorted Celene towards a pair of thrones at the end of the chamber. High Prince Damakos was seated on one of the thrones, the other was unoccupied.

'Welcome to Dra-Azun, Your Highness, I trust your journey was not too taxing?' the High Prince asked.

Celene curtsied politely, 'Thank you, Your Highness, no, the journey so far has been a pleasure.'

The High Prince smiled and said, 'I look forward to getting to know the daughter of High Prince Raparké at tonight's dinner.'

Celene must have given the slightest hint of the reservations she felt at attending another long banquet, because the High Prince picked up on this.

'Do not fear, Your Highness, State dinners in Dra-Azun do not carry on over-long, just long enough for everyone to get to know everyone else; I realise that you probably have a rather full schedule over the next few months, and the last thing you want is to sit through a long, boring state banquet where you don't know anybody!'

Celene blushed slightly, embarrassed at being so transparent. 'Your Highness is very perceptive, it is true that I do have a rather full schedule, but attending state banquets given in my honour is a royal duty, however, I do appreciate those with the fewest courses!'

The High Prince thumped the armrest of his throne. 'As I thought! Have no fear, my dear, we shall endeavour not to bore you. Prince Asmos will escort you to your chambers where you can freshen up. In an hour or so the prince will take you on a tour of the palace and its surrounding gardens.'

'Thank you, Your Highness, I would like that,' she replied. *Wonderful! Yet* another *tour of a royal palace!*

Prince Asmos escorted Celene from the audience chamber down a long corridor with walls adorned with more shields and weaponry to her chambers in the guest wing of the palace.

Stopping at an ornate double door Prince Asmos said, 'Here we are. It is a pleasure to meet again, Your Highness. I hope you will enjoy your stay.'

'Likewise, Prince Asmos. I am sure I will. I look forward to seeing the rest of your palace – so long as you don't have a large collection of paintings!' she added without thinking.

'Pardon?'

'Oh, nothing,' she replied quickly.

The prince thought for a second or two, then asked 'You have just come from Lephar-Nihkur, have you not?'

'Yes...'

'And you would have undoubtedly been entertained by Prince Rass?'

'Yes...'

Prince Asmos laughed, 'I understand your apprehension about the tour, but I assure you that you have nothing like that to fear here in Dra-Azun, Your Highness! You are not the first to have been bored by Lepharian art. The house of Lephar can be quite over-bearing at times, can it not?'

Celene paused, remembering that protocol prevented her from criticising a royal family of the angelic caste.

Prince Asmos smiled. 'You don't have to stand on protocol, Your Highness; you will find the house of Dra to be somewhat more easy-going! You may be frank with me.'

Celene visibly relaxed, 'Thank you, Prince Asmos, if the truth be told, I was dreading another *very* long banquet followed by an extensive tour of your works of art!'

'Ah, there is nothing of the sort here! What is arranged is just a tour of the palace and gardens this morning, dinner this afternoon and a tournament tomorrow.'

'A tournament?' Celene asked as Prince Asmos opened the door to her chambers for her.

'Yes, we have several tournaments each year that pit our best archers, riders, soldiers and athletes against each other. It really is quite exciting to watch,' he answered.

Celene sensed the enthusiasm in his voice and asked,

'Will *you* taking part, Prince Asmos?'

'Yes, I will be entering the bladed martial arts event.'

'Then I expect it *will* be exciting,' she replied, 'I will be ready to see your fine palace in an hour, Your Highness.' She smiled briefly before closing the chamber doors.

'That's a smile I've not seen before!' Arité commented as Celene closed the chamber door.

'Arité, I don't know *what* you mean!' the young princess replied.

'Oh yes you do! From what you have told me you were not *that* civil to Prince Rass!'

'Well, maybe not... anyway, I will need something nice for my tour of the palace in an hour's time, Arité,' Celene said, changing the subject before she blushed any more than she already was.

'Certainly, Your Highness,' Arité replied, smiling, 'is the dinner starting early?'

'No, Prince Asmos is showing me the palace and gardens beforehand,' she explained.

'Oh well, if Prince Asmos is taking you on a personal tour of the palace then we had better find you something extra-special!' Arité teased as she began to sort through Celene's wardrobe which consisted of a collection of dresses, most of which were green.

'Arité, don't tease me so!'

'You need to look your best, Your Highness, Now, get out of those clothes and into your bath before the water gets cold.'

Almost exactly an hour after he left, Prince Asmos returned to take Celene on her tour of the palace. Celene was rather taken by Prince Asmos although she refused to admit it initially, putting her feelings down to the fact that he was so very different from Prince Rass. For a start this young prince didn't feel the need to expound on his family's history and exploits. Another thing that Celene found quite refreshing was that the young prince's tour of the palace building was rather rapid, but when they got outside into the gardens he slowed his pace and allowed her to wander wherever she wished.

Prince Asmos suggested that they flew above the grounds so he could give Celene an aerial tour, but she declined saying she preferred to walk instead. Whilst there were orchards and vineyards that stretched far away from the palace, Celene ignored these and explored the formal gardens where there were flowerbeds and neatly manicured lawns. The prince and Celene had just entered a garden that was planted entirely with an exotic variety of rose with deep blue flowers, when a series of trumpet blasts sounded from the palace battlements.

'Has so much time passed?' Prince Asmos asked himself in surprise.

Celene was stooped over a rose flower, smelling the rich, heady fragrance, when she looked up and asked him 'Why? What time is it?'

'An hour before dinner!' he replied.

'How do you know?' she asked.

'Because the trumpets have sounded. Didn't you hear them?'

'Really? I didn't hear a thing except the buzzing of the bees. These gardens really must be enchanted. I had no idea that the time had passed so quickly. Can we return via the lily garden?'

'I'm sorry, but there is no more time, Your

Highness. I'm afraid I must insist that we return to the palace directly; we don't want to be late for dinner! You will need time to change, obviously.'

'Why, Prince Asmos, do you not think that I am dressed appropriately for dinner?' Celene asked with mock offence.

'Er, er, no, Your Highness. No, I mean yes, you are perfectly attired. I was only saying that, usually...' the young prince fumbled his words, desperately trying to undo his faux pas.

'Prince Asmos, relax,' Celene laughed, 'I *am* dressed for dinner; I have been since you called on me earlier this morning.'

The young prince, somewhat embarrassed, lowered his head and apologised, 'Forgive me, Your Highness; I meant no offence.'

'None was taken. Thank you for the tour of the palace and allowing me to enjoy the gardens. Now, Prince Asmos of Dra-Azun, would you be kind enough to escort me to dinner?' she asked with a coy look.

'Certainly, it will be my pleasure,' the prince replied, grateful of the opportunity to redeem himself. Taking Celene's arm he led her back through the gardens and into the palace where the pre-dinner reception was just beginning.

The dinner that night in the palace at Azun was much less grand than that put on by Prince Tamar, but much more enjoyable as far as Celene was concerned. The table was arranged in a large horse-shoe shape with people sitting on both sides. Celene was sat between High Prince Damakos and Prince Asmos. She found herself opposite two of the prince's three sisters and the High Prince's Lord Commander; an older man who was dressed immaculately in full-dress uniform. There was not a single crease out of place.

The two princesses were both older than her. Borana was quite tall with strawberry blonde hair. Her wings were also blonde in colour but darkened towards the tips. Mada was shorter than her sister, though not by much. Her hair was a darker shade than her sister's. Her wings were also darker towards the edges. They were both very friendly to Celene; having undertaken their tours of the principalities a couple of years before and therefore able to empathise with the young princess. They spent most of the meal telling Celene stories about their tours and what she could expect in the next leg of her tour.

The dessert plates were being cleared away when Prince Asmos turned to Celene, 'Princess Celene, there is a dance beginning in half an hour. You are by no means obliged to stay for its entirety but I would be honoured if I could have the pleasure of one dance,' he asked with a note of reservation in his voice.

'Are you asking me to dance, Prince Asmos?' Celene asked him, rather loudly, casting a sidelong glance to where his two sisters were sitting. Prince Asmos began to blush.

'Er, yes, Your Highness, I am... I do not believe it to be beyond the limits of propriety,' he replied, blushing more as he noticed his sisters across the table.

'Prince Asmos, it is an entirely decent proposal; I would be honoured to dance,' she replied, 'However, I do need to freshen up first,' before turning to Asmos' two sisters, 'Would you be kind enough to show me where I might be able to?'

'Certainly, follow us,' they giggled, getting up

from their seats and motioning Celene to join them.

Three quarters of an hour later the three young princesses returned to the ballroom, laughing. An orchestra was playing a waltz. Prince Asmos approached them and addressed his sisters.

'I do hope you haven't been gossiping about me, dear sisters?'

'Why of course not, Brother dearest, we wouldn't dream of such a thing!' Borana replied.

'In that case, Princess Celene, may I have this dance?' he asked, bowing.

'Certainly, Prince Asmos,' Celene replied, holding out her right hand, which was duly accepted. Together the pair disappeared onto the dance floor. They danced together for some time making small talk and acknowledging the smiles and greetings from the other guests. Before long, Celene felt tired and took the opportunity during a lull in the music to excuse herself.

'Prince Asmos, I have enjoyed myself greatly this evening but I am afraid that it is getting rather late. Will you excuse me? I am rather tired.'

'Of course. I thank you for the pleasure of your company and look forward to seeing you at the tournament tomorrow.'

'And I you,' she replied with a smile. 'Please pass on my compliments to your family for such an enjoyable evening.'

'I will. I'm sure they will understand. I will summon a maid to escort you to your chambers.'

She smiled again before turning to follow the maid, the other guests parting before them, curtseying and bowing as she made her way to her chambers.

The following morning Celene breakfasted with High Prince Damakos, Prince Asmos and

Princesses Borana and Mada in one of the smaller rose gardens close to the palace.

'I hear you enjoyed last night's festivities, Princess Celene,' High Prince Damakos remarked as a servant passed a bowl of fresh fruit around the table.

'Yes, Your Highness, I enjoyed it greatly,' she replied.

Princess Borana gave her sister a knowing look as her brother blushed slightly at Celene's comment.

'I am sorry my youngest daughter, Princess Layenne, could not be here, but like yourself she is currently touring the principalities,' Damakos explained.

'Well I hope she is meeting with such hospitality as I have so far,' Celene replied.

'You are too kind, Your Highness,' the High Prince replied. An instant later a series of loud trumpet blasts sounded.

'Ah, the call to contestants – the tournament begins in half an hour,' Prince Asmos announced. 'Your Highness, Princess Celene, dear sisters, please excuse me; I need to prepare for my event,' he said as he rose from the breakfast table. His father nodded his consent before turning to Celene.

'Will you be staying for the tournament, Princess?'

'Yes, Your Highness, I shall be, although I fear I must leave early tomorrow morning,' she replied, knowing full well that Captain Gadas would have preferred to leave later that evening to ensure their prompt arrival in Khalii. *I will just have to persuade my dear captain that we can afford to leave a little later; it is* my *tour after all!* She let her eyes follow Prince Asmos across the garden as she finished her cup of light herbal tea.

After breakfast Prince Asmos' two sisters offered to accompany Celene to the tournament. Celene gratefully accepted their offer and together they walked around the palace to the main courtyard where they waited for their carriages to be prepared.

'Where does the tournament take place?' Celene asked.

'There is a large meadow to the west of the city by the river. It is about an hour's journey from here,' Princess Mada explained. High Prince Damakos arrived in the courtyard just as their carriages pulled up.

'Ah, I am glad to see my dutiful daughters have taken you under their wing,' he remarked.

'Father! Of course we have!' Princess Borana pouted, with mock offence in her voice.

'I knew you would; you both have hearts of gold,' he paused before continuing, 'you both remind me so much of your mother sometimes,' he said with the faintest look of pain behind his eyes. Without waiting for a reply he turned and entered his carriage. Celene's look of puzzlement was noticed by Borana who answered her unspoken question in a quiet voice,

'Our mother died last year; her spirit has returned to Holy Ios.'

'I am sorry,' Celene apologised.

'There is no need – you weren't to know. Father kept the news from spreading beyond Dra-Azun because he couldn't bear to face the long processions of condolence from the other principalities. He withdrew from all official duties and sat for hours in the gardens by himself. Despite the fact that her soul has been re-united with our Holy Mother, father still feels her loss acutely.'

Celene was sympathetic, 'That's understandable; grief is a difficult emotion to manage.'

'Please, you two, can we concentrate on the here-and-now? Mother would want us to enjoy ourselves wouldn't she?' Princess Mada said, trying to raise the mood.

'Yes, you're right, Mada,' Princess Borana agreed, 'We have a tournament to attend and, Princess Celene, you have a martial arts event to enjoy, don't you?' she asked with a knowing look.

'Yes, yes I do,' she replied with a smile. The three princesses then entered their respective carriages.

The journey to the meadow took about an hour, just as Princess Mada had said it would. As the royal carriages slowed to a halt at the edge of the meadow Celene left her carriage and walked up to Captain Gadas.

'Captain, I intend to stay until the end of today's tournament. I trust that delaying our departure until tomorrow morning will not be problematic?' she asked with a smile.

'It will not, Your Highness,' the captain replied, knowing precisely what the young princess was implying.

The tournament was a much less informal affair than the Nihkur Grand Fête. Different events took place at the same time all across the meadow with the exception of the final bouts of the more popular events. These would take place towards the evening with the bladed martial arts final being the highlight of the tournament. Considering how the tournament was laid out and organised, there was no royal platform or box anywhere. This was one of the few events in the calendar of Dra-Azun where the royal family mingled with common folk, albeit accompanied by a royal guard detail. Celene was no different. She made her way around the meadow accompanied by Captain Gadas and ten of his men. After discovering that Prince Asmos' event was not starting for another hour, Celene decided to explore the rest of the tournament.

The tournament was really an exhibition of the martial skills of Dra-Azun. Celene saw events such as archery, jousting, wrestling and martial combat taking place. In addition to the arenas for the sporting events, the meadow was also packed with trade stalls offering every item imaginable from fine linen, exquisite foods, exotic spices and furs to finely crafted crossbows and the like. Celene smiled constantly as she revelled in the day's atmosphere; everything felt so alive. The young princess may have been enjoying herself but her captain had his work cut out ensuring that she was protected at all times. They may have been deep in the heart of the principalities but he was taking no chances with his High Prince's only daughter.

As soon as she approached the arena where the martial combat event was taking place several spectators immediately gave up their seats for her and her escort. She sat down as the last of the qualifying bouts was finishing. An older man was being helped out of the arena. Blood was running from his nose and he didn't seem to be able to use his left arm.

'This looks dangerous, do people get killed?' Celene asked her captain.

'Very rarely, Your Highness,' he said. 'The contestants wear full armour and the weapons all have a leather sheath fixed over the blades. Like judicial duels, bouts are fought to submission, but occasionally accidents do happen.'

'I hope he recovers,' she replied.

'He'll be fine, he's still walking. Besides, at these events there are always a large number of the priesthood on hand to heal any injuries the contestants may suffer.'

Celene sat up straight as the contestants involved in the first bout of the first round entered the arena. The first contestant was a large man in a long coat of mail. He had a large two-handed sword over his shoulder. The second contestant was Prince Asmos. He was dressed in a relatively light-weight coat of mail. A rapier hung in a scabbard from his belt whilst he held a long spear in his right hand. The two challengers walked out into the middle of the arena, bowed to the crowd and then turned to face each other. Each combatant held his weapon out in front of him and backed away from his opponent until the points of their weapons were just touching each other.

A single trumpet blast sounded and the two combatants began circling each other. The large mail-clad man struck first, bringing his sword round in a mighty arc aimed at the prince's chest. Prince Asmos easily evaded this first blow, spread his wings and jumped back a pace. As he moved back out of the sword's path he thrust with his spear and connected with his opponent's chest. A winded gasp was the swordsman's reply as he brought his weapon up into a high guard. The two warriors traded blows for some minutes, the prince lithe and nimble, the swordsman slower and much heavier. In time though the slower man began to tire and Prince Asmos eventually drove him to his knees after raining down a torrent of blows. Dropping his sword, his opponent raised his hand, palm out as a sign of submission.

The crowd cheered as the prince helped his opponent to his feet. The two clasped hands and then left the arena. Suffice to say Celene was impressed at the prince's display. She sat and watched as Prince Asmos won each round that he entered until he and another angelic prince were escorted into the arena by a man finely dressed in deep red robes.

'My Lords, ladies and gentlemen, may I present our two finalists: Prince Nabas Thorvath of Thorvath-Heshkar and Prince Asmos Dra of Dra-Azun!'

The crowds went wild; the applause was almost deafening.

'The final bout of this competition will take place here in one hour!' Again the crowds cheered wildly as the two finalists bowed and left the arena.

Celene took the opportunity of the break to stretch her legs and find something to eat. After wandering for a little while she found something to her taste and returned to her place by the arena. Although the crowds were gathering no one had taken her place. *Royalty* does *have its privileges!*

A vast crowd had gathered to witness this final bout. The cheer that erupted when the finalists emerged was cacophonous and Celene had to put her hands over her ears. Both of the angelic princes were identically armed with rapier and spear. After bowing to the gathered crowds they bowed to each other and, upon the sounding of the trumpet, they leaped into the air. Again the crowd cheered. Both princes circled each other, swooping and thrusting with their spears, testing each other's skill. All of a sudden combat was joined and blows were exchanged almost faster than the eye could see. Spear struck against spear as the two angels clashed in mid-air.

SNAP! Prince Nabas' spear shaft broke and he wheeled away, narrowly avoiding Prince Asmos' following spear tip. The prince of Thorvath-Heshkar dropped his broken spear shaft and drew his rapier. Prince Asmos nodded and, turning to the crowd cast his spear to the ground, drawing his rapier in the process. The crowd went wild at such a show of courtly etiquette.

The two princes came at each other and fenced with matchless grace in mid-air. The pair traded blows for nearly half an hour before, in a move that no-one down below was quick enough to see, Prince Asmos disarmed his opponent. The prince of Thorvath-Heshkar conceded defeat and, holding his hands palm-out towards Prince Asmos, descended to the arena floor. The prince of Dra-Azun joined him a moment or two later as the cheering erupted once again from the crowd.

Celene watched the whole spectacle awestruck and found herself on her feet cheering Prince Asmos as he was declared champion of the tournament. She loitered around the arena as the crowds dispersed, making a bad show of pretending to be interested in the few stalls that were still open.

'Princess Celene, I didn't think I would find you still here; most of the stalls have closed and the tournament is over,' Prince Asmos said as he exited the arena, evidently pleased that she *was* still there.

'I wanted to congratulate you on your victory, it was very impressive to watch.'

'Thank you, Your Highness, Prince Nabas is a worthy opponent.'

'I suppose you are heading back to the palace now, are you not?'

'That was my intention, are you not?'

'My captain is insistent on leaving early tomorrow morning, he is afraid a return to the palace would delay our departure over-much.' *Come on, dear prince, listen to what I am really saying!*

'I suppose I could dine here this evening, after all some of the stalls are still trading. Would you care for dinner, Princess?'

At last! 'What a lovely offer, why thank you Prince Asmos, I would.'

The meadow was nearly deserted by now and so Captain Gadas and his counterpart, the commander of Prince Asmos's escort, allowed the couple a little privacy as they dined at one of the stalls that had remained open. They talked for an hour or so before they got up and strolled back to Celene's carriage via the river bank. Captain Gadas watched as Prince Asmos took Celene's right hand and gently kissed it before bowing and leaving the meadow with his bodyguard. After the prince had left, the captain approached Celene.

'Your Highness, as you know we will be leaving tomorrow morning. Do you wish to spend the night here by the river or would you rather return to the palace?' he asked.

'I think I will overnight here by the river; it's peaceful, and besides, I have already said good-bye to Prince Asmos.'

'Very well, in that case I shall send a couple of my men up to the palace to arrange for the rest of your carriages to convene here tomorrow morning.'

'Thank you, Captain, good night,' Celene replied with a voice that betrayed how tired she really was.

The cool breeze blew gently through the open

windows of her carriage, whilst the gentle sounds of the river added an air of serenity to the night; the young Princess slept deeply and peacefully. She woke the following morning as the rest of the caravan that had remained at the palace overnight, made its way onto the meadow. A minute later her carriage door opened lightly and Arité stepped inside.

'Good morning, Your Highness,' she said as Celene raised her head from her soft down pillow.

'Good morning, Arité, have you just arrived from the palace?'

'Yes, just this moment. I believe that Captain Gadas wants to be away by mid-morning so there's no immediate rush, just you come to for a minute or two whilst I find you a basin of fresh water,' she replied before leaving the carriage with a silver bowl in one hand.

The caravan enjoyed a leisurely couple of hours by the water, before setting off south along a road that ran parallel to the river for some miles surrounded by mixed woodland. An hour or two had passed in this way when the sound of many galloping hooves suddenly became audible coming down the road from behind them. The caravan's rear-guard immediately turned about and formed a defensive ring around the rear-most carriage. Their caution, however, turned out to be unnecessary, as they soon learned when Prince Asmos came galloping round a bend in the road at the head of a score of royal knights.

'Ho! Well met! Take your ease!' the young prince called out as he slowed his charger to a halt. Captain Gadas came jogging up from the front of the caravan and rounded the rear of the last carriage just as Prince Asmos was dismounting.

'Prince Asmos!' he said with obvious relief. 'What brings you out this way?'

'I thought I might escort Princess Celene to the border of Ezné-Khalii. The roads are quite safe, Captain, I assure you. I simply thought that—' Prince Asmos stopped mid-sentence as Celene appeared from behind the rear-most carriage. 'Your Highness! It is a pleasure to see you once more. I was about to ask your captain for permission to escort you to the border,' the young prince said, trying to conceal the real reason for his being there.

'Prince Asmos, Captain Gadas may be in charge of my security but it is I who will decide whether this caravan has an additional escort or not,' she told him, sounding as imperious as she could. 'I think an additional escort would be welcomed, do you not, Captain? It would give your men a little time to take their ease,' she said to her captain before glancing up at Prince Asmos. Captain Gadas knew immediately that there was only one correct answer to this.

'It would indeed, Your Highness,' he said before turning to Prince Asmos, 'I thank you for your kind offer, Prince; my men will take their ease for a few hours.'

Prince Asmos rode down to the head of the caravan as his knights took up position on either side. He approached the front carriage and drew alongside as Celene was mounting its steps.

'I am so glad you accepted my offer of an escort, Your Highness…' He left the sentence hanging, hoping that she would finish it.

'It was a very kind offer, Prince Asmos, very kind indeed,' she said as she, smiling, entered her carriage. *A kind offer indeed dear prince, but I can't let you have* everything *your own way, after all I am a princess and we are notoriously hard to please sometimes!* Sitting down, she admired the prince as he led his knights in escort of her caravan.

'Oh you tease, Your Highness!' Arité said quietly as she prepared the princess a light brunch.

'Me?' Celene joked. *Mother would be so displeased if she heard me talking to a member of the priesthood so candidly!*

'Is there anyone else in this carriage who happens to be sitting by a window and admiring a dashing young Dra prince?' Arité asked. 'No! And you are quite right not to be so easily caught up in the young prince's affections,' she said maternally. 'Courtship should be a process that is longer rather than shorter; each person should discover who the other really is; that is its purpose,' she advised, handing Celene a plate of crackers and light cheeses.

'Thank you for your advice, Arité, I mean it.'

'Think nothing of it, I am your maid; it's my job to see that you are well looked after. Besides, I am also a member of the priesthood and so I am here to serve your spiritual needs as well as your pastoral ones.'

'I know, but I want to thank you anyway,' Celene replied before taking a bite of cheese, 'Where did you find this cheese? It's wonderful!' she exclaimed.

'I have my ways, Your Highness, to ensure that your *every* need is taken care of, even your love of soft cheese! As it happens I found an opportunity to visit the tournament yesterday too, briefly. Knowing your fondness for it I made a point of purchasing a small supply from one of the farm stalls. And before you ask, yes, I *have* hidden it and no, I will not tell you where! Now, eat up and go outside for a walk; the sunshine will do you good,' she teased as the caravan wound its way along the road.

The caravan proceeded alongside the river, its gentle sound, accompanied by the birds singing in the trees created an almost enchanted atmosphere as the afternoon wore on. Prince Asmos had given his horse over to the care of one of the caravan stewards and was walking alongside Celene. The two were talking together as the road cut across a bend in the river when Captain Gadas walked up to them.

'Excuse me, Your Highnesses, evening is drawing on. I would suggest we halt here for the night as there is enough room to pull off the road.'

'Very well, Captain,' Celene replied, stepping off the road onto the clearing around which the river wound. 'Prince Asmos, where will you and your men sleep tonight?'

'Oh, we shall camp out here overnight, Your Highness. My men brought their equipment with them. Every third man carries a tent on his saddle. They are made from a marvellously lightweight material that packs down to a very small size. I am not sure what the material is exactly but its qualities are extraordinary.'

'I see, I wondered what those small grey bundles were,' Celene replied, showing polite interest.

It was not long before a small camp had been set up just off the road, by the riverside. The prince's tents really were remarkable. Although they packed down into very small, lightweight packages, once erected they could just about accommodate three full grown men and their equipment. The knights had come prepared, and each carried several days' supply of dried meats and rice. In the evening four of the riders went out hunting and brought back some fresh game to supplement their rations, and shared some of this with Gadas' men and the princess. After their meal, the caravan guards set up a perimeter picket whilst Prince Asmos and Celene strolled by the river, under the watchful eye of Arité. An hour after dark the camp site was quiet except for the buzzing of insects.

The knights and the caravan guards were awake and packing up as the princess was waking. Her breakfast, consisting of fresh fish was already cooked; one of Gadas' men had managed to catch a couple using an improvised harpoon. With a routine thus established, Prince Asmos and his knights escorted Celene and her caravan all the way to the Ezné-Khalii border – a journey of around ten days. After five days the surrounding woodland thinned out and the road widened as the trees gave way to scrub; the caravan's pace picked up on the gently sloping ground until it reached a fork in the road. One arm wound east to the city of Mari and beyond, the other went west through flat, open country towards the southwest border with Ezné-Khalii. The caravan crossed a stone-built bridge over the river and headed west.

During this time Celene took every opportunity to engage Prince Asmos in conversation and he would often dismount to accompany her on foot. In the evenings they would either sit and talk on the steps of her caravan, or take short walks, enjoying the countryside, with Gadas and Arité following discreetly behind.

Once they reached the border the Dra knights rode ahead and formed an honour guard on either side of the approach road to the border post. Prince Asmos, who was escorting Celene behind her van, led her to the verge and allowed the rest of the caravan to proceed through.

'Princess Celene, it truly has been a pleasure to have met you. I can honestly say that I have enjoyed every minute of your company. I wish you well with the rest of your tour of the principalities and hope that you will remember Dra-Azun with fondness.' With that, he took Celene's right hand in his and gently kissed it.

'It has indeed been a pleasure, Prince Asmos. I have enjoyed your company, the hospitality of your family and that of your people. You can be sure that I will remember your principality with fondness. I do hope that it will not be over-long before we meet again.' She found herself blushing as she took her hand back. She wanted to leave it in his for longer, then realised that the last caravan had already passed and the soldiers of the rear guard had halted and were waiting politely for her several paces away. Turning, she walked through the two ranks of mounted honour guard who drew their sabres and held them aloft as she passed between them and crossed the border into Ezné-Khalii along with the last of her captain's soldiers.

Prince Asmos stood alone staring at her until she disappeared into the distance, obscured by the dust. The commander of the knights turned his horse and walked him back to where the prince stood. He was leading the prince's mount for him.

'She's gone, Your Highness, and we must go too.'

The prince suddenly looked up, as if awoken from a doze.

'Yes, I know. Thank you, Captain.' With that, he mounted up and cantered away with his knights following.

Chapter 20

The audience chamber was more akin to a charnel house than a palace hall. Seratos cast his gaze over the slaughter and recalled his earlier actions with grim satisfaction. He was finding this new-found power and freedom more and more intoxicating.

'So, once I have raised the bodies that are still in one piece, you will show me how to slave them to someone else, for example, her?' Seratos asked, gesturing to the reanimated body of his sister.

'Yes, My Lord, but first allow me to show you something that will become increasingly useful to you; allow me to show you how to re-knit the dead. Take that one for example.' Sisus gestured to the body of a priest whose left arm had been severed.

Sisus began to recite an incantation that was clearly second nature to him and stretched out his right arm towards the dead priest. A few seconds after he had finished the ritual ethereal tendrils began to creep out of both the dead man's wound and the severed arm that lay some feet from the body. Slowly the tendrils grew and began snaking through the air until they found each other whereupon they became one and the arm was drawn across the room. Seratos looked on in awe as the priest's wound was repaired, with only a thin band of necrotic scar tissue to tell of what had happened.

'Now you try, My Lord, with that one,' Sisus instructed, pointing to an elderly woman who lay disembowelled a few feet away. Seratos was silent for a moment or two as he recalled the precise words and intonations that Sisus had used only minutes before. This process, Seratos discovered, was far more straightforward than the reanimation ritual he had performed on his sister. Moments passed and, as they did, ghostly tendrils gathered up the corpse's entrails and closed the gaping wound in its chest.

'This will take a long time, re-knitting them one at a time Sisus, is there a quicker way?' Seratos asked.

'Yes, My Lord,' Sisus began, 'When you re-knitted the woman's corpse you were only concentrating on her. Now try to concentrate on more than one.'

Seratos did as he was instructed and found that re-knitting a dozen or so corpses at once was little more difficult than re-knitting one, so long as one's concentration wasn't broken. Seratos practised and practised until every corpse was whole again. Finally, he turned to the reanimated forms of his father and sister and re-knitted their wounds as well, undoing the damage he had inflicted when he slew them.

'Excellent; you learn fast, My Lord. I don't expect it will be long before your brothers arrive. I think that there is time however to create your first lieutenants,' Sisus said, eyeing the raised corpses of his lord's father and sister. 'Come,' he commanded. In response the two corpses shuffled over to Sisus and stopped a few feet away to look blankly at him.

'My Lord, please pay attention, this ritual is complex and somewhat involved. A person can only enslave corpses to their own will or the will of those already slaved to them. I, for example, cannot enslave your sister to you; you must do that yourself. I will take you through the ritual, stage by stage but you must perform it yourself.'

'I see.' Seratos crossed the audience chamber
and stepped outside. A few minutes later he returned
with a small pile of parchments, a quill and a bottle of
ink. 'You may begin.' he instructed as he dipped his
quill into the ink.

The ritual of enslavement was just as Sisus
had warned, long, involved, and complex. Seratos
recorded everything Sisus said and did in exacting
detail. Once his tutor had taken him through the ritual
Seratos spread his notes out on the floor and
commanded his sister to stand in front of him. Sitting
cross-legged on the blood-stained floor he began.
Perspiring with concentration, he concluded the ritual
quite some minutes later and slowly rose to his feet.
Where before his sister's eyes had been blank and
dead, now a dark light burned in them, she seemed
possessed of an unholy intelligence; that which was
dead now appeared very much alive, risen to un-life.

Tired as he was, Seratos felt compelled to
enslave his father's corpse as well, before his brothers
arrived. In like manner he commanded his father's
corpse to stand in front of him, sat down, crossed his
legs and began the ritual anew. He was almost
completely drained of energy by the time he had
finished, barely able to get to his feet.

'You need to rest, My Lord, your brothers will
be here soon,' Sisus reminded him.

'Thank you, Sisus, I am aware of their
impending arrival... but you are right, I need to rest.
Father, Aldene, remain here until I summon you.' The
two un-dead nodded crisply in response to Seratos'
order. 'Sisus, help me to my room and call me as
soon as my brothers arrive.'

'As you wish, My Lord,' he replied, leading

the exhausted angel from the audience chamber which was now beginning to smell of decay.

Sisus sent a servant to rouse his master around mid-morning with news that his brothers had arrived and were waiting for him in the audience chamber. After rising and quickly donning his formal robes Seratos strapped his sword to his belt and made his way to the audience chamber. As he approached he could hear the goat-like screeching of harpies.

Seratos entered the blood-stained audience chamber to find his father and sister standing on either side of his throne. In front of the throne his two brothers were kneeling, held down firmly by a large pack of harpies.

'Silence!' Seratos commanded as he entered the hall. The raucous rasping of the harpies slowly subsided. The room fell into silence as he strode over to his throne.

'I am so glad you were able to come, Brothers,' Seratos began with barely concealed contempt.

'What has happened here?' Goson, Serato's youngest brother asked, with tears in his eyes as he looked from his sister to his father and then to his blood-stained hands.

'Able to come? These devils broke into my palace, slew my guards and abducted me, Brother! What's happened to you?' Phadinus asked, obviously more aware of what was going on than his younger brother.

'What terrible malady has overtaken the palace that you have sought such aid as these... *creatures*?' Goson asked, 'Your priesthood stand statuesque and appear as ill as our father and sister...' the young prince trailed off, at a loss for words as he looked round the room as much as his winged captors would allow.

'Oh, Brother, open your eyes!' Phadinus snapped, 'the priesthood is not ill, it's *dead!*' He fixed Seratos with a withering gaze.

Seratos returned his brother's gaze as he sat down on his throne.

'Dear Goson, our brother is right. Our father is dead, our sister is dead and the priesthood is dead.' He watched the colour drain from Goson's face before adding 'I killed them.'

'Why?! What could have driven you to such... such... *madness*?' Phadinus asked.

'Betrayal, Brothers, betrayal and enlightenment. Ios betrayed me. She never really cared for me and so I was somewhat ambivalent regarding our faith, but when Saruké lay dying she did not answer my prayers and all attempts at transference failed. She was deaf to the prayers of the entire priesthood. I even sacrificed the best healers of the Order of Life, such was my love for Saruké and my faith in Ios. But when she let Saruké die I could take no more. I wandered lost and alone until I was found by someone who opened my eyes. Lord Dach of Emphar-Nek showed me the source of true power, he brought me before Nhurkhu...' Seratos let the name of his new patron hang in the air.

'The god of the dead?' Phadinus asked, aghast.

'And Lord of the Underworld. Brothers, you no longer kneel before Seratos Leznar, High Prince of Life but before Lord Leznar, Angel of Death.' Seratos rose from his throne as he made this last pronouncement, resting his hand on the hilt of his sword. 'You are no longer tied by your old pledges of allegiance to me since Ios no longer has a place in this principality. I am giving you this one opportunity to swear yourselves to me afresh. Brothers, I am offering you enlightenment. Witness the impotence of Ios to protect her sycophants,' he continued, gesturing to the dead priests, 'and the power of Nhurkhu over all that once lived.' He stepped down from his throne to stand before Phadinus.

'You have fallen far, Brother,' the young angel began, his anger now washed aside by grief, 'I only wish—' Phadinus was cut off mid-sentence as Seratos' sword plunged into his chest. Ripping his blade free, the Angel of Death shot a look to the harpies that were restraining his brother. They let go and he fell to the floor clutching his chest, choking on his own blood.

'Wishes are as smoke, Brother, intangible and blown away by the slightest of breezes.' He turned to his youngest brother, a questioning look in his eye.

'I... I... I—'

Seratos opened up the young angel's chest with a single vicious slash and turned away.

'Such weakness...'

Cleaning his blade on his robe he turned to the harpies' pack leader. 'You have done well; you may leave.' The pack left for their roost, the sound of wet gravel and claws scratching on the stone floor. Seratos gestured for Sisus to join him at the throne.

'I will re-knit and enslave these two and then you will show me how to bind the priests to them. I must begin to form the hierarchy you spoke of.'

'A sound notion, My Lord. The process of binding to an enslaved will is similar to binding to your own. I doubt you will have any problem mastering the process,' Sisus agreed obsequiously.

'May I also suggest that you give some thought to ensuring the loyalty of your military?'

Seratos was silent for a moment, considering if Sisus was over-stepping his boundaries. Eventually he decided that, though he may be, he did have a good point and was proving to be a most diligent tutor.

'Of course you may, Sisus. I have given some thought to the issue myself. I concur with the views you put forward earlier, I will share some of what I have learnt with my officers, giving them a taste of Nhurkhu's power. This should not only earn their loyalty but provide me with an initial core of necromancers for you to instruct.' Seratos paused for a moment as an idea took him. 'I think I will also teach some of what I have learned to my family; this will allow them a greater level of independence, will it not?'

Sisus nodded, waiting for his lord to finish before speaking further.

'You mentioned you had another idea regarding the raising of my new *priesthood?*'

'Yes, My Lord. When you raise a body from the dead you do just that, because the soul has departed. Any intelligence imparted to the body is derived from the will of whomever the body is enslaved to—'

'Yes, Sisus, I know, get to the point.'

'There are certain souls, My Lord, that remain in this world,' Sisus carried on, ignoring his lord's reprimand. 'These are the souls of men and women who worshipped no god whilst they were alive and who, by sheer strength of will, have not passed into the Underworld. They are fiercely independent spirits but they are also desperately lonely; devoid of purpose. They are neither alive nor can they pass on. You, My Lord can give them purpose again; give them a reason to exist.'

'Yes, yes I can...' Seratos replied, stepping over to the still warm corpses of his brothers. As he did, the genesis of an idea began to form in his mind and his countenance darkened...

Chapter 21

The country gradually changed from relatively flat to hilly as Prince Magrivald's merchant caravan travelled east. As the days drew on the hills became steeper until the caravan road snaked through a steep-sided valley. This narrowed in places as it wound its way through steep hills and the caravan's guards became visibly more alert whenever the valley narrowed ahead of them. It was as the caravan was entering one such narrow defile that Thurion spotted a lone figure atop one of the hills bordering the road. It was clad in a concealing green cloak; it was solely due to his hunter's eyes that he saw it at all. The figure darted between several points along the hilltop before mounting a steed and riding rapidly down the other side of the hill.

The small hairs on the back of Thurion's neck stood on end as he urged Rimehorn into a gallop, riding as fast as he could towards the head of the caravan, calling urgently for it to stop as he did so. The head of the caravan came into sight just as the hilltop exploded sending several hundred tons of earth and trees sliding down into the valley. There was nothing he could do but watch as the front wagons were buried beneath the landslide. The caravan came to an abrupt halt and guards ran forward in a vain attempt to dig out the buried wagons.

Confusion and fear were palpable in the camp for several days as Prince Magrivald waited for the road to be cleared. Eventually it became clear, even to him, that the guards could not clear the road and so the prince sent parties out to look for alternative routes. Thurion rode off too, as much to help the situation as to escape the raging temper of the prince.

Several days passed before the patrols returned. The news was poor. A single route had been found, though it wound through a narrow mountain pass that was only wide enough to permit a single wagon through at a time.

After conferring with the leaders of the patrols and his senior officers, Prince Magrivald summoned all of the merchants to a meeting. In the failing light of evening, flanked by flaming torches, he stood on the steps at the back of his carriage and addressed them.

'Gentlemen, a route has been discovered through the hills,' he announced, as if he had done the work himself. There was a mumble of approval from the gathered merchants. 'It is not ideal; it is narrow and difficult and progress will be slow, but—' his sentence was cut short as Thurion stepped from the shadows and addressed the prince directly.

'Prince, I would advise caution. The path winds through a narrow pass. The land there is nervous and speaks in hushed tones.'

'What nonsense! The words of a superstitious savage and no more! My men and I have assessed the risks and concluded that this is the only viable route to Hayesh-et-Kun. We will turn around and take this new route tomorrow. We will arrive at Hayesh Et-Kun no more than a week behind schedule.'

Realising that neither the prince nor the gathered merchants would listen to him further Thurion stalked away from the gathering and sought out the commander of the caravan guard. He found him sat around a fire in conversation with some of his captains. As he approached the officer looked up and the conversation around the fire petered out.

'May I help you?' the officer asked.

'I am looking for the commander of the caravan guard.'

'I am Commander Patos,' replied the officer, introducing himself.

'Good evening, Commander, I am Thurion. May I join you?'

'Of course,' the commander replied, offering him a place near the fire. He had heard about the young barbarian from Captain Guntono, and was anxious not to show his displeasure at having such a savage in the caravan.

Thurion sat down. 'You've probably heard that the prince intends to lead the caravan along the route that your men discovered a day or so back. I have come to warn you to take that route only with great caution. I don't think it is safe.'

Patos furrowed his brow. 'Why not? My men reported nothing but empty country for miles around.'

'Yes, too empty and too quiet. I do not like the pass. It has a bad air about it. I have travelled most of the lands from what you know as eastern Barbaria to the fur traders' camp, near the Widowmaker. I have seen country like that before, you must believe me. Take great care and be vigilant.'

'I have heard of your martial prowess from a musket captain, and you sound as though you know what you are talking about, barbarian. If I were to double the guard would that suffice?'

'It might, or it might not; it depends on what's out there. This is not my caravan to protect, but if it were I would do more than that. I would do all that I could,' he replied before rising.

'You're right; it's not your caravan. I'll take your warning under advisement though, and double the guard,' Patos called after him.

Thurion returned to where he had pitched his small tent, somewhat angry that the commander had not appeared to take him seriously. He eventually fell asleep and dreamt of many of the things that might be lurking in the hills.

The following day the caravan turned around and headed a few miles back down the road to a point where a smaller, poorly made track forked off to the north. Slowly the caravan left the main road and the wagons and carts made their way onto the small north track. Once the hills that flanked the main caravan road had dropped out of sight behind them, the land flattened until the track entered an area of light woodland.

Three days passed without incident although Thurion could not shake the uncomfortable feeling that they were being watched. During the morning of the fourth day the woodland petered out and the land opened up into a narrow plain several miles across. A range of low hills with steep, angular outlines was visible on the horizon and appeared to block the way ahead. The caravan encountered a boulder field as it approached the outskirts of the range, and the caravaners had some difficulty in negotiating the stones. Scouts rode ahead to guide the lead caravans towards the pass that they had discovered some days before.

As the leading wagons of the caravan approached to within a mile of the pass a cry went up from the rear. Thurion turned and looked behind him.

From the cover of the woods many horsemen could be seen galloping towards the caravan. They were naked from the waist up, daubed in red war paint and brandished bows and light throwing spears. Severed heads hung from their saddles. Hurriedly, the caravan guard dashed to the rear wagons to form a protective cordon. Realising what was happening, Thurion began urging the forward wagons to make for the pass as quickly as they could. Unless the caravan managed to make it into the pass it would be cut off and surrounded.

The leading wagons began to pick up speed but Thurion's heart sank as he watched a large number of dark figures suddenly appear at the mouth of the pass. With the majority of the guards formed up at the caravan's rear – and with the exception of a couple of mounted scouts – there were no soldiers available to engage the bandits who were forming a shield wall ahead of them. Their path was blocked. Realising what was happening, the unarmed merchants and drivers in the lead wagons began to panic and slewed the wagons off the track. Thurion quickly re-assessed the situation: There would be no escape from the inevitable bloodbath unless the pass could be re-opened. He dug his heels into Rimehorn's flanks and urged him on.

'Don't slow down! Drive hard, follow me!' he cried as he thundered away from the forward wagons, Rimehorn shaking the ground with each thunderous step. Turning away from the wagons Thurion fixed his gaze on the line of warriors holding the narrow pass. They were grim faced men in dark boiled leather armour. They stood behind a wall of tall, broad black shields and brandished spears. A tall pole could be seen rising above the mass of black armour and shields. It flew no banner, just the severed heads of previous victims. Thurion raised his axe high and roared as he closed the distance, the enemy shield wall faltering with each earth-shaking step of his enormous mount. To their credit the bandits holding the pass did not flee in the face of such primal fury, though their nerve did waver in the last few seconds before Rimehorn smashed into their line.

The pass was barely wide enough to admit a single wagon and so should have been a very strong position to hold. Rimehorn however, was almost as wide as a wagon and hit their line with the force of a battering ram. Shields splintered and men were crushed as Thurion's primeval companion careered through their midst. Thurion added to the devastation wrought by Rimehorn, attacking savagely to his right and left, his great-axe reaping a bloody harvest. Thurion turned to look back once Rimehorn had slowed down enough to turn. The entrance was a mess of mangled bodies, broken wood, twisted metal and spilt blood. Out a full score of bandits, six of them had survived Rimehorn's charge, and Thurion watched as they pulled themselves from the pile of crushed and mutilated bodies of their comrades. Dismounting, he strode back to the mouth of the pass.

The six survivors re-grouped and advanced warily towards Thurion, their spears lowered, their shields locked. A grim smile crossed Thurion's face as he strode towards them, swinging his massive axe in a deadly figure-of-eight pattern. He came at them with a roar, his swinging axe severing spearheads and splitting shields. The shield wall did not hold for long and then Thurion was among them, his axe rising and falling in fearsome arcs. Still dazed by Rimehorn's charge, they were no match for an experienced adversary like Thurion and soon enough the barbarian found himself standing amongst six bloody corpses. Grunting in satisfaction he cleaned the blood from his blade before climbing the left hand wall of the pass, eager to discover how the merchants were faring on the plain.

The caravan had not become surrounded, as he had feared. The forward elements had kept moving towards the pass allowing the rest to flee from the marauding horsemen to their rear. He watched as the first wagons rolled through the pass, over the remains of those that had sought to hold it against them. From his vantage point Thurion could see the fearsome power of the caravan guard. Formed up in a wide arc, muskets in front of pikes, the guard kept firing withering volleys of heavy lead shot into the enemy cavalry whenever they rode close. A few of the guards lay dead, arrows protruding from their chests, but the presence of the pikes meant the enemy cavalry were robbed of their ability to charge the musketeers once they had fired a volley.

As each wagon made its way through the pass the guard began to fall back in good order, maintaining its formation, laying down covering fire. Having taken heavy casualties and seeing their quarry had escaped, the marauders gave up their attack and rode back into the forest from whence they had emerged. Having survived what would become known amongst the guards as the "Battle of Headtakers' Pass" the caravan continued cautiously on its way. It took another three days of wary progress before they rejoined the main road.

As dusk fell at the end of their first day back on the main road Thurion was summoned by Prince Magrivald. Ignoring the urgent tone of the message,

Thurion finished his meal before making his way over to the prince's carriage. The prince was sat, as usual, on his richly upholstered settee, his golden eye glinting in the warm candle light of the carriage's interior.

'You wished to see me?' Thurion asked.

'Yes, please make yourself comfortable,' the prince replied, his tone far more amiable that it had been when they had first met. Thurion set his feet apart slightly and thrust his thumbs into his belt.

'I hear that you are the one I have to thank for leading my caravan to safety, you are a very brave warrior,' he said.

'Well, I opened the pass if that's what you mean – but it was your guards who saw off the horsemen.'

'True enough, but they were simply doing their job. Should I honour them simply for doing what I employ them to do?'

'You should honour them, Prince, because they risked their lives for the sake of your caravan. You are aware some of them fell in its defence?'

'Yes, I am. Commander Patos reported to me after the action, he said we lost eight men. But what of it? They knew the risks, such men are easily replaced.'

The prince's cold detachment incensed Thurion.

'How can you speak so disrespectfully of the dead? How can you value their sacrifice so poorly?' At this, Thurion could sense that the prince getting irritated. Perhaps he was supposed to be flattered by the compliment and take all of the credit for himself?

'I hire and fire men as easily as I buy and sell anything else, barbarian. Now, I wish to thank you for your assistance in seeing my caravan safely through that pass by means of a reward of some sort. What can I offer you?' the prince asked, interrupting Thurion's train of thought.

'I will accept nothing from you, Prince. Anything you could offer would be stained with the blood of those guards who died to protect it. They needn't have died if you had listened to me in the first place. You called me a superstitious savage and ignored my warning, and now several merchants, their drivers and a number of your guards are dead – all because of your arrogance! I did what I had to do at the time and for that I seek no reward, and I will not accept anything from a man of little honour!' Thurion snapped before storming out of the carriage.

For the remainder of the journey Thurion kept to himself in brooding silence. A week passed in this way before the Tented City, came into view on the horizon. Hayesh Et-Kun was not a city in the conventional sense, as in one built from wood or stone but rather – as its colloquial name suggests – one comprised of tents. The nomadic tendencies of the inhabitants, who were mainly travelling merchants and their families, meant that they could take all their worldly goods with them wherever they travelled. The city sat in a wide, gentle depression that had once been a floodplain of the mighty river that drained from the Widowmaker long ago. Over time, and due to seismic activity, the river's course had changed and shifted to the east, leaving the dry bed and its plains. Small pools of water were all that remained of the once-torrential flow that had carved the rock away, exposing the soft blue and yellow clays that lay beneath. The pools were an oasis on the plain, and the clays were now the reason for the settlement at Hayesh Et-Kun, being used in the making of dyes for cloth and in the fine glazes for pottery which was produced in the Port of the Merchants' Guild.

Thurion could see no set boundaries to the city: Lines of tents snaked out in all directions from a central cluster, which sprawled along the pool-sides and spilled out onto the surrounding plain. From a distance it looked like a veritable sea of cloth and canvas of all colours, shapes and sizes. He halted Rimehorn less than half a mile from the nearest line of tents and sat for a long time in contemplation. A voice from behind suddenly interrupted his thoughts.

'Will you not accompany me into the city, friend Thurion?'

Thurion turned, noticing Elaim's wagon for the first time.

'Ah, good morning, Elaim. Sorry, I didn't hear you pull up.'

'And what is it that makes a hunter like you so oblivious to the rattles and creaks of a hundred wagons and horses? Are you still troubled by Prince Magrivald's decision over the business at the pass?'

'I am not sure,' he replied. 'There are many things on my mind. Certainly, the prince is one of them, and I *am* sure that I would like to kill him if I ever saw him again, if the truth be told. He is a despicable man with no respect for man or beast. If that city up ahead is filled with more like him, I fear tonight will be bloody should I venture in. Thank you for your kind invitation, but no, friend Elaim, I think I will camp outside of the city this evening.'

'They are not all as bad as Prince Magrivald,' Elaim said. 'Trust me, I will show you.' He held up a small square of red silk and read the embroidered script "Do not judge others by the actions and words of one." – Bis'anturr, from his second memoir on the *Journey to Oblivion.*'

Grudgingly, Thurion agreed to accompany him and urged Rimehorn on to keep pace with Elaim's wagon as the caravan streamed into Hayesh Et-Kun. As the wagons trundled through the tented lines, some would veer off the main route and disappear down narrow gaps between the masses of poles and guy ropes. Most of the caravan had dispersed as Elaim's wagon reached the centre of the city where the tents became bigger and more opulent. The stench of human sweat and waste hit Thurion like an invisible fog and both he and Rimehorn recoiled at the sudden assault on their senses. Elaim and his driver didn't appear to notice the nauseating atmosphere and continued threading through the increasingly crowded streets. Every breath was torture to Thurion and the desire to turn and escape the foul odour was overwhelming, but, intent on keeping his word, he kept Rimehorn abreast the wagon. Then, as they turned off the street they had been following and left the remaining wagons of the caravan behind, wafts of incense and sandalwood began to mingle with the heavy ammoniacal smells and took the edge off the foul air, offering a little respite.

'I am bound for a district on the far side of the city, my friend,' Elaim said, clearly more at home here than he had been on the road, as the pair made their way slowly through the bustling city. Noting the look of revulsion on Thurion's face, he added, 'Bear with me, it gets better further on.'

As they trundled through the busy streets Thurion noticed for the first time that a group of small children were running behind Rimehorn. Their eyes were large with wonder and they shrieked as they ran. People stopped what they were doing and stared at the curious beast and its strange rider. Many gave him hard disapproving looks. Granted, some of the looks spoke merely of curiosity but many spoke of insults, unvoiced but obviously implied. Few dared to voice their opinion once they noticed his weapons. He grunted to himself in grim satisfaction, entertained by their lack of courage.

Whilst they traversed the city both Thurion and Elaim were constantly harangued by street hawkers, trying to sell them all manner of wares from exotic foods of varying quality to trinkets promising the bearer good fortune. Elaim turned them away with cordiality whilst Thurion tended to fix them with a dangerous, withering stare until they retreated back into the crowds. After some hours of slow progress Thurion and Elaim passed from the bustling heart of the Tented City into its more open suburbs. The smell didn't get much better, however.

'We are not far away now, my friend,' assured Elaim.

'Good,' replied Thurion. 'Not only am I getting hungry but I am also growing increasingly short tempered at this constant harassment.'

'Ah, you must expect it. Everyone in Hayesh Et-Kun has something to sell.'

'Yours, my friend, is a civilisation I doubt I will ever understand!'

'And yours, my friend, is a life I could never survive!'

At last they reached their destination. Elaim's driver halted the wagon outside a large red marquee.

'Stay here,' Elaim said to his driver as he

climbed down from the wagon and entered the marquee. A minute or two later he reappeared accompanied by a man clad in rich red and gold silk robes and a golden turban. The two were laughing and joking with a camaraderie that spoke of a long friendship.

'I always bring you the finest cloths, Saichur. Here – look,' Elaim said as he led his friend round to the back of his wagon. He removed the heavy canvas covering and drew out a bolt of cloth, revealing a deep green material.

'Southern velvet – very hard to come by.'

The other man's eyes lit up in delight. 'Where did you get this?'

'Ahh, I have a contact amongst the Corsairs of Eshund. He, in turn, has contacts further south. That is all I can say.'

'You have become quite the merchant since your days as a fur trader, Elaim! Come inside, and we will talk business. Your friend is welcome to join us, though I have no stable for his, er... mount.'

'That won't be necessary, Rimehorn can be trusted – so long as you leave him be, that is,' Thurion warned as he dismounted.

'You would do well to listen, Saichur, I have seen what happens when you try to tether the beast. He has quite a spirit,' Elaim said, motioning to his driver who handed him a thin leather satchel.

'As you say,' Saichur replied, looking Rimehorn up and down before turning and entering his marquee. Thurion whispered a few words into Rimehorn's ear before following Elaim. The norshorn watched Thurion enter the marquee and then sat down, resting his great head on his forelegs, to await his return.

Inside, the marquee was packed with racks and racks of cloths and furs of all colours and varieties. The two men passed these by as they were led through into a small curtained-off area. The chamber was illuminated by three small oil lamps which cast a warm glow over the elaborate drapes that hung down from the tent poles. Several low-cushioned couches were arrayed around a central space. An incense burner stood on a small pedestal in the middle and the air hung heavy with the sickly vapour.

'Welcome to my inner sanctum,' announced Saichur, 'A space where I can escape the bustle of the city.'

'Peaceful indeed,' said Elaim admiringly as he entered. Thurion did not comment.

'I had this part of the marquee extended some months ago. I found I really needed a private space to get away from my wives and children, and somewhere I could retreat to when the haggling with the hawkers and the marralos got too much for me. They're crooks, you know – every last one of them!'

Elaim sensed that Thurion did not understand and explained. 'Hawkers are those fellows who tried to sell us things on our way in, and marralos are the agents who come to buy plain cloth to sell to the dyers. The dyers buy the clays for dyeing the colours into the cloth from the clay diggers, and sell the dyed cloth on to be either embroidered or printed with designs. The embroidered or printed goods are then transported west to the Port of the Merchants' Guild where they are sold in the markets or traded overseas to the Empire of the Sun.'

Thurion nodded. 'But you brought cloth for Saichur, yes?'

'Indeed,' replied Elaim. 'But what I brought was a finer quality material for making superior clothing. My friend, here,' gesturing to Saichur, 'sells these on to the many seamstresses and tailors both here and in the port who make clothing for the more affluent among the merchants – including Prince Magrivald. I also brought some plain cloth for dyeing.'

It took Thurion a little while to grasp the commerce of cloth and was about to say something when Elaim politely interrupted him.

'My apologies, I am forgetting myself. I have been too busy talking to introduce you both. Thurion, this is my old friend Saichur Kalashabin.' Turning to Saichur he said, 'I met Thurion, here, on the way to Hayesh some weeks ago and invited him to join me in the caravan, with the approval of Prince Magrivald. He was instrumental in saving many of us during an attack on the road.'

'I am pleased to make your acquaintance. Any friend of Elaim is welcome in my house,' Saichur said. 'And how do you find Hayesh Et-Kun?'

'I prefer the clean open air of the wilds. I find this city stifling.'

'That is understandable. Many here say that you can buy anything you need in Hayesh Et-Kun, except fresh air. Please, take a seat, Thyron.'

'My name is Thurion, son of Ragna, son of Rannweig of Vorde – in Barbaria.'

'You are a long way from home, barbarian. What brings you this far east?'

'I am a wilder; the wilderness is my home. I am here simply because this is where I find myself.'

'And because I managed to persuade you to experience this fine city!' Elaim added.

'That too,' admitted Thurion.

Saichur smiled. 'Good. Now, for a little refreshment.'

Saichur produced three small finely-shaped wooden bowls. These he passed around, one to each man before taking a small, short-legged metal bowl and placing it in the centre of the room. He removed the bowl's lid and, taking a taper that stood smouldering in a stand close by, blew on it and lit the thick fluid within. This done he took another lidded metal bowl, this one having a long spout, by its handle, and placed it on top of the first. Then he poured in some water from a jug. Elaim and Thurion looked on with interest.

'During my travels in recent months I visited one of the Northern Islands' principalities. I don't care to go there very often because of their dislike of strangers, and the almost constant state of tribal warfare. However, on my last visit I stayed as a guest of the royal family of one of the more civilised of the Islander tribes, where, despite recent clashes, there was a profound sense of calm.' He produced a small pouch from his belt, shook its contents slightly, and tipped some small leaves into the warm water.

He went on, 'When I asked why this was they simply shrugged their shoulders and said that it had always been so. I asked how they fared in battle, because most of the young men had the scars of combat, to which they replied that whenever their warriors went into battle the tribe's medicine man concocted them a potent drink that gave them courage and strength in the face of the enemy. Intrigued by this, I made enquiries and – to cut a long story short – I discovered the secret: a herbal infusion that everyone drank after their evening meal. A few herbs, coarsely ground and boiled, that helped them sleep soundly.'

'Rather like a sedative?' Elaim ventured.

'Yes,' Saichur replied. 'But without the grogginess and lethargy. Their senses were still sharp and they could drive a bargain. What the medicine man gave the warriors reversed the effect and released the blood-lust. I secured a quantity of the herbal mix before I left, and I now find it helps me sleep when I am stressed.'

Soon, steam began to emanate from the spout of the top bowl, and Saichur lifted it clear of the brazier beneath and poured its contents into the three wooden bowls. Elaim and Thurion cautiously raised their bowls and took a small sip. The drink was warm and aromatic, possessing a slightly sharp but not unpleasant taste. Every sip tingled their taste buds and every swallow induced a calming sensation that neither man had experienced before. Whilst he lounged, drinking Saichur's hot infusion, Thurion listened as the two merchants discussed the transaction. The simple process of bartering had become something far more convoluted and, in his opinion, unnecessarily complicated. There were tariffs for certain bolts – but not on others, and premiums on most but not all. The whole affair was something Thurion found very hard to follow. At length, however, a price was agreed and the two men embraced warmly.

Saichur sent for a couple of servants to help unload the wagon whilst he counted out the money. Elaim produced a sheaf of papers from his leather satchel, loaned some ink and a goose pen from his friend, and started writing out a bill of sale. Thurion, who had completely lost interest, got up and followed the servants outside. Once he returned to the wagon he motioned to Jagada to help them unload the cargo. Between the four of them the contents of Elaim's wagon were unloaded and stacked in Saichur's marquee in no more than ten minutes. When the two merchant friends appeared from the marquee, Saichur held a sheaf of papers in his hand and Elaim now carried a heavy pouch as well as his satchel. Both men were smiling.

Saichur watched as Elaim handed his baggage to Jagada. He said 'I'm sorry that my wives were not here when you arrived, but they took the children with them when they went out to the pool to do the washing. You must come and visit after you have settled down somewhere, Elaim. You know how Ella, Ensaff and the children always look forward to your visits.'

'That I will, Saichur, you can be sure of it. But first I must find a suitable pitch, and then conclude some other business; I have the usual bag of letters and bundles for people here that I must deliver before I do anything else – you know the sort of thing. Please give my regards to Ella and Ensaff. Goodbye for now, old friend.'

With their business complete the two merchants embraced again before Saichur returned to his marquee and Elaim climbed back aboard his wagon. Thurion returned to Rimehorn's side and whispered softly into his ear. Snorting contentedly, the great beast got up onto his feet and allowed Thurion to climb onto his back. He kept pace with Elaim as they made their way down the street.

'Elaim, am I right in what I heard, that your friend Saichur has *two* wives?' enquired Thurion after some while in thought.

'Yes,' replied the merchant. 'He has two wives, as is the custom in these parts. If he were *really* wealthy, like Prince Magrivald, then he would have several more. I realise that this may seem strange to an outlander such as yourself, but wives and children are regarded as an emblem of prosperity here, and with prosperity comes respect and integrity. And integrity in business means everything to a merchant, as this builds a good reputation – something that it would be nearly impossible to survive without, in commerce.'

Thurion nodded, 'Elaim, my friend, you have a way of explaining things to simple folk like me – you would have made a very good teacher.'

'Hardly. I don't have the patience – for a start, and secondly, I don't like children! I can tolerate them for short periods but I could never sit with them for hours in a schoolroom. If I did, then it would not be too long before there were clipped ears and bloody noses in the class. That's one reason why I'm not married.'

'But Saichur said you got on well with his children, and that they looked forward to your visits! How do you account for that, if you don't like them?'

Elaim smiled and said 'Ahh! I said I can tolerate them in small doses. Saichur's children – he has five – are made to sit and listen whilst Saichur and I recount some of our experiences on the journeys we have undertaken, the sights we have seen and the people we have met. They dare not misbehave in front of their father, and I like that.'

Thurion remembered his childhood in Vorde. His father had taught him nearly everything he knew, but he had observed and listened to some of the elders and learnt by their example. As he recalled, there were few miscreants in Vorde – mainly because of the strict discipline imposed by the parents from an early age and the need to respect one's elders. From what he had seen of the children in the Tented City, running riot between the tents and in the streets, they were certainly in need of some discipline and felt that he too, would have little patience with them.

'Where will you go now, Elaim?'

'Well, Jagada and I will need to find somewhere to pitch our tent for the season. Then I will visit the families for whom I have bundles to deliver, and after that I will go in search of goods within the city for a while before filling my wagon ready for the return trip west. Will you join me?'

'No, I think not. I am getting restless for the open country, not to mention Rimehorn. I fear if we do not leave soon he will flatten these pretty little tents in frustration!' Thurion said, laughing.

'I fear those are not empty words, my friend. Do you intend to leave immediately?'

'I think so. I will continue along this road until it leaves the city and then head... south, I think.'

'Well it has been a pleasure to share your company, my friend. If you ever pass this way again please call on me. May the gods smile on you.'

'Aye, and you, merchant.'

Thurion waved as Elaim motioned for his driver to turn the wagon into a side street, and rode on through the bustling city streets as dusk began to fall. He ignored the petitions of all those who approached him, regardless of their reasons for doing so. As he approached the outskirts of the Tented City Thurion found himself riding through a suburb where all of the tents bore the same symbol above their doorways: a coiled serpent, embroidered in purple. He gave this little thought as he carried on riding until his path was blocked. A dozen men clad in loose fitting black robes stood brandishing thin-bladed pole arms.

'You cannot travel through this precinct without permission,' one of the men stated flatly.

'Why not?' Thurion asked.

'This precinct belongs to Prince Mondra Mar-Ethu. No one enters his precinct without his permission,' the man explained. 'Turn yourself around, barbarian. You are not welcome here.'

'You would do well not to threaten me, little man,' Thurion growled. Clearly, the effects of Saichur's herbal infusion had worn off. Unfazed, the black clad man jabbed Rimehorn with the tip of his weapon. The shaggy beast took a step or two back, releasing an angry, guttural noise from his throat.

'And you would be foolish indeed to taunt him,' Thurion said. 'Now, let us pass.'

The men paid him no heed and came at them with steady, measured paces. As they closed one of the robed men slashed at one of Rimehorn's front legs. The beast withdrew it, letting out a pained cry. Sensing their advantage, the others began to step in and swing for the legs of the colossal beast retreating before them. Rimehorn backed into a tent, flattened it and almost got tangled in the guy ropes before realising he could retreat no further. One of the warriors over-reached himself and Thurion struck, as swiftly as a serpent, removing the end of his weapon with a swing of his large axe. Seeing the man fall back Rimehorn let out a snort and rose up, rampant. It was all Thurion could do to hold on and avoid being thrown. Rimehorn pawed the air before crashing to the ground, crushing one of his attackers. With loud snorts of rage, the great shaggy beast flailed left and right with his great horn, hurling men through the air. In his rage Rimehorn trampled another four of the prince's soldiers to death before the rest turned to flee. Howling, Thurion gave chase, urging Rimehorn on, though the beast needed no persuasion. The fleeing men did not reach the end of the street before they were either cut down by Thurion or crushed by Rimehorn.

It took a long time for Thurion to convince his friend to ease his pace but eventually he did so and brought him to a halt. Thurion dismounted and inspected Rimehorn's wounds. The cuts were not deep for his hide was thick but Thurion cleaned them up nevertheless. Together the two walked through the remainder of Prince Mar-Ethu's precinct without incident, although they were eyed suspiciously from shadowy doorways. An hour later the two companions left the last of Hayesh Et-Kun's tents behind them. Both breathed deep of the fresh clean air as they made their way into the night, heading steadily south.

Chapter 22

Not long after crossing the border into Ezné-Khalii, the river that Celene's caravan had been travelling alongside, the Vashaka, fed into a wetland that drained into the ocean. The road veered away from the river, turning gently west to avoid the boggy ground. As the caravan plodded along the coast road the marshland gave way to rolling sand dunes dotted with stands of saltgrass, which formed a large headland. These gradually fell away to reveal long sandy beaches. Two days after crossing into Ezné-Khalii the capital came into view.

Khalii seemed to be Azun's antithesis. Where the capital of Dra-Azun had been heavily fortified Khalii was not even walled, it seemed to simply sprawl along the coast with the royal palace clearly visible at its centre, atop the only hill in the region. As the caravan approached what appeared to be the outskirts of the city a single rider came galloping down the road towards them. He was wearing loose fitting robes of pale blue and bore a standard pole from which fluttered a pennant bearing the arms of the High Prince of Khalii: a stylised fish, white on ultramarine. He pulled up just short of the Royal Guard.

'Greetings, I have the pleasure of addressing the caravan of Princess Celene-Nemeth, do I not?' the rider asked.

'You do, sir,' Gadas replied, 'I am Captain Gadas.'

'And I am Aspharos, herald to High Prince Achmek Ezné. I have been sent to escort you to the High Prince's coastal palace.'

'I was expecting to be escorted to the royal palace at the city centre,' Gadas replied, gesturing to the many-towered palace on the hill.

'That was the original intention, yes. However, the High Prince has changed his mind and decided that it would be far better to entertain Princess Celene on the coast rather than in the midst of the city.'

'Very well, Aspharos, Herald to the High Prince, lead on.'

They followed the herald to a point where the road forked and took what became the main coastal road which wound around the outskirts of the city. Celene had never seen the coast before and was enthralled by the myriad sounds and smells that assaulted her senses as she walked alongside her carriage. She looked on in wonder as white and grey sea birds screeched and wheeled overhead; huge flocks trailed small fishing boats that were returning to the city's main port. The coastal road entered the city at this point and skirted around the huge port. This time there were no large cheering crowds to greet her as Celene arrived in the capital. Everyone seemed very busy, caught up with loading or unloading the various ships that were currently berthed along the quays. The smell of fish was overpowering, and Celene was forced to return to her carriage in an attempt to get away from what was the strongest smell she had yet come across.

The road left Khalii and continued along the coast. Eventually it would lead to Sumir and beyond but Aspharos led them along another fork that led down to a secluded beach. The beach was vast, sandy and dominated by a small palace that stood on a stony platform at the headland.

'The coastal palace of High Prince Achmek Ezné,' Aspharos explained as the caravan made its way carefully along the hard sand towards the headland. Captain Gadas halted the caravan at a point almost adjacent to the palace where an area of sand had been cleared and paved with slightly rough marble slabs. Celene dismounted and followed the High Prince's herald into the timber-built palace.

Inside Celene was confronted by an altogether unconventional sight. There was no main audience chamber with formally arranged thrones. The majority of the ground floor formed a large open plan lounging area that opened directly onto the beach. High Prince Achmek was reclining on a luxurious settee along with his wife, High Princess Tigato. He was cradling their young son, Bochon, who appeared to be no more than six months old. Passing his son over to his wife, Achmek rose from the settee and waited for his herald to announce his visitor.

'Her Royal Highness Princess Celene Nemeth, of the Royal House of Nemeth-Sharrayah!'

'Ah, Princess Celene, you have managed to find my little beach front retreat I see. Welcome, please take a seat; there is no need to stand on ceremony here.'

The high prince's manner was so casual that Celene did not know quite how to respond.

'Thank you,' she replied, attempting to sit on the edge of one of the settees but instead sinking rather unceremoniously into an unexpected depth of cushions.

'I am sure you have come to expect formality,

pomp and ceremony, Your Highness,' Achmek continued. 'However, you will find we do things a little differently here in Ezné-Khalii. Please don't misunderstand me, we can be as formal as any other principality when need requires it, but our natural tendency is towards informality. So whilst you are here you can relax and be informal: we want you to enjoy your stay!'

Celene was still trying to keep her dignity amongst the voluminous cushions. 'Thank you, Your Highness, I will admit it is not what I am accustomed to, and it does seem rather peculiar not to have a formal audience at a royal court. Not that I find it unpleasant – it's just so *unconventional* – and unexpected.'

High Prince Achmek just laughed. 'Oh, Princess Celene, you have a way with words! That may possibly be the most polite response we have yet had to our way of life! Would you care for some refreshment?'

Before Celene had an opportunity to answer, the High Prince turned to one of his servants, 'Tilbes, some refreshment – if you would be so kind!'

The high prince then gestured towards his wife and son, 'Before we go any further, may I present my wife, High Princess Tigato, and my son, Prince Bochon?'

'Pleased to meet you, Your Highness,' Celene replied, finding it strange that the High Princess did not stand and expect a curtsy from her.

'Hello, Celene,' replied the High Princess, 'Bochon, say "hello" too!' She waved one of her son's little hands.

'Thank you, Your Highness, that's, er, very nice of him,' acknowledged Celene, still rather perplexed at the situation. The drinks arrived and Celene chose a tall glass filled with a clear yellow liquid which bubbled slightly and had a fruity aroma. She took a sip of the cool drink and was mildly surprised by the effervescence as it tickled the roof of her mouth.

The servant, Tilbes, placed the tray on a low stand in front of High Princess Tigato. Achmek walked over to her, took his drink and sat down.

'I am afraid we are a small family,' Achmek said, gesturing to his wife and child, 'In a small principality with a small population and a small economy, so we may have little to talk about. I fear Bochon will not prove much of a conversationalist quite yet!' he joked. 'But seriously, please, tell me of Nemeth-Sharrayah, it has been many years since I was there last, as a young prince. I was a guest at your parents' wedding. I remember meeting your father and enjoyed going fishing with him.'

Celene relaxed back into the cushions and took another sip of her drink, she felt comfortable talking about her family and people. She conversed with the High Prince and his wife for some hours before she was invited to dine with them on the beach.

The beach was sheltered and so the wind that cooled the rest of the coast was little more than a pleasant breeze. A couple of fires were lit in pits, lighted torches were erected along the beach and the evening meal was set to cook. Celene had not eaten much seafood before and was delighted to be able to taste some of the dishes beforehand. Being able to choose what she wanted to eat was informality as she had never known it. High Prince Achmek was so informal that he invited not only his own household staff to join him but also Captain Gadas, his men, Arité and her maids. The atmosphere that evening was very relaxed; there didn't appear to be a care weighing down on anyone.

The following few days passed in much the same manner; Celene relaxed in the company of High Prince Achmek, his wife and their infant son. The beach was so secluded that Captain Gadas found himself able to dismiss his men for a bit of much needed relaxation once they had brought sufficient fodder for their horses down from the nearby city. To his surprise none of them ventured into the city; usually the first port of call for soldiers given leave. Instead they all chose to relax on the beach. The fact that few, if any of them, had ever seen the sea may well have had something to do with their decision not to seek out a tavern in the city. The prince's butler, Tilbes, also kept them supplied with a drink, not unlike beer, from the royal cellars; possibly another reason why they elected to remain on the beach.

Celene discovered that her host had been very modest when he spoke of Ezné-Khalii having a small economy. She took this modesty as another example of the informality that the High Prince embraced. She learned that the principality derived most of its income from the sea; fishing was a large industry and catches landed in the capital's port were exported far and wide. High Prince Achmek informed her that salted fish was transported in small barges up-river as far as was navigable, and then in ox carts as far as the Fur Traders' camp at the foot of the glacier. Sea salt was another major export and much in demand to the north, as were dried vegetables.

Being predominantly a maritime nation, Ezné-Khalii maintained only a small standing army, but possessed a substantial naval flotilla that patrolled the shoreline and the territorial waters to protect merchant vessels from the ever-present threat of pirates and corsairs.

Celene listened for hours as Prince Achmek and his equerries talked to her about Ezné's economy, her people and her armed forces. Normally, she would have been bored fairly quickly with such detail, but she found herself comfortable in their company and with the way they treated her. They did not use the stiff, official delivery that she was used to, and their speech was not liberally interspersed with 'Your Highness' or 'M'lady'. She was beginning to like informality – she even took to walking barefoot along the beach and in the waves.

Captain Gadas delayed departure for as long as he could. Not only was it evident that Celene was enjoying her time in the house of Ezné, but the trepidation he had felt at the beginning of the tour concerning Leznar-Carchum, was once again beginning to gnaw inside him. On the morning of the fourth day he made preparations to break camp and travel west. It was with great sadness that Celene thanked High Prince Achmek and his wife for their hospitality, and walked back up the beach to where the carriages had been readied for departure. She saw Captain Gadas talking with Aspharos and the Captain of the Ezné Royal Guard; all three men wore grave expressions as they conversed. As she approached, they quickly shook hands and parted. With an air of reluctance Captain Gadas gave the order to leave the beach-front palace and make for the border with Leznar-Carchum.

Chapter 23

It took Seratos some hours to complete his work. He began by re-knitting his brothers' corpses, raising them from the dead and enslaving them to his will. This done he divided the un-dead priests between his father, sister and two brothers, and enslaved an equal portion to each. Once he had finished he practised giving commands to his family members. He found that if he, for example, commanded his sister to guard the entrances to the audience chamber, she would automatically delegate those priests enslaved to her to guard the doors rather than trying to guard the entrances herself. It would take some time for commanding his subordinates in this way to become second nature, but Sisus assured him it would become easier with practise. Indeed he began to suspect that the more second nature it became, the more independence his subordinates would exercise.

It was early afternoon by the time he had finished, taken something to eat and retired to his chambers. Before he retired however, he ordered Sisus to gather his generals, captains and lieutenants together so that he might reveal his new patron to them.

Rising in the early evening Seratos prepared to meet the commanders of his armies. Whilst he was dressing he happened to catch his reflection in a mirror; he had become rather gaunt and pallid of complexion. He had been resting less too, he noted, although he didn't seem to suffer from lack of sleep as much as he thought he might have. *It must be my desire to master my new-found powers and to reshape my principality* he mused. He left his chambers and made his way to the courtyard outside the palace's main gate where his commanders were now waiting.

The Angel of Death stepped through the palace entranceway as the doors were opened for him. A light breeze caught his blood-stained robes, ruffled his black feathers gently and caught his knotted hair. There was an audible gasp from the gathered men as they beheld the transformation in their prince.

'You are right to gasp, for much has changed since last you saw me. I have lost much but I have gained so much more. Doubtless you have heard about Saruké?'

Hushed murmurs assented whilst bowed heads showed their respect.

'What you may not have heard, and may have been kept from you, was how my beloved was betrayed to her death by the god she had revered all her life. I begged Ios to show her mercy, but she answered my cries with silence! The priesthood petitioned the Holy Mother for aid, but again she answered with silence!' Seratos spat, bitterness dripping from every word as he recalled the last hours of his wife's life. 'I summoned the most powerful healers in the order but they too failed. Ios betrayed Saruké to her death, she betrayed me and she betrayed her own priesthood. Who could do that and honestly call themselves a god? What has the Holy Mother ever done for you?' the now-raging prince demanded of his audience.

Silence.

'Answer me! What has she ever done for you, *personally?*' Again his questions were met by a wall of silence. Some among the gathered crowd muttered to themselves but no one spoke out.

Whilst it could be said that fear of their enraged prince kept some from speaking out, not daring to nay-say Seratos, the truth was that most could not think of an instance where the Holy Mother had intervened in their lives directly. The ruling angelic caste and the priesthood had frequent communion with the God of Life, but for the common man and woman, her relationship was much more distant and her benevolence was not tangible. For the men gathered before him, reverence of Ios was little more than a long-standing tradition. These military men tended to hold somewhat more pragmatic views, relying on steel more than prayers, unless one of the priesthood had been attached to their command, which was rare unless a major engagement was likely. A pensive silence therefore answered Seratos' shouted questions as his commanders waited for their prince to continue.

'Doubtless you would have heard rumours that I had fled in the wake of Saruké's death. These were not rumours, I was broken by grief and flew without direction for some time. Eventually, I was taken in by a kindly lord. He showed me that what I had known for many years, but had refused to admit, was in fact true; death is stronger than life, it always has been and it always will be.'

Many of the men exchanged worried glances that spoke of questions none dared ask.

'If you need proof watch now and learn the truth.' Seratos turned and motioned towards the shadows of the open palace doors. In response Sisus brought out a servant, bound and gagged, stood him before Seratos and returned to the shadows.

'Witness the weakness of Ios.' In one fluid motion Seratos drew his sword and disembowelled the servant in front of his men.

The cries of horror and outrage were many but fear of their prince, and a secret desire to see if their god would answer their prince's blasphemies, rooted the soldiers in place.

'Ios! I call on you now to save this poor wretch! Save him if you can!' Seratos cried mockingly at the evening sky. He allowed a moment or two of silence, broken only by the whimpers of the dying servant, before continuing his exhibition. After running his blade smoothly across the servant's neck he re-sheathed his sword and, with great ceremony re-knitted the corpse's wounds. Before the horrified expressions of his commanders could subside, he drew out a small amount of graveyard dirt from a small pouch on his belt and began the reanimation ritual. All the while his commanders looked on, both aghast and awed by their lord's show of new-found power. At length he finished the ritual and stood back as the corpse-servant struggled to its feet.

'Witness the power of death over life. You have all now heard what I have heard: the silence of Ios when she was needed most.'

A few nods of agreement answered him.

'I do not intend to keep this power selfishly for myself however, not like the wretched devotees of Ios. Your vows to me as your High Prince, made in the name of Ios are now null and void. All that you have seen here I promise to share with you, in return for fresh vows... in the name of Nhurkhu, God of the Dead and Lord of the Underworld. No longer will you be answerable to snivelling priests in expensive temples; *you* will wield the power! *You* will have the power to re-knit wounds just as you have witnessed this evening. *You* will have the power to raise the dead, just as you have witnessed *and more besides.* All you need do is swear to me fresh allegiance and I will make you as gods amongst men!' Seratos' voice rose to a crescendo as he concluded his speech.

Once again silence had fallen across the gathering as every man present considered the implications of the decision that lay before him.

'I will follow you, my prince!' a grizzled soldier shouted from the back of the gathering, 'Ios be damned; she's never done 'ought for me!'

'Aye, I'll swear to you!' another called out. One by one, Seratos bought his men's loyalty with the promise of power. Before long the courtyard was a raucous tumult as every man present voiced vows of loyalty and service. Seratos beat his wings and rose into the air, spreading his arms wide, motioning for silence.

'Men of Carchum, you no longer serve a High Prince of life, but an Angel of Death!'

A great roar erupted from the gathered soldiers that Seratos silenced with difficulty. 'I promised you power in return for your loyalty. I swear to you that I will set you on the path to power you can, as yet, only dream of. Before I do, however, I would ask one thing of you. Words and vows are all well and good but acts and deeds set all doubts to rest. Commanders of Carchum, gather your men and scour the city. Destroy every temple and shrine dedicated to Ios that you find. Once you have done this, return to me and I will see that you are rewarded!'

The roar of assent was deafening as the enlightened officers began tripping over each other in their haste to rouse their men. Within an hour fires were burning across the city as Seratos' troops ran amok. The Angel of Death stood and watched the destruction from a window high up in one of the towers, a look of satisfaction on his face. From the doorway behind him, a shadowy figure emerged and approached. It was Sisus.

'Congratulations, My Lord, you have ensured the loyalty of *your* troops.'

Without taking his eyes away from the fiery destruction Seratos responded, 'What is on your mind, Sisus? It is almost as loud when you say nothing as when you speak.'

'Only this, My Lord: you have bought the loyalty of your officers, and therefore their men, with promises of power. What about the armies of your two brothers? How do you plan to sway them? They may not be as easy to convince as these were.'

'Trust me, Sisus. My men were able to see the truth once I had demonstrated the weakness and frailty of Ios. All I need do is ensure the same truth is witnessed by my brothers' soldiers and I am sure they will see the light, so to speak,' Seratos replied, recalling a conversation he had had with Lord Dach back in Emphar-Nek.

'But how, My Lord? Those cities are still loyal to Ios, they are still overseen by the priesthood,' Sisus asked, clearly failing to see how such an undertaking would be possible.

'Wraiths, my dear Sisus, wraiths. You will show me how to summon them, and I will send them throughout the land to slay every single priest they can find,' Seratos explained, the light of the fires burning in the city below reflecting in his eyes.

'Masterful, My Lord, truly masterful.' *And with the death of the priesthood, Ios' influence in this principality will diminish, effectively to nothing.* 'And with your brothers absent their commanders will be forced to come to you for help...'

'Precisely, Sisus. Now, I believe you have a lesson for me?'

'But of course. Please, follow me, My Lord,' the necromancer replied, almost piously as he turned and walked away. Seratos surveyed the blazing temples once more before following his tutor back into the darkened palace.

Chapter 24

The land south of the caravan road was lightly wooded with many open glades. As the days passed, the first signs of autumn began to show. The leaves of the trees turned from deep greens to shades of orange, brown and red. Some had already fallen. It was as if Thurion was walking through a twilight world, somewhere between the living and the dead. It was a curious feeling, as if he too were somehow passing into autumn along with the world around him.

'Change is coming,' he said, as much to himself as to Rimehorn, who was walking beside him through a drift of dead leaves, kicking them up as he did so. Rimehorn didn't answer, as always, he just kept plodding. He seemed preoccupied however, not swinging his head as he usually did, nor did he flick his ears as much despite the flies that constantly plagued him. Sometimes the shaggy beast stepped out and went ahead of Thurion. As the days passed Thurion felt himself drawn inexorably south. He walked with Rimehorn plodding steadily beside him until late one afternoon, with the sun low over the trees, they came upon a large clearing. At its centre, towering above the trees of the wood stood a colossal standing stone at least two-score feet high. A ring of smaller stones surrounded it, themselves almost ten feet high. Rimehorn raised his head and sniffed the air. Then he bellowed loudly.

'What is it, Friend?' asked Thurion. 'What do you sense, that I cannot?' Rimehorn didn't answer, only shook himself and began to sniff the ground. 'Well, it's a good place to stop for the night, old friend.' Thurion removed the straps that held his few belongings to Rimehorn's sides and began to make camp. This done, he slipped quietly back into the wooded glades in search of supper. When Thurion returned to his camp Rimehorn was gone. He assumed that his friend had wandered off in search of some forage since neither of them had eaten since the early morning. He quickly re-kindled the fire and set his kill to cook once the flames had died down slightly.

The moon rose, full and bright over the outline of the canopy. As dusk fell the rocks began to emit a faint lambent green glow. The atmosphere in the clearing became charged with supernatural energy, faintly at first, then slowly increasing. It felt as if something was about to happen, though what that something was, Thurion could not guess and so he waited.

As the gloaming faded into darkness a solitary figure entered the clearing. An old man, clad in little more than a few furs with a set of antlers woven into his long unkempt hair, slowly walked in leaning on a gnarled wooden staff; the very embodiment of the wilderness. Thurion rose and approached the man.

'I see you – you are welcome at my fire.'

The old man stopped, leaned on his staff and replied, 'I see you too, barbarian. I sensed you coming some days ago and have been returning here every night so that I didn't miss you.'

'How could you? Even I didn't know I was coming here.'

The old man smiled through his thick beard, 'I sensed you when you were some way off, as only a wilder can. Now, have you anything to eat?'

The old wilder shuffled towards the warm fire and slowly sat down. He accepted Thurion's sizzling offering and bit off a large chunk. Chewing enthusiastically he said 'Ahh, tree rat. Good choice, barbarian, they are very tasty this time of year and extremely nutritious. I find that eating these helps fend off the effects of extreme cold.'

'How do you know?' asked Thurion, now even more curious about the man sat before him.

'Questions and more questions. Don't you know anything, barbarian? Has your wandering taught you *nothing* about the ways of the wild? The spirits should have shown you. I learnt about simple things like tree rats before I had reached my eleventh summer,' the old man replied.

Thurion didn't quite know what to say. He felt like he was a child again, sitting before the elders in Vorde, and got rather defensive, 'I have been travelling a long time – or so it seems. I have learnt many things but accept that there is more yet to learn.'

'That is always the case,' said the old man, sucking at the bones in his hand.

Thurion tried a different approach. 'I am Thurion, son of Ragna, son of Rannveig of Vorde. The spirits called me into the wilds as I completed my rites of passage into manhood.'

'Yes, I know,' the old man replied, wiping his beard with a flap of fur. 'I left my people when I was young too, I have forgotten exactly when and where, but I am a wilder too, like yourself.'

'What is your name?' asked Thurion, excited at the prospect of meeting a kindred spirit.

The old man frowned, 'My name? I haven't

used my name for a long time; I haven't spoken to anyone these last few years; there's no need for a name out here.'

As he listened, Thurion became more aware of the energy building up around him. It seemed to emanate from the standing stones.

'What is this place, old man?'

'Old man? Yes, I am old, older than you might guess I'd wager. This is the Moonstone and it stands at a point where a number of this world's ley lines converge. It is a place of great power to those that are aware and it is where some of the world's oldest creatures gather here on certain nights of the year.'

'And this night is one of those nights?' Thurion asked, not really understanding the old man's cryptic response.

'Yes, yes it is.'

'Why is it called the Moonstone? It looks like an ordinary standing stone to me, I have seen a few in my time; the ancients called them menhirs; I have also seen stones standing in circles, but I felt no power from them.'

'You felt no power from them because the time was not right. This one is the most powerful of all. It is called the Moonstone because once every one hundred and fifty years the moon aligns with the cardinal planets, and the tip of the stone when it is directly overhead. It is then at its closest to the Earth and exerts a strong force that pulls the weaker energy of the other stones along the ley lines to this one. That is the energy that you feel. Look at the moon. Do you not see its brightness?

Thurion looked up and suddenly noticed that the moon was indeed brighter than he had seen it before. He looked back to the old man who was licking his fingers. 'You said some of the oldest creatures will gather here tonight, but why am I here? I am not old.'

'No, but your friend is,' the old man replied, motioning to the tree line. Thurion turned to look in time to see Rimehorn walking out of the trees towards them, into the strange green light being cast by the gently glowing rocks. The old man pulled himself up using his staff and walked over to Rimehorn. Placing one hand lightly on the beast's forehead, he closed his eyes and concentrated. Rimehorn made a low, purring noise and gave a gentle snort. The old man hobbled back to the camp fire. 'Ah yes, I see now why you are here, barbarian.'

'Why *am* I here, old man?' asked Thurion, a note of concern in his tone.

'You are here because your friend brought you here, and he was drawn here by the energy of the stone, in the same way that he was drawn to you on the day you answered the call of the spirits. Your paths are about to diverge; a parting of ways has come.'

Thurion said nothing.

'The path you are following is leading you south from here, isn't it?'

'Yes, that was the general direction I was heading in,' admitted Thurion.

'Then yes, you have reached a parting of ways. Your companion will not travel any further south than here.'

'Why?'

'The spirits are leading you south – that is a path you must tread alone. To the south lie the Plains of the Dead. That is no place for so noble a beast.'

'But I would not leave him. Not alone,' Thurion said with emotion.

'Do not fear, barbarian, he will not leave this place alone. Look!' The old man pointed to the edge of the clearing, now illuminated by the glow from the stones.

Thurion turned to look where the old man was pointing. From out of the tree line came a great shaggy norshorn, a little smaller than Rimehorn. A moment later another appeared from the same gap. Thurion looked on in surprise and amazement, never having seen another of Rimehorn's species until that moment. By midnight, when the moon was overhead, a good-sized herd of two dozen animals had gathered around Rimehorn. There was clearly a close bond between Rimehorn and the herd, some approached and nuzzled him on the cheeks whilst others started to groom him like friends who had been apart for a long time. Gentle purring sounds came from the great beasts.

'You see, barbarian, your companion has returned home. Your paths must now diverge.'

'I see,' was all Thurion could say. Grief welled up inside him at the thought of losing the closest friend he had ever known. He turned away from the old man and walked up to where Rimehorn was standing surrounded by the herd. The other animals parted to allow him through. Placing a hand under his chin he spoke gently into the beast's ear. 'It's alright, old friend. I understand. I wish we could go on together but I realise that we can't. I shall never forget you.' Snorting affectionately, Rimehorn rubbed his head against Thurion's shoulder. His large eyes watering, he slowly turned and joined the others as they walked towards the gap in the trees. When they reached the path they all broke into a trot, shaking the ground gently, the noise of their hooves like distant thunder.

'Good-bye, old friend,' Thurion said as he turned away and walked back to his camp, tears rolling down his face. The old man was standing, waiting for him.

'The force that forged the bond between you was strong, but it needed a stronger force to break it. He sensed where the spirits were leading you, and he knew that he could not go there. That's why he led you here, on this night. He knew the force of the energy from the Moonstone was the only thing that could come between the two of you. He knew you would understand.'

'Just leave me alone!'

'As you wish,' replied the old man, 'The spirits go with you!' With that, he hobbled off in the direction from which he had appeared.

Thurion sat down next to the fire and stared at the ground. He sat there until the flames died and stared at the embers until they went out one by one. He didn't sleep. He didn't notice the glow from the stones grow fainter as dawn broke. He was still sitting there when a chilly breeze blew into the clearing and broke the spell. He suddenly shivered, goose pimples erupted over his bare arms and realised that he wasn't wearing his cloak. He tried to straighten his legs to get up and yelled out in pain; cramp had set in. He cursed his legs, he cursed the pain, he cursed the wind – he cursed everything and didn't stop until the feeling came back into his legs and he was able to stand. Slowly he gathered his things, shouldered his pack that Rimehorn had carried for years and started walking. He didn't bother to think about where he was going.

He walked aimlessly for many days and nights without stopping until eventually he collapsed in a small clearing and wept into the cold grass. He wept until he was too weak to weep any more. He lay there, sick and empty, until a cold wind roused him from his desolation and hunger gnawed at his stomach. He got up and surveyed his surroundings. He was in a clearing in a sparsely wooded area with grasses and rushes growing in large tussocks; a small brook flowed from the middle of the clearing and ran out of sight between the trees. The blades of frozen grass sparkled in the morning sunshine. He walked towards the brook but as he approached he began to sink in soft ground. Quickly back-tracking, he made for the edge of the clearing and started to explore the area. Small trees and bramble bushes grew profusely, making progress very slow but he persisted until he came to a large tree that dominated the periphery, and found the area under its branches was clear of undergrowth; there was a thick carpet of golden leaves on the ground. Though the sun was shining, he felt the winter weather approaching, and without his friend he knew he would not make the sort of progress that he had previously enjoyed. He decided to make camp here for the winter and wait until the snow cleared and made walking easier. He dropped his pack, gathered some twigs and lit a fire. He then went looking for tree rats.

Over the next few days Thurion built himself a shelter around the boll of the large tree and prepared the clearing for the coming winter; he laid a path to the brook, cleared some of the undergrowth and began gathering firewood. When the first real snow fell and covered the clearing he was ready to face the long cold spell that lay ahead.

Thurion reflected on his new situation for many weeks, he had, after all, nothing else to do. It wasn't until the latter weeks of winter that he ceased mourning the loss of his friend, and felt able to move on with his life. So it was on a bright cold morning after eating the left-over remains of yet another tree rat, that he packed up his things, left his winter camp and started walking resolutely south. As he walked his solitude became easier to bear. The memory of Rimehorn had taken its rightful place in his mind; it would remind him of the second season in his life, a very pleasant one spent travelling with a friend. As all seasons eventually come to an end, so had his time with Rimehorn. The last snow was soft under foot and the icicles had started to fall from the trees as he strode through the skeletal wood. Spring was coming as he walked south, wondering what this new season of his life would bring.

Chapter 25

Celene had expected to reach the border of Leznar-Carchum in just over a week, however, she noticed that contrary to expectation, Captain Gadas had directed the caravan north, passing Sumir to the south. Deviating from a plan was not like her captain and it unsettled her. One morning as they were travelling more north than west, Celene broached the subject with him.

'Captain, we are travelling north, are we not?'

'Yes, Your Highness, we are.'

'Leznar-Carchum lies to the west, does it not?'

'To the north west,' he corrected.

'Captain, please don't try to fool me, we could have crossed the border several days ago had we travelled directly west. Instead you have led my caravan along winding country lanes, and have yet to cross the border. This is not like you, what's wrong?' she asked, her voice gentle but firm.

Gadas paused for a few moments before answering. 'I asked Aspharos if he had received any news from Leznar-Carchum recently. He said nothing substantial of late, but travellers have told of a land in turmoil, and of the priesthood fleeing from an unknown terror. Tall tales, likely as not, but unsettling nonetheless. I feel a deep foreboding about this next leg of your tour.' He paused before continuing, 'May I be frank, Your Highness?'

'Please, Captain.'

'If it was my decision, I would turn this

caravan around, head back to Sumir, take the north road towards Dra-Azun and cut out Leznar-Carchum entirely. But it is not down to me, is it?' he asked, already knowing the answer.

'No, Captain, it is not; we are bound for Leznar-Carchum. That was the arrangement. Should we encounter anything untoward I am sure you and your men can deal with it. Fear not, captain, I have the utmost faith in your abilities. I honestly do not think I will be in any danger so long as you and your soldiers are here to protect me.' In an attempt to reassure him she asked, 'Do you recall what you said to me when we left Sharrayah?'

'I told you that my men were the finest soldiers in the whole of the principality,' he replied.

'You did. Have you changed your mind in the meantime?'

Gadas replied with conviction, 'Of course not, Your Highness. As I said, I have fought alongside every one of them; they are all solid, dependable souls.'

'That they are; just as you say. Therefore I have nothing to fear, do I?'

'No, Your Highness, you do not,' he conceded.

'Please cheer up, Captain, it is a wonderful day, your dour mood is spoiling it!' she said before turning aside to watch as a small flock of young birds wheeled in the sky above her.

Yes, I have *fought alongside all of my men. Yes, they are* all *dependable souls but I still fear what we may find once we cross the border,* Captain Gadas thought to himself. Later, with that foreboding gnawing away even stronger, when they reached the next junction he headed the caravan towards Leznar-

Carchum.

They were travelling along a small winding lane and so there was no formal border post to mark their passage into Leznar-Carchum, just a sign proclaiming the entrance into the principality. Perhaps it was just the gathering gloom of evening, but something did not sit well with the captain as he halted the caravan and made camp on the outskirts of a small hamlet.

Despite being midsummer the following morning was cold and damp. The horses were restless as they were harnessed and prepared for the day's journey. Celene was woken as her carriage left the rough ground and rejoined the road.

'Arité, what's going on?' she asked, tucking a lock of hair behind her ear.

'Captain Gadas seems eager to be on the move, and to be honest with you, Your Highness, I can't say I blame him,' her maid replied.

'Oh?'

'Well, I was up at dawn, as usual, and ventured into the hamlet a short while back to see if I might purchase a few supplies that we are getting a little low on. Well, everyone I came across seemed possessed of a strange mood. They seemed distant, fearful, depressed even – almost despairing...' she trailed off.

'Arité, are you alright?'

'No, Your Highness, I'm not, to tell the truth. As your head maid I could find nothing really wrong this morning; I managed to get the things I needed. As a member of the priesthood however, I was disturbed by what I saw. There was little life in the eyes of the people I met, and the hamlet's shrine didn't look like it had been used for some time.' She paused before continuing, 'I would ask something of you, Your Highness, as the highest ranking member of the priesthood present.'

'Go on.'

'Stay with the caravan. Do not venture from it whilst we are in Leznar-Carchum. If, for any reason, you need to venture away from the carriages, take a couple of Captain Gadas' men with you. I am not sure what it is that is weighing on my soul, but I have felt it since we crossed the border, and I am afraid that it is not good.' Suddenly Arité had become very serious, something she had not yet done during the tour.

Celene knew that what Arité had sensed was real to her, and that it troubled her deeply. 'I will,' she replied, 'I trust your judgement, Arité.'

The young princess was rather reserved that morning, and did not venture outside but watched from the carriage's windows as the countryside passed by. The more she looked, the more uncomfortable she felt. There was little of the life and vitality of summer in what she saw. What she saw was a sick landscape.

The further into Leznar-Carchum the caravan travelled, the sicker the land appeared. The few birds that Celene saw were all scruffy-looking crows that appeared to be diseased. Even the trees, the most enduring of Ios' flora, looked ill with many beginning to shed their leaves months too early. An eerie silence hung over the land that was broken only by odd, distant howls. The mood of those travelling with Celene was tenebrous. Captain Gadas kept his men busy, doubling the night watch in an attempt to keep their thoughts from wandering during the hours of darkness. Arité, likewise, tried to keep the minds of her maids from idle thoughts, setting them trivial tasks such as darning socks for the Royal Guard. Thoughts still wandered however, and before long, initial feelings of apprehension became outright fear; few slept well at all.

Four days after they had crossed the border, the city of Sursh came into view on the horizon. A few miles from the city limits the road forked but Captain Gadas did not need to give the order; those driving the carriages veered right, taking the road that circumvented the city. If anything the city appeared more drear than the surrounding countryside, especially as a dark heavy cloud bank had settled over it, casting an ominous shadow over the principality's second largest city.

The road leading around the city was almost as deserted as the city walls appeared to be. The caravan passed few figures on the road, most were hunched over and shuffled along under filthy ragged robes. One man that they passed had a donkey with him. The wretched beast looked terribly thin and ill, its ribs showing clearly through its parchment-like skin.

'Friend, what's happened here?' Captain Gadas asked the man as he approached the caravan. The man slowly looked up and considered the captain from under his low hood.

'The land is dying; Ios has abandoned us,' he replied, before turning and continuing on his way.

The captain made a mental note to talk with Arité later on. For the rest of the day those escorting the caravan kept to themselves, much as they had in previous days and did not look towards the city. Had they done so, they may have noticed a solitary figure leave the city on a coal-black horse and ride fast, heading north.

As it was, the caravan continued on its circuitous route around the city before following the road as it led north into the hills. As the afternoon passed into early evening Captain Gadas began to look for somewhere to make camp for the night. There was nowhere to pull off the road to make camp; the hills were all far too steep, so Gadas was forced to order the caravan to pull as far off the road as it could and make camp at the roadside. This was not ideal but the light was failing and he wanted to be encamped and to have set a watch well before nightfall.

The captain sighed with relief as the first watch of the night took up their positions, barely minutes before the sun disappeared below the hill-line. After making one last inspection of the camp's perimeter he headed over to Celene's caravan and knocked at the door.

'Ah, Captain Gadas, how may I help you?' Arité asked as she opened the door.

'May I have a word, *in private*?' he asked in a hushed tone.

'Certainly,' the head maid replied quietly, then, turning her head she said, 'I'm just popping out for a few minutes, Your Highness, there's nothing to worry about,' as she stepped outside, closing the carriage door behind her.

'How may I be of service, captain?'

'I would like your opinion on something, in your capacity as a priestess of Ios.'

'Go on, captain, you may speak openly and in confidence,' she replied, keeping step with him as he walked slowly past the carriages.

'Earlier today we passed a traveller on the road. He had an old donkey with him, do you remember?'

'Yes, he looked very old and his companion appeared malnourished and sick, as I recall.'

'That's him. Anyway, I stopped him as he approached and asked what had happened in Leznar-Carchum, for I felt sure that something had.' He paused for a minute as they passed one of the sentries standing watch.

'What did he say, Captain?'

'He said that Ios had abandoned them and that the land was dying. I have seen and heard many things in my time, but what he said – and the forlorn manner in which he said it – shocked me.'

Arité did not speak immediately. When she did her tone was solemn. 'What you have just said confirms a fear and a suspicion that has been growing inside me for the past few days. Look around you, captain, what do you see?' she asked.

Gadas did as he was asked, straining his eyes in the darkness. 'The land appears…' he struggled to find the right word, 'sick, almost.'

'Quite so, Captain. The traveller's words are, for me, the last piece of the puzzle. I believe I now know what has happened here.'

'And what is that?'

'The traveller you met was right, the Holy Mother has abandoned this land. How much do you know of the gods, captain?'

'Little; I am a soldier,' he admitted.

'Each god's power and influence is directly proportional to the size of their following. For example Sol, the sun god, has great influence within the Empire of the Sun and will answer the supplications of those who revere him, but has little influence elsewhere and will not hear those who hold no reverence for him. Likewise Ios, the Holy Mother, is sovereign within our principalities and hears our cries and those of her children, but her power does not reach into the Plains of the Dead, for example.' She let the implications of her words hang in the air.

'So what you are suggesting is that... surely not?' Gadas said in horror, not daring to voice his fear.

'Yes, Captain, there is now no one in Leznar-Carchum who reveres the Holy Mother. She therefore has no power or influence here any more.'

'But how can that be?'

'The answer to that, Captain, I do not know.'

'But why this sickness? Why does the very land itself appear to be dying? Has the Holy Mother cursed this land?' he asked, not really believing that his god would do such a thing.

'No, Captain, that is not the way of Ios. Some other power has taken hold. Something dark, and altogether quite sinister.'

Gadas was stunned. 'So all this sickness and decay are signs of this other power's increasing influence?'

'Yes, Captain, I fear that is true.'

'In that case we must leave this principality as soon as possible. I will not escort the princess any further into this sick and dying land than I already have. This road leads directly to Carchum. I do not really wish to approach the capital, but we cannot turn east towards Nemeth-Sharrayah at the moment; the mountains prevent it until we pass Carchum. Once we reach there, however, it is a shorter journey north to the border of Varga-Shemshah than east to Nemeth-Sharrayah,' he said, more to himself than to Arité.

'That would seem like the wisest course of

276

action, Captain.'

'Thank you, Arité, I have been in two minds for some days now, but no longer. You may return to Princess Celene.'

'What would you have me tell the princess?' she asked.

'Tell her... tell her only what we know for certain, and keep her calm,' he commanded, adding, 'Please inform her that we will be travelling as fast as possible. I expect to cross the border in a few days' time.'

'The High Prince's trust was not misplaced in you.' With that, she left to return to Celene's carriage whilst he turned to make one final inspection of the camp before retiring for the night.

Arité told Celene everything that she and the captain had discussed. It was clear to her that the captain still entertained a faint hope that what he secretly knew to be true might still turn out to be false. Arité, however, *felt* that it was all true; the evidence was all around her. Celene took the news rather well, considering its implications. She was obviously shocked and she grieved for all that was being lost but did not become hysterical, probably due to her captain's cool head and seemingly calm acceptance at the changed circumstances.

As the night drew on, the sporadic howling that had been heard since they had entered Leznar-Carchum became more and more frequent, until Celene found herself lying awake, unable to sleep.

And then the screams started. Screams of fear became screams of terror echoing through the night. Sounds of steel on steel and the splintering of timbers caused Celene to shrink in fear, close her eyes and beg for the sounds to stop. They did, sometime later, although she was not sure how much later. She began to hear voices outside, voices raised in panic. An urgent knocking at her carriage door brought her to her senses.

'Your Highness! Your Highness! Are you alright?' It was Captain Gadas.

'Yes!' she replied, her voice quivering.

'May I come in, Your Highness?' He sounded urgent. Slowly she got out of bed, wrapped a blanket around herself, walked across the carriage and opened the door.

'What's happened?'

Gadas was ashen. 'Something terrible, Your Highness.'

'Captain? What is it?' Celene asked, trying to sound stern.

'It's the maids, Your Highness.'

'Arité!' Celene cried as she pushed past her captain and ran to the maid's carriage.

'Your Highness! NO!' Gadas shouted, but it was futile. She was already down the steps and running. In the half-darkness Celene almost tripped over something lying on the ground. Looking down, she screamed as she saw what she had tripped on. Two of the Royal Guard were lying dead at her feet. Both men had been cloven nearly in two. Only their mail shirts held their two halves together. The princess turned, and backed away from the dead men, stepping over their smashed tower shields as she approached Arité's carriage. Light from the flames of two small fires flickered over the scene and she was able to make out some detail.

The maids' carriage was virtually destroyed, one side had been completely torn away and pieces lay all around, little more than matchwood. Celene didn't immediately notice this however, as her gaze was transfixed by the scene inside. It was like an abattoir. Arité and all of her maids had been slaughtered; they had been cut to pieces. Blood coated every surface, and body parts lay strewn all around. Celene could not believe what she was seeing; she had never imagined that such carnage was possible. Tears streamed uncontrollably down her face. She lost control.

'ARITÉ! ARITÉ! ARITÉ! ARITÉ!' She screamed at the top of her lungs. She tore at her hair, 'WHY? WHY?'

Gadas tried to restrain her. 'Your Highness! PLEASE! I tried to tell you.'

Celene wasn't listening. She hammered on his chest as he held her elbows.

'WHERE WERE YOU? YOU WERE SUPPOSED TO PROTECT HER! WHERE WERE YOU? WHERE WERE YOUR MEN?'

She was hysterical with rage and struggled against his grip. Gadas manoeuvred himself behind her as she flailed at him and herself.

Suddenly her knees gave way and she collapsed. The captain caught her and picked her up. He shouted to the guards who had gathered around their dead comrades.

'You men! Form a perimeter around the princess's carriage! Stay alert.' Looking around, Gadas called his senior non-commissioned officer to him. 'Sergeant Capelas!' A tall, burly man with huge square shoulders ran up to him.

'Captain?'

'Find out what happened here. I want a situation report as soon as possible. Put everyone on full alert. I'll be in the princess's carriage.'

'Yes, sir! Right away, sir!' Capelas saluted smartly, turned and jogged off into the smoky haze.

Gadas carried Celene gently back to her carriage. Her body was shaking. He laid her carefully down on her bed and offered her some water but she just shouted at him, so he reluctantly backed off. He wished they had brought a physician with them but immediately banished the thought. *Why would we need a physician when we have a child of Ios?* The answer came to him. *A child of Ios cannot administer a sedative to herself.* Celene kept sobbing uncontrollably.

'Rest, Your Highness, please rest. There is nothing we can do. I am so very sorry.'

Gadas had never been in a position where he had to soothe and reassure a grieving member of the opposite sex, let alone a child of Ios. He didn't know what to say or how to say it. Had she been one of his troops it would have been easy. He had done it many times before. Quite a few times during a skirmish he had had to grab a junior officer by the lapels and scream at him to keep fighting. It often happened when young subalterns had their first taste of actual combat; the sight of a friend being killed in front of them traumatised them and they just froze. He would yell at them. *He's dead, there's nothing you can do for him. Now pick up your weapon and fight or you'll end up like him. This is not a game, Lieutenant.* A few choice oaths thrown in for good measure would often do it.

This was not the same situation, but she was suffering from the same kind of shock. Shock at seeing the body of her best friend, brutally dismembered. Even he hadn't seen such gruesome brutality perpetrated on women. He couldn't understand what had happened, so he could hardly tell her to "pull herself together and get on with it." Somehow that wasn't quite right. She was his responsibility though, as had been Arité and the other maids, and he had to face up to it. He did what he thought was best – he sat on the edge of the bed, held her hand and waited.

Gadas was still sitting next to her when Sergeant Capelas and another soldier brought in one of the Royal Guard. He appeared to be in a daze.

'What's wrong with him?' Captain Gadas snapped at the two men.

'He saw everything, Captain, but he won't say what he saw,' Capelas replied.

'Sit him down here, next to the princess. Wait for me outside,' he commanded before turning back to Celene, 'Your Highness, what can I do?' he asked. He felt helpless; he was a soldier not a maid. Celene turned from where she had been staring at the floor to regard him.

Placing a trembling hand on his shoulder she said 'Keep doing what you're doing, Captain.'

'Thank you, Your Highness. I will have one of my men stay with you. I need to go now and sort things out,' he replied, before leaving her with the dazed soldier.

A few minutes passed in silence before Celene turned to the soldier sitting next to her. He was staring at the floor muttering to himself. She saw he had cuts over his head and arms. She reached out and touched him, then prayed silently to Ios. She found it difficult but, eventually, the man's wounds began to heal.

'What did you see, soldier?'

He didn't reply but kept muttering and staring

at the floor. Celene gently place her left hand under his chin and brought his head round, held his gaze and asked again, as kindly as she could.

Slowly, he began to speak. 'Those eyes... those burning green eyes. It came out of the night, wrapped in shadows. Silently... so silently we never heard it coming. It killed Goson and Maas with its huge broadsword before they could raise the alarm. I heard them die and came running but I was too late; they were already dead. It was ripping the side of the carriage apart as I charged. It stopped and turned on me... I tried to fend it off but it smashed my shield and sliced the head off my spear... I turned and ran. I've never run from anything in my life, Your Highness, nothing, but I ran from this.'

'There was nothing else you could have done. You were unarmed. Had you not run, the captain would now have three dead men rather than two,' she said trying to console the distraught man.

'I ran to the rock face and hid. I heard the women screaming but I couldn't do anything. I couldn't help them. I'm sorry, Your Highness,' he sobbed.

'What is your name?'

'Ratha.'

'Now, Ratha, What was it that attacked you? Did you get a good look at it?'

'I'm not sure, Your Highness, it seemed to come out of the night. I didn't hear or see anything get past me. When I heard the yells from Goson and Maas... well, when I got there, there was hardly anything to see but blackness. It looked like a figure in a loose, hooded robe – but made out of the night... all swirling. All I really saw were the eyes... glowing green... piercing. It was like trying to fight something that wasn't there. I can't explain it any better, Your Highness. Do you know what I mean?'

'Yes, I do, Ratha. Don't worry any more. You did all you could do.'

'Thank you, Your Highness. So I have not failed you?'

'No, Ratha, you have not failed me. You are here, now, by my side and I thank you for that.'

Guardsman Ratha could not find the words to thank his princess, but the look in his eyes spoke for him and Celene smiled, letting him know she understood. At that moment Captain Gadas returned, a serious look on his face.

'I would speak with you, Your Highness,' he said. Understanding the unspoken order Guardsman Ratha got up, bowed to Celene, saluted his captain, and left. When he and the other guard had left the carriage and closed the door behind them, the captain continued.

'Princess, I realise that you must be traumatised by what you saw but I need to ask you something.'

'Of course, captain. In all honesty I don't think it has sunk in yet; go ahead.'

'Thank you. Did Arité voice any concerns to you about our entry into Leznar-Carchum?'

'No, she didn't – but she was very worried by something. I saw it in her face. When I asked her what was wrong she said that the land was sick, and that we were not to continue our journey in Leznar-Carchum; that we were to leave with all haste.'

Gadas nodded. 'Barring my two men, who I believe were simply in the wrong place at the wrong time, all those killed tonight had one thing in common. They were all members of the priesthood.'

Celene understood his implication immediately.

'So you think this was an attack on the Holy Order, rather than on myself or the caravan?'

'You tell me – I'm just a soldier, not a politician or a priest. But it certainly looks that way.'

'Captain, there is something that Guardsman Ratha said to me that you should know. When I asked him if he saw what attacked the carriage, he said that he didn't see it as such. He said that it came out of the night, almost as if it was part of it: a darkness with green eyes. I don't know much about these things but that sounds evil.'

'I questioned the rest of my men and none of them saw anyone or anything enter the camp. They're all good men, hand-picked and I believe what they said. Arité told me that she believed that a dark force was present here, perhaps it was this force that did it?'

Celene looked very worried. 'We must bury the dead and leave immediately, Captain; I think Arité was right. Once all the priesthood are dead, then all that is good resides in the Children of Ios – we must waste no time.'

'Your Highness is correct to suggest leaving as soon as we can, but we have no time to dig graves to bury the dead.'

'Captain, I will *not* leave our dead for the wolves and crows,' there were tears in her eyes, 'I simply will not.' She broke down and began to cry again.

Gadas thought for a moment of two. 'A pyre, we can build a pyre from the remains of the wagon.'

Celene simply nodded weakly as she cried. He left her to grieve. The wagon was quickly converted into a funeral pyre and set ablaze. Captain Gadas ordered two men to stand guard over the princess as the rest prepared the caravan for travel. Very quickly, with dawn approaching, they were under way again, heading north.

Chapter 26

The ritual that had summoned the dozen wraiths now haunting the palace library had taxed Seratos to his limit, and he felt mentally drained. Sisus had tried to persuade him to summon only one of these ethereal assassins at a time but he needed more to accomplish his aims, so the warnings had gone unheeded. The ritual itself involved less liturgy and mystical symbolism than others he had learned, but required far greater mental concentration and extreme psychological aggression. It involved casting one's mind into the underworld and trawling for a wraith. Then, once a wraith had been found, wrestling with it in order to drag its essence into the mortal world. A successfully summoned wraith would perform almost any task in order to earn its passage back to the underworld. In this way wraiths were not so much controlled, as unleashed, and Seratos had sat for hours wrestling one after another until a dozen stood before him, all hooded and robed in darkness, their burning green eyes blazing with evil intent, all desiring to get back to, and haunt, the underworld.

'Wraiths, I have a task for you,' he began in an authoritative tone. 'I have called you forth for one purpose. Nhurkhu is now my patron but the priesthood of Ios is still strong outside of this city. Slay every priest of Ios in Leznar-Carchum. When they realise what is happening they will flee and try to hide but you will hunt them down.'

The wraiths did not bow to Seratos, but

instead departed immediately. They drew enormous great-swords from the darkness that enveloped them, then turned and melted through the walls of the library. Seratos stood alone in the library as a smile – entirely devoid of humour – crossed his face. The removal of the priesthood from his principality would cause his people's faith in the Holy Mother to collapse, thus allowing him to install Nhurkhu as their new patron with little opposition. As he stood there a thought crossed his mind. *Imagine how the steady assassination of Ios' disciples in the neighbouring principalities would weaken their faith...*

It was in this state of reverie that Sisus found his master, and was taken aback when he learned of his prodigious feat.

'My Lord, evidently I owe you an apology; I underestimated your talents,' Sisus began.

'Thank you, Sisus. Your apology is accepted. Now, what was your actual reason for disturbing me?'

'It would appear that everything is going according to plan, My Lord, though I am not yet sure of that plan's ultimate goal. I would ask you to forgive me if I overstep the bounds of propriety, My Lord, but I am uncomfortable when I do not know what I am working towards.'

'Sisus, you are right to ask for enlightenment, I have so far kept my ultimate ambition secret. But more of that in a moment. I trust that everything is in place regarding the induction of my officers into the necromantic arts?'

'It is, My Lord. As soon as they return, their training will begin. I have also managed to entice those few shades that still haunt this city's graveyards to join our cause. I will begin training these spirits alongside your officers.'

'Excellent, Sisus, excellent. I see that you have not only done what I have asked you to do, but more. In return for your diligent service to me, allow me to explain how I plan to put the Holy Mother to the sword... so to speak.' Seratos began, resting one arm lightly on Sisus' shoulder as he led him deeper into the library where he took him into his confidence.

Seratos and Sisus walked the quiet corridors of the palace library for some hours. Sisus listened as Seratos explained to him what he was planning. The necromancer remained silent for the most part as his master spoke, only speaking to clarify a point or suggest an alternative that his lord had overlooked.

'So now you understand?' Seratos asked as they finally made their way out of the library.

'I do, My Lord. It is a sound plan though an invasion of this scale will require us to begin preparations immediately if we are to be able to march by next spring,' Sisus pointed out.

'*Crusade,* Sisus,' Seratos corrected his mentor. 'What I am planning is a crusade. Some might call it a holy war, but there is nothing holy about what I am about to begin. I think it is time that you take up the mantle of Seneschal of Carchum. This was to be your position from the beginning. Now you have proven yourself I think it is only right that I make your position official. I will have a declaration published and sent out through the city.'

'Thank you, My Lord, I am honoured.' Sisus' tone might have been fawning but there was a hint of malevolence behind his grin.

Chapter 27

It took several months to raze every shrine and temple in Leznar-Carchum. To begin with the soldiers met with resistance when they began their acts of desecration. Though given the nature of Ios' followers this resistance was entirely ineffectual. The resistance they met swiftly fell away, to be replaced with fear and then terror as the wraiths that now haunted the principality went about their grim task. Seratos had been right; it did not take long for the priesthood to work out what was going on. The news of the desecrations and assassinations spread like wildfire, and before long priests were fleeing the temples and shrines they had tended since they were ordained. Some fled for the sanctuary of neighbouring principalities, whilst others were hidden in cottages by devout citizenry or simply took off and hid themselves in the expanses of Carchum's wilder parts.

None of those that rode for neighbouring borders ever saw what killed them. Trusting in the speed of a horse had seemed a sound notion, but neither horse nor rider can continue indefinitely; both need rest. Wraiths, however, do not and overtook the fleeing priests as they slept by the roadside, hewing them apart with their enormous broadswords.

Those priests who went into hiding fared better than their fellows who took to the road. Seratos' wraiths scoured the countryside all winter, mercilessly terrorising outlying settlements and larger towns alike. By spring those few priests who had survived the harsh winter found that very few people were now willing to aid them for fear of the wraiths.

Seratos and his seneschal had been far from idle during the winter months. Sisus began the instruction of Seratos' officers and the shades in the necromantic arts, whilst Seratos found that the officers in command of the garrisons in Sursh and Laho were not as difficult to turn as he had feared. Evidently their faith in Ios had been severely undermined by the actions of his soldiers and the wraiths. By midwinter he had ensured the loyalty of every officer in the principality, started their training in the necromantic arts and had begun expanding his standing armies until the entire principality was effectively on a war footing.

That winter, the people of Leznar-Carchum began to doubt their faith in Ios. What little faith remained died as the wraiths spread terror far and wide. As the people's faith in the Holy Mother died so too did the land; the once-beautiful trees, shrubs and grasses began to sicken and die – a visible sign that Ios' influence on this principality was fading whilst Nhurkhu's was strengthening.

It was a cold winter's morning when Sisus informed Seratos that the commanders of Carchum's army had been trained to a competent level, the ethereal shades had mastered what they had been taught and that by early spring the remainder of his commanders would be ready.

As midwinter drew close Seratos ordered that, barring the citizenry that were essential, everyone was to leave the capital. Some left willingly, others had to be forcibly evicted. With the city virtually denuded of its population, Seratos began organising its conversion into a colossal barracks. This confused Sisus.

'My Lord,' he asked one afternoon, 'the conversion of the city into a barracks is almost complete. It would appear that you have far more capacity than is required... unless you are planning on assembling the armies of Sursh and Laho here in Carchum?'

'No, Sisus, I am not. They are to remain garrisoned in their respective cities. I will, however, require the *extra* capacity... please have my commanders meet me in the audience chamber at midnight,' he ordered without giving further explanation.

'As you wish.'

The audience chamber was still blood-stained. The stains on the floor had worn off but the spatters and streaks that covered the walls had darkened to a deep red-brown. Once Seratos' officers had assembled, he explained the reason for the extra barracks capacity.

'Men of Carchum, I understand that your training is progressing well. I promised you power, did I not?' A chorus of appreciative agreement erupted from the gathered commanders. Seratos indulged it for a moment or two before raising his hand for silence. 'You will no doubt have noticed that I have had the entire city converted into a barracks, easily large enough to house twice the number of soldiers currently under your command.'

Silence.

'There are many *recruiting grounds* lying both within this city and without. I am assured by my seneschal that you are all competent enough now to raise and command troops for yourselves.' Seratos paused for effect. 'Scour the city's graveyards. Raise the dead and incorporate them into your companies and regiments. The living will fight alongside the dead. Barracking all of your men within the city walls will hide our numbers from prying eyes. I want everyone under your command equipped and ready to march by spring.' The assembly saluted crisply together and left the hall as Seratos dismissed them.

The weeks that preceded the onset of spring were buzzing with activity within the walls of Carchum. It was not long before all the graveyards within a mile of the city were emptied. Soon the living and the un-dead were drilling alongside one another; man's natural aversion at being in the presence of death was slowly eroded.

It was difficult to tell exactly how many troops were barracked within Carchum's walls by the time recruitment was complete, but a conservative estimate led Sisus to report a figure of eighty thousand to his lord. Seratos smiled without mirth as he listened to Sisus' report. Soon his crusade would begin.

Chapter 28

By dawn the caravan was some miles from the valley they had passed the night in and was travelling as fast as Captain Gadas could safely manage. The soldiers of the Royal Guard were mounted on the caravans and the horses were being urged to step out briskly. By mid-morning the capital city, Carchum, appeared on the horizon.

If anything, the countryside surrounding the capital appeared unhealthier than the rest of the principality. As the caravan drew closer to the city the last vestiges of life disappeared altogether and the land appeared dead. Trees were no more than leafless skeletons providing perches for crows and the meadows had become arid dust-bowls. They passed few other travellers on the road. Those they did pass did not stop to greet the passing caravan but continued on their way with lifeless expressions on their faces. Celene had remained in her carriage since last night, not wishing to venture outside to see what had become of this once-beautiful, verdant land. Guardsman Ratha and another man had been ordered to wait on the princess as they travelled. Owing to the impracticality of carrying weapons inside the royal carriage, they had been forced to leave their broad shields and tall spears in one of the supply wagons, but the swords hanging from their belts imparted a measure of reassurance for the princess.

Despite the fact that he was a soldier, and not a maid, Guardsman Ratha did his utmost to see that

Celene's needs were taken care of. *Bless him,* she thought as he left to fetch her some fresh water from one of the supply wagons. *He seems to carry so much guilt from last night.* She smiled as he returned with the water.

'Thank you, guardsman, I appreciate everything you have done for me; you are a credit to your captain.'

'Thank you, Your Highness,' he replied quietly.

Some short time later a knock sounded at Celene's carriage door.

'Come in!' she said, as the other guardsman opened the door. Captain Gadas bowed as he entered.

'Your Highness, I am proposing a short break to rest the horses and prepare some hot food.'

'Thank you, captain. A hot meal would be appreciated. How close are we to Carchum?' she asked.

'No more than a mile or so, but the road forks away to the north permitting us to circumvent the city.'

'I think I should like to see what has become of Carchum, Captain. I will take my meal outside,' she said. Despite the surrounding lands being desolate and uninviting she felt the desperate need to leave her carriage and breathe some fresh air.

The meal she was served was typical military fare; a plainly seasoned broth, prepared with dried vegetables, dried salted fish from Khalii with a little barley thrown in. Nothing special, however, it was hot and filling so she did not complain. Whilst she was eating she turned to regard the principality's capital city. A sense of foreboding came over her as she gazed over its features. The bright banners and pennants that had once flown from its walls and towers appeared to have decayed. They were now little more than wisps of mottled cloth flapping in the unseasonally cold breeze. She could not exactly say why, but the city seemed to have a rather disturbing air about it that made her feel distinctly uneasy.

Celene was watching the city walls as the servants cleared away after the meal, and Captain Gadas' men prepared the caravan for the road. She was about to return to her carriage when she thought she saw a figure on one of the battlements.

'Captain, a moment if you please,' she said, catching Gadas' attention.

'Yes, Your Highness?'

'What can you see on the battlements just to the left of the main tower?' she asked.

Gadas squinted at where the princess was pointing. 'Very little, Your Highness; my eyes are not what they once were,' he replied, 'KARSZAS!'

'Yes, Captain!' A young soldier came jogging over to where the captain and Celene were stood.

'Guardsman Karszas, please tell me and the princess what you see on the battlements, just to the left of the main tower.' They young man strained his eyes as he peered at the city's wall.

'Guardsman Karszas has the best eyes in the regiment,' Gadas explained quietly to Celene as the young man concentrated on the city.

'I can see a couple of figures, Your Highness. One is a member of the royal family; I can make out his wings quite clearly from here. He is pointing towards us. The other is a just a man as far as I can tell... Wait, there is a third figure, also winged, though it looks like no angel that I've ever seen.' He turned to face Gadas. 'Who could it be Captain? What does it mean?' the young soldier asked.

'I do not know, Guardsman – but whatever it is, it means we must leave immediately, we have stopped here too long,' Gadas replied. He then ushered Celene into her carriage and started barking a series of orders for the caravan to be on the road within minutes.

Gadas was right to get the caravan moving again. The carriages were just re-joining the main road, having passed by the city, when a large number of winged figures became visible on the battlements. Even the captain could make them out. He urged the carriages and wagons of the royal caravan to greater speed.

The Royal Guard were ordered to ride in the carriages as they fled for the border. Guardsman Karszas, however, had been stationed in the rearmost wagon and ordered to watch the city for any signs that they were being pursued. It wasn't long before he spotted something.

'CAPTAIN! CAPTAIN!'

Captain Gadas came galloping down from the front of the caravan riding one of the horses that had originally been employed pulling the maids' carriage.

'What is it, Guardsman?'

'Look, Captain!' he replied, pointing towards a dark cloud that was some way behind them, moving swiftly. 'What is it, Captain?' Kaszas asked.

'Harpies!'

'Where did they come from?'

The captain's countenance darkened, 'The city,' he replied. He was already turning his horse as he said it, before galloping back to the front of the caravan. *We're in trouble now,* he thought. He had faced harpies before on the edge of the Plains of the

Dead, and knew they were a formidable and deadly enemy. He prayed that the caravan would reach the border before they were overtaken.

Are you listening, Ios?

Ios was not listening. The cloud of harpies continued to close on the fleeing caravan until the sound of leathery wings was heard flapping overhead. The rangy looking creatures soon began dropping on to the carriages and wagons, ripping at the roofs with their wickedly sharp claws – some used long serrated swords. The creatures' screeching and hissing unnerved the draught horses causing them to buck and kick off the traces, bringing the caravan to a halt. The Royal Guard began to pile out of the carriages they had been travelling in and form up into small groups, locking their shields together whilst defending themselves with their spears.

'To the Princess! Form up around the royal carriage!' Captain Gadas cried as he hacked his way towards Celene's carriage.

Inside the royal carriage Guardsman Ratha and his comrade were sheltering Celene as claws and sword blades broke through the windows. A tearing, snapping sound caught Ratha's attention. He looked up and watched in horror as the roof of the carriage was torn to matchwood. Celene was terrified and screamed when something began pounding on the carriage door.

'Your Highness! You must come with me!' Captain Gadas shouted. The young princess was too distraught to do anything other than cower on the floor. Fortunately, Guardsman Ratha also heard his captain's cry and began ushering her towards the front of the carriage. His comrade opened the door and Celene fell into the waiting arms of her captain who pulled her onto his saddle.

'You men! With me!' he commanded. Ratha's comrade responded immediately, leaping clear of the stricken carriage but Ratha found himself overrun as the last of the carriage's roof was torn away. Celene looked on in horror as the guardsman was set upon by half a dozen winged fiends. His screams did not last long.

'To me! Form up on me!' Gadas commanded in a loud clear voice as he kept his foes at bay with his longsword. His men responded immediately and began to encircle their captain. They had almost managed to lock their shields together around Gadas and Celene when a harpy, much larger than the rest landed in front of them, blocking the road.

There was little in the creature that confronted Captain Gadas and his Royal Guard that would have made them think it was a female. It was clad from chest to ankles in a suit of ancient bronze armour. Its bare, muscular arms clutched a corroded, horrific-looking pole arm. The screeching, ear-splitting cry that emanated from its bestial face caused men to wince and the captain's horse to rear. The captain and Celene were both thrown to the ground whilst the horse bolted, breaking through the protective ring of guardsmen.

Rising to his feet Captain Gadas looked about him. His men were surrounded and embattled but managing to hold the harpies at bay. The countryside in their immediate vicinity was mostly flat and sandy except for a huge outcropping of rock around fifty feet across and easily a couple of hundred high. It appeared to be riddled with caves – caves that could be defended much more easily than the open ground they were now on.

'To the rocks!' he bellowed.

Slowly, whilst still engaging the harpies, the tight circle of guardsmen moved towards the rocky outcropping. The harpies' commander seemed to sense Gadas' intentions however, and took to the air, screeching. Around a score of the winged beasts joined it as it fell upon those men closest to the rocks. Their stout shields may have been proof against the harpies' blades but against their commander's archaic pole arm they were a less sure defence. That awful weapon, swung with consummate skill, rent a guardsmen and his shield in twain. The adjacent man looked on in horror as his comrade collapsed to the floor spilling blood and guts everywhere. That slight opening was all that was needed. In the blink of an eye the shield wall broke and the formed defence became a desperate fight for survival.

'Fly to the caves!' Gadas shouted at Celene, cutting another harpy down in her defence as he did so, 'Fly to the caves!' he repeated in a tone so commanding that Celene found herself obeying him without thinking.

Spreading her snow-white wings she took to the air and sped towards the rocky outcropping. Espying a cave at ground level she sped towards it and retreated inside. A screech of anger and frustration went up as the harpy pack leader realised what had just happened. Another cry and it leapt skywards, flying straight for the caves followed by the rest of its pack.

'To the Princess! Make for the caves!' Gadas cried as he saw the harpies break away from his men to follow their leader. They responded at once and immediately began to make their way after the princess and her assailants. They found their path blocked, however, as the harpies' leader turned and, leaving the princess to the attention of its minions, led a counter-attack that stopped the captain and his men in their tracks. Though they fought like men possessed, they could not reach their beloved princess and were helpless do anything as her screams filled the air.

The cave was barely large enough for Celene to enter. Warily she peered out, trying to see what had become of her captain and his men. She leapt back in terror as the cave entrance was suddenly filled with long claws and thin blades, as far too many harpies tried to enter the small space at once. Some of those claws and blades were longer than others, however, and the young princess of Nemeth-Sharrayah soon found herself bleeding from numerous stabs and lacerations. Screaming, she shrank back into the cave as far as she could and drew her wings about her. As filthy claws began to tear at the feathers of her beautiful wings she continued to scream, trying to drown out the flapping of those leathery wings and the infernal screeching that accompanied it.

Chapter 29

'My Lord, a messenger has arrived from Sursh. He is demanding an audience with you immediately,' Sisus reported.

'Very well, show him in.' Seratos looked up from a large, detailed map of the Principalities of Life as a tired man in weather-beaten robes walked into his study.

'My Lord,' the man began, dropping to one knee.

'Rise and report. What is so important that you see fit to disturb me?' Seratos snapped.

'My Lord, a couple of days ago a train of carriages passed by Sursh. It did not enter the city and so my commander ordered me to investigate. The caravan belongs to a royal princess. My commander didn't know what she was doing here but ordered me to ride north as quickly as I could.'

'You did not announce your presence in any way did you?' Seratos asked.

'No, My Lord, I observed them under cover of night. Not even the sentries they posted suspected my presence,' the messenger replied.

'Good, good. Thank you, you may leave.' Seratos dismissed the man as he plumbed the depths of his memory. Yes, he remembered receiving a missive from High Prince Raparké Nemeth regarding the imminent tour of his daughter. He had ignored the message, having more important things to deal with at the time. *What an opportunity* he mused, as he waved

Sisus over to him.

'Sisus, double the watch on the walls and inform me as soon as the princess's caravan comes within sight.'

'Yes, My Lord,' Sisus replied before excusing himself and making directly for the city wall.

Seratos was notified of the princess's approach a couple of days later. Before heading out onto the wall he summoned the harpy pack leader.

The mottled, rotting banners mounted on the walls were moving gently in a cold breeze as Seratos and the harpy walked over to where Sisus was observing the caravan.

'Ah, My Lord, our guests are just breaking camp. It does not look like they plan to visit.' Sisus' voice was deadpan and betrayed no emotion at all. Seratos did not respond to his seneschal but instead turned to the she-beast standing next to him. Gesturing to the departing caravan he gave her very explicit instructions before stalking from the walls and returning to his study.

Chapter 30

As Thurion walked he noticed a change in the flora around him. The low trees that had been plentiful around the Moonstone had given way to stubby, coarse grasses whose leaves crunched and cracked under foot. These brown swathes were very different from the verdant grasslands that stretched from Hayesh Et-Kun to the Moonstone woods. It was as if the area was suffering from a prolonged drought. Gradually the land became more and more desolate until the dry ground could support little more than a few sickly grasses and the odd short, gnarled tree. No birds flew in the sky save for the occasional crow. He saw no deer, no wild oxen or wandering bears. This land appeared to be home to little more than bats and vermin. Even the sky took on an unhealthy dark pallor, like that of old parchment. He found himself walking down a dry, cracked road that wound steadily south. Thurion knew for certain he had entered the Plains of the Dead.

The only signs of civilisation were run-down settlements, seemingly abandoned and now crumbling. As Thurion trudged down the rutted road he entered what may at one time have been a thriving hamlet. All that now remained was a cluster of old huts showing signs of decay. The settlement's few residents slunk in doorways and watched Thurion as he passed, eyeing him with cold, dead eyes. Rags hung from their thin frames, and lank hair fell across their faces in thin, knotted ropes. Thinking he might at least find some shelter for the night, Thurion strode up to one of the huts.

'Excuse me. I have travelled far today. Is there anywhere I might find shelter for the night?' he asked the sickly-looking old woman lurking in the doorway.

'Nowhere here,' she replied in a dry, rasping voice.

'And where is here?' asked Thurion. The woman ignored his question and retreated back into the gloom of her hut, shutting a mould-wracked door as she did so. Turning, Thurion carried on down the road and left the hamlet.

The land south of the hamlet was even more desolate than that to the north, it was no more barren but it seemed sicklier. As dusk fell, Thurion left the road and climbed a small hill on which grew a single, squat tree. Its branches were low, twisted and devoid of leaves. Thurion could not tell if it was dead or had merely shed its leaves early. If it was alive it would not live for much longer, he concluded, as he set up camp under its shadow. The air was cold and damp and his fire refused to do anything more than smoke heavily, giving off little heat. The night was full of strange, unsettling noises that kept him awake, despite his many years of living in the wilderness. Dawn brought a cold, pale light to the land and he woke stiffly. After a meagre breakfast of dried meat and seeds he set off southwards once again.

It was mid-morning when Thurion turned a bend in the road and saw an old man walking towards him, travelling north. He was clad in a traveller's cloak and carried a worn staff. There was nothing about him that could mark him out as individual in any way. He was entirely nondescript. Indeed, Thurion almost lost sight of him as he approached; he appeared to melt out of sight unless great attention was paid. The traveller would have passed without a word had Thurion not broken the heavy silence that accompanied him.

'Good morning, Friend. I am a stranger here, what can you tell me of these parts?'

The figure stopped and turned to face the barbarian, his face hidden in the deep folds of his hood.

'There is little to tell. This is a dead land. Those who live here are dead as are those who tarry here over-long,' the figure replied, his voice hollow and entirely devoid of emotion.

'But you, sir, are not dead,' Thurion replied.

'Are you sure?' the figure asked before turning and carrying on up the road. His reply gave Thurion pause for thought, and it was a few seconds before he turned back to the wizened old man. However, he was nowhere to be seen. *Truly this is a strange land*, Thurion thought, *where the living and the dead may walk side by side.*

He found himself standing at a fork in the road. The main road he was on was flat and continued south but the other began to incline slightly into the distance. Leaving the main road, he took the sloping route. At length the road began to wind up a steep-sided hill on the top of which stood an old timber keep. Not wishing to spend another night outside in this forsaken land, Thurion made towards the keep. As he climbed he approached what at one time would have served as the keep's gatehouse. Now however, all that remained was a pair of rusted gateposts and a pile of rotten timbers that spoke of the one-time existence of the gatehouse itself. As he passed the old gateposts he felt the unpleasant sensation of being watched, though from where not even he, with all the keen senses of a wilder, could tell. Shivering, in spite of the warmth of his cloak, he carried on up the hill towards the keep.

The keep stood alone, possessed of an air of ancient nobility despite its derelict state. The keep's gates – though still standing – had rotted through and collapsed when Thurion tried to push them open. He entered the main audience chamber. In the gloom he could make out a large object on the far side of the chamber and as his eyes adjusted to the dim light he was surprised at what he saw. A throne stood at its far end on which sat the skeletal remains of the fort's former lord garbed in all his mouldering finery. A thin circlet of silver sat at an angle on his skull whilst moth-eaten robes of faded crimson hung from his shoulders. His right hand rested on the pommel of a large, rusted great sword whilst his left grasped the arm of the throne.

'Who enters my domain?' a deep voice demanded. Thurion looked around for the source of the voice but could not find it. He answered regardless.

'A traveller. I am seeking a night's shelter.'

'You are not welcome here. You must leave.'

'I simply seek shelter, nothing more.'

'You must leave,' the voice repeated.

'Who are you? Show yourself!' Thurion demanded, anger keeping his growing apprehension at bay.

With the dry scratch of bone on bone the skeletal lord rose to his feet and took his sword in both hands. Dust fell from his bones and robes in a thick cloud as he walked towards Thurion.

'I am Sir Vasik Bresa, and you trespass in my

realm,' the dead knight said as he advanced.

'I meant no offence, sir knight,' Thurion said, taking a few steps away from the un-dead knight.

'Offence has been taken, traveller. Defend yourself!' the knight cried before charging Thurion from across the audience chamber. Drawing his great axe, the Northman deflected the knight's initial attack before returning a strike to the side of the head. Sir Bresa, however, fought with consummate skill and avoided Thurion's counter-attack. The two warriors fought back and forth across the audience chamber for a long time, tables and benches collapsing into rotten piles as they clashed.

At length, Thurion managed to land a number of blows and saw that his adversary's grasp on the realm of the living was beginning to fail. The end came as Thurion easily sidestepped what should have been a decapitating strike and returned with one of his own. The knight's skull crumbled to dust as it rolled across the chamber floor followed soon afterwards by the rest of his body. In moments, there was nothing left to mark the knight's passing except for a pile of disintegrated robes and a rusted great sword with its tip embedded in the floor. Returning his axe to its shoulder strap Thurion began, cautiously, to climb the stairs in order to explore the keep and ensure it was now entirely unoccupied. The stairs creaked and cracked under his weight as he climbed, but they held.

Thurion found nought but rot and vermin as he explored the other rooms. After setting a few traps he prepared a small fire on the stone dais next to the dead knight's throne. There was no shortage of dry kindling and firewood in the old keep. Tonight his fire did burn, not as well as it should have, but sufficiently well to cook the few rats he managed to trap. Thurion heard little before falling asleep. He was woken once or twice by a distant howling but other than that, the night passed without incident.

The dawn air was cold as Thurion left the keep. A heavy fog had settled on the land, limiting visibility to little more than a few yards. He found his way back to the main road with the intention of continuing south. Around mid-morning he reached the fork in the road, and was beginning to wonder whether the fog would lift at all.

Travelling the south road for many days, Thurion survived on nothing but trapped vermin and boiled grasses. Life in this land was truly miserable; it was no place for the living. He remembered the words the old wilder had said at the Moonstone; that the land he was heading for was no place for such a noble beast as Rimehorn. *How true indeed,* Thurion thought. His friend would have died of starvation by now, and the notion of such a lingering death for his companion made him shiver.

The road eventually came to an abrupt end on the shore of a wide, stagnant lake. He found a rough track which took him around the eastern shore. The lake's margins were shallow and marshy. The air around the lake was foetid, the thick mud gave off a foul stench with every step. Dead reeds crunched under his boots sending hundreds of fat black flies buzzing all around, landing on his clothes, his face, in his ears and eyes. Once or twice Thurion saw ripples across the lake's surface that were not made by the wind, indicating that *something* was living in the apparently lifeless water.

Thurion soon turned away from the dying lake which he named Deadwater, and headed in a more easterly direction which took him out of the valley the lake was situated in, where the air was cleaner. As dusk fell he turned to look back over the land through which he had just passed. He could just make out the outline of the lake's near shore in the half-light of evening. He saw small lights hovering over the still waters. Even from this distance, he felt a strong sense of unease when he looked at them for too long, and was glad that he had not tarried long in those dreadful stinking marshes.

By dawn the next day he was making for what appeared to be a ring of hills. From there he believed he might get a better idea of the lie of the land; an urge to leave this cursed place was building inside him. It took him the best part of three days to reach the ridge he had been making for. As he approached, the ground ahead of him appeared to be populated with what looked like termite mounds. Lots of them. Close up he could see mounds of earth situated everywhere; they were piled next to roughly oblong holes. What struck him most —more than the apparent regularity of the excavations— was the sheer number of them. They stretched for as far as he could see. It was as if these hills were surrounded by many thousands of graves. Each one that he passed was empty. *What kind of disaster would prompt the digging of so many graves? Why were they all empty? Where were the gravediggers?* There was no sign of them, not even a footprint. The sheer scale of the graveyard was almost too much for the young wilder to take in. Suffice it to say that Thurion was greatly relieved to reach the solid ground at the foot of the hills.

It was late morning when he finally reached the ridge top. What he saw made him gasp: the hills formed an unbroken ring. They descended steadily onto a plain that was obscured from view by a thick layer of black fog. A little way down the hillside, visible above the concealing fog, was a ring of standing stones each carved with runes that he could not read, though he felt uneasy when he looked directly at them. As he watched, a column of soldiers in baroque armour marched out of the fog and up the far side of the depression. Thurion could make out little from his position on his side of the depression, but what he saw was enough to convince him that the troops and their commander were all dead men. Not covered by armour, their hands were white bones clutching spears. Their spear tips did not glisten in the pale sunlight; neither did they march in step. They did however, march at pace, not slowing as they climbed the hill, for the dead do not know fatigue.

Thurion stalked along the ridge top, around the ring of hills, following the army as it marched out of the fog-covered depression. Ranks of cavalry followed the infantry. Armed in an equally baroque fashion, the knights rode skeletal steeds that were clad in ancient, moth-eaten caparisons. Behind them loped packs of slavering wolves. Thurion was hard-pressed to keep pace with the army of the dead, for though a single man may travel faster than a large body, the dead did not rest come dusk. If anything, they seemed to travel faster as night fell.

The army's route was not difficult to follow, however, and Thurion followed it easily in the dark as it made its way east. It marched relentlessly east for three days before it halted at a large obelisk carved from something akin to sandstone, but the stone was not dull like sandstone – it glistened faintly in the sunlight. As the army stood, standard poles were raised in each regiment and banners were unfurled. Each banner bore a red runic device on a black field. The air was still but the banners flapped as though a strong wind were blowing. Indeed, the wind appeared to come from the banners themselves, for a faint smoke began to emanate from each regiment's colours. Once the colours were flying a single trumpet sounded and the army advanced as one. As they passed the obelisk the wolves began to yelp and falter, not wishing to pass the great stone. In response, the knights sounded their trumpets and the wolves slunk into the midst of their ranks; the knights themselves now concealed under the smoke given off by their banners.

The army had clearly just crossed the border from the Plains of the Dead into another realm. Thurion had no idea into whose realm he was now entering, though he immediately felt at ease as he passed under the shadow of the obelisk. Compared to the Plains of the Dead this land seemed to glow with life. As he travelled east, following the dead army he noticed the land becoming more and more fertile. Rivers were no longer dry beds. The sky was home to birds other than crows and the land seemed blessed with abundant life. Thurion stopped that afternoon to make camp and hunt. He ate well that night, but real sleep eluded him.

Two days later Thurion found himself cresting a hill that had been rising steadily for some miles. On reaching the top he gasped in amazement: on the opposite hill a vast fortress rose majestically from the summit. He had never before seen such a structure. Easily able to house an entire tribe, its towers stretched up into the sky, seemingly high enough to kiss the clouds. The fortress was constructed from the same pale stone as the obelisk he had passed a few days before, and it glistened, as if it were covered by a light autumn frost.

Below him, arrayed between the advancing army of the dead and the great fortress, was a force the likes of which he had not witnessed in all his life. Ranks of spearmen in shining armour and white tabards were formed up in front of crossbow men, likewise garbed. Cavalry units were positioned at each flank. Caparisoned in white, their armour gleaming, they stood as still as statues, the very essence of nobility. It was the commander of this force that held Thurion's gaze, however. Clad in bright golden armour he wielded a long spear. Thrusting it skywards he spread a great pair of white-feathered wings and took to the air.

Thurion watched from the crest of the hill as the army of the dead deployed for battle. The infantry columns formed into wide-fronted combat formations, locking their shields together as they did so. The cavalry took up positions on either flank of the main force whilst the wolf packs slunk away, lurking in the wings.

As he watched, Thurion saw a lone figure walk out from the front rank of the centre-most infantry regiment. His armour was as old as that of the rest of the army but it was far more ornate, the verdigris of its bronze trappings clearly visible. The figure, undoubtedly the army's commander, advanced until he was a dozen or so yards ahead of his front line. Raising his ornate halberd into the air he began to chant in a long-forgotten language. A minute later the ground in front of him began to shake and soil was heaved out of the ground, as the bodies of the dead lying in a long-forgotten cemetery began to pull themselves free of the ground, reanimated to serve their new master. Before long, hundreds of corpses had been raised and stood facing the defending army. The un-dead commander lowered his halberd and, in unison, the army began to advance towards the ranked lines of the defenders.

Where the dead walked the grass under their feet sickened and withered. As the screen of corpses shuffled into range the ranks of defending spearmen dropped on to one knee and the men behind them raised their crossbows to their shoulders. A single trumpet sounded and the crossbow men opened fire, peppering the advancing dead. Scores and scores of the newly-animated corpses fell, pierced by heavy bolts. Astonishingly, the defenders' fire did little to thin the ranks of the advancing un-dead.

Eventually the two battle lines clashed. The defenders fought with grace and finesse whilst the dead fought with relentless ferocity, clawing at shields, trying to pull the defending spearmen to the ground. Time and again they crashed against the shields of the defenders. Time and again the tides of the dead were repulsed.

As the infantry clashed, cavalry on both sides began advancing down their respective flanks. Steadily their advance increased in pace until they were galloping towards each other at full speed. With a crash that resounded across the battlefield the charging cavalries collided. Lances were splintered and men, both living and dead, were pitched from their saddles. The fighting was ferocious; finely wrought straight-bladed cavalry swords clashed with rusted long axes. Slowly, the tirelessness of the dead began to take its toll on those noble knights and their numbers began to dwindle.

It was as the battle was raging at its fiercest that the gates of the fortress-city opened and a small band of robed men rode out, racing for the battlefield. The approaching riders were clad in robes of gossamer white and held golden sceptres aloft. As they approached the defending army their formation split, each rider making for a different part of the battle line.

Thurion watched as one of these men rode down the infantry's right flank making for the beleaguered knights. He almost reached them when a large pack of wolves leapt from a small copse of trees and raced to cut him off. He did not check his steed's pace however, but simply brandished his sceptre and cried out a command that Thurion could not hear from where he was. A blinding flash of light sprang from the sceptre, and the charging wolves stopped dead, howling and pawing at their eyes, before retreating as best they could from the brilliant light.

As he approached the knights the robed man once again raised his sceptre and called aloud another command. A golden brilliance emanated from him and began to engulf the dead knights, who disintegrated to dust as he advanced through their ranks, escorted by a handful of knights.

Similar events were unfolding on the opposite flank; the magick animating the dead cavalry was undone by another of these strange, but clearly powerful men. The battle raged fiercest however, between the lines of infantry. Shield walls clashed time and again and the noble defenders were slowly pushed back by the unrelenting tide of the dead.

The dead commander stood behind the main battle line protected by a bodyguard of a dozen wraiths wielding long, ethereal blades. As his infantry was cut down he would raise them again and send them back into battle. In this way the defenders were slowly ground down by attrition.

A couple of the strange white-robed men had made their way into the centre of the battle- field, and were directing their attention towards the slowly retreating spearmen. Raising their sceptres together they gave voice to a single command. A faint mist descended on the defending infantry, and began to swirl until it coalesced into many fine spectral swords. Guided by an unseen force, the swords hovered above the heads of the defenders then, with lightning speed, engaged the weapons of the advancing dead. With the clash of steel on steel, each enemy blade was blocked, lunges were parried, thrusts were deflected and the relentless advance of the dead was halted. The beleaguered infantry took heart, rallied and took the fight back to the enemy.

From his vantage point Thurion watched as the battle raged, noting how the advantage oscillated between the two forces. He sensed the battle was reaching its climax when he saw a spear slam into the ground – mere yards from where the dead commander stood. Looking up, Thurion watched as the defenders' golden-armoured commander flew down from the lofty heights above the battlefield to land facing his opposite number. Striding forward he calmly withdrew his spear from the ground and stood facing the commander's spectral bodyguard. At a gesture from their leader the wraiths advanced on the angel and spread out to surround him.

Taking his spear in one hand he raised the other and pointed at one of the advancing wraiths. At a word a strong wind sprang up, and the wraith dissolved until nothing remained. Then battle was joined. Eleven spectral blades flew at the angel, wielded by spirits so bitter they cared not for the beauty they now sought to bring low. The angel defended himself with preternatural speed, his spear moving in golden arcs, almost too fast for Thurion's hunter's eye to track. A moment passed and one wraith – having been impaled on the angel's golden spear – dissipated, its form melting into nothingness. Stepping back from the press of his enemies, the angel voiced another command. A mist appeared above his head and took the form of a long sabre. The weapon moved swiftly in the angel's defence, deflecting many deadly blows whilst he concentrated on one individual at a time. The fight raged for some time, the sabre whirling in the black midst, the angelic commander despatching his opponents one by one, until the last wraith was impaled on his spear. As the last wraith disappeared, the ethereal sabre above the angel's head dissipated.

Uttering a curse the dead commander raised his halberd and advanced slowly towards the angel. The two combatants circled each other warily for a few minutes, each testing the other's guard. A low sweeping strike saw the angel leap into the air, his wings holding him aloft for a second or two as his enemy's halberd sliced the air where he had been standing moments before. Holding himself aloft the angel thrust down towards his opponent. The dead man turned his opponent's strike, deflecting it with his pauldron. A return strike saw the angel take the full force of his adversary's blade in the chest, it striking him just as he landed. The noble warrior was thrown to the ground, his breastplate split by the force of the blow.

Rising to his feet he threw himself at his

enemy, landing blows quicker than the eye could see. Sparks flew as blow after blow was deflected by the dead commander's armour. Staggering back under the torrent of blows the dead warrior reached out and grasped the angel's spear, halting his attack. Then, with a strength no mortal could hope to possess, he brought his halberd round with one hand and struck the angel in the side of the head, knocking his helmet off and drawing a gush of blood. The blow was tremendous and would have felled lesser mortals, but the angelic commander did not relinquish his hold on the spear. Wrenching his weapon free, the angel thrust at his opponent, forcing him to back away, giving him time to gather his senses.

Again and again the two mighty warriors clashed, both receiving grievous wounds. Steadily, however, the angel ground down his opponent with determined, accurate blows, until the dead commander's wounds began to tell. His grip on his halberd loosened and his movements became slower. The angel parried the arcing blade and quickly thrust his spear through the dead man's visor, twisting as he did so. The commander staggered backwards, dropping his halberd as he stumbled – his head and shoulders arching back. With a flap of his wings, the angel leapt in the air still pushing and twisting the spearhead, grinding the skull within the helmet to dust. Using his momentum he propelled his dead foe rearwards until he fell. The angel's hands slid down the spear shaft as he quickly descended to the ground, landing astride the commander's head. He rapidly jerked his spear out of the helmet and thrust down again. The commander's body stopped thrashing and fell limp as the dark spirit that had animated his corpse slipped away and, immediately, his body began to crumble into dust, his halberd and armour collapsing into a pile of rusted metal.

With their commander vanquished the dead soldiers started to disintegrate. Thurion watched as, over the course of no more than ten minutes, the entire army was reduced to piles of dust and corroded metal. The relief amongst the defenders was clear; many jubilant trumpet blasts were sounded.

With the enemy defeated the victors set about retrieving their dead. Thurion watched as graves were dug and the burial rites administered by the strange white-robed men. The rusted arms and armour of the vanquished army were collected and loaded onto carts, and then driven into the city. The ground over which the dead had walked still looked sick. As the wagons pulled away, more white-robed men rode out of the city, dismounted and began to walk across the battlefield, praying over the ground. Before nightfall the dead had been buried and the detritus of battle had been cleared.

As the last of the wagons rolled back towards the city, Thurion descended from his ridge-top vantage point to walk the battlefield. He wished to learn all he could of those who had defended their land from the walking dead. As he walked he was surprised to find that where the ground had suffered under the feet of the walking dead, it now appeared healthy, almost fully restored. Clearly these people had a great command of some of the world's restorative powers.

Exploring the land beyond the battlefield Thurion found that the fortress-city stood on a rise in a country of rolling hills. Setting up camp in a small copse Thurion spent the night in peace, the first since he had entered the Plains of the Dead. The following morning he set off keeping the fortress-city to his left. Not wishing to attract attention he kept to the natural cover, intending to give the huge settlement a wide berth before he headed out into open country.

The land here was fertile and full of many living things; nowhere did he feel any hostility to life. *This is a good land to travel* thought Thurion, as he walked in the dappled shade of a small wood. He passed through many small settlements as he travelled. Each settlement seemed to comprise of a number of small houses and a shrine of some sort. Whether small or large these shrines would often be decorated with flowers or small trinkets. Unsure of the significance of these shrines he did not approach them, and left them well alone.

He travelled south-east and the fertile grasslands gave way to wetlands. Varied was the wildlife that called these lands their home. Indeed he had not seen such creatures before. He spent hours under the shade of trees and watched as large-scaled, reptiles came to drink from the waters. These great beasts were squat and their mouths ended in bizarre wedge-shaped beaks, their purpose becoming apparent when they ate. Thurion watched as these large reptiles dug their lower beaks into the ground and took great mouthfuls of mud. The mud would be pushed out through filters in the sides of their heads with any prey being retained and consumed. Whilst these were by far the strangest creatures Thurion saw, they were by no means the only ones. Life here was as varied as he had seen it anywhere.

Eventually the wetlands gave way to scrubby grasslands again and one morning Thurion found himself walking south along a well-made road. He believed himself to now be roughly south and west of the fortress city he had seen when he had crossed the border. The road cut a roughly straight path through the desert and headed south-west and passed another great fortress-city. As he walked, the road curved around a vast outcropping of rock some tens of feet across and maybe eighty feet high. If he could climb it, he thought, this rocky formation would afford him an excellent view of the surrounding land. Concealing his possessions in a small crevice at the foot of the formation he began to climb. The ascent was not unduly arduous as there were many hand- and footholds.

Upon reaching a plateau some fifty feet up, Thurion stopped and listened. He thought he heard something on the wind. Then he heard it again, clearly this time. He could make out the sounds of battle; steel on steel and cries as steel tasted flesh. The sounds were coming up from the far side of the outcrop but from his position, he could not see where they were coming from. Not wishing to be caught in combat without any protection, he quickly descended the rock face, returned to the cave in which he had concealed his possessions and donned his war gear.

Keeping to cover wherever he could, Thurion stalked around the outcrop. As he reached the far side of the rocks he came across a small group of soldiers in bright armour and white tabards in a desperate struggle against a horde of hideous harpies. They were clearly trying to fight their way to a cave in the side of the rocky outcrop, but were being held at bay as the foul creatures struck out at them from all sides with long wicked blades. The harpies had the advantage, using their black leathery wings to hold them aloft.

What were these soldiers so desperately trying

to reach?

Thurion could not immediately see, as the cave mouth was swarmed by more of the winged she-beasts. Every few seconds, a white feather would fly out and float gently to the ground. Suddenly a cry came from inside the cave, a cry of fear and pain that he could not ignore. Adjusting his grip on his great-axe, Thurion stalked out from where he had been concealed and with grim determination advanced towards the skirmishing soldiers and harpies at the cave mouth.

Chapter 31

She shrank back, pressing herself against the cold cave wall, as black talons tried to pry her out. Her white dress was ripped and bloodstained, her wings dishevelled with feathers bent and missing. She dropped to the floor and, drawing her knees up to her chest, began to cry.

As he strode towards the fight, Thurion raised his axe high above his head and bellowed a challenge at the pack leader, who was battering the small troop's commander to the ground with the haft of her pole arm. She looked up to see from where the strange battle-cry had come. *Who was this interloper who dared challenge her right to a kill?* Angered, she leapt into the air, leaving Captain Gadas free to struggle to his feet. With a wet, gravelly shriek she landed a short distance ahead of Thurion, posturing in a show of bestial bravado.

With a long, bounding gait she charged the lone warrior, holding her weapon low, intent on disembowelling him. Thurion stood his ground and loosened his grip on his axe. She tried not to telegraph her strike, but the slight movement of her weapon's tip was enough to alert Thurion and he stepped round the gutting slash and slammed the haft of his axe into her bronze-helmeted face. The blow would have stopped an ordinary man in his tracks, but despite a mouthful of blood and smashed fangs, the harpy hardly stumbled and maintained her momentum, just managing to escape Thurion's spine-splitting follow-up strike.

The she-beast turned to face him again, this time holding her weapon in a more cautious guard. Thurion, on the other hand, began swinging his weapon in a deadly figure-of-eight pattern in front of him and began to advance. It happened almost too fast to see; Thurion altered his grip on the axe and brought it down right in front of him, intending to split his enemy from brow to navel. The she-beast was fast however, and one flap of her dark, leathery wings pulled her just out of reach as Thurion's axe slammed like a thunderbolt into the ground. Her riposte was swift, a slicing stab which would have opened Thurion's right side were it not for the protection of his mail coat. Leaving his great axe stuck in the ground, Thurion recoiled from the thrust and drew a small hatchet from his belt which he hurled at her with a serpent's swiftness. The small axe crashed into the harpy's chest plate, not injuring her greatly but wrong-footing her nonetheless. Seizing his opportunity Thurion wrenched his axe from the ground and leapt at his foe. One titanic blow severed the she-beast's right wing, right arm and bit deeply into her side. A second split her open from neck to chest.

After stooping to recover his hatchet, Thurion charged the harpies who were assaulting the cave entrance, slamming into the mass of slashing blades and flapping wings like a man possessed. With the brutality of a true son of the north, the barbarian laid into his enemies, his axe rising and falling in deadly arcs. Trusting to the protection afforded by his mail coat and spectacled helmet, he split skulls, severed limbs and disembowelled his way to the cave. Once he had planted himself firmly at its entrance he cast the briefest of looks inside.

Her blonde hair was blood-matted in places and the wings which she had wrapped around herself were torn. He saw terror in her eyes but also a sweet innocence. Something awoke inside him in that instant, something that had remained dormant all his life. His heart caught in his throat as he beheld her; bloodied and dishevelled as she was, she was still the most beautiful thing he had ever seen.

His reverie was quickly broken when a sabre slid around the haft of his axe, and stabbed into the mail that hung from his helmet's spectacled rim. Turning back to the fight he brought his axe down in a swift arc, cutting deep into a harpy's neck. Thick dark blood jetted from the wound as the beast fell back clutching its open neck. There was no respite however, as another winged fiend took its fallen comrade's place at the cave mouth. And so Thurion fought on.

* * *

Her unknown saviour, this grim warrior who had appeared out of nowhere, who now fought to protect her had been knocked to the ground, again. But once again he rose to his feet, clutched his axe tightly, and fought on like a force of nature. He was not comely to look at, his coat of steel rings and spectacled helmet were spattered in dark blood, matted hair hung down his back whilst a wild beard flecked with blood, some of it his own, protruded from under his helmet. But the look they had shared seemed to speak volumes and sparked questions in her mind. *Who are you? Where did you come from? Why do you fight for me?* She prayed that Ios would spare her mysterious champion; she prayed that the Holy Mother would save them all.

* * *

Spitting a mouthful of blood, he looked up as the last beast flew down at him; this one had a sword aimed straight for him, lance-like. He turned the thrust at the last second with the haft of his axe, allowing the blade to bite deep into the earth. Thurion raised his great-axe above his head and brought it down in an arc that sliced wings, broke armour and cut deep into the beast's back. It gave a wet cry before collapsing to the ground in front of him. Wrenching his axe from the beast's spine he swung again, severing the head from the body. Black, foul-smelling blood gushed from the open neck, spattering his armour.

As the last of the harpies bled out, he turned back to regard her; this beautiful creature for whom he had fought so hard. She looked up at him fearfully, unsure what to make of the bloodstained warrior standing over her. He was breathing heavily, blood trickling down his beard. She looked into his eyes, the only part of him visible under his amour. Although he appeared to be quite the most fearsome person she had ever beheld, his eyes spoke of care, of a deep concern and possibly of... she turned away briefly and might have blushed had she not still been in shock.

Thurion wiped his axe blade on the harpy's leathery wing and slipped it back into its harness. Then he leant down and offered his hand to the angel cowering in the cave. Meekly, she accepted his proffered hand and allowed herself to be helped out.

'How badly are you hurt?' Thurion asked her.

'I…, erm, I, I think I'm n-not hurt really,' she sobbed.

Time stopped for them as they stood and regarded each other. He, his armour covered in black blood, blood running over his chin and down his beard, in torn leggings and worn boots, rough and powerful – every inch a savage. While she, in her dirty, blood-stained dress, her wing feathers in complete disarray and her hands bleeding from numerous cuts, crying, trembling from fright – completely dishevelled: the very antithesis of what an angel should look like. She looked up at him.

'But you're hurt, you're bleeding,' she said putting her hand up to his face. He instinctively put his hand up over hers, but before he could answer, time started again.

'MY PRINCESS, ARE YOU ALRIGHT?'

It was Captain Gadas. He was several paces away, limping painfully towards them.

'Yes, thank you, captain,' she replied. She took a couple of steps towards him but her knees almost buckled as she did. Thurion immediately put his arm around her, supporting her.

'Get her some water,' Thurion said to the captain.

Gadas took exception to this… this… barbarian who was trying to give him orders. He was the princess's protector after all. He ignored Thurion completely.

'Please, Your Highness, take my hand. I will help you back to the carriages; you must rest for a while.'

'Thank you, Captain, but I think…' Celene looked up at Thurion questioningly.

'Thurion,' the barbarian replied, understanding

the angel's side-long glance.

'I think Thurion can help me.'

Gadas looked outraged but a dangerous look from the blood-stained barbarian silenced him. He was, after all, in no condition to take on the barbarian who had just slain several harpies single-handed.

Thurion helped Celene over to what remained of her caravan; a few supply wagons and a couple of carriages originally set aside for the guards. Water was brought up and after a few minutes Celene began to recover. Thurion collected his belongings from where he had stowed them and dressed the worst of Celene's cuts, ignoring the outraged looks of her guards. Her wounds were superficial and looked far worse than they really were. Just as he was binding a gash on Celene's left shin Captain Gadas drew his sword, holding it threateningly at Thurion's back.

'Put it away,' Thurion warned without even turning around.

'Captain, please!' Celene protested.

'Your Highness, this is an outrage! You know as well as I do that none but the priesthood may directly attend the Children of Ios. I have already made far more concessions during this trip than I would ordinarily care to. This is too much! This... this savage has overstepped the bounds of propriety!' the captain snapped, his sword quivering in his hand.

Thurion finished dressing Celene's leg and turned his face up to her.

'I've finished, Your Highness. You'll be fine, so long as you keep the dressing clean.' Despite his still savage appearance, Thurion's tone was calm and kind. She wanted to tell him that she could heal her wounds herself, but something made her hold back; she was rather liking the attention this strange warrior was lavishing on her. He stood and turned to face Gadas.

'Now, *Captain*, I believe you had a problem with me tending your princess's wounds?' he asked, loosening his hand-axe and hatchet from their belt loops.

Captain Gadas was a brave man who had proved his mettle many-a-time in battle, but this barbarian gave him cause to stop and think; despite having sustained a head wound that was bleeding profusely under his helmet, he was still prepared to fight and was squaring up to him. The slash on Gadas' leg was bleeding badly and he was finding it difficult to stand. Picking a fight with a much younger and fitter opponent who had already shown great courage and skill would only end in serious injury or, worse still, death.

If that happened, who would look after the princess? I would have failed in my duty! Thinking about it that way, Gadas relented a little and decided to stamp his authority over the situation.

'None but the priesthood may attend the royal family,' he stated firmly. Thurion looked around briefly, never once taking his hands from his axes.

'I see no priests, Captain, and your men are busy seeing to their own dead and wounded. Why shouldn't I tend the princess?' Thurion asked, honestly bemused.

The captain paused for a moment, searching for some precedent that would support his argument. Suddenly feeling overwhelmingly tired his shoulders slumped and he lowered his sword.

'It is simply the way that it has always been. Our society is built on clearly defined structures and hierarchies. We are a *civilised* people and order is central to our way of life. The last few days have not been easy, however. I apologise if I have been short with you. Some little time ago I commanded two-dozen soldiers and a dozen of the princess's priesthood. Now ...' the captain turned and looked about him where his men were dressing their wounds, '... about half of my men are dead along with every priest I set off with.'

'How far are you from safety?' Thurion asked, letting go of his axes and instead thrusting his thumbs into his belt.

'The border with Varga-Shemshah is close. We should be safe once we cross it.'

'*Should* be safe, Captain? You don't sound very sure. Now that our paths have crossed, I think that our fates are entwined. I will travel with Princess...err'

'Princess Celene Nemeth, daughter of High Prince Raparké Nemeth,' Gadas informed him. Thurion looked somewhat nonplussed upon hearing Celene's official title.

'I will travel with her and keep her safe until either she is safely home or our paths diverge,' he announced.

The captain, hearing in Thurion's words a slight that was not intended, decided that he had taken about all he cared to from this arrogant savage.

'She is *quite safe*. Your help, although appreciated, is no longer required,' he snapped.

'Look at your men, captain, how many do you now command? Ten? Twelve? And how many are uninjured? You do not have the strength to repel another attack. From where I'm standing if it had not been for my intervention, you, your men and the princess would likely all have been killed. *I* will see the princess safely home. I assume that is where you're going?' Thurion replied in a tone that indicated that the matter was not up for discussion.

Gadas was about to argue the matter when Thurion very deliberately removed his thumbs from his belt and replaced them on the heads of his axes.

'Are you going to argue with me, captain?' he asked, his voice a betraying a fraying patience.

Gadas felt the effect of the adrenalin from the battle starting to wear off, and the wound on his leg suddenly becoming very painful. Reluctantly, he relented once again.

'We are heading north to Shemshah. I would expect us to be safe once we cross the border. From there we will turn south-east and head for home,' he said, before limping off to the back of the caravan.

Celene had been listening to the exchange in silence and watched as her captain stalked off. She made a mental note to heal the wounded before they moved off again. The young princess breathed in deeply through clenched teeth as Thurion removed his helmet. A couple of strikes had found their way under his helmet's mail and the lower half of his face was a mess of matted hair and blood.

'It's probably not as bad as it looks,' he said, trying to reassure the young angel. He then proceeded to remove the rest of his equipment and armour until he was standing in just his cotton trousers. Taking a fresh bowl of water from the caravan's supplies he proceeded to wash himself, checking for cuts and abrasions as he did so.

Meanwhile the captain and his men either tried to ignore this uncivilised stranger or busied themselves preparing what remained of the caravan for departure. They quickly converted one of the soldiers' wagons into a makeshift caravan for the young princess.

'You must forgive Captain Gadas, Thurion,' Celene said. 'He is simply trying to discharge his duties as best he can. He means well, but we have been through so much and lost a lot of friends in the last few days; he is under a lot of pressure. Please try to understand,' she asked smiling, her tone gentle.

'I will try,' he replied.

'He is grateful, the captain. He just finds it difficult to acknowledge the acts of a...' Celene trailed off, embarrassed.

'Barbarian?' Thurion suggested.

'Yes, and a foreigner. I am sorry, but that is simply how it is.'

Thurion did not look up. *Were these people all so conceited? Was Captain Gadas a typical example?*

'We are not all like the captain,' Celene said, as if in response to his unvoiced question, 'I am both grateful for what you have already done and would be honoured if you would accompany me. Would you see me safely home?'

'Thank you. I will,' Thurion replied. *Perhaps there is more here than I have yet seen.*

'You have not yet told me your full name.'

'Yes, I have. My name is Thurion.'

'Well, Thurion, by now I would expect the good captain to be making final preparations for our departure. Please stow your belongings anywhere you can find space.'

Thurion made to collect his belongings and look for a stowage space amongst the wagons when Celene stopped him.

'Oh, and Thurion, when we reach Varga-Shemshah I would like to be able to introduce my saviour to the High Prince, but I know nothing about him at the moment. Would you tell me your story as we travel north?' she asked, her smile melting what reservations Thurion still held regarding this princess and her people.

He thought about it. These might be a strange people with what he feared to be an overly complex society, but telling tales and sagas was something that the people of the north were naturally adept at.

Smiling, he replied, 'I would be pleased to, Your Highness.'

Chapter 32

After stowing his few belongings in one of the supply wagons, Thurion returned to the carriage that had been set aside for Celene. Ignoring the two guards at the door Thurion knocked.

'Enter.'

'You wished to hear my tale, Princess?' Thurion asked as he entered, closing the door behind him.

'Thank you, I would like that very much,' the young angel replied, catching his eye, 'Please take a seat, there's no need to stand on ceremony.'

Thurion looked around the carriage, and finding a spot to his liking, sat down on the floor with his back resting against the carriage wall. A look of surprise crossed Celene's face which she failed to conceal.

'I am perfectly comfortable, Your Highness, I assure you,' Thurion replied, concealing his humour far better than Celene had contained her surprise. 'I will start at the beginning if you have no objection? Have you eaten?'

'I have no objection at all, Thurion. And no, I have not eaten; considering the current circumstances I am content to eat at the same time as the captain and his men. He will inform me when the evening meal is ready.'

Thurion was somewhat confused by the inference that in other circumstances she would have eaten at a separate time to everyone else. He let the issue pass however, preferring to begin his saga.

He began by explaining to Celene a little about the practices and beliefs of his people. This background given, he began his saga at his coming of age. He was just about to re-tell the story of his first attack on a slave train when a knock at the carriage door interrupted him.

'Come in,' Celene responded. The carriage door opened and a guard thrust his head into the candlelit interior.

'Please forgive my interruption, Your Highness, but the captain wishes me to report that the evening meal is ready. Should I have it brought in?'

'Thank you, I will take dinner whenever it is ready,' she replied, dismissing the guard with a slight wave of her hand.

'If you are eating now I'll go and prepare my own meal, Your Highness, if it's all the same with you?' Thurion asked, still not entirely sure how to address the beautiful angelic princess.

'If I am honest, I am not sure whether the captain will have made provision for you or not. Please, feel free to go and prepare your meal but I would welcome your company whilst I dine,' Celene answered, her tone was courtly but a thread of shyness ran through it.

'As you wish. I will return,' Thurion replied slightly more gruffly than he had intended.

Rising, he left the carriage with little ceremony and made his way to the storage wagon where he had left his baggage. He did not even ask whether Captain Gadas had ordered him to be provided for, preferring rather to support himself. He had found little time to hunt in the last day or two, and so his dinner consisted of some dried meat he had prepared some days previously and the last of his supply of dried vegetables boiled together in a broth, to which he added some edible herbs and roots that he found growing nearby. The men of the caravan guard proved more open than their captain, and so, consequently he found that he did not need his own fire to cook on that night. He was, however, as good as his word, and after thanking the guards for the use of their fire, he returned to Celene's carriage.

He found Celene already dining on what appeared to be a much larger portion of the stew that he had seen the other guards eating earlier.

'Please, sit and eat,' Celene said invitingly as he entered.

'Thank you,' he replied as he once again settled onto the floor, then pulled a finely carved wooden spoon from his belt.

'You made that yourself?' Celene asked, gesturing to his spoon.

'Yes, several days ago, why?'

'It's beautiful.'

'It's functional,' the barbarian replied, 'I make things as I need them.'

Celene was about to say something but continued eating her meal instead, her cheeks flushing ever so slightly as she did so.

'I can show you how, if you like, when we have a little time,' Thurion offered.

'Thank you, perhaps after we have crossed the border?'

'Of course. Now, I believe I promised to continue my tale?'

Celene smiled, 'You did.'

Taking this as an invitation to move closer, he edged nearer to her and continued his tale from where he had left off. He regaled her with his attack on the slave train and his journey to the glacier. It was late by the time Thurion had finished his tale for he told it like a true Northman – grandly.

'Where will you sleep tonight?' Celene asked as he opened the carriage door and stepped out into the night.

'Wherever I can Your Highness, I may even enjoy the comfort of a supply wagon given that your dear captain is undoubtedly asleep by now!' Thurion joked as he left.

The comfort of a wagon? Oh, the poor man. Truly he is a fine man, very fine if the truth be told, but how he must have suffered to think of a wagon as comfort... Celene reflected as she climbed into her comfortable, warm bed and blew out the last remaining candle.

Thurion woke a little before dawn and after performing his morning rituals gathered up his hunting kit and stalked off into the nearby countryside.

'I don't know, Your Highness, when my men and I awoke this morning he was gone. I mean, most of his baggage is still here but he's disappeared,' Captain Gadas explained to Celene with barely concealed contentment. Citing their desperate plight as reason enough, the captain saw that their camp was struck as soon as was practicable, and ordered the mid-morning meal be taken on the march. Although it was true that he owed a great deal to the strange savage from the wilderness, the captain was glad to be rid of him, at least for the moment.

Celene remained in her carriage that morning, reflecting on what she had learned the night before about her barbaric saviour and hoping that he would return.

Thurion smiled to himself as he watched Captain Gadas try to explain his disappearance to the princess. He had concealed himself behind a clump of bushes and was watching them, like a lion watches the herd. Whatever the captain or the princess thought, the truth of the matter was simple: he had almost run out of supplies and had needed to go hunting. By the time the captain was rising he had already laid his traps and was going about gathering whatever edible vegetable matter he could find. In a little while he would go back and check his snares and traps before returning to the caravan.

The road the caravan was following wound round a hill which gave Thurion all the opportunity he needed to catch it up. Climbing straight over the hill he intercepted the princess's caravan, startling several of the soldiers as he appeared from out of the undergrowth onto the road.

'Don't worry, friends, I was getting a little short on supplies that's all!' Thurion announced, gesturing with a brace of small animals. The guards' surprise and alarm quickly turned to relief when the news of his return became known. Captain Gadas received the news as neutrally as he could, whilst Celene made her way immediately to the supply wagons where she found Thurion preparing his morning's kills.

'I'd stay to that side if I were you, Your Highness,' Thurion advised her, as he hurled a rabbit's gastrointestinal tract over the side of the wagon and into the bushes. The young princess looked on, horrified, but quickly took his advice and crossed to the other side of the wagon. Thurion stopped to help her up. She sat down and looked at what he was doing with a mix of admiration and revulsion.

'I'm sorry,' she replied quickly realising what she had done.

'You've never prepared your own meal before?' he asked her.

'Emm... no,' she admitted.

'It's not always this involved,' he explained as he carefully sliced the rabbit meat into thin strips with a stone knife, and laid them out to dry in the sun on the face of a spare shield. 'I need to dry it in order for it to keep,' he explained. Celene watched him work with a new-found respect, almost awestruck as he prepared and preserved his morning's catch. *There is far more to this man than meets the eye.*

Chapter 33

Captain Gadas marched up to the gatehouse that marked the border between Leznar-Carchum and Varga-Shemshah ahead of the caravan. The princess had healed his wound once she had felt strong enough to do so. The gatehouse was a small, unfortified structure that was home to a handful of border guards. The gate itself was open and looked like it had been for some time, given the weeds that were growing around it.

'Welcome to Varga-Shemshah!' a guard called out from the gatehouse. Gadas reached the house just as the unarmed guard, dressed in uniform but no armour, stepped out onto the road.

'I am Captain Gadas, Commander of the caravan of Princess Celene Nemeth. I am escorting Her Highness as she undertakes her tour of the Principalities of Life. We are not due to cross into your principality for another fortnight, however we stand at your border asking for sanctuary,' the battle-weary captain announced.

'Er...' the guard began, 'Yes, Captain, of course. What's happened?' his face paled as he saw the battered caravan roll into view round the bend in the road. It was obvious that all the Royal Guards in the escort had seen action recently. They were clearly tired and their grim demeanour lifted slightly at the sight of the friendly border.

'We were attacked by harpies outside Carchum, but we managed to fight them off. I intend

339

to make my report directly to your High Prince. I would ask you to send immediate word to Shemshah, announcing our imminent arrival.'

The guard faltered before regaining his composure. He was clearly not used to having to deal with situations like this.

'Yes, Captain, I will send word at once. Do you require aid? We have little here but what we have, you are welcome to,' the young man offered.

'Thank you, but no, I intend to keep moving and make for Shemshah with all speed.'

'In that case I will send word at once.' He saluted the captain before rushing back inside the gatehouse. A minute or two later a door to the rear of the house could be heard opening and closing. Some minutes later a mounted guard appeared from behind the building and galloped along the road towards the capital city.

The journey from the border to Shemshah was mercifully quiet, and within a week Captain Gadas was leading the caravan through the opalescent gates of Varga-Shemshah's beautiful capital. A wave of recognition came over Thurion as he beheld the walls of the principality's capital city. This was the city that he had seen attacked by the army of the dead some months back. He had given the city a wide berth then and had therefore not fully appreciated its grandeur. Even the vast tented city of the merchants was nothing compared to this. Indeed, he found himself gawking at his surroundings as much as its inhabitants gawked at the savage stranger that walked through their streets, apparently in the company of foreign royalty.

There were a LOT of people in this city. Truly Hayesh Et-Kun had been a buzzing metropolis, so full of people it was a wonder they didn't keep falling over each other. But here, here it was different; they were all looking at him – all of them. Faces stared from the roadside, from windows and doorways, and all of them were fixed on the battered caravan that wound its way through their city.

Very soon, awe and wonder gave way to suspicion and wariness. Many voices bubbled through the crowd, and Thurion found that his years of hunting in the wilds had attuned his ears such that he could pick out single voices from amongst the hubbub. He heard people saying things like 'Whatever happened to them?', and 'Look at him! What's a savage doing in the company of royalty?' Most of the comments made it clear that they did not like the look of the barbarian. Keeping his hands firmly on the heads of the axes hanging from his belt, Thurion returned their disapproving looks with glares of his own. The crowds made him very uncomfortable and he stayed close to Celene's carriage.

After half an hour, but what seemed like an eternity to Thurion, the caravan eventually passed through the imposing white stone gate house of the Shahrim, the Varga Royal Palace. An impressive guard of honour had been assembled to greet Celene and her attendants. Ranks of pristinely turned out soldiery lined the sides of the square into which they now entered. At the far end of the square, members of the royal family assembled to greet their impromptu royal guest. As the caravan came to a halt, Celene stepped out and walked to where her captain had stopped. A man wearing highly decorated armour marched out to meet them. He stopped in front of Celene, came smartly to attention and bowed low. He tried not to show his horror at her appearance, but could not conceal it entirely. She looked like she had slept in her dress for days, her wings were dishevelled and her hands and arms were covered in scabs.

'I am Sirnean, Seneschal of Shemshah and High Priest of the Varga Order of Life. On behalf of High Prince Lautos Varga and his wife High Princess Boreana Varga, I bid you welcome to Shemshah and the Royal Palace of the House of Varga. If there is anything I can do to make your stay more comfortable, please let me know.'

'I thank you for your kind words, Seneschal Sirnean. I am pleased to be here, if somewhat a little earlier than expected,' Celene responded. 'I have one immediate request, Seneschal – if you don't mind.' Turning to Gadas, she beckoned him to her. Gadas took one pace forward. 'This is Captain Gadas of the Royal Guard of Nemeth Sharrayah, commander of my caravan.'

Gadas saluted smartly, the Seneschal offered his hand and Gadas shook it firmly.

'Captain, welcome to Varga Shemshah. We are all glad that you are here.'

Gadas thanked him for his kind welcome, but before he could say anything else Celene interjected.

'Seneschal Sirnean, we were attacked outside Carchum. I would ask that you make him and his men as comfortable as possible; they have endured a lot in recent days.'

Sirnean responded immediately and decisively, 'I will see that they are well-billeted, that the wounded are taken care of and that a hot meal is prepared immediately, Your Highness.'

The seneschal motioned to a couple of the assembled soldiers and ordered them to fetch stretchers, summon the priesthood's healers, and then to guide Captain Gadas and his men to the palace's barracks. An officer with an enormous handlebar moustache came marching up to the group. He stopped and saluted in the direction of Celene.

'Ah, General Cordobas, this is Her Royal Highness Princess Celene of Nemeth Sharrayah...' Seneschal Sirnean said.

Celene didn't know what to do; she had never met a general formally before. She didn't know whether to salute back, curtsy or shake his hand. *If only Arité were here – she would know what to do.* She opted to smile at the general, and just said, 'Pleased to meet you, General.'

Sirnean continued, '...and this Captain Gadas of—' before he could finish General Cordobas had stepped forward and offered his hand to Gadas.

'There's no need, Sirnean. Gadas and I are old friends – we've fought together for heaven's sake. Gadas! How are you, man? I heard you ran into some trouble outside of Carchum but you seem to have come out of it alright!'

Gadas saluted and appeared to relax, 'General, good to see you! Yes, we did but it would not be appropriate for me to divulge any details before speaking with your High Prince. I can say that Leznar-Carchum is not a place that I would want to visit again.'

A small party of soldiers and white-robed priests came running at the double to the caravan. Captain Gadas and General Cordobas turned to meet them and the general issued orders for the priests to attend to the wounded, and for the carriages and wagons to be driven round to the barracks. The two officers bowed to Celene before turning and walking in front of the lead carriage when Gadas noticed the general fix his gaze on Thurion as he passed his eyes over the captain's tired men. A question passed unspoken from Cordobas to Gadas.

'A wandering barbarian; normally I would have nothing to do with such people. This one, however, has earned the respect of my men and, seemingly, the favour of the princess,' Gadas admitted with barely concealed contempt.

'I see... very well. I will see that he is watched closely; I doubt he understands the nuances of civilised living,' the general replied.

As they moved away Seneschal Sirnean tried to usher Celene in the direction of the palace entrance, 'Your Highness, plea... the Royal Family is waiting to see you.'

Thurion did not follow the captain and his men but instead stayed where he was at the rear of Celene's carriage. He didn't do this out of fear for the princess's safety; he was sure that she would be safe here, but rather because where he found himself now was so utterly alien to him.

As the captain and his men marched out of the square, Celene was about to walk across to the palace steps when she stopped and noticed the uncertainty on Thurion's face.

'My dear Thurion, I did not see a single trace of consternation in you during all our time in Leznar-Carchum but now, here in Varga-Shemshah, where we are perfectly safe, you look troubled.' Her tone was light, almost playful and so Thurion took no offence at the jibe.

'If our positions were reversed, Princess, how would you feel?' Thurion asked.

'I understand, just follow me. Allow me to

introduce you and... trust me!' she said with a wry little smile.

Thurion did as he was bade and, placing his trust in the young princess, followed her across the square to the waiting royal party. The High Prince was the first to greet her.

'Princess Celene Nemeth, it is so good to see you safe! We received word from the border a few days ago that you had been attacked in Leznar-Carchum. I was questioning this report before I saw the state of your guards, not to mention the rest of your caravan,' High Prince Lautos said, his dark-brown hair catching in the slight breeze.

'I am afraid to report that it is all true, Your Highness. Indeed, it is doubtful whether I would be here at all if a saviour had not appeared out of nowhere and delivered me,' Celene began, motioning to Thurion.

Thurion immediately recognised the High Prince as the angelic leader who had vanquished the un-dead commander in single combat during the battle he had witnessed. High Prince Lautos eyed Thurion. He appeared surprised but regained his composure quickly.

'In that case...'

'Thurion,' Thurion answered. Giving no clue that he had seen the High Prince before.

'In that case, Thurion, I am as indebted to you as Princess Celene is. Her gratitude is my gratitude,' he announced grandly, though, Thurion thought, with the slightest hint of insincerity. 'Please, allow me to introduce my devoted wife, Boreana, and my youngest daughter, Lemadia. I must apologise that my three sons are not here; they are currently involved in state affairs. Come, you both look travel-weary.' With a grand gesture he turned about and led the assembly up the stairs and into the royal palace.

The palace was as grand on the inside as it was on the outside. The floor was polished marble overlaid with richly coloured rugs. Fires burned in ornate sconces along the walls illuminating the finely worked white stone walls. Thurion walked past ornately carved furniture made from a warm red-brown wood.

'Princess Celene, Thurion, please follow Sirnean, he will escort you to the guest quarters. Dinner will be served at sunset, I will send word an hour beforehand but until then please make yourselves at home and relax,' High Prince Lautos said before nodding to his seneschal and excusing himself.

Sirnean led Celene and Thurion along a number of richly decorated corridors until they reached the guest quarters in one of the many wings of the palace. Celene's quarters were grand, as befitting someone of her standing. Thurion was led to an adjacent set of rooms. Though he didn't know it, these rooms had originally been designed as lodgings for the servants and maids of whoever was currently residing in the adjacent suite. Sirnean had offered to provide Celene with some maids from the household staff but she had declined; she still hadn't gotten over the horrific murder of Arité and the rest of her maids. Not being privy to her situation, Sirnean had taken offence to Celene's declining of his offer and had retaliated by lodging Thurion in the adjoining servants' quarters. It was a puerile action but he felt slighted and didn't believe that either Celene or her attendant savage would notice.

Celene did find out however, but elected not

to make an issue of it; she was exhausted and was quite simply content to be safe and comfortable for the first time in weeks.

Thurion had never seen rooms so large or so lavishly furnished. His quarters comprised of two rooms. The first was a large, spacious lounge with several comfortable chairs, a large round table and an ornate fireplace. A second door led into Celene's quarters. The second room, the bedroom, was just as lavishly set out with a large set of double doors that opened out onto a balcony. The room itself contained three two-tiered beds, several cupboards and washing facilities he had never seen before. He found that if he turned the metal device above the wall-mounted bowl, water flowed freely out. He had no idea that these taps were simply fed by a large water butt in the palace's attic space that was filled daily by the palace servants.

Celene set about making herself comfortable. She ran herself a bath and did her best to allow the past week's cares and worries melt away. By the time she had finished her ablutions she was once again the very epitome of an angelic princess.

Make yourselves at home and relax. Thurion recalled the words of his host and began to unpack his belongings. Having laid them out on the large table in the lounge area, he began meticulously cleaning what was dirty and sharpening what had become blunt. After this he cleaned and repaired his armour, working on it until it was as good as new.

Standing up, he stretched, letting out a contented sigh as he put down the oiling cloth for the last time. Walking into the bedroom he lit a couple of candles to banish the encroaching gloom of evening before opening the balcony doors and breathing deeply of the fresh, cool evening air. A knock pulled him from his trance-like state of relaxation. He returned to the living room and was about to open the door leading out into the corridor when the knock sounded again. It was coming from the small door that led into the adjacent chambers. He turned, crossed the room and opened the door.

'I have just been informed that dinner will be in an hour's time,' Celene announced. Thurion was too taken aback to reply. He had never seen her in all her regal finery before. If he was honest he hadn't ever thought that it was possible for someone to look so beautiful.

'Are you alright, Thurion? What's the matter?' she asked.

'Er, nothing, Your Highness, nothing at all,' Thurion blurted, covering his shock badly.

'You heard what I said though? That dinner is in an hour?'

'Yes, an hour,' he paused and looked down at his grubby, oil-marked hands, 'I'd better try to clean myself up a bit, hadn't I, Your Highness? I won't be able to stand up to you though,' he replied, casting his eyes to the floor.

'My dear Thurion, all you need do is clean yourself up as best you can. I would not have you compare yourself to me, you're a different person with strengths I couldn't begin to understand,' she replied.

'But, I am to accompany you to dinner, am I not?'

'Yes...'

'And you're so beautiful...' Thurion tried to vocalise the conflict that was raging inside of him but he failed to find the words. Celene understood well enough to blush.

'I have presented myself as well as I can, all I am asking is that you do the same. It would be an honour to be accompanied to dinner by your good self, arrayed in all your finery. I see that you have already returned it to a pristine finish,' she observed, looking over his shoulder to where he had arrayed his cleaned and repaired equipment on the large table.

'I will do my best, Your Highness, you may believe me,' he replied. With that, he closed the door and went about his task.

A search of his apartments revealed a large metal bath, which he filled with water from the room's taps, and some cloths and brushes that he could use to scrub the trail dust off with. The water wasn't as fresh as some of the mountain streams he had washed in – nor as refreshing – but it would suffice.

Almost an hour later Thurion was standing on the balcony feeling fresh and clean, adorned in his full war gear. His long handed axe and hatchet hung from his belt but he had decided not to strap on his great axe; he did not expect to need it at a royal dinner. *Besides, if I do need to persuade someone, I'm sure these will suffice,* he thought with a smile as he rested his hands on the heads of his smaller weapons. Hearing a knock at his chamber's main door he turned, leaving the balcony doors wide open. He picked up his helmet, tucked it under his arm and made to leave for dinner. As he opened the door into the corridor he felt suddenly nervous.

Celene took a small breath as Thurion opened the door and stepped out into the corridor.

'You look so... noble,' she complimented, allowing her blonde hair to fall from behind her ears as she turned to conceal a reddening in her cheeks that she felt… again.

'Thank you, Princess, you reassure me,' Thurion admitted.

The steward that had been sent to collect the pair of guests for dinner, did his best to conceal any feeling of surprise he felt at what he saw passing between the two of them.

'Now, please take my arm, Thurion, tonight you are my escort,' she said smiling. Thurion had not come across the term before but did as he was told and escorted the radiant young princess to dinner. As the steward led them through the corridors of the palace to the grand dining hall, Thurion, surprisingly, felt his anxiety and nervousness dissipate. Whether this was the result of a growing determination to present himself with dignity and honour – and to not be found wanting – or the calming aura that the princess seemed to exude, he couldn't be sure. As they reached the great hall, he concluded that it was probably a combination of the two.

Chapter 34

The grand dining hall was vast. An enormous dining table occupied fully one half of the great room. Roaring fires burned in several large fireplaces and ornate candelabras holding more candles than Thurion cared to count, illuminated all but the darkest corners. As Thurion led Celene into the hall, he could see a seemingly endless procession of servants loading the dining table with a multitude of hot and cold dishes. The High Prince's guests, dressed in their finery, mingled in the other half of the room, sipping wine and eating canapés whilst they waited for the servants to finish.

As Thurion and Celene crossed the threshold into the hall a steward announced them.

'Princess Celene Nemeth and escort!'

Thurion looked round at the steward, somewhat startled. The steward, in turn, took an involuntary step back.

'It's customary to be announced,' Celene whispered, 'Just in case someone doesn't know who we are,' she added with a chuckle. 'Now, head straight into the hall and follow my lead.'

As Thurion, with Celene on his arm, slowly made his way towards the milling crowd a steward approached them to serve sparkling wine and a small mushroom-based canapé. Thurion, following Celene's lead, let go of her arm and accepted both. The nomadic Northman tried to adopt an air of grace and elegance, but after trying and failing to emulate those around him, he decided that it simply was not who he was.

'Just be yourself,' Celene whispered as a group of smartly presented dignitaries approached.

An older member of the group got to them first and introduced himself.

'Princess Celene, please allow me to convey what an honour it is to finally meet you. I am Councillor Durane.'

'It is a pleasure to meet you, Councillor. May I present Thurion?' she motioned to Thurion who bowed respectfully in response. Councillor Durane eyed Thurion with suspicion, who returned his gaze evenly. 'I owe a great deal to this man, Councillor,' Celene declared, in an attempt to defuse the situation.

'Then you are welcome, Thurion... ?' One of Councillor Durane's colleagues interjected, understanding Celene's intentions immediately.

'Just Thurion,' Thurion replied accepting another glass of wine and a canapé from a passing steward.

'Indeed!' Councillor Durane acquiesced, 'you appear to be a long way from home, Thurion, what brings you to Varga-Shemshah?'

'I am a nomad, Councillor, the wild spirits are my gods and the wilderness is my home. I was raised in Vorde, a village a long way to the west,' he explained.

Councillor Durane's face went blank; he had clearly failed to understand a word Thurion had just said.

Another of Durane's colleagues interrupted to rescue the councillor, 'I believe Vorde is one of the settlements of the Northmen that lays to the west of the Northern Islands, am I right, Thurion?'

'Aye, that you are, sir,' Thurion confirmed, before eating his canapé whole, draining his wine glass and returning the empty vessel to a passing steward. The assembled councillors tried, with varying degrees of success to hide their surprise at this show of poor manners. Celene tried in vain to suppress an amused smile. Thurion didn't notice a thing.

'Princess Celene, how wonderful to see you refreshed and radiant!' High Prince Lautos said as he glided through his gaggle of councillors, took Celene's hand and gently kissed it.

'Thurion, welcome,' he added.

'High Prince Lautos, you honour me with your presence. I thank you for your welcome and hospitality,' Celene replied.

'High Prince,' Thurion replied simply, bowing.

High Prince Lautos drew Celene a little closer and lowered his voice. 'You must forgive me, my dear, but normally, I would not discuss matters of state at an informal dinner such as this, however, your current situation is somewhat singular, and there is a question of a matter of diplomacy. If you don't mind?'

'If the situation warrants it, then please feel free, Your Highness,' Celene agreed.

'Your captain has apprised me of the events in Leznar-Carchum and what brought you here in your current circumstances. From what I understand dark forces have taken control of the region, and the two unprovoked attacks were clearly directed against yourself and the priesthood, by extension, this aggression was aimed at the Children and followers of our Great Mother. We, ourselves, have frequently had to repel attacks from the Plains of the Dead, but this was an assault on a member of the angelic caste and, as such, cannot go unpunished. However, I cannot take punitive action against Leznar-Carchum before your father has had an opportunity to act. It is protocol, you *understand* my situation?' he asked.

'I do, High Prince.' Though she wasn't privy to the official workings of her father's principality, she knew enough to realise something of the situation her host now found himself in.

'Thank you, I knew you would. With regard to your tour, I realise that the situation is somewhat delicate, but if you choose to continue with it, I am afraid that you will have to wait for my sons to return to Shemshah, and that may not be for some weeks. Of course, you are welcome to stay here in Shemshah for as long as you wish.'

'Truly, I would like to stay for a little while, what I have seen of your principality is beautiful. If I am honest, however, my greatest desire is to get back home to my father and the rest of my family,' she admitted.

High Prince Lautos placed a hand on her shoulder. 'I understand, Your Highness, I do. After such a horrendous experience, I agree that home and family are the best therapies for a speedy recovery. I have conscripted wagon-makers and wheelwrights and I am having your carriages repaired as we speak. They will be ready by tomorrow morning. Please, enjoy this evening's entertainment at least, and if you wish to begin your homeward journey tomorrow I will not take offence.'

'Your words lift my heart, High Prince; I had been concerned that I might have appeared ungrateful had I left for home too soon after arriving.'

'I am glad to see you so uplifted, Your Highness.' High Prince Lautos turned to regard the huge dining table that had by now been fully laid. 'Come,' he said, 'dinner is served.'

Thurion followed Celene as the High Prince escorted her to her seat. As far as he understood this, admittedly, rather complex arrangement, *he* was supposed to have escorted the princess to her seat. He was, however, wise enough to say nothing and let the High Prince act as he saw fit. Thurion may not have been *civilised* as these people understood the term, but he did understand respect and manners; something that seemed to take second place to protocol and unnecessarily complex social formalities here. Taking an empty seat next to Celene, Thurion found himself sitting amongst several high-ranking councillors and a few other assorted guests. In any other setting he would have felt cripplingly out of place.

Surely this *dinner* would be fundamentally no different from the feasts he had experienced as a child?

Drawing on his childhood memories Thurion prepared himself for what was to unfold.

Chapter 35

The confidence Thurion drew from his memories of feasts in Vorde faded, as his gaze passed from the plethora of dishes arrayed along the table to his place setting. He was used to having a wide, shallow bowl, a spoon, a knife and a goblet. After all what more could you need? In front of him he found a stack of shallow plates topped with a small bowl surrounded by a half a dozen sets of cutlery and four glasses of differing sizes. *What possible reason could anyone have for needing this much crockery?!*

'Just start from the outside and work your way in!' Celene whispered in his ear with a light laugh.

'Your Highness, are you making fun of me?' Thurion asked lightly, knowing that she was not.

'Of course not, Thurion. I am just amused – given what you have shown me over the past few weeks.'

'How so?' he asked, leaning back as a servant filled the small bowl atop his stack of plates with a cold soup.

'As far as I have been led to believe, you have survived out in the wilderness with a knife, a bowl and a spoon; all of which you have made yourself!'

'Yes?' Thurion replied, at first not grasping the point she was making. Then, as he picked up a spoon, only to put it down again and pick up the smallest one in response to a pointed look from the young princess, he understood and began to laugh.

A number of the conversations that were

going on nearby fell silent as Thurion's laugh rang out.

'Your friend is somewhat raucous, is he not?' A lavishly presented old man commented to Celene. The young princess did not immediately know quite what to say.

'It's my experience...' Thurion began, taking a spoonful of soup as he did so, '...that you have only two choices in life: laugh or cry.' He began to eat as the old man considered Thurion's words.

'Very profound, sir,' a middle-aged woman in the white robes of the priesthood commented from across the table. Thurion nodded. Swallowing, a strange look crossed his face and he turned to Celene.

'It's cold.'

'It's supposed to be cold,' she replied quietly, trying not to be overheard. A couple of muffled laughs indicated that she had not succeeded.

As the stewards came round offering wine, the soup bowls were cleared away and the meal began in earnest. Not wanting to show the princess up again with his ignorance of her customs, Thurion sipped his wine whilst he watched how those around him served themselves. It seemed that the different-sized plates were intended for different types of food. After looking around for a couple of minutes he decided he had understood enough of the protocol to serve himself.

For the most part, Thurion managed to serve himself without drawing too many disapproving looks from the other guests. By the time he had navigated the minefield of serving the correct food onto the correct plates, he realised that he had no idea which of the sets of cutlery to use to eat what; it seemed that certain cutlery was used to eat certain foods so that a person might use as many as four sets of cutlery at a time. Sighing in resignation Thurion picked up the inner-most knife and fork and decided to use them for everything.

Immediately, looks of disapproval were directed at him. Subtly he glanced over to Celene, but she was in conversation with Lemadia, High Prince Lautos' daughter. Feeling rather tired of the condescending attitudes of those around him, he took a bread roll from a basket without using the silver tongs lying next to it, then turned to a young man in a sharply pressed military uniform, who was staring at him in disbelief.

'Can I help you?' he asked, trying to keep his tone neutral but failing to repress a slight slight growl that accompanied it.

'You have no manners, sir! Do you not know how to act with decency?!'

'Of course I do, *boy*; Honour your gods, your family and your elders. All else is secondary. Why do you ask?' he replied, deliberately baiting the impetuous young man.

'You, sir, are a barbarian! You speak of honour but you shame Princess Celene by your conduct!' the young officer snapped.

Thurion calmly set down the bread roll he was holding and rose to his feet, all the while fixing the young man with a smouldering gaze.

'Dare you question my honour, *boy*?' Thurion growled. Across the room conversations fell silent, and the tension built as the young officer squirmed in his seat not wanting to back down and lose face, but at the same time realising that he had seriously underestimated this savage stranger.

A hand gently took hold of Thurion's right

hand.

'Thurion, please! He meant no offence, he is just young,' Celene implored gently.

'Yes he did, he implied that I was a man of no honour and that I had shamed you.'

'I have never met a more honourable man.' Celene gently squeezed the barbarian's hand, 'Thurion, look at me. I have never met a more honourable man than you in my life.' She turned to the young officer who was still sitting nervously in his seat, 'I owe this man my life. He is a man of nobility and honour and I would have you treat him as such. Please apologise for your rash words.' Celene fixed the man with an imperious look that would brook no arguments.

'I... I'm sorry; I spoke out of turn,' the young man stammered. The Northman's fierce gaze calmed as he looked into Celene's eyes. Eventually he sat back down.

'Learn from your mistake, lad.' Thurion offered the bowl of bread rolls to the young man who looked at it uncomprehendingly.

'Is this some strange custom of yours I am unaware of?' he asked.

'No, boy! You have drunk your fill of wine and your tongue has started wagging. If I were you I'd eat something – before you get yourself into trouble!' Thurion laughed. The burly Northman's mirth was soon accompanied by several other laughs and the tension in the room rapidly dissipated.

Although he was quick to anger, Thurion was also quick to forgive; he had heard many tales of how destructive a grudge could be. True enough, if there hadn't been a wide table between the two of them, he would have knocked enough sense into the young officer to give him something to think about for a good few months.

After that incident the other guests seemed not to notice Thurion's rather informal dining manners. The rest of the dinner proceeded without incident; indeed, as the evening progressed a few of the guests even went as far as to show a genuine interest in his background.

As the final course was being served Celene surreptitiously glanced over to Thurion, who was currently explaining to the middle-aged priestess what life was like for a nomad. *He seems to be holding his own, despite nearly attacking General Asaros's son!* she thought, smiling.

Chapter 36

ot formally conclude for quite some
the final course had been cleared
stayed and chatted, and the topic on
s was that of the Princess of Nemeth
that overcame her entourage. By the
nd Celene retired the hour was late and
exhausted. Having seen Celene to her
nurion returned to his rooms and
d down for the evening.

still warm inside despite the fact that he
balcony doors open. Granted it was
r as stifling as the dining hall had been,
ill too warm for him to sleep comfortably.
y he was forced to take his sleeping cloth
to the balcony and sleep there. Although the
mn was drawing on, it had not yet gotten cold
ough at night for him to unroll the blanket he
carried with him.

Waking with the dawn Thurion rose, washed,
and packed his belongings exactly as he had done
every morning for years. This done, he tucked a few
items into his belt and ventured out of his apartment
in search of food. The palace, he found, was a warren
of passages and halls. He wandered around until he
eventually found himself in the kitchens; admittedly
more by luck than by judgement.

'Good morning, sir. I'm sorry, we weren't
aware anyone was awake yet. If I may beg your
patience for a few minutes I will see that breakfast is

brought up to you,' a startled he said as Thurion
entered the vast kitchens.

'It looks like you're quite bu
without feeling you have to treat me lrough here
Thurion commented, gesturing to the wot man,'
a dozen servants were busy preparing where
the palace. 'Don't think me ungrateful; where
used to being waited on. In honesty it for
nervous. All I ask is a little of your t
permission to hunt on your grounds.'

'You must be Princess Celene's ε
you'll pardon my curiosity. You're welc
anything you'd like, so long as the seneschal ε
find out. We won't say anything,' the chef repli

Several of the servants who were pre
the breakfast made a show of suddenly
deliberately paying much more attention to t.
tasks.

'I thank you for your kindness, sir,' replie
Thurion, 'I wouldn't want to see you fall foul of the
seneschal on my account. I would be grateful for a
few herbs, some vegetables and access to one of your
stoves in an hour or so, depending on how charitable
the spirits are feeling this morning.'

Thurion smiled at the chef, then left through a
door at the far end of the kitchens. The chef bowed as
he passed. The door led directly into the palace's
vegetable gardens and poultry coops. The early
morning dew was still on the grass, and it did not take
Thurion long to notice rabbit tracks leading away
from some chewed cabbage. Keeping upwind he
traced the tracks back to their warrens where he
constructed and set simple snares and waited
patiently.

He returned to the kitchens about an hour later

with a brace of rabbits hanging from his belt and asked for some work space.

'You have some skill, I see,' the chef commented as Thurion began to prepare the rabbits with his seax.

'You could say I've had some experience,' Thurion commented as he expertly skinned and gutted the two carcasses. 'Normally I'd slice and dry one of these for leaner times, but somehow I don't think I'll need to whilst I'm here.' Thurion looked around the room at the kitchen staff, and asked 'Are any of you hungry?' The servants looked first at Thurion in surprise and then nodded at the chef.

'You have a generous soul, sir, thank you,' the chef said, accepting the gift.

An hour later, as Celene was breakfasting with the High Prince and his family, Thurion was sharing rabbit broth with the kitchen staff. After exchanging thanks with them, he left the kitchens and wandered the gardens, relaxing in the peace he found there. Although he desired to go in search of Celene, he guessed she would be in the company of the High Prince and his family, and he didn't have the stomach for more etiquette; last night had drained him emotionally and physically. It was a strange thing, he thought to himself as he walked through a rose garden, that he could outlast the bitterest winter and still find himself as alive as ever come the spring, but just one evening trying to simply survive a royal dinner had exhausted him.

It was Celene who found him a couple of hours later, sleeping under the low boughs of a broad-leafed tree. He opened a single eye as the princess approached, her light steps almost silent.

'I thought I might find you somewhere in the

gardens,' she said. 'You did not join me for breakfast?' she asked, puzzled.

'I rose with the dawn and breakfasted with the kitchen staff. I thought you would be entertained by the High Prince. I'm sorry, I didn't think I would be welcome at a royal breakfast,' he admitted as he stood up.

Celene's shoulders dipped almost imperceptibly.

'I admit it would have been awkward for you,' she said, 'I imagine our social structures and formalities must seem very complicated. Indeed, some of them confound me if I am honest. But they have formed the foundation of these principalities for many centuries and so they are respected. I am sorry if you are feeling out of place, but please try to understand that this is the sort of world I was brought up in, and to bring a stranger into it is very difficult.'

Thurion tried to find the words to explain how he felt and found himself staring into his hands. Gently he took Celene's hand in his.

'What do you see?' he asked.

Somewhat confused by the question, she answered 'I see a small delicate hand in a large, powerful hand. One soft, the other weathered.'

'I see two hands,' Thurion replied simply. 'Granted these hands belong to two different people and that is where my illustration breaks down, but fundamentally I see two hands. I don't wish to offend you, Your Highness, but that is not the view of many in this palace.'

'You may have spent your adult life so far in solitary wandering, Thurion, but you can be rather tactful when you put your mind to it. Did you know that?' Celene asked as she closed her hand around his and began to walk through the gardens.

'I did not. I was simply trying not to offend you. I understand that you have your ways and I have mine. I simply wish to show you the respect you deserve, not by virtue of your birth but by virtue of what I have seen in you: your kindness, your generosity...' His voice trailed off as an unusual shyness came over the usually confident Northman.

'And you have too, Thurion, you have. I must admit when I first laid eyes on you, you scared me half to death, I had never seen a show of such fury. You were like... a force of nature. I have heard some referring to my *savage* companion... and other less-becoming appellations. Do you want to know what I see?'

Thurion's silence spoke for him.

'If you are a savage, then you are a noble, honourable savage. You are a very complex man, Thurion. Do you know why I was touring the principalities?'

'No.'

'I have come of age. I am now able to sit at court with my father, my mother, and my brothers. It is customary, upon coming of age, to tour the principalities, both to officially introduce yourself to the other ruling families and also to...'

'... choose a husband?' Thurion asked, finishing Celene's sentence for her.

'That's one way of putting it, yes,' she admitted.

'And have you found yourself a suitably noble prince?' Thurion asked, the slightest note of humour in his voice.

'Are you teasing me?'

'Would I?'

'My customs then?'

365

'I wouldn't dare,' Thurion responded deadpan.

'No, no I have not *found a husband yet*. I have met some charming princes but I have not *found a husband*,' she repeated, her tone light. For some reason the image of Prince Asmos Dra entered her mind. She shook her head, dismissing the image.

'Are you expected to select a prince before you return home?'

'No, not immediately. It is customary for a princess to be wed within a few years of her coming of age, however.'

Thurion was silent as he tried to understand this strange, formal people.

'May I speak plainly, Thurion?' Celene asked after they had been strolling for a little while in silence.

'Certainly, Your Highness. Please, always speak plainly, it leaves less room for misinterpretation.'

'Yes, of course, thank you.' She paused and composed herself, 'I would like very much to get to know you more.'

Thurion would have teased her for blushing so much had he not felt a tell-tale warming of his own cheeks.

'Thank you,' was his only reply.

As they strolled back towards the palace Captain Gadas marched up to them.

'Princess… you have not forgotten our conversation with the High Prince over breakfast, I trust?' he asked, bristling as he saw the princess, who was supposed to be under his protection, walking hand-in-hand with the barbarian. 'It's almost noon!' he seethed, still ignoring Thurion.

'*Is* it? Why, my dear Captain, we had

completely lost track of time!' she replied, turning to Thurion. Looking up into the clear blue sky Thurion noted the position of the sun. He tried his best to hold his tongue but couldn't help goading the captain.

'Aye, it is nearly noon. You didn't tell me we had to be somewhere, Your Highness. Shall we?' he asked, gesturing to the palace with his hand that still held the princess's hand. Captain Gadas was almost apoplectic but, to his credit he managed to turn smartly on his heel and march back towards the palace before he did something he would, more than likely, regret.

'That was mean, Thurion,' Celene chided as the captain passed out of earshot.

'I know. I apologise, but your captain has been deliberately difficult and confrontational since the day we met. I couldn't help myself,' he admitted as they approached the palace.

'It was funny though, wasn't it? I thought he was going to explode! Imagine me, a princess, holding hands with a commoner! What a scandal!'

Chapter 37

After Thurion had escorted Celene to her room to freshen up, he returned to his own rooms. It did not take Thurion long to pack up his belongings, it never did. As he washed, he replayed the conversation he had shared with the princess before Gadas had interrupted them. It made him glow inside. As he made his way to her rooms, she met him in the corridor and they both smiled.

'I wish to get home to my family as soon as I can, Thurion. I have asked the High Prince to arrange for my carriages to be ready by this afternoon. We will take lunch with the High Prince and his family and then depart,' Celene told him as she led the way through the palace to a small, private dining hall.

'*We* will be taking lunch?' Thurion asked.

'Just the two of us. Captain Gadas is busy preparing the carriages,' the young princess explained, as they entered the hall just as High Prince Lautos and his family were sitting down at the table.

'Princess Celene, welcome!' The High Prince bowed, smiling as Celene walked in.

'*Thurion,*' he added, nodding politely.

'High Prince, once again your hospitality does you credit. High Princess Boreana, Princess Lemadia, good afternoon,' Celene replied.

'High Prince, High Princess, Princess,' Thurion managed, bowing slightly as he acknowledged each one. In the midst of all this formality he felt awkward but he did his best to conform. They sat down and ate. Lunch was light, just some cold meats, a few late season vegetables and fruits, followed by sweet curds and plums in a sweet conserve. The conversation involved a great deal of small talk. He remained silent throughout most of the meal, not finding much that he could intelligently contribute to many of the topics of conversation.

Thurion was the last to leave the palace and join the princess's caravan since he needed to return to his chambers after lunch to retrieve his belongings. Thurion stowed his pack in one of the newly-repaired baggage wagons and climbed aboard just as a score of knights rode into the courtyard. Thurion recognised these horsemen in white caparisons as the same knights that had vanquished the army of the dead some months previously.

'An escort,' explained one of Captain Gadas' men when he saw Thurion's questioning look.

'An honour guard!' the captain corrected his man as he marched past.

Whether they were acting as an escort or as an honour guard was really rather irrelevant, since the Princess was in no danger on the journey to the border of Nemeth-Sharrayah, but the High Prince was being careful to make Celene feel secure about travelling again. In the end her journey proved to be entirely uneventful.

Thurion spent a lot of time in the company of the princess, much to the disapproval of Captain Gadas. During the week or so they spent winding their way through Varga-Shemshah, Thurion learnt a good deal about the young princess, especially regarding her faith in Ios. Celene, for her part, learnt a lot about the mysterious nomad who had so suddenly entered her life.

At the border with Nemeth-Sharrayah the caravan was greeted by what was clearly another honour guard. Resplendent in the livery of royal palace guard, two dozen knights in gold trimmed myrtle-green robes waited, statuesque, for the caravan to pass. The messenger from Shemshah had evidently arrived in plenty of time. And so it was that Princess Celene Nemeth returned home prematurely from her tour of the principalities, escorted by her father's household knights and accompanied by a nomadic wanderer from the far west.

News travelled fast; the streets of Sharrayah were thronged with cheering crowds as Celene returned home. The young princess was greatly relieved to be home, for she spent most of the journey through the city walking alongside her carriage, waving at the adoring crowds. Thurion, on the other hand, still felt nervous receiving such attention. He kept himself occupied in one of the baggage wagons whittling a couple of hunting javelins from some dead-fall he had picked up on the outskirts of the city.

As they passed through the ornate gates of the royal palace into the courtyard Thurion heard Celene cry out.

'Father! Mother! Brothers!'

Several flaps of her snow-white wings carried her across the courtyard and into the arms of her father. A few seconds later, she was surrounded by the loving arms of her mother and brothers. Thurion dismounted from the wagon, stowed his javelins and dusted the wood shavings from his clothing as best he could.

After some minutes Celene emerged from the family huddle, and led her family across the courtyard towards where Thurion was waiting nervously.

'Father, I would like to introduce Thurion. He... saved my life.' Celene lowered her voice so her words did not carry to her captain's ears. Raparké looked first at his daughter, and then, realising that she was either being economical with the truth or deliberately placatory, turned and addressed Thurion.

'I welcome you, Thurion, and from what my daughter tells me I have you to thank for her safe return. I have, so far, only received the briefest of reports from High Prince Lautos of what transpired in Leznar-Carchum. I intend to learn of everything that has happened to my daughter since she has been away.' Raparké's stern tone was that of a concerned father.

'You will know everything that I know, High Prince, you have my word,' Thurion promised.

'Good. Let me introduce you to my family. This is my wife, High Princess Tamara and my two sons, the princes Erakos and Iraudis.'

'Your Highnesses, I ampleased to meet you.' Thurion bowed slightly as he acknowledged Raparké's family.

Raparké' turned and beckoned to his seneschal who was a discreet distance away.

'This is Seneschal Sandar, he is responsible for the running of the palace. He will arrangeyou're your accommodation, and some refreshment after your long journey.'

Celene impressed upon Seneschal Sandar that Thurion was to be treated just like any other royal guest, and that despite his outward appearance, he was not an uncouth savage. Thurion politely turned down the offer of personal servants, that were assigned to royal guests, saying that he did not need any help with washing or dressing himself, as he had been doing both since he was eight years old. Sandar was a rather pragmatic individual; he saw to it that Thurion was found lodgings on the ground floor. Whilst still suitable for royal guests, these apartments were not as plush as those on the palace's upper floors.

Whilst Celene was spending some much-needed time with her family, Thurion settled into his new chambers. The rooms were much more richly furnished than those he had been allotted in Shemshah. The bedroom, he was pleased to find, had a double door that opened not onto a balcony as in Shemshah, but directly out into the palace gardens. After unpacking his belongings and removing his mail coat, he relaxed in a reclining chair looking out over the gardens. An hour later he was disturbed by a knock on the main door. Getting up, he made his way to the door. A steward in green and gold livery stood there.

'My umm... please, I beg your forgiveness, sir. I do not know your title. How should I address you?' the embarrassed steward faltered.

'There is nothing to forgive, I have no title. I am just a man, the same as you. My name is Thurion,' Thurion replied.

'Thank you, Thurion, your presence is requested in the Council Chamber,' the steward announced.

'Certainly, lead on.'

'Please forgive me, sir, but I noticed that you have left the doors leading into the garden open.'

'Yes, I have. It's a little too warm so I'm cooling the place down,' Thurion explained, noting the steward's puzzled expression, 'I am used to sleeping outside. I find the air inside dry and stuffy.'

'I didn't mean to criticise, sir,' the steward apologised.

'No offence taken, you weren't to know.'

The steward remained composed as he led Thurion down the maze of corridors.

When they arrived in the council chamber High Prince Raparké was already present, as were Celene, her brothers, her mother, Captain Gadas and most of the privy councillors. As Thurion was escorted to his seat, another group of councillors arrived and took their places around the great dark-wood table that dominated the room.

'Now that we are all here, I call this council to order,' Raparké began. 'I have summoned you here because of the distressing events that took place in Leznar-Carchum during my daughter's grand tour. I am aware of the barest of details but I want to know everything. Once all the facts have been determined, only then can a suitable course of action be decided upon.' The High Prince's countenance was grim as his gaze passed over those assembled. 'You may begin,' he said to no one in particular.

'I believe I am best placed to brief the council, Your Highness, having witnessed the events first-hand,' Captain Gadas began.

The captain recounted how he had led the caravan from Ezné-Khalii into Leznar-Carchum, how he had felt a deep foreboding about crossing the border and had ordered the caravan to take the shortest route through the principality. He then summarised the night Celene's attendant priests had been massacred. Celene began to cry at the memory of that awful night. Iraudis held her hand whilst her mother passed her a handkerchief to dry her eyes. To

Thurion's ears the captain's re-telling of the battle at the cave mouth wasn't quite accurate; he was painting himself in a finer light than he should have done. Still, what did it matter? The facts were all sound. Captain Gadas concluded his report with their arrival at Sharrayah.

Raparké was silent for some minutes before he spoke.

'Thurion, how was it that you were present when my daughter was attacked?' The High Prince's tone was accusatorial and warned Thurion to pick his words carefully.

'Amongst my people I am known as a wilder,' he began. Several of the faces of those present were blank with incomprehension. 'A wanderer,' he added, 'I have been wandering the wilds for some years now. For a season I was the slaver's bane, but my path took me north towards the Widowmaker glacier before turning south again. I spent some time travelling with a merchant's caravan but turned due south when I reached the Tented City.' Thurion's eyes became damp, his voice quivering with emotion as the memory of Rimehorn came flooding back. 'I entered your lands from the west after crossing a grim, desolate land. It was by chance that I came across your daughter when I did, Your Highness.' At hearing this, a number of voices began murmuring.

'You crossed into the Deadlands?' Sandar asked; his voice cutting through the murmurs.

'The lands that lie due west of here?' Thurion's questioning look was met with a nod from the seneschal. 'Yes, I crossed them. It is a desolate land, almost devoid of life. I have never before seen such a border as the one that exists between your principalities and those plains—'

'My daughter, Thurion,' Raparké interrupted, as Thurion began to go off on a tangent.

'I'm sorry, Your Highness. As I said, I entered your lands from the west. I crossed the border into what I now know to be Varga-Shemshah. I was following a great army and watched as it assaulted Shemshah. That was when I first laid eyes on High Prince Lautos; I saw him defeat the dead king in single combat.'

Another stern look from Raparké brought Thurion back to his original point. 'I was resting by a rocky outcrop when I heard the sounds of battle on the far side. When I investigated, I saw Captain Gadas and his men fighting to reach a cave at the foot of the outcrop. I couldn't see your daughter, Your Highness, but I heard her cries and so I intervened. I had to. I could see that the captain, as valiant as he and his men were, would be unlikely to reach the princess in time.'

Hearing this, Captain Gadas glared at the barbarian. Thurion looked back and directed his remark at him, 'I do not speak ill of you or your men, Captain; you all fought bravely, but if I remember correctly you were on the ground and your foe was winged and had the advantage when I intervened.'

'Carry on,' Raparké interrupted, silencing the protest that his captain was threatening to raise.

'I cut my way to the cave entrance and vanquished the she-beasts, Your Highness,' he concluded modestly.

'And how was it that a single warrior was able to achieve what a score of professional soldiers could not?' a councillor interjected.

'Have you seen a Northman fight, sir?' Thurion retorted, a note of pride in his voice.

'I have not,' the old man was forced to admit.

'We are like a force of nature, born to fight, fearless and unstoppable, even in the face of overwhelming odds. I did what I thought was right at the time,' the barbarian replied proudly.

'Perhaps there is something you can learn from this man, Captain?' Raparké suggested.

'Your Highness.' Gadas could hardly conceal the icy tone in his voice as he smiled through gritted teeth and deferred to his prince and commander.

Raparké addressed Thurion, 'I am not usually given to overt displays of gratitude, especially to commoners and foreigners; however, I am grateful to you, Thurion, for saving my daughter and delivering her to me safely.'

Thurion nodded respectfully as the High Prince thanked him. Tamara smiled at him, her look conveying everything she wished to say. Iraudis simply nodded in acknowledgement. Erakos however, fixed the barbarian with a disapproving look that spoke volumes.

Raparké quickly changed his mood to one of extreme seriousness, fixed his eyes on the centre of the table and addressed the council in a solemn tone.

'Gentlemen, we have heard what happened in Leznar-Carchum from two reliable witnesses who fought off creatures we know to be evil. These forces were no doubt responsible for the massacre of the priests accompanying the caravan and the attempt on my daughter's life. Whether these unprovoked attacks were carried out without the knowledge of the authorities in Carchum, or not, remains to be seen. The murder of a member of the priesthood is a very serious matter, but an attempt on the life of a Child of Ios is an abhorrent act and one that cannot go unpunished. We must now decide what is to be done.'

Chapter 38

Winter was beginning to take hold in Leznar-Carchum, though the trees had long since lost their leaves to death's cold embrace. The country had become desolate. Its towns and villages were no longer populated by a lively and vibrant people. They were now haunted by husks: shells that used to be men, women and children but were no longer truly alive.

An old woman, or so she appeared to be, dressed in dark, stained rags was bent over from the weight of the bundle of firewood she carried strapped to her back. From under her hood her pale face stared directly down at the ground as she shuffled along the hard clay road. She met few travellers on the road, and those that she saw – apart from the odd word of greeting – paid little attention to her as she made her way towards Carchum. Which was good, so she thought; the fewer people who looked at her, the better. Once the walls of Carchum could be made out in the evening light, she slipped into a ditch and removed her load. She tore her long skirt further down the middle and tied the two halves around her legs. Scraping some of the dark soil from the ditch, she daubed her face with it. Cautiously raising her head out of the ditch, she waited some minutes before carrying on with her mission.

Stanara had crossed the border from Nemeth-Sharrayah some weeks ago on the orders of High Prince Raparké himself. She had been summoned to the palace along with eleven other scouts. Ordinarily their role would be to reconnoitre ahead of the High Prince's army, gathering intelligence regarding the disposition and movements of enemy forces. Her entire career so far had involved riding fast to the far borders of Leznar-Carchum, and reporting on enemy movements in the Plains of the Dead. Now she was being given a direct order from the High Prince to spy on Leznar-Carchum itself. Though she was a scout and not a spy, she had followed her orders to the letter; she had heard what had happened to the princess and was as horrified as everyone else in Sharrayah.

The twelve spies had parted company just outside the palace's main gates. They each made their own way into the neighbouring principality, some riding and some on foot. Stanara was one of the last to cross the border as she had elected to go in disguise on foot. She had spent the first couple of weeks observing the principality's outlying settlements and acquiring a broad idea of how things had changed since she was last here.

Frankly, what she saw shocked her. She had expected to see small vibrant towns and villages alive with the hustle and bustle of rural life. What she discovered were settlements that were populated almost solely by women and children who appeared close to death. They did not seem merely malnourished but appeared to be suffering from a malady that had sapped their vitality, their very life essence. The poor, wretched souls that still called these crumbling settlements their homes appeared to exist in a kind of half-life, somewhere between life and death. The state of the shrines and temples unsettled Stanara deeply too. She had not yet come across one that was intact and undamaged. Every single shrine had been desecrated, some had been burned, some had been torn down or defaced, others were missing entirely with just their plinths remaining. The temples had fared no better; many were just boarded up and daubed with blasphemic slogans whilst others had been torn down or were being used for military purposes.

She had been ordered to report back to Sharrayah by mid-winter. It was imperative therefore that she infiltrate one of Leznar-Carchum's cities and learn all she could before she turned for home. Since the closest city to where she had crossed into Leznar-Carchum was Carchum itself, it was towards its foreboding silhouette that she now headed.

A dank aura of death and decay hung over the capital city like a shroud. Stanara stalked towards its walls under the cover of a setting sun, carefully keeping to the scant cover provided by the little vegetation that had not yet rotted away. None of the gates leading into the city were barred or obviously guarded. All of her senses, honed by years of scouting, screamed at her not to approach them though. Instead she perambulated the city walls until she found a section of the outer wall that was lower than the rest. From a small backpack she pulled out a length of rope with a grapnel attached to one end, and hurled the triple hook over the city wall. It landed with a dull thud and she thanked Ios that the rags she had tied over the prongs had done their job. Pulling the rope taught she anchored it in place, then nimbly ascended the wall and slipped over the parapet.

As darkness fell Stanara began her reconnaissance of Carchum. What she found further disturbed her. The city was almost devoid of civilian life and it had the appearance of a military barracks; men in uniform thronged the streets and market squares had been transformed into parade grounds. She ducked into the shadowed doorway of an abandoned bakery as a column of soldiers marched past. She noticed that the heraldry emblazoned on the soldiers' tabards was not that of Ios but something else altogether. What held her attention – and horrified her in equal measure – was the sight of living, breathing men marching alongside soldiers who were clearly dead. She knew reanimation was a black art, practised solely by the disciples of Nhurkhu. In her mind this could only mean one thing: that Leznar-Carchum was in the grip of the Lord of the Underworld. What she was witnessing was evidence of practices that were abhorrent to the Children of Ios, and were expressly forbidden by the priesthood. The decay of the land, the malaise of the people, and the destruction of the shrines now made sense to her. The Holy Mother had been driven from the land.

But why? *What had happened here?*

Once the column had marched past and turned down into a side street, Stanara edged out from the cover of the bakery and silently made her way deeper into the city. The more she saw, the more certain she became of the intentions of High Prince Seratos Leznar: he was preparing for war. The only question now on her mind was when, and where? Shops and houses had been turned into billets, and many small fires burned in makeshift smithies where blacksmiths were forging weapons. Shop fronts were piled with new weapons and armour; the air was full of the sound of hammers beating steel on anvils; the stench of hot metal was everywhere. She had been in the city less than half an hour and she had seen enough.

At length she found herself back on the city wall. A little exploration revealed a circular building whose conical roof reached almost up to the wall itself. Climbing carefully onto this she was afforded an excellent view of the square immediately outside the royal palace. Dozens of torches blazed around the square illuminating the palace. He was there, the High Prince, on the palace steps. A few paces behind him stood a figure she had not seen before, which surprised her, because she had served alongside the soldiery of Leznar-Carchum for most of her professional career, and knew most, if not all, of the serving and retired officers. He was bald and clean-shaven; clearly not Seneschal Tiran. From this distance however, she could not tell much more than that. The High Prince was receiving a report from one of his officers who, like the soldiers she had observed from the shadows of the bakery earlier, wore a macabre new uniform.

A snapped command from the officer brought a line of soldiers marching into view. The squad halted in front of the High Prince. From within their ranks, eleven naked prisoners were frog-marched into view, then beaten onto their knees. Stanara felt suddenly sick. She strained her eyes in the darkness, hoping that she could not identify the poor souls that were now kneeling at the foot of the palace steps. Her heart caught in her mouth, she could just about see the nearest prisoner clearly enough and she recognised him at once. It was one of the scouts. They had all been captured, every one of the scouts that had left Sharrayah with her in the autumn.

How could this be? They were all experienced soldiers.

Her thoughts were suddenly interrupted as, in response to a nod from their High Prince, the soldiers behind the captives stepped forward, drew long daggers and slit the throat of every scout. She looked on, her gaze transfixed by the horror of what she was witnessing. She clamped her hand over her mouth to stifle the screams. She saw the High Prince reach into a pouch on his belt and draw something out. He began moving his hands over the bodies of the slaughtered prisoners, chanting. *What is he doing? What new horror is this?*

Stanara, the last of Raparké's spies, watched with stunned amazement as the slain captives rose unsteadily to their feet. The once-noble High Prince of Leznar-Carchum had just reanimated the corpses of eleven men. This was *definitely* enough. If she stayed any longer her nerve would certainly break. Edging her way back onto the city wall she froze as a roof tile came loose and slid away to smash on the street far below.

At first there was nothing to suggest that her slip had been noticed by anyone. Then a crow squawked. And then another. Seconds later the air was full of circling crows. In the square far below the High Prince looked up at the flock of circling birds and raised one hand in their direction. Stanara did not need to hear what he had said to know that she needed to leave the city immediately.

Chapter 39

'Thank you, Sergeant, please see that these new recruits are fully integrated into your unit—' Seratos paused, mid-sentence as a squawking crow caught his attention. By the time he had turned and pin-pointed where the noise was coming from, a small flock of the black birds could be seen circling a solitary figure as it climbed onto the city wall.

'Sergeant!' Seratos bellowed, pointing to the figure on the wall, 'bring me that spy.'

The sergeant saluted smartly and issued a number of clipped orders to his men. By the time Stanara was fleeing along the wall, Seratos' men had sprinted out of the square in pursuit.

Trading stealth for survival Stanara cut down any who got in her way, leaving a trail of dead and wounded guards in her wake as she fled along the ramparts. The first of the pursuing soldiers reached her position just as she had finished rappelling down the outside of the wall. As she fled into the night the sergeant recalled his men and returned to the palace.

Seratos fixed his sergeant with a piercing gaze as the man reported his failure. After a long pause he dismissed the shaking man and summoned Sisus.

'You sent for me, My Lord?' Sisus asked as he entered the audience chamber.

'Yes, Sisus, I did. It would appear that there is still at least one more of Raparké's spies at large. My men failed to apprehend her, fetch me the huntsman,' Seratos commanded.

'At once, My Lord.' Sisus bowed low before retiring.

Seratos was in the library examining various maps of the neighbouring principalities when a forbidding figure entered. He was over six feet tall and clad from head to foot in leather. A fur cloak hung from his shoulders. His skin had the appearance of old, dry leather, pulled too tightly over old bones. His eyes were dark pits and he spoke in a dry, rasping voice.

'You called for me, Lord,' the huntsman said, resting the base of his fetish-adorned staff on the polished library floor.

'I did,' Seratos said, not looking up from his maps. 'A spy has escaped my men and fled the city. It is believed to be a woman. I do not want her crossing the border with the information she has. Stop her,' he ordered.

'It will be done,' the forbidding figure promised before turning and leaving the library without ceremony.

* * *

Stanara stopped running and dived into an abandoned cottage to catch her breath. Gulping lungfuls of air she tried to slow her heart rate. She had to think clearly if she was going to make it back alive. In the distance she could hear the drumming of hooves. Her flight from the walls of Carchum had been headlong into the night. Now, however, she had to think carefully. She could head south-east to make straight for the border using the roads. However, that route would take her across fairly open country until she reached the border crossing point at the bridge over the Icerain river, leaving her exposed and with few hiding places. Besides, judging from the numbers of horses she had heard, the roads would be swarming with patrols. Or she could head due east and follow one of the small rivers that wound its way through what was once a verdant forest, until it joined the Icerain further south. As long as she could somehow cross that mighty river where it intersected the border, then the rest would be easy. The easterly route was more arduous and the least obvious, but it was also the one where she would be least likely to be spotted.

Her decision made, she peered out of the cottage and into the night. The moon was full and the sky was clear. Not useful if she were honest; if she could see where she was going, then so could they. She began to calm down; there were no signs of a pursuit – yet. Suddenly the silence was shattered as a number of howls drew her attention to the skyline. Silhouetted in the moonlight she could just make out a figure holding a staff aloft, surrounded by shapes that had to be dogs.

So I'm being tracked, she thought. *Got to get going.*

A long howl sent a chill through her body. She recognised the sound of a wolf pack leader initiating a chase.

No, I'm not, I'm being hunted.

As the figure of the huntsman and his pack disappeared from the horizon, Stanara darted out of the abandoned cottage and ran, listening for the sound of running water. The forest that the small rivers wound their way through was dying, and fallen branches littered the ground. Eventually she found a small river and even though the water was freezing she made a point of crossing it, and doubling back several times in an attempt to cover her tracks and throw the pursuing wolves off her scent.

She did not succeed. Soon she could hear the yelps and howls of the pursuing wolf pack. As the sounds of her pursuers came closer her careful route to the border became a panicked flight. Dead, leafless branches whipped and clawed at her face and hands, whilst tree roots tried to trip her and tangle her as she ran. Fortunately, she was wearing low-cut riding boots and made good progress. *At least the undergrowth is mercifully thin* she thought, as she tripped on yet another tree root.

It was no use; despite the lack of undergrowth in the dead forest her progress was still painfully slow. She needed to move faster and to somehow throw those accursed wolves off her trail. As the Icerain came into view she had an idea. At this time of year it was at its lowest. If she could find a point where it was wide and very shallow, instead of crossing it and continuing through the forest, she could cross it, double back and make her way upstream as fast as she could. Hopefully the wolves would be sufficiently delayed trying to pick up her scent again, and then she could make relatively good time whilst the river remained shallow.

Although she could not feel her feet, she somehow managed to jog upstream for about a mile before the water became too deep and the river bed became treacherously uneven. The yelps and howls of her pursuers had grown distant; evidently her ploy had succeeded in putting some much-needed distance between her and her pursuers. Eventually the forest thinned and she entered open country. Gradually she got her bearings and, her lungs burning in her chest, she began to jog towards the east.

As dawn broke over the horizon Stanara found one of the narrow roads that led into Nemeth-Sharrayah; it was no more than a cart track and nobody had used it for quite some time. She had been running all night in wet clothes and badly needed to rest but desperation drove her on. A sudden burst of yelps gave her cause to turn. In the lightening skyline her pursuers were just visible racing towards her across the open countryside some distance away. Turning back, she continued her desperate attempt to reach safety.

Rounding a bend in the track it came into view. A small border crossing which allowed farmers to take their stock to water. She would have wept in relief if she had had the energy. All of the official border crossings with Leznar-Carchum had been closed and their guards doubled whilst she had been away. She stumbled up to the gates that barred her way to safety and hammered on the timbers. A peephole behind a metal grille slid open and one of the guards on the night watch challenged her.

'Who goes there?' the young soldier demanded.

'Stanara Kipilis, First Scout Company, Second Infantry, I am one of the High Prince's scouts. Open up, please!' she gasped, glancing fearfully over her shoulder.

'I'm sorry, I cannot let anyone across. My orders come directly from the seneschal. This border crossing is closed,' the guard responded, his hand straying to the hilt of his sword. By now several other guards had joined him.

'Please, I am being chased, you must help me; I am on the High Prince's business, and I must deliver my report in person. It is of the utmost urgency!' she pleaded.

The guard was not convinced. The woman was in obvious distress but she did not look like she had business with the royal family. She looked like a vagrant. Her clothing was filthy and ripped – it looked like it was made of rags, her hair was wild and matted and her face was covered in mud. And she was armed. He was still deliberating when suddenly the yelps of the wolves became louder and louder, and the first of the pursuing pack loped into sight.

His stern expression slackened slightly. Then the huntsman appeared atop a small hill overlooking the road. The fetishes adorning his staff moved gently in the light morning breeze.

'What in Ios' name...'

'Open the gate! Quickly!' One of the other guards shouted as the rest of the wolf pack came into view.

The gate was opened just wide enough to allow Stanara to slip through. Another guard in the watch tower began ringing an alarm bell. The gate was quickly slammed shut and the locking rail dropped into place, as the rest of guard detail came running out of the gatehouse in varying states of undress. Despite their apparel, or in some cases, lack thereof, they were all armed with swords, spears and shields. The wolves cautiously approached the gate and growled menacingly, they seemed to be considering leaping over when a shrill whistle from the huntsman stayed them. Another whistle caused them to turn and lope away, back to the solitary figure on the hill top. The huntsman fixed Stanara with a penetrating stare before turning and disappearing below the far side of the hill.

'Who did you say you were?' one of the half-dressed guards demanded of Stanara, who had fallen to knees onto the cold ground.

'My name is Stanara Kipilis, First Scout Company, Second Infantry, I am a scout for the High Prince. I have been on a mission across the border for the past month or so. I am heading for Sharrayah to make my report directly to High Prince Raparké,' she explained.

'You don't look like a scout.'

'I know,' she panted. 'My mission was secret –that's why I had to adopt this disguise.'

'I'm sorry, I didn't know about any missions or the like. All I was told was that the border was closed until further notice and that we had to report any suspicious activity. Then last week we had to find billets for another ten men.'

'Do you have a horse?'

'We do,' an older man said, resting his spear in the crook of his arm and holding out his hand. Stanara shook it.

'I am Sergeant Kason, commander of this border guard.'

'Thank you, sergeant. I would also appreciate a little food and water; this last night has been... long.'

'Of course. I will see to it at once,' the sergeant replied.

Within an hour Stanara had changed into a spare uniform which was too big for her, but she didn't care –it was dry and that was all that mattered. She had eaten a hurriedly prepared breakfast and was galloping up the road towards Sharrayah. She rode as rapidly as she could; even in her exhausted state, the journey to the capital took only a few days.

Chapter 40

Once it had been decided that agents would be sent into Leznar-Carchum to learn more of High Prince Leznar's intentions, Raparké concluded the meeting and dismissed his officers and councillors.

'Thurion, I wish to convey my profound gratitude to you for the care you have shown my daughter. I am holding a state dinner this evening and I would be honoured if you would attend,' Raparké said as he rose from his seat, signalling the official end of the assembly.

'I would be honoured, Your Highness,' Thurion replied, bowing as he rose. Once again Thurion noticed Erakos fixing him with a look of utter contempt.

'It is a great honour, you know,' Celene began, as she accompanied Thurion back to his chambers.

'It is?'

'My father is a very conservative man. Although he holds many state dinners, his guest lists are... how shall I put it? *Selectively considered*,' Celene answered as diplomatically as she could as they reached the door to his apartment.

'What does that mean?'

'It means that you have made an enormous impression on him,' Celene answered trying to emphasise *enormous*.

'I see. Thank you for the warning.'

'Warning? I was just trying to convey the

magnitude of the honour my father has bestowed upon you,' Celene replied, not quite following Thurion.

'I do not intend to belittle the honour, Princess, but it is helpful to know that there will, in all likelihood, be others in attendance tonight who are not as tolerant as your good self,' Thurion explained.

'My father is not bigoted, Thurion. I am fond of you but I will not hear you speaking ill of my father, especially unprovoked,' the young princess snapped.

'I was not referring to your father, Your Highness; he has been nothing but courteous and gracious toward me since I arrived. I am referring to your brother, Erakos.'

'Aah, I see. I'm sorry, I misunderstood.'

'Forget it, it was nothing.'

'Yes, Erakos can be difficult. He is over-confident and ambitious, which is a combination that has gotten him into trouble before now,' Celene admitted.

'But since he is the High Prince's son...'

'...he has avoided too much chastisement,' Celene finished. 'Please, promise me one thing?'

'Of course.'

'Don't bait my brothers. Iraudis can take a joke and has a measure of self-restraint. Erakos has neither in sufficient measure.'

'Princess, have I yet shown you up? I have been doing my best to follow your complex customs. If my word will set your mind at ease then I will give it. I will not bait either of your brothers. I warn you though, there are limits to how far I can be pushed.'

Celene suddenly felt guilty; deep inside she had known that Thurion was a man of honour and would not act unreasonably. In truth she was more concerned that her bellicose brother would look for any opportunity to make an example of him.

'You have always acted with impeccable manners. I should not have doubted you.'

'You don't trust your brother to behave this evening, do you?'

'If I am honest, no, I don't. At least I know I can trust you though,' she replied, smiling.

'Aye, you can.'

'Until this evening, then.' Celene gently squeezed his hand and was about to turn to leave when Thurion, impulsively, drew her hand to him and kissed it. His heart pounded like a drum in his chest; the next few seconds seeming to pass inexorably slowly. And then she smiled, blushed and hurried off down the corridor.

You lucky bastard, that could have been disastrous! Aye, but it wasn't, was it?! Thurion thought to himself as he entered his chambers. He spent the next few hours outside washing his clothes and cleaning his kit ready for the evening's meal. He did not want to embarrass Celene tonight; a savage wilder he might be, but he was reasonably confident he could put on a good courtly show. He did, after all, have a little experience from his stay in Varga-Shemshah.

* * *

Erakos watched from a window overlooking the garden as the barbarian oiled his mail shirt on the patio just outside his chambers. *Pitiful, look at him trying his best to appear nobler than he is! And for what? To try and impress father? Or Celene?* He had seen the way Thurion had looked at his sister and how she had, in turn, looked at him in the meeting. What was his father doing inviting him to a state banquet? He had never heard of his father agreeing to anything quite so improper before. He was obviously still traumatised by what had happened to his daughter, which was understandable. It simply meant that he, Prince Erakos, would have to ensure that that crude, uncultured nomad behaved himself and knew his place.

* * *

Celene was also watching Thurion from a high window overlooking the garden. Unlike her brother however, she was gazing down with adoration. *He actually kissed me! What do I do now? Who do I tell? No one you fool! No one. But what if father found out? What if Erakos found out? Oh that Arité were here, she would know what to do.*

She missed Arité; she missed her a lot. Though she had known her only for a few months she and the priestess had become close. She had had a cheeky grin, and a wicked sense of humour for a member of the priesthood. Arité had quickly become her friend and confidante, and apart from her mother, no-one else shared her sense of humour – not even her girl friends at court. Celene still felt traumatised by what had happened to Arité, and often woke up crying when the memory of that night returned in her dreams. Now she had Thurion to dream of. She could have taken Sara into her confidence, though her former lady-in-waiting had been assigned other duties now that Celene had come of age. As it was, she dared not take her newly appointed maids into her confidence; she didn't know them well enough yet.

* * *

The hour of the banquet was approaching and just as Thurion was buckling on his cloak, a knock sounded on the door. He opened it and was met by a steward.

'The Princess wishes to announce that she is ready to attend the banquet.'

Thurion looked somewhat blankly at the steward. *Well... good! Why are you telling me?*

'She would be pleased if you would escort her to the banquet hall,' the steward added helpfully.

'Ah, thank you. Lead on,' Thurion replied, stepping out into the corridor and closing the chamber door behind him. This time it was the steward's turn to look slightly blank.

'I find places like this somewhat of a maze. I could wander for days and still not get to where I'm trying to go!' Thurion laughed as the steward led the way. 'I'm sorry if I didn't follow you back there; your customs are new to me,' he said, trying to break the uneasy silence as they walked.

'Of course, sir,' was the steward's only response.

After what felt like an age they arrived at Celene's chambers. The steward hurriedly returned the way he had come, as if on some vitally important errand. Finding himself alone in the corridor, Thurion stood up straight with his chin out and shoulders back, took a deep breath and knocked on the door. A slight maid of no more than sixteen opened it and invited him in.

'Your Highness, er...err...your friend is here,' she announced in a small voice.

'Thu-rhy-on,' he enunciated in a voice that seemed to rumble in comparison to the girl's.

'Theerion. Yes, sir, thank you, sir. I'll remember next time,' the young maid replied.

Celene's voice floated from the next room. 'Thank you, Nee. That will be all.'

Thurion glanced around the room in absolute amazement. He thought that his rooms were lavishly furnished, but the exquisitely-carved furniture and the gold-trimmed upholstery of Celene's richly decorated apartment were beyond his comprehension. He had never seen such opulent luxury.

'I will be back late; you may leave a little early if you like,' Celene said to the maid as she glided into the room. Nee curtsied slightly and mumbled 'Thank you, miss,' before withdrawing.

'Do you like it?' she asked Thurion, motioning to her myrtle-green dress, 'It's father's favourite colour.'

'You look... more than beautiful,' Thurion replied, struggling to find the words to best describe, quite literally, the angel who now stood before him. He suddenly felt very under-dressed and began fidgeting with his mail shirt.

'Relax, my dear Thurion, you are every inch the noble I know you to be,' she soothed, holding out her right arm for him to take.

'I notice that you are unarmed this evening,' Celene pointed out as they walked along the corridors.

'Almost. I've left my hand-axe in my chambers. After our conversation earlier I didn't want to end up in a situation where I would be tempted to use it!'

'Thurion, you have a very dark sense of

humour!'

'I wasn't joking, Your Highness. I vowed that I wouldn't goad your brothers, but neither of us knows what they might do. If the worst were to happen it would be ill if I were armed.'

Celene was silent for a minute or two.

'You are unarmed on my account?'

'Yes,' he replied. She placed her left hand on his and looked sweetly up at him.

'Thank you,' she said. Then her look became quizzical, '*Completely* unarmed?'

'My hatchet is on my belt, further round, under my cloak. It's not really a weapon though; a carving knife's just as dangerous!'

'Honestly!' she laughed, 'There.' She pointed down the length of the corridor to where a pair of liveried stewards stood outside a large hall with open wooden doors. Beyond them, High Prince Raparké's banquet was about to begin.

As soon as they entered the hall a steward escorted them to their seats.

'Almost respectable,' Erakos complimented with false sincerity.

'Almost,' Thurion replied with a grin.

'Behave, Brother!' Celene replied as Thurion saw her into her seat.

'I was merely complimenting our *honoured* guest on his grasp of our customs,' her brother replied, feigning hurt.

A bell rang, interrupting Erakos.

'Your Highnesses, lords and ladies, your host High Prince Raparké Nemeth!' the master of ceremonies announced. The hall erupted in a riot of applause as Raparké entered and took his seat between his wife and his seneschal.

The banquet itself was in a similar style to the one that had been held in Varga-Shemshah, and so Thurion was not at a complete loss.

'So are you of noble birth, where you're from, Thurion?' Erakos asked, subtle barbs in his question.

'My father is a respected and honoured member of the tribe, as was my grandfather – his prowess was well known,' Thurion answered Erakos directly.

'So your grandfather was a noble?' Erakos continued, trying to show Thurion up in front of everyone present.

'No, I said my grandfather's prowess was well known. You can be a man of honour; valiant in battle, honest in life and true in spirit without being noble-born.'

Erakos seemed somewhat affronted by this response.

'*My* grandfather was High Prince before my father, he was a great poet and playwright,' the young prince boasted.

'Mine died in battle, delivering our tribe from daemons from the Shadow World,' Thurion replied grimly, glancing at the gold ring that his father had given him. A number of those that had been listening in fell silent at Thurion's last statement.

'Legends told by mothers to their children; stories – nothing more!' Erakos announced, dismissing Thurion with a wave of his hand. Thurion fixed the young prince with a dangerous look. Celene immediately stopped eating and prayed that her brother would push Thurion no further.

'In every legend there is usually at least a seed of truth,' she interjected.

'Nonsense!'

'Tell me, Prince Erakos, do you believe in ghost stories?'

Erakos did not answer Thurion's question.

'The dead can walk alongside the living, I have seen it. Now if that can be true, why cannot other legends be true?'

The entire hall had now fallen silent.

'Your humour does not amuse me, Thurion. There are certain things about which one does not joke, especially in my halls.' Raparké's voice carried across the table. Thurion turned to address the High Prince.

'I was not making a joke, High Prince. I *have* seen the dead walking this side of the Underworld. My eyes have not deceived me. I know my father did not deceive me; my grandfather did give his life liberating our tribe from Nightmares of the Shadow World. I was simply pointing out to your son that a wise man should keep his mind open, that is all,' Thurion explained, nervous at finding himself the centre of attention but holding Raparké's gaze nonetheless.

'Very well; that is sound advice, especially in times such as these,' he said after a slight pause. Once Raparké had resumed his seat, the hubbub resumed and the banquet hall's atmosphere returned. Celene breathed a sigh of relief. Erakos' supercilious countenance gave way to a look at once embarrassed and angry at his father's siding with the barbarian. He said very little for the rest of the evening which suited Thurion, who was finding it very hard to keep his vow to Celene that he wouldn't goad the arrogant young prince. He was relieved to be able to talk of his travels with some of Raparké's councillors who were sat near by.

As the banquet drew to a close Erakos shot Thurion a venomous look and stalked out of the hall accompanied by several young guards.

Chapter 41

Thurion walked Celene back to her rooms once the banquet had finished.

'I hope I didn't speak out of turn earlier,' he asked her.

'No; you were honest. My father is a hard man to please but I think you have earned his respect.' She took his hands in hers, leaned up and kissed him.

'Thank you for accompanying me this evening, Thurion,' she said, before turning and entering her chambers.

Had he met anyone on his way back to his rooms, they might have wondered why the big barbarian was grinning behind his beard. Fortunately for Thurion he met no one. When he returned to his room he found that it had been cleaned, tidied and the doors to the garden had been closed. Once he had reopened them he stripped, wrapped himself in his sleeping cloth and fell into a light sleep on the bed.

In the early hours of the morning four men in lightweight leather armour, armed with short-bladed stabbing swords and lengths of rope, approached the open doors of Thurion's bedroom from the garden. Cautiously they stepped inside.

'I thought Erakos said these were his rooms?' one of the men hissed.

'They are, I checked,' another voice whispered.

'Look, someone *was* here,' a third man said, pointing with his sword at the creased bedding.

Thurion was crouching naked on the table in the adjacent room, watching them as a mountain lion watches its prey. His years in the wilderness had taught him to sleep lightly. These soldiers, for that is who they undoubtedly were, had made a poor attempt at stealing into his room undetected. They had woken him as they crossed the garden, the wind had brought their scent to him and their forms had blocked out the moonlight. This had allowed him to slink out of the bedroom unobserved. Slowly he reached for his great axe that was lying on the table a foot from him. The slightest sound of steel on wood gave him away and he cursed himself for his carelessness.

Immediately the four men started and peered into the next room. Silent surprise was quickly replaced by gasps of alarm.

'There, on the table, those eyes… it's a…'

'…panther or… something…'

'How in the name of Ios did that get in here?!'

'Forget how it got here, let's get out!'

The four men slowly backed away from the shadowy form of the big cat that was crouching on the table in the other room, and retreated into the garden. Once he was sure that they would not return, Thurion jumped off the table and landed with a cat's grace before returning to bed.

The following morning he rose as usual with the dawn, and after getting dressed, went in search of the kitchens. He found them and discovered that the chefs and servants who worked there were of a similar disposition to those he had met in Shemshah. So, just as he had done previously, he offered to provide the bulk of their breakfast in return for the use of the kitchens. So it was that as Celene was sitting down to eat with her family, Thurion was sharing the pigeons he had trapped with the kitchen staff.

After breakfast Celene found Thurion, returning from the kitchens to his rooms.

'I presume you ate with the staff this morning, Thurion?' she asked.

'I enjoy their company.'

'It wasn't a criticism,' she reassured him in her sweet voice. 'Would you like a tour of the palace grounds?'

'Thank you, I would like that very much; I haven't seen much of them yet.'

They entered the gardens through Thurion's chambers where he dropped off the equipment he had used to prepare breakfast. The patio that his bedroom opened out onto led, in turn, onto a vast lawn of lush grass.

'There is much to see, though we are in no rush,' Celene explained, as she took his hand in hers.

'Oh?'

'No, father won't make any decisions about what happened in Leznar-Carchum until his scouts have returned. He does not tend to make rash decisions,' she explained as they passed under a bare rose-arch that led into another part of the gardens.

'This garden is beautiful in the summer.'

'There is beauty here still. The frost settles in exquisite patterns, though it has all melted away now. I also find that when the air is still, winter brings with it a silence that is almost divinely serene. Then, even the wild spirits' voices are stilled and you can almost feel the potential growing in the earth, preparing itself for spring,' Thurion said, his voice far off and his eyes staring into the middle-distance.

'You really do see beauty in *everything*, don't

you?' Celene asked.

'In everything that grows, and in every creation of the wilderness, yes. There I find a balance and a peace that I have yet to find in more *civilised* places.'

'I understand, at least a little of what you have said. You have heard that we, the children of Ios that is, can channel her power?'

'Yes, you can cure the sick and heal the wounded; I have heard a little and seen some of the power of your priests on the battlefield,' he replied.

'The priesthood are not as close to Ios as we are,' she said, gesturing to herself. 'But even we, Ios' spiritual children, must learn her arts. Do you know what the first thing was that I healed?'

'No.'

'It was a little bird with a broken wing. I was walking in these very gardens when I found the poor creature crying out in pain in the shadows of a great old tree. My heart broke for it.' As Celene spoke she recalled how it had flitted about her in delight once she had re-knit its wing.

Thurion looked over at her then said 'I see kindness and compassion in your eyes that I have not seen in anyone else's.'

Celene blushed as Thurion drew close to her. The atmosphere was shattered as Erakos strode into the rose garden.

'So, *this* is where you have led her?!'

'Excuse me?' Thurion replied calmly, drawing slightly away from Celene and squaring up to the angry young prince.

'I knew you would try something like this! I have seen the way you look at her! It's clear that your intentions towards my sister are entirely dishonourable! Step away from her, you animal!' Erakos fumed.

'Are you impugning my honour, *boy*?' the barbarian asked, in a threatening tone.

'No, of course he's not, are you, Erakos?' Celene intervened, trying to defuse the escalating situation.

'I'm saying that you're nothing but an uncultured savage! Celene, I thought you had *some* standards, get away from him!' Erakos shouted as he grabbed his sister's arm and pulled her violently away from Thurion.

The Northman's hand moved with a serpent's speed and gripped Erakos' wrist in a vice-like grip.

'Let her go,' he warned. Erakos refused at first but quickly relented when Thurion's grip tightened.

'Let go of me, barbarian, I won't ask you again,' Erakos replied.

'You accuse me of being a man of no honour; nought but a savage and *you're* threatening me?!'

Thurion's blood was up. Despite the promise he had made to Celene last night he desperately wanted to beat this brother of hers to within an inch of his life. An instant later Erakos gave him the opportunity. With one deft move the young prince drew a long-bladed knife from his belt and thrust at the unarmed Northman. Erakos was fast but Thurion was a heartbeat faster and twisted aside, the steel cutting air instead of flesh. Thurion countered with a quick chop that sent the knife spinning to the ground followed by a savage jab to the face which sent the young prince reeling.

Erakos was clutching his bloodied nose as Thurion took several deep breaths and fought the urge to complete what he had started. Celene had only just realised what was happening as it finished.

'I accept!' Erakos spat, his hand over his nose.

'Oh no…' Celene whispered.

'What? You want some more, boy?'

'At noon, savage…' the prince replied before staggering away.

'What did he mean by that?' Thurion asked.

'You have just challenged Prince Erakos to a duel,' she replied weakly.

'What? He treated you contemptibly and tried to run me through with this,' Thurion said as he picked up the prince's knife. 'So I hit him. That was all.'

'I'd better have that,' Celene said, holding out her hand and accepting the knife from Thurion.

'I'm sorry, Celene, but I what else could I have done?'

Celene was silent for a moment or two. 'Nothing,' she admitted finally.

Raparké was unsurprised to hear that his eldest son had got himself into yet another duel, and therefore decided to let his seneschal handle the affair.

'I am afraid I must place you under guard, Thurion,' Seneschal Sandar announced as he entered Thurion's chambers accompanied by four soldiers.

'You needn't be afraid, Seneschal, I'm not going anywhere,' the Northman replied, as he began checking the straps on his armour.

'You have been made aware of the rules, I trust?' the seneschal asked.

'Rules? It's a fight isn't it?'

'You do know what a duel is, don't you?' Sandar asked, his tone carefully conciliatory.

'Aye, Seneschal, I do. They were rare in

Vorde; not uncommon, but usually fatal,' Thurion replied without a hint of consternation.

'Ah… There are various degrees of duel in the principalities. We *usually* duel to first blood. However—'

'—however, given Prince Erakos' state of mind…' Thurion finished the Seneschal's thought for him.

'You are being rather frank and seem rather calm given the circumstances you find yourself in, if I may say so.'

'You may. Put it this way, how much worse can it get? And besides, I have faced worse things than this young prince in combat before,' replied Thurion as he checked the underarms of his mail coat.

'For your sake I hope you're right, Prince Erakos has sparred against every prince in the principalities and has only ever been beaten by one: Prince Asmos Dra. You will be escorted to the palace forecourt in a little under an hour,' the seneschal announced as he turned to leave.

Aye, sparring is one thing, but actual close combat is something else entirely. Thurion finished checking his armour and picked up the first of his axes.

The palace forecourt was empty except for Seneschal Sandar and his officials who were present to oversee the duel, Celene, Prince Iraudis and half a dozen of Erakos' friends. The High Prince and his wife, whilst fearful for their son, preferred to stay away so as not to be seen to show favour to either of the duelists, and thus not upset their daughter. The pervading silence was broken only by the bubbling of water flowing from the tall fountain in the centre of the forecourt. Once Thurion had approached Sandar, the seneschal began the proceedings.

'The matter, gentlemen, is a question of honour. Prince Erakos, you claim that Thurion attacked you whilst you were defending your sister's honour?' Erakos nodded his assent.

'Thurion, do you deny this charge?'

'Of course not, I struck the young cur, and with good reason – he tried to stab me,' he responded. Erakos seethed.

'Prince Erakos, is this true?'

'Only to stop him ravishing my sister!' Erakos shouted for all to hear.

Sandar turned to Thurion, 'Thurion?'

'The honour of Princess Celene was never at stake, and he knows it.'

'LIAR!! SAVAGE!!' Erakos was beside himself.

'Gentlemen, it appears that this matter might be the result of a misunderstanding, if this can be settled in any other—'

'NO! Get on with it, man!' Erakos demanded.

Sandar sighed, 'Very well. Do you still demand satisfaction, Prince Erakos?' the seneschal asked.

'YES!' Erakos' reply was spat from between gritted teeth.

'Very well, to first blood.'

'No! To submission! I want to see this savage beg for mercy!'

The seneschal's shoulders slumped. 'Very well, it is your decision. PRINCE ERAKOS NEMETH, THURION – YOU DUEL TO SUBMISSION!'

Prince Erakos was garbed in a suit of finely wrought plate armour and a plumed half-visor helmet. An elegantly curved blade hung from a scabbard on his belt. In his left hand he held a small buckler, whilst in his right he brandished a long spear.

Thurion, on the other hand, was wearing his long mail shirt and mail-adorned spectacled helmet, his axes hanging in their belt loops. As he removed his great axe from the belt strapped across his back the young prince shot up into the air on dark-brown wings. Thurion kept his grip loose and tracked the young angel as he posed in the sky above.

Erakos' attacks were swift, swooping strikes that Thurion found difficult to counter; by the time he had deflected the incoming thrust the prince was already outside his reach. Thurion gradually tired and Erakos's confidence waxed; his attacks becoming more sensational. As he parried another thrust, a predatory gleam entered Thurion's eyes and he backed towards the fountain, seemingly fatigued. Erakos attacked again and this time drove the barbarian down onto one knee. Thurion let go of his huge axe and appeared to rest his right hand on the fountain wall for support.

'So, you are beaten at last, barbarian! You have stamina, I will grant you that, but you lack skill and breeding!' the prince boasted as he hovered above the exhausted Northman. Thurion crouched, exaggeratedly panting.

As the prince turned to swoop again, Thurion struck, serpent-like. His right hand had not been seeking purchase on the fountain wall but had rather been drawing his hatchet. His powerful legs uncoiled underneath him, sending him shooting into the air. He hurled the small axe at the prince; it flew straight and true, slamming into the prince's chest and splitting his breastplate. Shocked and surprised, Prince Erakos stalled and fell from the air landing on the hard ground in a cloud of dust and feathers. Thurion landed a few feet away and was on top of him before he could recover. Not bothering to draw his hand axe, the enraged barbarian grabbed hold of the prince's gorget and head-butted him repeatedly until he lay unconscious on the ground, his face a bloody mess.

Thurion stopped smashing his heavy helmet into the prince's face only when Erakos stopped struggling. Breathing heavily, he got to his feet, retrieved both of his axes and staggered over to the seneschal.

'He submitted,' Thurion announced, thrusting his axes into their respective loops.

'So I see. Somewhat unconventional but arguably effective,' the seneschal replied, then, turning to address the spectators he announced 'The result of this duel is indisputable: Thurion of the wilds has prevailed and carries no slur. Unless there are any other matters outstanding...' looking in the direction of Prince Erakos' entourage who, to a man, cast their eyes to the ground, 'then I hereby declare this matter closed. Gentlemen, please see to the prince,' the seneschal concluded, motioning to Erakos' shocked comrades.

Celene was unsure quite what to make of the whole affair. She had just seen her brother brutally beaten by someone she had begun to develop deep-seated feelings for. She knew that he was capable of such violence, indeed, she would not be alive today if he were otherwise. But to see such savagery unleashed against her brother was a shocking experience.

Chapter 42

Seratos fixed his stony gaze on the far wall of the audience chamber as the huntsman explained how his quarry had escaped. There was silence in the hall for several minutes.

'Leave,' the Angel of Death commanded, his eyes still fixed on the far wall.

'Sisus, follow me. Our timetable has just changed.' Rising from his throne Seratos strode out of the audience chamber and headed for the library. Sisus followed his lord into the palace library and closed the door behind him.

'Originally, I was intending to begin my campaign at the first sign of spring. Now however, thanks to the failure of a few, my hand has been forced. I want both armies to be at their allocated border crossing points as soon as possible,' Seratos stated, his tone final.

'But, My Lord, there is still much to be done, and the weather – it is only just past mid-winter...' his seneschal began.

'Then work day and night... and to hell with the weather! If it kills the living, have them raised! I will hear no more excuses or complaints! Now, summon my commanders!' Seratos snapped. Sisus bowed obsequiously and left the library.

Some little while later Seratos' father, Abragon, his sister, Aldene and his two brothers, Goson and Phadinus, arrived at the library. They all had the appearance of desiccated corpses. Their skin clung tightly to them; in places it had split, showing fraying sinews and white bone. In place of their regal apparel they were now clad in ornate armour which, though it had been only recently forged had already begun to show signs of age. With dead eyes the four commanders beheld their lord.

'Our timetable has had to be brought forward due to circumstances beyond my control. You will therefore begin readying your troops for action immediately. Commander Goson, Commander Phadinus, take a seat at my left hand and study these maps.' Seratos indicated a pile of maps detailing one of Leznar-Carchum's neighbouring principalities. 'Commander Abragon, Commander Aldene, take a seat at my right and study these.' He gestured towards a second pile of maps, detailing another neighbouring principality. 'I want you to memorise these maps, we don't have the luxury of waiting a couple of months for copies to be made.'

'When do you want us to march?' Commander Abragon asked. His once-noble, measured tone now sounded like two pieces of sand paper being drawn across one another.

'Both forces should begin mustering immediately and be ready to march within a week,' Seratos answered. He waited for his commanders to voice any objections they might be harbouring. Silence was their only reply as they studied the maps laid out before them. They then discussed strategy and tactics between themselves in dry, broken voices.

Chapter 43

Celene was a little withdrawn in the days following Thurion's duel with her brother. She was having trouble marrying what she knew to be true about the noble-hearted wanderer, with the brutal savagery he had displayed in the duel with Erakos. The duel didn't seem to have affected Thurion in the slightest. Erakos, however, made a point of keeping out of the Northman's way. When their paths did cross however, the young prince made an effort to be rather more respectful than he had been previously.

The snow was gently falling as Celene wandered the palace gardens looking for Thurion. She had finally worked up the courage to ask him about the duel, and found him sitting under a tree by a frozen pond. He was working on a lump of ice he had broken from the pond's surface. As she approached she could see that he carving a norshorn bust.

'That's beautiful,' she complimented, as she walked up.

'An old friend,' Thurion explained simply as he put his knife away.

'How are you?' Celene asked, at a loss how best to broach the subject.

'As always, though you're not, I notice,' Thurion replied, resting the ice carving on a tree root, 'You've been avoiding me.'

'No, I... Yes, yes I have; I'm sorry. It's just I had never thought...' Celene stumbled over her words. Thurion rested his hand gently on the carving of Rimehorn before rising to his feet.

'—that I was capable of such violence? You have seen me fight before, back at the cave.'

'But then you were protecting me against those, those monsters,' Celene countered.

'And a few days ago I was protecting myself from your brother. Celene, there is a great difference between knowing how to fight and kill and finding enjoyment in it. I know how to fight, and fight well; if I didn't, I would be long dead. Do I enjoy it? I will admit that there is a certain rush, a certain feeling of being very much alive... but no, I don't enjoy it. If I did, I would have toyed with your brother as he tried to toy with me. Look into my eyes, what do you see?' Thurion turned to her.

Celene looked deeply into his eyes and saw a man who was far more than any other she had ever met.

'I... I do not see violence. I'm sorry, I was shocked to see you transform so quickly from the noble warrior I had come to know, into a brutal savage that I barely recognised, that is all. Can you forgive me?'

'Forgive you? Your Highness, there is nothing to forgive.' There was kindness in his voice. He drew her close to him.

'You're cold, here take this,' he said. They broke their embrace, Thurion unclasped his cloak and wrapped it round her. Together they walked back to the palace.

As the pair entered Thurion's chambers from the garden they met Seneschal Sandar walking towards them.

'I apologise for entering your chambers uninvited, Thurion, but I was looking for Celene, the

High Prince has summoned her to the council chamber.'

'You had better go,' Thurion said, letting go of her hand.

'Is it urgent, Sandar?' Celene asked.

'Yes, Your Highness, it is; one of the scouts has returned from Leznar-Carchum.'

* * *

Celene left Thurion and followed Sandar to the Royal Council Chambers. When she arrived she found that her father had called a full meeting.

'I'm sorry I'm late, Father.'

Raparké acknowledged his daughter's apology with a slight gesture of his hand.

'Now we are all here, I will begin. Less than an hour ago a scout returned from Leznar-Carchum. I have received her report and intend to act upon it.'

'Your majesty, if I may interject...?' a councillor began, 'would it not be wise to wait until the rest of the scouts return?'

'No other scouts will return to Sharrayah. Scout Stanara reports seeing them all executed,' Raparké said, censoring the details somewhat.

'Surely High Prince Seratos is unaware of this? We must send a deputation immediately,' another of the councillors interrupted.

'High Prince Seratos *was* the one who executed my scouts, councillor.'

His words silenced the chamber. Celene's face paled as she recalled her flight through Leznar-Carchum. Raparké noticed his daughter's countenance and turned to her.

'Celene, I think that we can now be sure who

was behind your attack. I think that we also now know why.'

Celene looked up at her father, a question evident in her eyes.

'High Prince Seratos Leznar has forsaken the Holy Mother and is, at this moment, amassing a great army, one so large that his major cities have been converted into barracks,' Raparké announced.

'But where? How? Surely this cannot be so!' a councillor stammered.

'My scout reports seeing the living marching and training alongside the dead. It would appear that our once erstwhile ally, the High Prince of Leznar-Carchum, has forsaken life and embraced death.'

The chamber suddenly went quiet; the atmosphere could have been cut with a knife.

After letting the full implications of what he had just said sink in, Raparké continued. 'I want our full military strength mustered. I want all of the old bastions along our border with Leznar-Carchum reinstated, and I want them garrisoned as soon as possible.'

Sandar stood up. 'Your Highness, the old bastions were converted into private homes centuries ago, to reinstate them as military outposts would require the current owners selling them back to the royal estate. That process could take months, if they decided to sell at all.'

'Have them seized, seneschal, and relocate their current owners. They may grumble now but if we do nothing they will, rightly, condemn us for not acting when the dead march across the border and begin putting towns and villages to the sword. See that is is done. I have, this morning, sent envoys to Shemshah, Khalii, Azun, Nihkur, and Heshkar, requesting the High Princes gather here as soon as possible to form a Council of War. This is something none of us will be able to face alone.'

The chamber was silent as Raparké finished speaking; a pin could be heard dropping.

'You have my orders, councillors, I expect regular and rapid progress reports on their execution before the arrival of the heads of state. Until then, gentlemen, you are dismissed.'

* * *

The first of the neighbouring princes began arriving in Sharrayah within a few weeks of Raparké sending out his messengers. It took a further week for everyone else to arrive before matters could begin. Once again Celene was summoned to the Council Chamber. This time however the council meeting was a much grander affair; food had been prepared and servants waited on the delegates.

Raparké brought the meeting to order before he began formally, 'Your Highnesses, gentlemen. I have asked you all here in response to a number of disturbing events which have taken place over the past few months. As you are all no doubt aware, my daughter, Princess Celene, began her tour of the principalities last spring. I wish to express my thanks to High Princes Taran, Damakos and Achmek for their generous hospitality during her visit. However, upon entering Leznar-Carchum, her caravan was attacked and all of her attendant priestesses were slaughtered in a single night.'

Immediately a bubble of speculative conversation erupted across the length of the chamber.

'Please, please!' Raparké raised his voice, restoring order. 'In response to this her captain ordered the caravan to make for the principality's northern border with all speed. Unfortunately they were attacked a second time, and were it not for the timely intervention of a wandering nomad I fear she would not be sitting here now.'

'Who was he, this wanderer?' High Prince Asmos asked.

'A barbarian, originally from the west,' High Prince Lautos answered.

'So the caravan made it safely to Shemshah then?' Asmos continued.

'Yes, it did. And I thank High Prince Lautos for his understanding and hospitality in receiving my daughter after suffering such trauma,' Raparké interrupted, taking control of the discussion. Lautos nodded respectfully, acknowledging Raparké's thanks. 'As soon as Celene had returned to Sharrayah and I had learned what had happened, I dispatched twelve scouts into Leznar-Carchum.' Raparké paused for effect, 'One returned. She reported that Carchum had been turned into a colossal barracks. She also reported witnessing living soldiers drilling alongside the dead.'

Every High Prince present started at once, some nearly choking on their food or spilling their drink, as Raparké revealed the depth of Seratos' betrayal.

'Are you suggesting that...' High Prince Taran began.

'High Prince Seratos Leznar has abandoned Ios, forsaken the Order of Life and embraced the ways of death. He now treads a different path. It is with a heavy heart therefore that—'

Raparké was interrupted by a knock at the chamber doors. A steward opened the door and spoke with someone outside. After a second or two the steward stood aside and a bedraggled messenger in the livery of Varga-Shemshah walked in.

'Begging your pardon, Your Highnesses, but I must speak with High Prince Lautos.'

Raparké motioned for the man to approach the table. High Prince Lautos' face became ashen as the messenger whispered his message. The High Prince's face was downcast as the messenger bowed and left the room.

'Your Highness?' Raparké prompted. All eyes in the chamber focused on High Prince Lautos.

'My lands have been invaded. Shemshah lays besieged and legions of the dead advance, razing and burning as they go.'

Everyone in the council chamber was momentarily silent – almost paralysed with shock. The High Prince stared ahead.

'They say that dead troops fight side-by-side with living troops, led by High Prince Abragon and even Princess Aldene; both of them looked to be dead. I find it hard to believe. We are used to assaults from the Plains, of course, but not from a neighbour and angelic ally. I do not have exact numbers yet but losses have been high and I fear for my principality, Your Highness.'

Raparké was silent for a moment as he absorbed this new information.

'Before requesting your presence here, I ordered my own military to begin mustering so I am in a position to lend aid. However, if what your messenger reports is correct, this will require more than just a token relief force. High Prince Nabas, can you send aid?' Raparké asked the High Prince of Thorvath-Heshkar.

'I can, not a great deal though; I don't maintain a large standing army. We are far from the Plains of the Dead and see little need for maintaining a large standing army. However, I will send what I have. The people of Thorvath-Heshkar extend their heartfelt commiserations, and pledge their support to their neighbours in Varga-Shemshah.'

'High Prince Taran, are you able to help?' Raparké asked. The High Prince of Lephar-Nihkur thought for a minute or two before responding.

'It will take some time to muster my troops, most of them are currently deployed in the east,' he replied. Raparké noticed his evasive tone but did not press the matter.

'In that case, Your Highness, I would ask you to muster what strength you can as soon as you can.'

'I will see what can be done. I will send as many men as I am able to. Lephar-Nihkur will stand by the principality of Varga-Shemshah,' the High Prince replied.

'So, the intentions of our former brother become clear. It would seem that he intends to march on the northern-most principalities first before turning south. At least, that is how it appears at the moment, Your Highnesses,' Raparké continued. He turned to address the High Princes of Dra-Azun, and Ezné-Khalii, 'Highnesses, may I suggest that you too, begin mustering your armies?' The two princes looked at each other and were about to respond when a second knock at the chamber door interrupted them.

Another messenger was admitted into the chamber and, after bowing, approached both High Princes Damakos and Achmek.

'Your Highnesses, I have ill tidings. May I beg a moment of your time?' the exhausted man asked. Both princes nodded and the messenger passed a rolled parchment to them. After reading the rapidly penned missive their faces paled as High Prince Lautos' had.

'We too have been invaded, Your Highness,' Prince Achmek began, addressing Raparké. 'Sumir has fallen, but the advance of the dead legions appears to have been checked some miles west of Khalii.'

'Likewise, it would appear that we have been able to hold the High Prince's legions back along a similar front. Although we are holding our ground we will need help if we are to drive them back,' High Prince Damakos added.

Raparké's countenance was grim as he took in this new report.

'I will send you as much aid as I can spare; I will not denude my own border, however. It is possible that I have not yet been attacked because the High Prince is well aware of the strength of arms I can bring to bear – we have a long history of fighting side-by-side. It would seem that he is attempting a pincer movement with the aim of catching me in the middle...'

There was silence as Raparké made his pronouncement. A minute or so later he closed the formal part of the meeting. Immediately a hubbub of raised voices filled the hall as princes sent for their messengers and advisers, and began discussing the sudden events that had overtaken their principalities.

Chapter 44

Seratos watched from the window of one of the palace's high towers as the army, led jointly by Commanders Abragon and Aldene, marched out of the city and began mustering on the plains to the east. This was a vast force, many tens of thousands strong at least; the graveyards for miles around had been emptied in order to amass such an army.

Company upon company of infantry began mustering as squadrons of knights trotted along the main road to form the army's vanguard, the flesh of their starved, rotting mounts peeling and tearing as they rode. Packs of hounds from the Plains of the Dead barked and howled as they ran alongside.

'Sisus, have my carriage made ready, it is time,' Seratos ordered, without turning away from the window.

'Yes, My Lord.' The necromancer bowed before turning to leave.

Seratos' macabre carriage was brought round to the front of the palace, and the coachman and the groom waited for their passenger. With its black curtains and gharish ornamentation it resembled a hearse more than a royal carriage. Indeed its driver, far from wearing the ornate uniform of a royal footman, wore a long black coat and a wide brimmed hat that concealed his features.

'Driver, form up ahead of my commanders,' Seratos commanded before entering the carriage. The coachman driving the horses slapped the reins on the lead horse's rump, shouting 'Get on there, Zheros. Haa!' The hearse-like carriage pulled out of the palace courtyard and set off on the main road into the near-deserted city.

The interior of Seratos' carriage was no less macabre than the outside. Arcane texts lined shelves on one wall panel, whilst all manner of bizarre and unwholesome items could be found lining a number of shelves opposite. At the far end of the carriage Seratos knelt in front of a heavy wooden trunk. Opening it, he began to mark a pattern of runes into the earth that was contained inside.

'Commander Phadinus, I compel you to answer me,' Seratos spoke into the casket of graveyard earth. A moment later the impression of a face began to form in the dirt, obliterating the runes that had been drawn into it.

'My Lord?' Phadinus' face replied.

'How is the muster at Laho proceeding?'

'Everything is in order, My Lord. Commander Goson should be preparing to march on Dra-Azun as we speak. I expect we will cross the border at our respective locations at around the same time, in a few weeks.'

'Excellent. Keep me informed of your progress, commander.' Seratos replied, evidently pleased with how smoothly events seemed to be progressing in the south.

'As you command,' Phadinus' image replied before it disintegrated back into formless earth.

It took a further day for the northern army to muster outside Carchum and prepare itself for the march north. Eventually, preparations were completed and the ground shook to the beat of thousands of marching feet and trotting hooves.

Progress was slow with such a large force and it was two weeks before the border was reached. Seratos had instructed that the border post be taken by surprise. Although he was marching at the head of an army many thousands strong, he wanted to advance as far as possible before he was discovered.

To this end Commander Aldene dispatched a small cohort of knights, and several packs of hounds, with the task of silencing the border guards and preventing word being sent back to Shemshah.

It was dusk when the ten knights, their attendant hounds slinking silently around them, approached the border crossing. High Prince Lautos had reinforced his border with Leznar-Carchum after learning what had befallen Celene earlier in the year. As the knights reached the edge of light woodland that had, so far, concealed their presence, they beheld for the first time the well-lit, strongly guarded border that was their objective.

The sergeant in command of the knights tightened his grip on the reins, turned his pale, dead eyes to the sky and rasped a command that sent the hounds loping off into the darkness. A few minutes later, challenges could be heard being shouted into the night. These challenges were quickly followed by calls of alarm, the barks and howls of hounds and the sounds of combat. These sounds prompted the sergeant to kick his decaying mount into a trot and he led his knights out onto the road.

The gate was illuminated by burning torches and manned by a score of well-equipped soldiers. The men guarding the gate heard the sound of hooves long before they saw anything. Prepared as they were for an attack on the gate, these men had not before faced the dead in combat and shrank back from the gate as the dead riders galloped into sight.

Jumping clean over the gate the knights set about the terrified guards, their long-handled maces swinging in deadly arcs. The skirmish was short and brutal. The sound of hooves disappearing into the distance brought the sergeant's head round sharply. A snapped command sent six knights galloping up the road in pursuit of the fleeing guard.

The knights caught up with the fleeing soldier some miles down the road where tall trees blocked out the moonlight. He had been forced to slow his pace in order to pick his way carefully along blind stretches of road, whereas the dead knights had no such trouble, being as able to see in pitch darkness the same as in bright sunlight. Both guard and horse were brutally beaten to death, their bodies discarded a little way from the roadside.

The army's vanguard crossed the border later that same morning and Seratos' crusade began in earnest. Once across the border, several smaller forces splintered off from the main army and began marching on the nearby towns and villages. With no warning from the border post the settlements were caught unprepared. Entire populations were put to the sword or simply burnt alive as they cowered in their homes. The pace of Seratos' advance was relentless and in a little over a week he had reached the walls of Shemshah. With his ranks bulked out with the dead of the settlements he had razed, the Angel of Death could afford to lay siege to the city and continue his crusade into Varga-Shemshah.

Seratos was taken a little by surprise at the ease with which he was able to surround Shemshah. He had expected High Prince Lautos to march out and meet him in open battle, where he excelled, but instead everyone had withdrawn into the city and seemed prepared to endure a lengthy siege. Indeed, as he thought about it, Seratos was not at all sure he had seen any evidence to persuade him that the High Prince was in residence.

As smaller forces set about the systematic razing of the lands surrounding Shemshah, Seratos and his commanders began preparations for the siege. Although the employment of artillery was completely unknown in the principalities, Seratos was not entirely without weapons capable of breaching the city's formidable defences. He began by ordering the construction of many scaling ladders. Although it was looking to become a lengthy siege, with his smaller forces laying waste to the surrounding countryside, it was unlikely any relief would be forthcoming. The palls of black smoke that rose from the burning crop stores and villages blotted out the sun and caused the morale in Shemshah to wither.

* * *

'Commander Goson, report!' Seratos addressed the face in the dirt-filled chest.

'I crossed the border on schedule, My Lord, but we have encountered determined resistance from the enemy,' the face of Commander Goson replied.

'What is your current position?' Seratos asked, irritated.

'My advance has been checked some miles into Dra-Azun. I have, so far, been unable to pin down the armies of the High Prince and engage them in extended combat. They attack us briefly before withdrawing rapidly,' the commander complained.

'And what of Commander Phadinus?'

'He has managed to raze Sumir but has also met unexpectedly determined resistance. It is almost as if both principalities are acting together in an attempt to thwart us.'

'Do not fail me, Brother,' Seratos said coldly, before dashing his hand against the image of his brother in the dirt and breaking the communication. His advance in the south seemed to have stalled; however, that wasn't a complete disaster. Even if the entire southern campaign achieved no more than draining the neighbouring principalities of much-needed man-power, then it would still have achieved a great deal. It was to the north where the real thrust was coming from. Once Varga-Shemshah had fallen, Thorvath-Heshkar would be next. This would provide the Angel of Death with a strong position from which to lead further crusades into the central and southern principalities.

Chapter 45

With the meeting concluded a steady stream of messengers was sent out from Sharrayah to all of the principalities. The city itself was buzzing with gossip and speculation. Thurion sought out Celene once he learned that the meeting had ended.

'What have your scouts reported?' he asked as they walked through the palace towards Celene's chambers.

'*Scout* – only one returned. High Prince Seratos Leznar, once one of my father's staunchest allies, has forsaken his faith and invaded Varga-Shemshah, Dra-Azun and Ezné-Khalii. My father is sending reinforcements both north and south. Knowing him, it would surprise me if he didn't lead one of the relief forces himself,' Celene replied, somewhat troubled.

'If he does march with the army, will you be going too?' Thurion asked.

'I don't know. Father has marched with the army before but that was always west, into the Plains of the Dead and we were always safe here in Nemeth-Sharrayah. Now though... there's a chance that we will be invaded too, and if we have sent our armies to relieve our neighbours...'

Celene was clearly worried. Thurion placed a hand on her shoulder trying to comfort her.

'From what little I know of your father he will have already have considered this. You can trust him to ensure that you're kept safe. Besides, I have no plans to leave, not for a while yet at least.'

Celene embraced him, holding him tight, his words reassuring her.

The mustering of the two relief forces began almost as soon as the meeting was concluded. With the exception of High Prince Lautos, all the other delegates immediately returned to their principalities. High Prince Lautos sent messengers to his three sons ordering them to immediately march and rendezvous with Raparké's relief force south-east of Shemshah. Oddly, High Prince Taran didn't seem as concerned to return to his lands as the other princes had been. Raparké made a mental note to investigate this at a later date, but for now, it was far more important to secure what aid he could from the High Prince of Lephar-Nihkur.

It did not take long for the two relief forces to assemble and depart for their respective destinations. Celene discovered that she, along with her mother and the rest of the household staff, was to travel with the army tasked with the relief of Varga-Shemshah; Raparké was not sending a mere token force, he would be leading the army himself. Seneschal Sandar was given the task of running the palace until Raparké returned, and it was with a tear in his eye that he watched Raparké march out of the city at the head of an army many thousands strong.

Thurion was neither allocated a position or rank within the army nor did he request one. He simply travelled within sight of the royal carriages and kept out of the way. Although he would often stray away from the main marching column he was always able to see Celene's carriage, though she was not always able to see her nomadic protector.

The army steered a more-or-less direct course

towards Shemshah, depending on the lie of the land and availability of maintained roads. High Prince Lautos had initially objected strongly to Raparké's intentions, insisting that his capital city could endure a siege for many months, even years. It was the surrounding settlements that desperately needed aid, he argued.

'Your Highness, we have both fought against the denizens of the Plains of the Dead before, and so we both know that the soundest way of defeating a foe such as this is to cut off it's head. We must confront High Prince Leznar; it is my firm belief that should we slay him then his entire campaign will crumble too,' Raparké explained to the distraught High Prince. It was a sound tactic and despite his current indisposition High Prince Lautos eventually saw sense.

Within a little over a week of leaving Sharrayah the army crossed the border into Varga-Shemshah. The first settlement that lay along their route to the capital was the town of Nimram. As the army's vanguard trotted ahead of the main force towards the town they passed outlying farmsteads that had been burnt to the ground. Cautiously the light horsemen approached the outskirts of the town itself. What they saw shocked them. Nimram was not a walled town, it had not been built to withstand a concerted attack, but it now found itself besieged. Every road into the town had been blocked by overturned carts and wagons. All around the town's perimeter small battles raged as the townsfolk strove to drive off unrelenting attacks by the living-dead. Raparké's light cavalry observed all of this from the cover of a small copse before turning and galloping back to the main force.

Immediately upon hearing his vanguard's report, Raparké ordered a flying column to be organised and despatched immediately to relieve the town. In a little over an hour, most of the pack horses in the column had been unharnessed and reassigned to a couple of infantry companies who were ordered to attach themselves to a squadron of knights under the command of Marshal Xobas.

The morning was wearing on by the time the flying column was galloping towards the beleaguered town. The rest of the army didn't reach the outskirts of Nimram until later that afternoon but the sounds of battle, carried on the wind, had been audible for hours. Thurion was a little way from the roadside when a knight came galloping up the road, past the advancing infantry towards the royal carriages.

'I bear tidings from Marshal Xobas,' the knight announced formally to one of the footmen at the rear of Raparké's carriage. A second later, before the footman had had an opportunity to reply, one of the carriage's side doors swung upon and the High Prince leaned out.

'Report!' Raparké commanded.

'The town is taken, Your Highness. We suffered some losses amongst the infantry but nothing particularly concerning,' the knight announced confidently.

'None of the enemy escaped?'

The knight paused for a moment before replying awkwardly. 'There was one, but we lost track of him in the surrounding countryside.'

Raparké was silent for a moment.

'Tell Marshal Xobas that he is to secure the town and prepare for our arrival. We shall camp at Nimram tonight.'

'Yes, Your Highness,' the knight replied, snapping a crisp salute before turning his mount about and galloping back down the length of the column.

Before he returned to his plans, Raparké ordered the footman to send word to Captain Gadas to have the guard doubled that night: everyone was to be on high alert.

The army of High Prince Raparké made camp in the countryside surrounding Nimram. Pickets were put up and the sentries on guard were changed every four hours. Thurion made his camp within a stone's throw of Celene's carriage. They had had few opportunities to spend any time together since they had marched north with the army, and he was hoping that tonight might be different.

The spirits were with him for, just as he was about to strike flint to steel, a soldier in the livery of the Royal Guard came marching up to him.

'Thurion?' the man asked in a deep voice.

'Aye, that's me.'

'I have a message from the Princess Celene. She requests the pleasure of your company at dinner this evening,' he announced somewhat reluctantly.

'Is there a problem, soldier?' Thurion asked.

'Er... no, Sir, not at all,' came the hurried reply.

'Then lead on, man, lead on,' he replied with a grin.

Thurion removed his furs as he entered Celene's carriage.

'Ah, Thurion, come in. I'm *so* glad you decided to accept my invitation,' she said, greeting him in her sweet voice.

Was that really a seductive tone, or am I imagining it? The spirits are playing with me.

'Was there ever really a chance that I would have declined, Your Highness?!' Thurion replied, smiling.

'No, I suppose not.' Celene blushed. They enjoyed the next few hours, relaxing in each other's company before Celene reluctantly admitted to how tired she was. They embraced, kissed, and Thurion returned to his camp.

The following morning the army was marching again as dawn broke over the horizon, the mist still a thick carpet on the ground. The town of Nimram was left behind as the army continued its journey north-west towards Shemshah. A few miles outside of Nimram they were forced to march through a narrow defile that was heavily wooded on both sides. Tension filled the heavy, silent air as Thurion walked alongside Celene's carriage, hand-in-hand with the young princess. The trees to either side cut out most of the early morning sunlight, adding to the forbidding atmosphere. Thurion, at Celene's behest had stowed his belongings in her baggage wagon. *Why carry them if you don't need to?* she had asked.

A rustle of leaves from the roadside immediately drew Thurion's attention and he walked over to investigate. He had almost reached the source of the rustling when a pale skinned, bloodied corpse rose up and attacked him.

'Get back in the carriage!' he yelled as the slain of Nimram rose up from the undergrowth all around them. It was no use, Celene quickly found herself backed against her baggage wagon, boxed in by a couple of guards.

With most of his weapons stowed in the wagon Thurion was forced to fight with his trusty hatchet, and did so with a will until it became lodged in the skull of a dead villager. He was about to tear it loose when he heard Celene scream. Punching a burnt corpse square in the face and crushing its tissue-thin skull, he turned and looked for the princess. Both of her guards were dead, pulled down by the weight of the dead attacking them. She had lost her grip on the wagon and was being carried away, screaming, into the tree line.

Thurion couldn't help himself, he let out a terrible bestial roar and plunged into the trees after her. Sprinting through the undergrowth with natural ease, it did not take him long to catch up to the princess and her kidnappers — two dozen burnt villagers armed with an assortment of improvised weapons. He laid into them with his bare hands, roaring with a rage born out of love. His eyes glazed over as he tore heads from bodies and dismembered Celene's assailants, oblivious of the blows raining down on him. A shadow swirled around him but vanished as he barrelled through it to finish off the last of the un-dead.

At first he didn't recognise the Royal Guard as they stood around him, the tips of heavy spears levelled at him. He simply roared at them and stood protectively over the cowering princess. A hand gently took hold of his wrist and drew his attention away from the spearmen. He looked down at Celene, she was crying and she was trying to say something.

'Th... Thu... Thurion... Thurion, I'm alright. I'm alright.'

Slowly the rage drained away from him and he found himself panting heavily, his hands covered in cold viscera and surrounded by aggressive Royal Guardsmen. Celene got to her feet and stood in front of Thurion.

'Put your weapons down... PUT THEM DOWN!' she screamed. She then placed her hands protectively round the exhausted Northman.

'It's alright, he wasn't going to hurt me. He never would. Now, lower your weapons.'

Slowly the guards did as the princess demanded. As the tension eased one of the guards stepped forward and spoke to her.

'Your Highness, my name is Captain Ramphien, Commander of the Royal Guard. We heard you screaming and found the two dead men by the roadside. We feared the worst—'

'What happened here?' An authoritative voice demanded.

Captain Ramphien turned around to see who had interrupted him, and saw half a dozen knights come tramping through the undergrowth. Celene quickly recognised the commander.

'Marshal Xobas, I was attacked by these... these... things, but thanks to Thurion I am safe and unharmed.'

The marshal bowed to the young princess before turning to Captain Ramphien.

'Captain! Report.'

'Marshal, I heard the princess screaming. My men and I got here as fast as we could but it was pretty much all over by the time I got here...' the captain trailed off, at a loss for words, 'Guardsman Balos was one of the first here,' he said, gesturing for a younger soldier to come forward.

'Guardsman, tell the marshal exactly what you saw,' the captain ordered. The young soldier paused for a moment before beginning.

'Well, er, yes, I was the first here, Sir. The princess was on the ground, just over there,' the young man pointed to a where a small depression had been trampled in the undergrowth, 'There were bodies strewn everywhere, and there was a bear standing right over her, sir.'

The marshal did not look impressed by the young man's testimony.

'A *bear*, guardsman?'

'Yes, marshal, a bear, clear as day, standing over her. It seemed to be protecting her from the dead, marshal.'

'This is your report, guardsman? This is the report you expect me to relay to the High Prince?' Marshal Xobas asked accusingly. The young man was initially cowed by the marshal's presence but finally stood tall and replied.

'Yes, marshal, that's exactly what I saw.'

'And where did this *bear*, that you say you saw, disappear to?'

'Well, marshal, by the time the captain got here there was just a bear standing over the Princess surrounded by a load of bodies. He ordered us to kill it and we would have, marshal, we would have, only it...'

'Don't try my patience, guardsman, I haven't got all day.'

'Well, I don't know how to explain it, marshal, other than it only seemed to respond the the Princess. It was roaring and bellowing at us, but as soon as Her Highness touched it and spoke to it, it... it...' the guardsman trailed off again, lost for words. He pointed at Thurion,

Marshal Xobas turned to Thurion and fixed him with a stern gaze. Thurion returned the look without emotion.

'I think you had better come with me, both of

you,' he said, indicating Guardsman Balos and Thurion. Thurion seemed about to challenge the marshal when a gentle touch from Celene caused him to turn. Her smile spoke a thousand words and reassured him, he allowed himself to be led away by Marshal Xobas' knights.

Thurion and Guardsman Balos were led to Raparké's carriage where the marshal recounted what he had seen, and Guardsman Balos gave his testimony. Raparké didn't speak for a while as he mulled over what he had just heard.

'Bring me Father Xathos, he is the acting head of the Nemeth Order of Life in Sandar's absence, is he not, marshal?'

'He is, Your Highness, I shall fetch him at once.'

It was a couple of minutes before the old priest arrived at Raparké's carriage, a couple of minutes that passed in awkward silence. At length, however, Father Xathos did arrive and heard both the marshal's report and that of Guardsman Balos. After giving it some thought, he began explaining.

'Taking the guardsman's report as being true, and I have no reason to doubt his word, Your Highness, I think the explanation lies with our friend, Thurion, here,' he began before turning to the barbarian, 'Thurion, as I understand your culture, upon coming of age, among other things, you decide upon a patron god?'

'Aye, in a manner of speaking,' Thurion confirmed.

'And from what I have heard, upon your coming of age, you chose the spirits of the wilderness as *your* patron?'

'Aye, that's true.'

The old priest turned his attention back to the High Prince.

'In which case, Your Highness, I believe I can explain what happened in the woods. As you are aware we, as devotees of Holy Ios, can channel some of her power.'

'Yes, what of it?' Raparké asked.

'It is my understanding that among the Northmen of Barbaria, those who devote themselves to the wilderness can, after a fashion, channel some of its power. This channelling however, tends to be less driven by conscious thought and more by emotions. It is my belief that the kidnapping of your daughter, elicited an emotional response from Thurion that was so powerful it triggered the change that Guardsman Balos witnessed, only reversing when the princess calmed him down,' the priest concluded.

Raparké looked to be in deep thought, and then nodded.

'I see. That explains what Guardsman Balos saw, and why the bear, just… disappeared.' Turning his attention to Thurion he continued, 'I think I am beginning to understand you a little better, Thurion. My daughter is right, there is more to you than meets the eye.' Raparké turned back to his priest. 'Thank you, Father, this goes some way to explaining how he was able to banish a shade back to the underworld.'

'A *shade*, Your Highness?' the priest asked.

'The shadowy figure Guardsman Balos saw was in all likelihood a shade; an ethereal necromancer. They are immune to mundane weapons…' The High Prince turned again to Thurion, 'It would appear that your transformation, Thurion, is far from mundane. I thank you again for saving my daughter. It would seem that you *are* wherever you are needed… which is a curious thing indeed.'

Turning to address them all he concluded this impromptu meeting, '*That*, however, is a topic for another time. We have been stationary too long, marshal. See to it that we are moving again as soon as possible. You are dismissed.'

Chapter 46

Celene kept to herself after her attempted kidnapping, not due to the trauma of the event itself, but rather due to the change she had seen come over Thurion. Her feelings towards the strange wanderer had been growing ever since they had met. Even his duel with her brother, and the savage aggression he had displayed that afternoon had done little to diminish the way she felt. Indeed, last night, when they had shared dinner together in the quiet serenity of her carriage, she had discovered that her feelings were far stronger than she had previously admitted.

But now though, now that she had seen what he was capable of, given the right emotional stimulus, she was suddenly entirely unsure just how she felt. On the one hand she knew, deep within her, that he would never hurt her, nor allow her to come to harm if he could at all prevent it. On the other however, there was always the chance that, should he become sufficiently emotionally worked up, he could change form with no warning. And so, in her state of confusion, she kept very much to herself.

Thurion, for his part did not try to impose himself upon the princess, sure that she was simply coming to terms with what she had witnessed. He spent the days after his transmogrification walking close to Raparké's carriage in order to overhear the reports that were regularly brought to the High Prince.

Some days later a rider in the livery of Varga-

Shemshah came galloping down the road, stopping only when he drew alongside High Prince Lautos' carriage.

'I bring tidings from Prince Nabas; I must speak with the High Prince immediately,' the rider demanded.

A footman informed him that the High Prince was in a meeting with High Prince Raparké at the moment. Pointing towards Raparké's carriage he said 'You will find him in that carriage, over there.' The messenger turned his mount and rode up to Raparké's carriage. A few moments after announcing himself, High Prince Lautos emerged and addressed him.

'You have a message for me? From whom?' the High Prince demanded.

'From Prince Nabas, Your Highness. He reports that he expects to rendezvous with you as planned. Prince Thulganos, however, has been delayed by a day or so, though he is marching his men hard.'

Lautos received this news with a grim acceptance. He was pleased to hear that Prince Nabas would reach Shemshah on time, irritated by the delay of his second son but very concerned that he had heard nothing from his third.

'Thank you. Get yourself a fresh horse and return to Prince Nabas. Inform him of our current situation and tell him that we expect to reach him in about two days.'

The rider gave his High Prince a smart salute and trotted off to replace his tired mount.

The High Prince's estimate had been correct, Raparké's army sighted Shemshah two days later. Prince Nabas' much smaller force was waiting for them a few miles from the city, concealed behind a line of low hills. The prince commanded two companies of regular infantry, two companies of irregular militia, two squadrons of heavily armed knights and a single squadron of light cavalry. The regular infantry was a mixture of lightly armoured crossbowmen and more heavily armoured spearmen with tall, broad shields. This combination of arms was favoured in many of the principalities. The irregular militia had been rapidly raised and were, for the most part poorly equipped and far less reliable than their regular counterparts. It was obvious that the prince's knights had seen heavy action, their armour had been extensively repaired and was, in some places, badly scored or dented. The squadron of light cavalry looked skittish and nervous and had clearly suffered during the recent invasion.

Prince Nabas embraced his father warmly.

'Oh, father, I am so glad to see you, especially in such company!'

'And I you, son, you're looking well—' Lautos pulled a broken feather from his son's left wing, '—given the circumstances. Have you heard from either of your brothers recently?' the High Prince asked.

'Thulganos is a little over a day behind me, though he is marching hard. He should arrive by noon tomorrow if he is not delayed further.' Prince Nabas paused and lowered his voice, 'I have not heard from Rodemos. The last I knew he had marched out of Ibukar with a small force of cavalry to reinforce Thulganos, that was some days ago now...' the prince was downcast as he thought of his youngest brother.

'Try not to worry, Nabas, Rodemos is resourceful and intelligent, he may yet surprise us all.' Lautos tried to reassure his eldest son, but his words didn't convey much conviction. 'Now, however, we must turn our attention to more immediate matters: the relief of Shemshah.' Father and son turned to view the battered capital city.

A smoky haze hung over the city, testament to Seratos' razing and burning of everything he possibly could. It seemed that the fallen angel was intent on turning Varga-Shemshah into a burnt, lifeless wasteland. Slowly, Raparké's army formed itself up facing the city and, with Prince Nabas's force to its right, began to advance. There could be no surprise assault with such a large force and so Seratos' legions of dead soldiers managed to retreat in good order. The siege of Shemshah was, in this way, lifted with no loss of life. Knowing that he would have to face Seratos in battle the following day, however, Raparké ordered that his army camp in the shadow of the city's western wall. High Prince Lautos insisted however that Raparké and his household be put up in the royal palace rather than camping outside with the rest of the army.

Thurion followed the royal carriages into the city and was immediately assaulted by the stench of a city under siege; human and animal waste mixed with smoke and blood. The streets were lined with tired, battered soldiers, every one of them showing deep relief as the city's saviours rode past. When they reached the palace Thurion was treated as one of Celene's attendants, his presence wasn't questioned by anyone. He couldn't explain this – given the prejudice he had experienced in the past. He hadn't noticed the look of approval Raparké had given him when he saw that he was still at his daughter's side. And if Raparké approved, then everybody approved.

As dawn broke the city was already bustling

443

as men prepared to meet their macabre enemy in battle. Thurion breakfasted with the rest of the servants and, after donning his war-gear, he accompanied Celene to the palace courtyard where she tearfully embraced her father and brothers before they departed for the battlefield.

'Oh! I cannot bear it!' Celene admitted to Thurion as they climbed the steps back into the palace, 'It is always the same when they leave for war.'

Thurion thought for a moment.

'The battle will be some distance from the city walls, and so they should be well out of bow shot,' he said.

'So?' Celene asked, wiping a tear from the corner of her eye.

'We could watch the battle from the city wall. You'll be safe there and you won't have to wait in anxiety,' Thurion explained.

She placed a hand on his mail-covered arm. 'Thank you, Thurion, I would like that.'

And so Thurion and Celene watched from the city wall as Raparké's army formed up, flanked to it's right by Prince Nabas' detachment. Across from the city, the self-proclaimed Angel of Death began to deploy his vast force. High Prince Lautos was busy organising the surviving units of his city's soldiery; they were to remain as a reserve, out of sight within the city until required.

Chapter 47

Raparké deployed his army along the length of the western wall, between the city's south-western gate and the wall's furthest northern extent. The centre of the battle field was dominated by a single huge outcropping of rock surrounded by what was once a small wood. Now however, all that remained was a smouldering, ash-choked graveyard of burnt tree trunks. A deep, sluggish river wound its way from the west, its course bisecting the southern end of the battlefield before curving away to the south. A small farmstead and bridge were located on its banks, nearly opposite the city gates. Besides these terrain features the rest of the battlefield was a burnt, blackened wasteland.

Thurion and Celene watched as Raparké formed his battle line. Three squadrons of light cavalry and two squadrons of knights formed up on the far left, in front of the city gates. Some one thousand, two hundred and fifty cavalrymen in total. It was the role of these units to support the advance of the infantry and counter any attempts by the enemy to turn Raparké's left flank. To the knights' right a detachment of three companies of mixed infantry were formed up. Led by the newly-promoted Marshal Gadas, these soldiers were equipped the same as Prince Nabas' regular infantry. Raparké led the main infantry detachment, deployed to the centre. This was also comprised of three companies of regular infantry but was supported by the palace Royal Guard – the

High Prince's personal bodyguard. Wearing heavy scale mail armour and armed with halberds, these were veteran soldiers who had seen many years' service and could be relied upon. Two loosely-formed units of skirmishers loitered in front of the High Prince's main detachment.

Raparké's right flank was anchored by two further detachments, each led by one of his sons. Prince Erakos commanded a detachment of three companies of regular infantry whilst Prince Iraudis commanded two companies of regulars and a squadron of knights and had deployed behind his brother, ready to reinforce him if it became necessary. Prince Nabas deployed his detachment to Prince Erakos' right, on the far right flank.

As Raparké scrutinised the dead legions deployed opposite him he ordered his priests to prepare themselves. Each priest rode off to his or her appointed company or squadron and began praying for Ios' blessing. Once battle was joined they would beseech their holy patron for aid and to intervene more directly.

* * *

Seratos watched as his army deployed, a mirthless smile crossing his face. He saw how Raparké's priests prayed so arrogantly to their weakling god. Normally these conduits of the God of Life would pose a very real threat. Today, however, would be different. It was typical for Lords of the Dead to guard their knowledge jealously and so they often found themselves commanding the entire army themselves, something which required great concentration. Seratos, however, had decided to break with tradition and take his officers and commanders into his confidence, revealing to them some of what he had learned. In this way he would not be forced to try and counter each and every action of Ios' cursed sycophants.

As the last of his legions deployed, Seratos looked over his force one last time before giving the order to advance. Commander Aldene's detachment of mixed infantry mirrored that of the detachment deployed opposite her. She had advanced her infantry almost to the farmstead by the river, anchoring Seratos' right flank. Three squadrons of knights were concealed behind her infantry, dismounted until they were required. Two large packs of hounds lurked in the cover of the farmstead. Between the river and the burned wood Seratos' two companies of archers had been deployed. Lacking any armour, these lightly-armoured soldiers were armed with powerful bows, easily able to out-range the crossbows of either force. Seratos himself commanded a detachment comprising two companies of mixed infantry supported by his own heavily-armoured bodyguard armed with colossal two-handed weapons. This detachment was currently out of sight, deployed behind the burnt wood and the rocky outcrop.

His Seneschal, Sisus, was deployed to his left and commanded the largest detachment in the army; two companies of regular infantry and two companies of archaically equipped heavy infantry armed with pole-weapons. Commander Abragon had deployed his detachment of four infantry companies aggressively, in front of Sisus' infantry. Seratos' left flank was was held by the majority of his cavalry; four squadrons of knights stood sentinel-still, whilst two packs of hounds loped around nearby.

447

A single brass horn sounded in the cold morning. In response, the dead began to advance. Moments later several other horns responded and Raparké's army also advanced to meet their foes. Marshal Gadas and his High Prince advanced steadily whilst the head-strong Prince Erakos advanced rapidly towards Commander Abragon's detachment. In response, Princes Iraudis and Nabas were forced to follow suit so as not to leave the young prince stranded.

Observing Raparké's advance, Seratos once again smiled to himself and watched as his forces advanced; following the order of battle they had drawn up the previous night. Commander Aldene advanced her infantry to the river bank, still keeping her knights concealed. The hound packs loped through the farmstead but stopped short of crossing the bridge. Seratos ordered his own detachment forward in support of the archers. Commander Abragon advanced, successfully drawing the rash young Prince Erakos out of position whilst Sisus advanced in support. The cavalry on the left flank suddenly roused themselves, their mounts rearing and flailing at the air before galloping towards Prince Nabas and his men.

The light cavalry on Raparké's left flank and the skirmishers in the centre were the first troops to advance within range of the enemy. The former took the full brunt of Commander Aldene's crossbows and broke whilst the leftmost unit of skirmishers was targeted by both units of archers and was slain to a man.

Marshal Gadas' detachment continued to advance despite the loss of its light cavalry. As it did so, the hounds that had been lurking in the farmstead suddenly began racing across the bridge. They tried to outflank the marshal but were cut down by well-disciplined crossbow volleys. Raparké's detachment doggedly advanced in the face of the archers' fire.

Prince Erakos had advanced too rapidly and too far, however, and his detachment was trading crossbow bolts with Commander Abragon's infantry and coming off worst. The surviving skirmishers tried to advance in support of the prince, but several volleys of crossbow bolts drove them back. Prince Iraudis found himself stuck behind his brother's infantry, whilst Prince Nabas was forced to check his advance as Sisus' detachment wheeled round Abragon's, and he found himself suddenly facing the seneschal's infantry as well as the rapidly closing cavalry.

* * *

Celene and Thurion watched from the city wall as the battle unfolded. Thurion watched with interest, since he had only ever witnessed a pitched battle with formations once before. Celene, however, was watching with rising concern.

'Oh, no...' she whispered.

'Princess?' Thurion asked.

'It's my brother; he's always been rash and headstrong. He's in trouble.'

They watched as Erakos' detachment began to fall back under a relentless rain of crossbow bolts, fired in orderly volleys from Commander Abragon's detachment. The legions of the dead rarely fielded mixed infantry, traditionally favouring fewer units of archers supported by massed ranks of spearmen. Seratos, however, was no traditional Lord of the

Dead. Prince Erakos, it seemed, had severely underestimated his foe.

Celene watched with horror as her brother's detachment began to retreat, its flanks crumbling until the main body of infantry was falling back to the relative cover of the burnt woods.

'Thurion, you must do something!' she cried.

'Do something? What do you expect me to be able to do?!' the Northman asked, incredulous.

'Can't you see what's happening? My brother may be killed if someone doesn't do something! Look around, there's no one else! Please!' she cried, tears running down her cheeks.

Thurion looked over the battlefield and then down to where the army of Shemshah was forming up behind the city gates, ready to reinforce Raparké. She was right, Erakos was being pushed back against the monolithic rock formation and there was no one that could reach him in time. His countenance became grim as he realised what he had to try and do.

'Get me a horse, now!' he yelled, before turning and running in the direction of the south-western gate. Celene spread her wings wide and threw herself from the city wall. She flew swiftly into the city in search of any horse that could be spared.

* * *

As Prince Erakos fell back towards the towering rock and blasted woods, Sisus' detachment engaged Prince Nabas' infantry at range, causing both units of militia to break and flee. The prince's knights wheeled, taking up position behind the infantry, as their more lightly-equipped counterparts drew the advancing enemy cavalry on.

To the south, Marshal Gadas' infantry had begun exchanging fire with Commander Aldene's detachment on the far river bank, with both sides suffering considerable losses. Where the commander's subordinates could resurrect their fallen troops, the marshal's priests found their attempts to heal the wounded hampered by the full force of their enemy's considerable necromantic capabilities. The marshal's knights had, by now, scattered the few remaining hounds that still lurked around the bridge near the farmstead.

High Prince Raparké was experiencing similar difficulties as he exchanged crossbow fire with Seratos' detachment and the supporting archers. All of the High Prince's units of regular infantry were driven back by the weight of fire rained down upon them, leaving only the Royal Guard to advance on Seratos' heavy infantry.

* * *

In the time it took Thurion to make his way from the wall, past the mustered reinforcements and reach the south-western gate, Celene had already commandeered a horse and was waiting for him.

'Save my brother!' was all she could manage as she thrust the reins into his hand.

Thurion mounted without a word. The gate was opened and he galloped out of the city just as High Prince Lautos gave the order to advance. Thurion did not see the High Prince leading his two companies of foot knights and five companies of regular infantry out of the city in support of his embattled ally.

By the time the horns of Sharrayah,

451

announcing the presence of High Prince Lautos on the battlefield had sounded, Marshal Gadas' infantry was in full retreat, unable to withstand the punishment being meted out to them. As they retreated, Commander Aldene reached out her hands and, an incantation on her lips, raised those whom her troops had just slain. The newly animated dead immediately began advancing on their former comrades. The marshal's knights, unaware of what had just befallen their supporting infantry galloped across the bridge, intent on engaging the commander's infantry from the rear. Instead they found themselves counter-charged by the commander's knights that had until now, remained hidden from view. The ensuing battle was savage.

Raparké's Royal Guard were still locked in bitter combat with Seratos's heavy infantry, when their own supporting infantry – who had already been driven back by concentrated crossbow fire – were charged. Having already suffered heavy casualties, Raparké's supporting infantry were savagely cut down. This loss allowed Seratos' archers to begin raining arrows on the advancing army of Shemshah.

* * *

As Thurion galloped across the battlefield, a single figure unnoticed by either side, Prince Nabas' infantry barely withstood the charge of Sisus' detachment. Both of his fleeing militia units were cut down by the pursuing dead who, finding themselves in no immediate danger, resurrected the slain militia, swelling their own ranks. Despite withstanding the charge of Sisus' heavy infantry, the prince's infantry was cut down, falling beneath the pole-arms of the seneschal's heavy infantry. Prince Nabas was the last to fall, dismembered by many vicious, heavy blades. To the right, the prince's light cavalry successfully drew the dead knights into range of their heavily armoured fellows, but found themselves pulled from their saddles by the packs of pursuing hounds.

With a thunderous crash, Prince Nabas' knights thundered into the rear two squadrons of dead knights. Here the desperate fury of the living met the unrelenting savagery of the dead. None rode away from that charge, neither living nor dead. As the High Prince's right flank began to crumble, it was all Prince Iraudis could do to wheel his own detachment round to face Sisus' rampaging infantry, before he too was engaged.

By the time Thurion reached the charred forest, Prince Erakos' infantry had been pushed back amongst the burnt trees themselves. No longer able to hold their ranks, the battle had transformed into a number of small, desperate skirmishes as bands of soldiers fought to hold the inexorable tide of dead at bay. The surviving unit of skirmishers tried to circle round to reach Commander Abragon. The commander however, had raised so many of the recently slain that the lightly-equipped skirmishers were, once again, forced to fall back.

Thurion leapt from his horse as it careered into the burnt wood. Landing with feline grace the Northman drew his great-axe and ran towards the sounds of battle in search of Celene's brother. The fighting was fierce and had kicked up so much of the thick carpet of ash that covered the ground, that the prince's soldiers found they could barely breathe, let alone fight. Thurion found Erakos surrounded by two dozen enemy spearmen. To the prince's credit, he fought with peerless skill coupled with a desperation born of mortal dread. He was horribly outnumbered though and was eventually driven to his knees.

Thurion entered the small clearing and initially thought that he was too late. A bright sabre tip appearing through a dead spearman told him that he was not, and with a roar he charged into the meleé and began hewing at the prince's un-dead assailants. Thurion fought like a demon, barely stopping to breathe as he cut down the dead, fighting his way through to the prince. As the last of the prince's assailants fell, cloven in two, Thurion made the most of the brief respite to haul the near-senseless prince away from the swirling, chaotic battle. Thurion hauled the badly wounded prince up the pillar of rock, like a panther might a fresh kill. Then, looking about him he espied the skirmishers loitering in cover, on the far side of the outcrop.

'You there!' Thurion bellowed. The scouts looked up in surprise and not a little consternation.

'I have the prince here. He's wounded but alive. Climb up and guard him while I clear us a path out of here!'

'Who are you?' a voice called.

'I am the one who has just pulled your beloved prince from the jaws of death!' Thurion bellowed, lifting the prince's body enough for them to see that he was telling the truth. A couple of them immediately ascended the rock face to tend the prince, whilst the rest took up positions at the foot of the rocky formation. Thurion leaped down and jogged back to the battleground looking for the enemy commander.

Not wanting to have to cut his way through an endless tide of the walking dead, Thurion slunk in and out of cover, dodging the desperate skirmishes. Where he could not sneak past, he would attack suddenly and without warning, charging through the haze of disturbed ash to cut his way through, disappearing as suddenly as he had appeared. Moving in this way, he quickly worked his way through the enemy formation and found himself face-to-face with Commander Abragon.

The commander had thought himself safe behind his troops, confident that he had pinned the young prince and his troops against the rock face. His look of shock had not quite turned to one of anger when Thurion, his stride unbroken, barrelled into him. Both commander and barbarian fell to the ground. Thurion was quicker to his feet though, and didn't wait until the corpse-commander had gotten to his before raining a torrent of blows down on him. Abragon was wearing well-made heavy armour but even the toughest tempered plate could not withstand the rain of blows. Thurion didn't give his opponent the chance to gather his thoughts, let alone regain his feet. Eventually the commander's armour failed and Thurion's massive axe split him in half at the waist. Another blow decapitated Seratos' father, killing him a second time.

Thurion breathed heavily, spitting a mixture of spittle and ash through his helmet's mail and watched as the commander's detachment began to crumble. In a matter of minutes, the few dozen men that were still alive found themselves alone in a sea of corpses.

* * *

Although Seratos had just lost an entire detachment of infantry and one of his senior commanders, it mattered little — the way the battle was progressing. The dead that Commander Aldene had recently raised had drawn all of Marshal Gadas' crossbow fire allowing her own troops to rain steel-tipped death onto the marshal's battered troops with impunity. Before long, the marshal's effective fighting strength had been reduced to a single company of infantry. The marshal's knights had finally succumbed, dying to a man on the outskirts of the farmstead.

Raparké found himself suddenly isolated, his Royal Guard alone, fighting a bloody battle with Seratos' heavy infantry.

High Prince Lautos took to the air briefly to gauge the situation on the ground. Once he returned he immediately ordered three of his units of regular infantry to peel off and march in support of Prince Iraudis, who was now out of position and heavily outnumbered due to the complete collapse of their right flank. The High Prince then led his two units of foot knights, and his two remaining units of regular infantry, in support of Raparké and his beleaguered Royal Guard.

Chapter 48

Thurion unexpectedly found himself taking charge of the situation. He had set out to save Celene's brother, and had managed to save him from being butchered like most of his men, but he was still far from safe. Those few of Erakos' men who had survived the disastrous charge against Commander Abragon's detachment now looked to Thurion for guidance, as did the skirmishers who were still standing guard over the wounded prince.

'We need to get the prince back to the city. Bring him down here,' Thurion ordered. The prince's men quickly made a crude litter and laid their prince on it. Cautiously, Thurion's rag-tag band of survivors crept out of the burned forest and onto the open battlefield. What they saw shocked them.

To their left, Prince Iraudis' infantry was being overwhelmed. As the last of the prince's banners fell, the young angel took to the air and flew away from Sisus' rampaging heavy infantry, back towards the relief force from Shemshah. The young prince's knights desperately charged the surviving squadrons of dead cavalry that had annihilated Prince Nabas' knights. The crashing sound of steel on steel was tremendous; they fought bravely but were not able to halt Seratos' marauding cavalry.

To Thurion's right, the battle-weary soldiery had suffered heavy losses as they fought Seratos' infantry. However, they had slowly gained the upper hand and were able to kill the enemy faster than their commanders could resurrect them.

With the battle still raging Thurion led his small troop out towards the city. Suddenly, one of Erakos' soldiers cried out, pointing to his right.

'Look!'

Everyone stopped and looked in the direction the man had indicated, in time to see the enemy's standard waver and fall where their High Prince's Royal Guard battled Seratos' own bodyguard. A great cheer went up from the survivors. Their cheering was quickly silenced as the sound of battle erupted again to their left. The relief force sent to support Prince Iraudis had been charged by Sisus' unstoppable infantry. Without warning, the young prince's massacred detachment slowly rose to their feet and began marching towards Thurion and his company.

'We can't make it to the city, not now! ... Back to the forest! Get back!' Thurion bellowed. His men needed little convincing; not wishing to be caught in the open and surrounded by the relentless dead, they turned and carried their wounded prince back to the burnt wood.

* * *

Seratos did not see Commander Aldene lead her infantry across the river to finally annihilate Marshal Gadas' detachment. Neither did he see her knights cut their way through High Prince Lautos' remaining foot knights. He was only dimly aware of the sound of horns blaring in the distance announcing the arrival of Prince Thulgano's relief force. All his attention was focussed on High Prince Raparké who had stepped out from the ranks of his bloodied, but victorious, Royal Guard to challenge him.

So it has come down to this.

'What has happened to you, my old friend?' Raparké asked, lowering his long sabre, sadness evident in his tone, 'look around you.'

'Look around me?! Look around yourself, High Prince! Is your Holy Mother anywhere to be seen? Where is the evidence of her presence? I can't see it. No, Raparké, she has abandoned us. I have seen it and it is time you did too. Your army is defeated; your god and your priests have failed you. Submit to me, forsake that weak old hag you call your god and allow me to enlighten you,' Seratos implored.

'I cannot bear to hear you speak thus, brother. Have you really fallen so far?' Raparké asked.

'Fallen? I have not fallen. I have risen to such great heights, surely you can see that?!'

'I weep for you, Seratos, truly I weep for you,' Raparké replied, his heart grieving.

'Weep not, old friend, for I am free. Now... allow me to set you free,' the Angel of Death announced as he took to the air, his archaic bronze armour creaking. His long pole-arm, unnaturally, reflected no light at all as he came at Raparké.

Chapter 49

Raparké drew a second, shorter blade; his sabre's twin, as Seratos swooped towards him. With a crash the two angels clashed, blades moving almost too fast for the eye to follow. Sparks flew as steel met steel, the mêlée flowing back and forth between Raparké's Royal Guard and the archers behind Seratos, who were still sending flights of arrows into High Prince Lautos' infantry.

As he fought, Seratos' movements began to trail black fumes that poured from the Angel of Death with no visible source. Raparké, as he fought with greater and greater conviction, seemed to be surrounded by a faint golden aura that blurred his movements some-what. It seemed that the Gods themselves were intervening in this epic duel.

Blows were traded and armour scored and dented. More than once the elegant aerial duel came crashing to the ground. The two winged warriors grappling in the ash, blood and mud of the battlefield until one or other broke away and took to the air once again. The decisive blow, when it came, was so quick and so fast that none saw it. Raparké, flicking his wrist and sending the blade of his sabre around the shaft of Seratos' pole-arm, severed his opponent's right wrist with a pin-point strike. The Angel of Death cried out and, dropping his pole arm, fell from the sky. Raparké however, had run him through before he hit the ground.

Seratos hit the ground with a crash, blood

pouring from his chest and the stump of his wrist. The fumes that had been emanating from him as he fought settled over his body. Raparké looked on, a deep sadness etched across his features, as the Angel of Death breathed his last and the fumes that had gathered over his body began to float away, westwards, towards the Plains of the Dead.

Barring Sisus' infantry and cavalry, the army of Seratos, Angel of Death, began crumbling to dust.

***

Thurion, alongside his band of battered survivors, prepared to meet the charge of the dead once again. Even though every man in that small, desperate band had suffered numerous wounds, was bleeding and exhausted, a grim determination still smouldered in their eyes. With a cry of defiance Thurion led his adopted men as he counter-charged the advancing dead.

As Sisus was driving his heavy infantry forward against Prince Iraudis, High Prince Lautos and the Shemshah relief force, he felt a profound shock, such a shock that could only have one meaning.

It's over… it's all over…

With a thought he summoned his remaining two squadrons of knights and their trailing hound packs to him. Pulling a skeletal knight from his steed, Sisus mounted the dead warhorse and fled the battlefield surrounded by his remaining cavalry, leaving his infantry, leaderless, to their fate.

Sisus' abandoned infantry were finally overcome, though the cost was high; fully a third of the men who had marched to Prince Iraudis' aid lay dead or dying around him.

Thurion and his ragged band fought like cornered beasts around the prone form of Prince Erakos. By the time High Prince Lautos had reformed his two remaining companies of infantry, noticed Thurion's plight, and had marched to relieve him the barbarian's battle was almost over. The sight that confronted the High Prince as he led the Shemshah infantry into the burned-out forest shocked him. Bodies of friend and foe alike were strewn everywhere, blood covered the ground forming a red-brown ashy-sludge.

Thurion alone was still on his feet, straddling Prince Erakos, his long-handled axe in one hand and his hatchet in another fending off blows from two opponents. He was covered from head to foot in blood. His mail was torn and he was breathing heavily. As Prince Iraudis led a score of spearmen into the clearing, Thurion split the skull of the last of his assailants. It was suddenly so very quiet, barring the moaning of the wounded.

Iraudis ran over to the barbarian.

'Thank you...' the young prince was too overcome by emotion to say any more.

'He still lives,' Thurion replied, still somewhat out of breath, in answer to the prince's unasked question. Iraudis immediately fell to his knees at his brother's side.

'We need to get him back to the city immediately,' he announced. In response several soldiers jogged over and picked up the litter on which the prince still lay.

'There's still a battle going on isn't there?' Thurion asked, recalling his previous attempt to reach the city with the wounded prince.

'We must try! We need to get him to the temple at once.'

Painfully, Thurion limped over to where his great axe was stuck in the head of a corpse, and pulled it free before following Prince Iraudis and his infantry as they cautiously marched out onto the battlefield once again. However, when no evidence of any enemy formations could be seen, their natural caution slowly transformed into confidence. As they were marching back to the city, a rider galloped over and delivered the news of Raparké's victory over Seratos. A great wave of relief swept over the tired, wounded soldiers as the news spread through the ranks.

Upon their return to the city the prince's detachment was met by a large number of the city's priesthood who were ready to tend to the wounded. Thurion escorted Prince Erakos as he was taken straight to the temple. Celene and her mother were waiting there for them. Four priests took the prince's litter from Iraudis and the soldiers who had carried him from the battlefield, and laid him on a low altar. Celene and High Princess Tamura approached the altar and began to pray.

Thurion watched in silence as the prince's mother and sister called on their god to intervene. Slowly, a golden aura settled around the young prince and his wounds began to close up. The aura moved over and settled on Celene and her mother. They both cried out in pain as Erakos' wounds were transferred to them. Horrendous cuts appeared on their exposed skin, and their wings contorted as the bones broke. Thurion made towards Celene when she cried out but Iraudis restrained him.

'Wait, wait. It will pass,' he whispered, and

Thurion was compelled to stand back and watch as the healing ritual was carried out.

As the Erakos' wounds were assumed by Ios through Celene and Tamura, so their wounds and injuries closed and healed.

Seeing their prince healed, the soldiers who had carried him to the temple were filled with joy and relief, and gave thanks to Ios for restoring their commander. Iraudis dismissed them so they could tend to their own needs. Thurion turned to leave with them when Celene's hand grabbed him.

'Thurion, wait.'

Slowly, painfully, the battle-weary Northman turned his bloodied form to the princess. He was about to say something when a wave of exhaustion overcame him and he nearly collapsed. Celene fell to her knees as she tried to support his weight. With the help of several priests, she helped him up the steps that led to the altar, where they sat him painfully down.

'I'm sorry, I'm bleeding all over your nice clean temple,' he smiled, attempting humour – but grimaced suddenly.

'Shh...' Celene quietly told him. She turned to her mother, 'Mother, help please!' she implored.

High Princess Tamura walked over to where Thurion was reclining against the altar steps.

'I would look into the face of the man who saved my son's life,' she announced, resting one hand gently on her daughter's shoulder.

Painfully, Thurion removed his helmet, grunting loudly as he did so. Laying his helmet on one of the altar steps, he turned his bloodied face up towards the High Princess. Tamura's usually measured expression gave way to one of compassion as Thurion looked up at her, one eye sealed closed by a thick layer of drying blood.

'You have given so much, for us, for my son. Allow me to give you something in return,' she said, kneeling. She placed her hands on his head.

The experience of being healed was surreal, like nothing he had ever felt before. The golden aura that enveloped him felt warm and calming. He felt the pain leave his body, his wounds flushed hot, and the flesh flowed together like molten wax. He was not expecting to be able to stand easily, never mind feel as fit as he ever had. Stand up he did though, albeit somewhat shakily. After thanking the High Princess, who was herself still slightly traumatised from the healing, he was escorted out of the temple by Celene.

'You almost died today. Why did you do it?' she asked once they were out of earshot of Tamura.

'You asked me to,' he replied simply.

'But you don't even *like* my brother...'

'I have nothing against your brother. The fact that he doesn't like me is something entirely different. We Northmen don't die easily, and besides, I wasn't going to die without seeing you again,' he admitted. Celene was about to respond when Prince Iraudis interrupted her.

'Sister, I expect that father will return soon. We should be at the gates to welcome him.'

'Yes, of course.' She motioned to a priest that was leaving the temple, beckoning him to her, 'Please see that Thurion has quarters in the palace tonight.'

'At once, Your Highness,' the priest replied.

'I am going to welcome my father at the gates. I'm not sure what his intentions are but I expect he will want to thank you personally. Please come to my chambers either later on this evening or tomorrow morning and we shall go and find him together,' she said before joining her brother on his way to the city gates.

Thurion was shown to a small apartment where he removed his battered and bloodied armour, before returning to the site of the previous evening's camp to retrieve his belongings. That didn't take him long, but it did take him several hours to clean and repair his clothes and armour as best he could. To repair his armour properly would require the use of a blacksmith's forge, but that could wait until tomorrow. The battle had lasted until the early evening and it was some hours past sunset by the time Thurion finally finished cleaning his equipment. Given the late hour, he thought it best to wait until the following morning before calling on the princess.

Thurion slept late the following morning and it was some hours after sunrise before he rose. Despite expecting to be staying in the palace for a few days at least, he packed his belongings regardless, out of force of habit, before departing to find Celene.

He was admitted to the princess's chambers by one of her maids.

'She's out on the balcony in the next room with Prince Iraudis,' the maid explained as Thurion looked around the empty chamber. He walked into the next room but decided not to interrupt the princess and her brother.

'How is Prince Nabas?' Celene asked.

'Distraught, as is his father; they recovered barely half of the prince's body from the battlefield,' Iraudis replied.

'That's awful...'

'Celene, I've known you for many years; it wasn't out of concern for Prince Nabas that you sent for me, was it? What's wrong?' the princess's brother asked.

'It's Thurion, I... I don't know how I feel about him,' she began, uncertainly.

'What is it that's confusing you?'

'Well... he's a fine man; honourable, strong of mind and body. I could trust him with my life... but...'

'He's not one of us?' Iraudis offered.

'That sounds so awful when you put it like that,' Celene replied, tears in her eyes.

'But it's true, isn't it? His ways are not our ways. You know that I would support you whatever you decide, but few others would. You would always be the princess who married a barbarian. At best you'd never be taken seriously at court, at worst you would become a laughing stock,' Iraudis explained as gently as he could.

'So it's not really my decision to make, is it?' Celene burst into tears, burying her head in her brother's shoulder. 'I've been fooling myself, haven't I? I could never really be happy with someone like Thurion...' Celene continued to weep as Iraudis held her.

Thurion, having overheard everything, turned slowly away and silently left the princess's apartments.

***

How could I have been so stupid? She never really liked me, how could she? Think about it, a princess, well-bred, cultured and beautiful. And me... what am I compared to her? A wandering barbarian, a 'savage' nomad, not of royal blood and certainly not a Child of Ios...No, it wouldn't have worked out. We are too different; worlds apart. My spirits led me to her when she needed help and our paths crossed for a while, now she says what we had wasn't real. I have stayed in these lands, amongst these people for too long! I need to get back to the wild and the spirits. At least, I can rely on them!

Thurion strode back to his apartments, bitterness and disappointment in his heart. The princess's words had wounded him deeply. For a little while he had begun to entertain the idea that he might actually have found someone who really understood him. Only his parting with Rimehorn had hurt this much, it was almost a physical pain he felt. Tears welled up in his eyes as he donned his armour and strapped his belongings to his back. Pulling on his helmet to conceal his tears he left his chamber and made his way to the city gates.

***

'Celene, oh dear, Celene, of course it's your decision,' Iraudis said, soothingly. His sister was still crying as he continued, 'You are third in line to father's throne after Erakos and myself.'

Celene looked up at her brother, tears running down her cheeks. 'So?'

'So you will never be under as much scrutiny as father is or Erakos will be. If your feelings for Thurion are as strong as I suspect they are, then admit it, first to yourself, then to Thurion. Father will understand... eventually. Erakos may take some persuading though his experience on the battlefield may have changed some of his preconceptions somewhat.'

'I... I love him, Iraudis, I really do,' Celene admitted for the first time. 'Thank you, without you I may have made a terrible mistake.'

She hugged her brother before leaving the balcony and returning inside, 'I should tidy myself up, I asked him to come by yesterday afternoon,' she said, drying her eyes.

'Er, Your Highness?' A maid began, interrupting the princess.

'Yes, what is it?'

'Please, forgive me, I wasn't meaning to over-hear your conversation but...' the maid tried to explain.

'It's fine, what is it?' the princess pressed.

'Well, Your Highness, Thurion was just here.'

'He was WHAT?! He didn't... did he?' she asked, her eyes wide with fear.

'I think he heard everything, Your Highness. He left just after you started... well... crying,' the servant answered awkwardly.

'Oh, no, no!' Celene cried. Leaving her apartment doors wide open behind her, she ran to Thurion's apartment, desperate to find him and explain everything.

**

Thurion left the palace and marched across the city towards the south-western gates, tears running down his face and beard. He didn't notice the soldiers of Shemshah who now wore black arm-bands in memory of Prince Nabas. As he passed through the gatehouse and out onto the mist-covered battlefield, he barely noticed Marshal Xobas directing the digging of a mass grave. Indeed, Thurion noticed very little of the morning's activity as he strode away, vaguely due east.

***

Celene ran along the corridors of the palace like a woman possessed until she came to Thurion's apartments. They were bare. As she looked over the empty rooms a terrible thought struck her and she sprinted out of the palace, leapt into the air and flew as fast as she could towards the city gates. She looked around helplessly for a minute or two before spotting Captain Ramphien talking with a number of other officers by the roadside.

'Captain! Captain!' she shouted, landing on the road, 'Captain, have you seen Thurion this morning?' she asked anxiously.

'No, I'm sorry, Your Highness, I haven't,' the captain answered.

'The barbarian? I saw him a few minutes ago. He went that way,' one of the other officers interrupted, pointing towards the city gates. Without even thanking the officer Celene ran headlong through the gatehouse and out onto yesterday's battlefield. She wandered the bloody field for an hour looking for Thurion before collapsing onto her knees and weeping uncontrollably.

Chapter 50

She didn't recall how she got back to the palace but woke to find herself in bed, her father standing by her bedside.

'I've lost him, father,' she said weakly. Raparké knelt down and took his daughter's hand tenderly in his own.

'Some of life's most important lessons are painfully learned. I'm sorry, Celene, but you *have* lost him. If I thought there were *any* chance of finding him, I would send out every soldier who can still walk across the length and breadth of the land.'

Raparké felt helpless; there was little he could do. He had heard what had happened from Iraudis. If it were anyone else he would feel confident that he could track them down, but this mysterious nomad, if the reports were true, could simply melt into the wilderness and disappear at will. His daughter had made a terrible mistake, it had broken her heart and there was little he could do except to comfort her. The pain would ease, he expected, with time; she would be stronger and wiser, having learned a valuable lesson. Many burdens weighed heavily on the High Prince's shoulders; he had to help High Prince Lautos as the grieving father laid his son to rest and began the long, arduous task of rebuilding his principality. He also felt that he should be the one to approach Prince Nabas' widow who, as the oldest surviving member of Seratos's bloodline, stood to inherit the throne of those ravaged lands. The next few years would be some of the most difficult he had yet known, but he vowed then and there, to make time for his daughter whenever she needed him.

* * *

As Celene lay in bed, her heart broken, Thurion found himself answering the call of the wilderness yet again, its embrace an analgesic to his wounded spirit. He was as broken now as he had been when he had parted ways with Rimehorn, and knew full well that the pain and the heartache would take a long time to heal.

He had set out from Vorde as a young man, more at ease in the wilderness than in the settlements of men. Now, however, he was becoming more and more a *part* of that wilderness. Leaving the Principalities behind, he entered the Kuna Plain to the northeast before heading for the truly wild lands of the far east, the next season of his life unfolding before him.

Also by the same author

Pandemonium Ascendant

A dark fantasy set in a world of swords and sorcery.

Fleeing the Corsair Coast, the fugitive sorcerer Dakuran El-Alamir and his companion Mikhael travel west towards the Plains of Madness in search of power. Seeking to unite the might of the Abyss with that of Pandemonium, Dakuran would rule the whole of the known world. Standing in his way, however, is the kingdom of the Eittendorfer and the fastness of Castle Wundigstein.

Will the stone of Wundigstein and the mettle of those who defend it turn the chaotic tide that has been unleashed, or will the streets of this mighty fortress-city echo with the cries of daemons; a foretaste of the doom to come?

Paragon of Order

A dark fantasy set on the western border of
Pandemonium.

Relations between the Paladins of Order and the
Lords of Chaos have always been hostile with both
sides turning a blind eye to cross-border raids, or
actively sponsoring them. Despite this, a fragile
balance of power has existed for a century or more
that has kept their borders fairly unchanged. This
balance is threatened when Sir Thomas D'Brentieu,
Paladin of the Greater Prefecture of Brentieu, seeking
to emulate the deeds of the ancient heroes of Order,
begins planning a crusade against the heathen tribes
of Pandemonium and their dark lord, Legion.

Sir Thomas' neighbour, the newly appointed
Paladin of the Greater Prefecture of Valan, find
themselves with an unenviable choice: side with the
orthodox, some might say fanatical, Sir Thomas and
become embroiled in a war with the Lord of Shadow
Keep, or remain neutral and risk attracting the ire of
both sides?

Dr S. Fern

Beyond Earth
The collected tales, volume 1: New Earth

A collection of science-fiction short stories set as
humanity leaves Earth to colonise the galaxy.

As Earth breathed her last mankind finally began
considering its future: could it survive off-world, and
if so, where would it go and how would it get there?
Fortunately United Industries, a trans-national
corporation with a monopoly on deep space
technologies, was on hand to provide its assistance,
for those who could afford it. And so the great
migration to New Earth was undertaken and the next
chapter of mankind's history began, at least it was for
those fortunate enough not to get left behind with
their dying mother...

Will mankind make the most of the fresh start that
New Earth offers?
What about those who were left behind?

The Barbarian and the Angel

Dr S. Fern

Lightning Source UK Ltd.
Milton Keynes UK
UKOW04f2114020218

317310UK00001B/187/P